RIPTIDE

CATHLEEN COLE
FRANK JENSEN

Copyright © 2023 by Cathleen Cole

All rights reserved.

No part of this book may be reproduced in any form or by any electronic or mechanical means, including information storage and retrieval systems, without written permission from the author, except for the use of brief quotations in a book review.

Any references to historical events, real people, or real places are used fictitiously. Names, characters, and places are products of the author's imagination.

Publisher: C&J Novels LLC

Cover designed by: Kari March Designs

ASIN: B0BHTY7G25

This is dedicated to my family. Thank you for all your love and support.

TRIGGER WARNINGS

This book is meant for readers 18+. Some content may be unsuitable for some readers. Due to the nature of the cult in this book, there are some heavy topics discussed. Please find the list of trigger warnings below.

ENDS in a cliffhanger (Couple gets their HEA)
Strong language
Explicit sexual content
Religious Cult
Gun violence
Knife violence
Fighting
Murder
Death
Sexual assault (off page)
Rape (off page only)
Physical abuse (whippings, beatings, child off page only and adult on page)

Mental abuse (Child and adult)
Neglect (child and adult)
Death of a child (happens on and off page)

CHAPTER 1

Riptide

I'd lost my mind. I was sure of it. But ever since I'd seen the beautiful woman out in the desert I hadn't been able to get her out of my thoughts. She was with me during every waking moment and throughout the night. It could be any one of my brothers preparing for this mission, but because of Sloane, it had to be me. I just had to convince my brothers to vote for me to go.

Never did I think I'd be doing something as crazy as this. Yet here I was, preparing to immerse myself into a way of life I knew nothing about. Sure, I was doing it as a way of rescuing anyone I could—including the woman who'd caught my eye—and taking out those who were a danger to anyone who stumbled upon them, but still... I was about to join a cult.

Everyone was slowly piling into the meeting room. Apprehension made me hyper focused. It was an unusual and almost foreign feeling for me. Covert Operations hadn't really been a thing for Green Berets. Our main function had been to train other troops. We'd trained our own men and other countries' armies on how to effectively fight. The best way to train those forces was to fight alongside them, but nothing was ever undercover. That kind of work was for the Feds.

Go behind enemy lines, lay up in the woods, hide out in an abandoned building and prepare an ambush? That was too easy. I'd done that more times than I could count. But to actually go into the enemy's lair and pretend to be one of them? That was new for me. And yeah, I was nervous. My life, the lives of my brothers—if the cult found out who I was working with—and the lives of innocents out there on the compound could be at stake if I fucked this up.

I thought about the woman I'd seen only a few weeks ago. They'd called out her name and it had been echoing in my head ever since. *Sloane.* I'd only seen her for a few minutes. She'd been trying to stop the cult mob from beating a kid. She'd taken the punishment instead.

At the time I'd tried to run in and save her, but my brothers had pulled me back. I couldn't recall ever going into a blind rage like that in my life. But when I saw her—that gorgeous long brown hair glinting in the light, eyes so blue they shone from a hundred yards away, and a heart big enough to care about a child that way—I hadn't been able to help myself. To see those men hurt something so perfect had me seeing red. It was time to go undercover, into the cult. To take them down. I would need to contain my anger, or else I would never be able to rescue her.

As if my own imagination wasn't enough to keep me on edge, Butcher, our resident psychopath, was serious and somber. That was never a good sign. I took my seat at the table, directly across from him. He had some expertise in this area, so as much as I appreciated the others being there, I needed to be face to face with him. None of the rest of us had dealt with cults before. At least not in this capacity. He was the one who was going to help me get through this, hopefully alive.

"Alright, everyone, settle down. Sit down and shut up." There was instant silence at Lockout's order. "It's time to vote. Are we sending Riptide in?"

He didn't need to clarify. We'd been thinking about nothing else since he'd announced two days ago that we'd be putting this to a vote. It was time to decide and I sure as hell hoped the others were on the same page.

Unease was heavy in the air as everyone looked around to gauge what the general consensus was. We never sent our brothers out alone. The guilt was heavy on their faces. They didn't like that I was going into the lion's den without them. Shit, if I could figure out a way to bring one of them along with me, I'd jump at the chance. Unfortunately, Chet only had one cousin that was supposed to be joining him. We'd had no trouble tracking the cousin down and handing his location over to the cops. Anonymously, of course. There was a rap sheet on him a mile long that would keep him detained long enough for me to get through this mission.

That meant that my brothers would have to sit back and wait, powerless, until I was able to bring them something actionable on the cult. In that regard, I had it easy, and didn't envy them. I would be too busy trying not to blow my cover to ever get bored and feel powerless.

Before I could answer, Toxic spoke up. "We could still kill the bastard outright. There's no need to send Rip in alone. He would still get his girlfriend and the cult would be done."

I ignored the dig about 'my girlfriend'. Everyone at this table knew the reason I'd volunteered was because of her. Her stunning beauty, her courage, her defiance, she was pulling at me, drawing me in. I needed to figure out what it was about her that had me so wound up. Once I knew, I could go back to my normal life. A life without her haunting my dreams.

"Won't work." Butcher's tone was wooden. "Back when I worked for the secret squirrel agency more than once we ran across these Jonestown type cults."

My lips twitched as Butcher used the secret squirrel reference. It was a way to make fun of anyone in law enforcement or military who was overly paranoid or enthusiastic about a mission. Everyone knew the CIA was the epitome of paranoid.

Butcher's eyes locked on me, his brow raising, but he didn't stop his explanation to ask what was so funny. "All over the damn world.

For as much as they seem different, they really are all the same. They all have a basic religion they start from, Christian, Muslim, Hindi, whatever. They begin with the accepted religion, but then pervert it into a worship of the cult leader himself."

"That tracks," Dash said, interrupting my thoughts. "This guy frequently calls himself the Earth God."

We'd been listening in on the recordings Dash and I had managed to get off the cult. It wasn't much since they rarely held their weird ass meetings out in the open. We hadn't infiltrated the camp, so I hadn't been able to set any surveillance equipment up in any of the buildings.

Butcher shot him a look so stern that Dash almost fell out of his chair. "Don't get ahead of me, I'll get to that."

"Sorry."

"Butcher," I muttered, getting him back on track. My muscles were tense and I was practically vibrating in my seat. I was amped up to ten and itching to go. The sooner I started, the sooner I finished. Everyone just needed to agree first.

"Anyway," Butcher said, focusing back on me, "these guys prey on the weak and disenfranchised. You'd think that they'd go after the dumb and gullible, but that's never how it works. The cultists tend to be smart, capable, and fanatically dangerous. It's like once they have something new to set their sights on they come alive again. In a way that usually isn't good for anyone." He looked over at Toxic. "It's why you can't just outright kill their leader. The consequences are always unpredictable and violent. They might commit mass suicide, killing off the women and children first. They might engage in ritual sacrifice. Or they might attack. Randomly kill dozens or hundreds of civilians that aren't even connected to the cult."

Butcher stopped and rubbed his forehead, as though he needed a minute to shove down whatever memories were battering at him.

I pushed down the thought of her getting killed by the other followers. I couldn't focus on that right now, or I'd drive myself crazy. If killing Ethan would put her in jeopardy, then that option was off the table. No way would I let her get hurt. I looked back at Butcher. I was left with the feeling that, more than once, he'd tried the direct approach by killing a leader, and that it had backfired. That he was talking from personal experience. We all stayed silent while he gathered himself.

"We only have one real option here, and that's to send Riptide in. Let him become part of the cult. Identify the members that are there against their will. Once we get them out, then, and only then, can we take on a direct approach. Kill them all."

It still seemed like an extreme approach. Priest spoke up. "Far be it for me to advocate for police assistance, but we're talking about dozens of people here. How is this not mass murder?"

"Mass murder?" Butcher's head snapped up and locked onto Priest. His normal, wild eyes were back, pupils so blown they nearly looked black with just a thin blue ring noticeable. "Have you been listening to Dash's recordings of these guys? Have you listened to his 'sermons'? This isn't your run-of-the-mill scam like a pop-up church. Some hillbilly preacher, rolling into town and filling the collection plate before bailing. This is the real deal." He looked back towards me so he could really emphasize his next words. "Ethan is a believer. A true believer. He believes that he is God incarnate, flesh and blood on earth. That's why he calls himself the Earth God. That's not some hippie tree hugging term. No, he believes that he is God, here on earth. And they believe it too. Most of them anyways. Hopefully not all of them."

"What about gettin' the innocents out, then lettin' the cops handle it?" Hush suggested.

We weren't the kind to go to law enforcement with anything. We handled our own shit. So for some of our brothers to consider bringing in the police it spoke to how dangerous all this was. How much they didn't want to have to send me into that place alone. It wasn't my idea of a fucking good time either, but I was the best choice. I came closest to fitting Derek's—Chet's cousin's—description. Hell, our first names even matched. Add to that I was the VP for the club and had more authority to take action than anyone—other than Lockout. It meant I wouldn't need to check in before making decisions. Lockout and I had already talked and he was giving me full approval to do what needed to be done while I was in. If I fucked things up we'd handle them once we took out the cult.

"The cops would get slaughtered. Oh sure, eventually they would call in the FBI and end up taking them down. But it would take years of surveillance before they even attempted to arrest or kill the members. In the meantime, any of the cultists who aren't there by choice would be subjected to this sick fuck's every whim. Besides all that, cops are stupid, and they have rules to follow. How many would die before they figured out what they were dealing with? Remember Jonestown? They killed a U.S. Congressman. The part they leave out is how many CIA and FBI tried to infiltrate the place. Over a dozen agents. All of them were killed. Better that we just take care of it ourselves."

Butcher's outlook made sense. He'd been part of a team that hadn't needed to follow any kind of procedure while he'd been in the military. The rest of us still had to follow those 'rules' so we knew exactly what he was talking about and how those protocols had bound our hands so many times in the past. He was right and I saw the resignation on everyone's face. We had to do this ourselves.

I thought of the woman again. The way she took a beating for that child. It left me with a selfish hope that maybe she wasn't one of them. Maybe I could save her. A pang of guilt struck me as I realized that I almost didn't care if no one else there could be saved. So long as I could get her out. That didn't mean I wouldn't try. The more people we saved the better. One, because it would make what I was about to do worth it if we could help them. And two, because that meant less people for us to fight in the end.

"But if they really do think he is their God, wouldn't killing him break them out of their trance? Prove that he isn't their 'Earth God'?" Ricochet insisted.

"You'd think so, but too many times that has proven not to be the case. They're too far gone, too obsessed with him to see it like that. Their minds will collectively create a story around it. He returned to heaven, rejoined the spiritual plane, blah, blah, blah. The end result is the same, mass murder or mass suicide. And the mass suicide is almost never voluntary."

"Time to vote," Lockout said, putting an end to the other options. "All those in favor, raise your hands." He started it off by putting his in the air.

I gave him a grateful look. He didn't want to send me in there any more than the other men did, but I'd pulled him aside yesterday and asked him to do this for me. With him voting in favor the others were more likely to do so as well. He hadn't asked me to explain. He trusted that I knew what I needed and I had to do this.

Looking around, I relaxed a fraction. Every hand at the table was up. No one looked pleased about it, but they'd voted in favor. I was going in.

Lockout stayed quiet for what felt like a whole minute, watching me, before he spoke again. "Last chance. It's not too late to pull the plug on this."

"I'm good." I said definitively. "I've made up my mind. Butcher, run me through this. Tell me everything you know about cults. I don't want to end up buried out in the desert because I don't know what the fuck I'm doing. We know there's no taking him down, not by assassination. I assume that discrediting him and making his worshippers abandon him is out of the question?" I asked, already knowing the answer.

"Not a chance. Chet Holden killed his wife and was going to kill his daughter for this creep." Butcher was watching Priest as he said it.

Priest was squeezing the end of the table so hard I thought that he might snap it. He'd adopted Chet's daughter, Caitlyn. The thought of anyone hurting that girl was enough to send him flying into a rage. But it rammed home Butcher's point. The 'true believers' were beyond our ability to help. All we could do was rescue the children and those kept there against their will.

Butcher focused back on me. "Don't forget that. You aren't smart—or crafty—enough to discredit him, and he'll kill you if you try."

Don't forget about the woman. One way or another, she's coming with you.

"How do I fit in once I'm there?"

"That's going to be the fun part."

I groaned inwardly. Butcher's idea of fun wasn't what the rest of us would consider a good time. It always turned out to be horrible in one way or another.

"You're the new guy, everyone will be suspicious of you. Play stupid, apologize for everything. Only ask *him* for forgiveness, though. The other members are going to test you, try to assert dominance over you. Stand your ground to a point, but don't attack them. You may even have to take some punishment at the beginning."

Gritting my teeth, I thought again about the woman, and how they had circled her and kicked her for standing up for the girl. *This is going to be hard.* Not losing my shit over that kind of behavior would take all my willpower. It was one thing to let people beat on me, but to stand back and watch them hit women and children went against everything I believed in. I sighed and relaxed my hands, which had balled up into fists at the thought.

"Oh, another thing. They'll have a strict set of rules. Guaranteed they'll be bizarrely contradictory. Like, don't touch the children, but women are fair game. Don't rape a married woman, but an unmarried one has no protections. Never mind the contradictions, don't try to make sense out of them. Just don't violate the rules, and never point out the contradiction. They might kill you on sight. Just nod and agree."

Fuck. Me. How the hell am I going to pull this off?

It didn't matter. I'd figure it out. In the end I knew helping Sloane would be worth whatever I managed to get myself into.

CHAPTER 2

Riptide

"You have twenty minutes," the prison guard muttered, giving me a hard look before glancing back at Static, "or until he asks you to leave."

Static gave the guard a nod, then motioned for me to follow him. "Don't say a fucking thing at first. Let me get through the shit I need to, then you can ask questions."

I nodded in acceptance while we waited for the guard to open the cell. Derek Holden—also known as Derek Johnson, and a slew of other names—looked up as we entered. He'd been told his attorney was here to speak with him and Static had managed to get himself placed as such not long after the cops took him into custody. It wasn't a coincidence. There were things we needed from Derek to pull this off.

We sat down and Static introduced me before handing over some paperwork. "These are the charges being filed, Derek."

The man's eyes scanned the page, his face getting more and more grim as he went. When he finally looked up there was a finality in his gaze. He was fucked and he knew it.

They spoke back and forth as they went over the charges, the potential sentences—this guy was looking at being an old man or dead before he got out of prison—and what the plan would be for the eventual trial.

I watched his mannerisms. If anyone in the cult—other than Chet—had met him before, I was finished. The only way I was accessing the cult would be by pretending to be this guy.

Static cleared his throat and shot me a pointed look. Derek's eyes followed the movement and he stared at us with mistrust flashing over his face. "What's going on?"

"We have an offer for you," I told him.

"Who the fuck are you to offer me shit?"

"Someone who can help you," I said with a shrug. It was important that I played this right. He needed to think that we could help him, but he had to be the desperate one here. If he knew how much we needed his cooperation we were screwed.

"How the hell could you help me?" His dark brows pulled low over his eyes as he stared down at his handcuffs.

Pasting a bored look on my face, I sat back in my chair. "We can get you out of prison and get the charges on you dropped." I crossed my arms over my chest, biting back a grin when his eyes snapped up to mine.

"Bullshit. They have me dead to rights."

"We have someone that can make it all disappear," I replied.

Rat was a techie who was better than everyone. The cops, FBI, CIA, none of those agencies had anyone working for them who could outsmart the kid. He'd already agreed to help us with the Austin Chapter President's approval. Those guys were out of the life, but it didn't mean they couldn't occasionally dip their toe in when their brothers needed it. They agreed that the termination of this cult was worth Rat playing around in the FBI's databases for less than an hour. He could make the evidence disappear, leaving the FBI holding their dicks.

Hope flickered there in Derek's blue eyes. There was heavy suspicion to go with it. "What do you need me to do?"

"A few things," Static said, taking back over. "We need information. And we need you to fucking behave in here until we finish up what we need to do. Only after that's been concluded will we get you released."

Fucking lawyer speak. Derek looked back at me since I was giving it to him straight. That desperation I was hoping for was pouring off him in waves now. He wanted to take this deal. "What kind of information do you need?"

"It's about The Silverbells Cult."

Derek sat frozen. "How do you even know about them?"

"You think if we can erase what you've done, we can't find out about a cult?" I asked.

He shook his head. "You don't want to go fucking around with them. They're not-" He paused as a guard walked by, checking on us. Shifting in his seat, he waited until the guard was clear of the area. "They play for keeps. You cross them, you end up dead."

We figured that was the case. This wasn't news to us.

"Do they know what you look like?" Static asked.

"Not likely. Maybe an old photograph from one of my old jobs. Nothing recent. I just got into town. Was supposed to meet my cousin then head out to meet the big wig himself."

"Ethan."

"Ethan Hargrove," he confirmed with a nod. He looked around again as though he expected someone to be crawling along the walls trying to listen in. "Guy's nuts. Something fucking weird is going on out there. Turned Chet—my cousin—into a raving fucking lunatic."

"Why were you going to join them then?" I asked.

He shrugged. "Money. Fucking loads of it. They were willing to pay me a small fortune to manage their finances for them. Set them up with shell corporations that would funnel their money from wherever they're getting it back into legitimate businesses. From there it would return back into their hands. Clean as you please. Plus, they were going to set me up with a real hottie for a wife. I mean, look at me, I'm not exactly pulling the ladies."

I ground my teeth as I tried to calm myself. Her face appeared before me again, and the thought of her—or any other woman—being forced to marry this pile of shit made my blood boil. I silently counted to ten, and studied him while doing so. He was right about one thing, he was no prize. He had a gut, receding hairline and a pathetic attempt at a comb over to hide it. That made me feel a little better.

"What were the terms?" Despite his less than desirable appearance, he still was clearly successful financially. It fascinated me why someone with as much going for him as Derek would do this.

He shrugged again. "Had to live out there in the desert with them for a year. Get everything set up. Easy peasy. Once I did that, I had to train someone—probably would've been Chet—then I could leave."

"What do you mean get everything set up?"

"Well, all I've seen is photos so far, but they're not exactly roughing it out there and they plan on making it as comfortable as they can. He's got a semi-modern set up, electricity, water, food, and ammunition. It takes some doing to hide all that, considering they're not on private property. To build that kind of infrastructure on federal land and keep it secret takes more than money laundering. You need contractors that work outside the law, that can get permits with no questions asked. Shit like that. That's my other specialty."

This was an interesting dichotomy. They needed him and his weaselly skills and connections, but they were still fanatics. Considering what Butcher had told me about these guys I doubted he would train someone and then leave. He'd have either been assimilated into the cult, or they'd have learned his techniques and killed him, guaranteed.

"When were you supposed to meet?" Static asked.

"Was going to meet with Chet tomorrow at noon. He was going to bring me out. Show me the ropes. Introduce me to Ethan. Haven't been able to get a hold of him." He played with the chain connecting his cuffs. "I'm willing to play ball to get myself out of this." He motioned to the paperwork still on the table. "I don't want to go to prison for that long…or at all, but there's no way Chet will go along with it. From what I can tell he trusts this Ethan guy and is loyal to him."

I cleared my throat and shifted. "Hate to be the one to tell you this, Derek, but Chet is dead."

His eyes widened, mouth falling open as he looked between us. "What? What the fuck happened?"

"We don't have answers for you," Static said, evading the question. The last thing we needed was for him to find out we'd been responsible for Chet's death. That would shut down his cooperation instantly.

"Do you think Ethan would accept you joining the cult without Chet bringing you?"

Derek's brows rose and he huffed out a breath as he thought that over. "Maybe…if he thought it was his idea. I mean, they still need me."

"You haven't spoken to him?"

"No, but Chet would have given him a way to contact me."

I leaned forward, putting my elbows on the table and glanced over at Static. He gave an almost imperceivable nod. "You're going to tell us everything you know, tomorrow, when we come back."

"Why not now?" he asked, anxious to make a deal with us that would ensure his freedom.

"Because for now, you're going to give me the location of all your shit. Your laptop, your cell, everything you've hidden in preparation for joining that cult."

"You want to make sure I'm not jerking you around."

"Exactly Derek," I told him, giving him a wide grin. "Once we know you're in this fully, then we'll talk."

* * *

"Take everything," I told Static, as I started loading up duffel bags with Derek's things.

"How are you going to keep Ethan from finding out about Derek being in prison?" Static asked as he packed up clothes.

"Seek spoke with her contacts. The police are holding him under one of his many aliases, one not associated with the cult. It's a simple clerical error that will buy us time. Plus, they're keeping everything on the down low as much as possible, as they investigate and gather the evidence they'll need to prosecute Derek."

"That usually lasts for about seventy-two hours." He glanced down at his Rolex. "That gives us about twelve hours."

I grinned over at him. "Press got wind of it about five hours ago."

He straightened up and cocked his head. "I haven't seen shit. It's my client-"

"Thank Rat for that. He's keeping an eye on things and anyone who tries to break the story keeps ending up with a virus shutting down their company."

His lips tipped up into a smile. "You guys have some impressive friends."

"You mean like a badass lawyer who gets paid more than most make in a lifetime to represent a single client?" I arched a brow at him.

"Something like that."

"He doesn't blame you for making the choice you did, you know. Lock's always been proud of you."

Static went back to throwing clothes into bags. "We need to be out of here as fast as we can."

I let him change the subject. He would talk about it when he was ready. If he ever was. "The others are heading over to help us out."

Static cursed and gave me a dark look. "You sure you're ready for this Rip? This isn't a fucking game."

I'd known Static almost as long as Lockout. Many of our brothers didn't know him—that had been a choice he'd made—but I'd always looked at him as an older brother. At twenty-eight years old, I was one of the younger members of the club, but Lockout had still made me his VP back when he'd taken over.

When I'd told him there were others who could take the position he just shook his head and said, "I need someone I know will have my back no matter what. Someone that would kill for this club. Die for this club. For its members."

I was a surfer kid. Had grown up in Washington State riding the waves until circumstances forced me into the military. From there I'd found the brotherhood I'd been searching for, yearning to have. Once my enlistment contract had been fulfilled I'd walked away from the military. The retirement couldn't hold me, neither could a promise of a fat reenlistment bonus. I'd been done, but that was only because I had this club to walk toward. It and my brothers were my life. Nothing would ever change that. I slapped a hand on Static's shoulder and just went back to cleaning out Derek's apartment, leaving his question hanging in the air. Her face, that gorgeous, innocent, and defiant face hung in my mind. I was ready for this. I needed to get in there. Get her out.

CHAPTER 3

Sloane

Something was going on. There were stirrings around the compound. There was a shift in the energy that even I was able to feel despite my nearly outcast status.

I crept around the building that Ethan used as his main office, eyes darting around to make sure no one had seen me back here. The last thing I needed was to be caught listening in. My bruises had only finished healing mere days ago from the last beating I'd taken. It'd been for a good cause—letting Abigail be punished by the men had been inconceivable—but it had still been hard for me to get out of bed for days afterward. Bella, Abigail's mother, and a few of the other women had been there to take care of me. Bella had been nearly inconsolable when she'd seen the injuries I'd sustained on behalf of her daughter.

I'd gotten accustomed to the beatings. It went hand in hand with being an outcast. Ethan was so quick to beat the children into submission, and the zombie-like mothers were all too ready to let him. I couldn't blame them. They were good women at the core, but they knew if they interfered they'd receive the same treatment. At this point I knew that any time I opened my mouth, I would get hit. It was better me than the children. I'd learned how to, quite literally, roll with the punches. To let Ethan's blows land in the least damaging ways, thus I would walk away with bruises but no broken bones.

I wouldn't forget though. I certainly wouldn't forgive. Make no mistake, I knew I didn't *deserve* this. I was doing this to protect the children, and the mothers who were still salvageable. I took the beatings and whippings to keep them safe and alive until I could escape. Until I could get them all out of here.

The air was warm and still as I rose on my tiptoes to listen in at the window that had been left slightly ajar. The summer heat had passed us by and soon winter would be settling in. I was grateful the winters here would be so much milder than the last place we'd settled. North Dakota had been brutal and though the Tucson summers were no joke I'd take them over those harsh winters.

We hadn't been here long. The men were still in the process of erecting all the buildings and our utilities were still mostly temporary. We were all grateful to have them, but we needed something more permanent if we were going to stay here long term. It was always the plan when we moved somewhere new to remain permanently, but just the nature of our community ended up making us enemies. We would settle in a place and inevitably be run out some time later. Big surprise that Ethan and his 'acolytes' weren't good at making friends.

"What happened?"

I froze at the sound of Ethan's voice as he and his right-hand man, Jacob, walked into the room. This was it. I was about to find out what had caused the tension in the air today.

"I don't know, Ethan. Chet isn't answering his cell phone. I haven't been able to get a hold of him."

There was silence as Ethan absorbed that information. I wished I could see them, but honestly, after growing up with this group of people I knew them so well I didn't need the view. Ethan would be rubbing his jaw as he thought about why one of our newer members might have abandoned the faith, and with it, us.

"Do you think he's betrayed us?" Ethan finally said, breaking the silence.

Jacob sighed. "I don't know. As far as I can tell, everything is still where it should be and nothing has changed. That's not really my field of expertise though."

"That's why we needed Chet, or more importantly, his cousin."

"Exactly. The loss of Chet—as long as he hasn't taken anything from us—is something that we can recover from. But losing Derek..." Jacob trailed off.

I wondered who Derek was—obviously Chet's cousin—but why was this man no one seemed to know so important to our group? Rarely did Ethan place real value on anyone other than himself.

"It's long past the meeting time." Ethan would be digging his fingers into his temples right about now, something he only did when he thought no one was watching. "If we don't have Derek then we're going to have to find someone new."

Jacob sputtered. "Ethan, that's...not going to be easy. That man had a plethora of skills that would have-"

"I'm aware of that," Ethan snapped. "That's why I'm going to initiate the backup plan. I don't fucking like it, but it's necessary."

Silence fell again and I wondered if they'd left when I heard Ethan speak again. "I'm calling for Derek Holden." I held my breath and waited. "I see. This is highly unusual, but I'm willing to give this a second chance as long as you can prove to us that you won't be as unreliable as your cousin." Another lengthy pause. "Be that as it may, Chet has left us in quite the predicament. If you wish to secure the funds I've offered, you'll meet my man in two hours at the address I'm texting to you."

It was all I could do not to pull my hair out by the roots. I couldn't hear both sides of the conversation and my curiosity was killing me. What funds? Who was Derek Holden?

The sound of someone coming toward me had my head snapping in that direction. I gave a little frustrated growl under my breath and backed away from the window. I edged my way around another building as one of the men walked by, doing a sweep of the perimeter. Once Bruce had come around and joined our group he'd convinced Ethan to secure our community better. There'd been guns and round the clock guard rotations ever since.

It was a damn inconvenience for someone like me—who did her best to cause trouble as much as she could and not get caught—but I'd learned over the years to flit through the shadows, to pocket things here and there so I could squirrel them away for 'someday'.

I lived in a cult. The Order of The Earth. They didn't think they were, but that was exactly what this place was. They worshiped Ethan as though he were the reincarnation of a god on Earth. Not a messiah, prophet, or anything remotely reasonable. No, a god as flesh and blood, here on Earth. It was ridiculous. It was insane. It was downright dangerous. But I couldn't leave. Not yet. There were too many here who needed my help. Women and children who weren't here of their own volition.

My whole life I'd been a part of this group. I was born into it. I didn't intend to die here as well. It'd been years of planning and prepping, but every day, I did what I needed to in order to survive and prepare. I would get out of here. One day.

Today wasn't that day. I hurried away from the main office and made my way across the camp. Hissing as an errant cholla spine stabbed through my boot, I bent and carefully plucked it out before tossing it away. Many of the women hated the desert. It was hot and everything poked, stung, prodded, and tried to kill you out here—even the damn plant life—but oh it was so beautiful, too.

The sunrises gave me life each morning. The way the colors painted the sky in their oranges, pinks, and purples was truly a testament to all the wonder that existed here. The monsoons—while deadly—were such a need in this arid environment and they provided everything the inhabitants of the desert required. I felt connected to the land here, loved it. This was where I would make my escape and I'd disappear into this desert where Ethan and his group of nut jobs would never find me again. I just needed to make sure I was ready when that time came.

"Sister Sloane!"

The cries of the children as I walked into the schoolroom made me smile. They were why I was still here. One thing about Ethan was that, though he refused to ever integrate us into whichever cities we lived near, he refused to live without amenities.

That refusal had been my salvation. My mother had believed in this life with her whole heart and soul. Even as a child, I couldn't understand how any kind of god would want people living the way we did. The men weren't kind, gracious, or pious.

My doubts were the first thing that had me learning how to sneak around. I'd creep into Ethan's office while he was occupied and use his computer. This started when I was around thirteen years old. I'd taught myself more than our pitiful excuse for a schoolteacher back then and had learned a little about the outside world. Now the children benefited from the things I'd managed to learn. There were still so many things I didn't know. I thirsted for the knowledge, but creeping around was getting harder and harder. I'd finally realized that if I wanted to stay and teach the children, then I'd have to stop sneaking into his office. There wouldn't be any more access to the computer.

The kids were all I cared about. It had taken years of convincing Ethan that our children would be able to better serve The Order if we educated them on more than just life here. He'd put me in charge of teaching them one day after he realized the decrepit old school teacher had done more napping than teaching.

Education was a fine line for Ethan. Too smart and people asked questions, learned to think for themselves. That was bad for him. He needed devout, gullible, and unquestioning followers. Too little education, and you wound up with mindless drones, not unlike a few of the men around here. Obedience was good, stupidity was not.

I was happy with my job here. Most of the time the men expected the women to clean, cook, and make more babies for The Order, so being a teacher gave me something to do. It worked for Ethan because it was a means of control over me. If I over-educated the children, if they learned to think critically and ask questions, they would get beaten. I had to be careful with my teachings.

Somehow, I'd managed to avoid the usual path for women in this community and I was still unmarried at twenty-two. Probably had something to do with the fact that I was a known trouble maker and most of the men didn't want me. That was just peachy as far as I was concerned.

I didn't want to get married. The men here were disgusting. They thought they owned their wives and they mistreated them. I'd known the majority of these men for most of my life and wanted nothing to do with them. The women would flutter their lashes as a handsome man walked past. The only reaction I usually had was disgust. It made me wonder if there was something wrong with me. I'd never giggled and flirted with a man, not even as a teenager.

Even though I wanted nothing to do with the men, I longed for children. It was why I bonded so closely with the kids. It wasn't hard to deduce that I'd never have children of my own—I refused to give myself over to these cretins—and that made the yearning that much more difficult to bear.

Ethan often forced marriages upon our community, but he had yet to find a match for me. I hoped to keep it that way. As long as I was doing my job by teaching the kids they left me alone to keep planning my escape. I smiled and stepped up to the chalkboard that was at the front of the classroom.

"Alright. Where did we leave off yesterday?"

The chorus of voices answering me was music to my ears. They made this place bearable. I knew I needed to do my best to take as many of them with me as I could when I went. My heart sank as I thought about it, because I knew I wouldn't manage to get them all out.

CHAPTER 4

Riptide

A bead of sweat rolled down my temple as we made our way out toward The Silverbells. Ethan had contacted me like we'd hoped he would and I'd met with Jacob at the designated spot. It hadn't taken long to load my—other Derek's—shit into the pickup and head out into the desert. It was beginning.

Luckily other Derek hadn't known much about these guys because I'd had precious little time to study the information he did have. I was going into this almost as blind as other Derek would have.

The drive was filled with tense silence. I knew other Derek would have been babbling like a magpie after the first twenty minutes, but I remained quiet. It gave me time to think. I needed to somehow pull this first meeting with Ethan off. If I could do that, I might make it out of this alive. If I failed, well… I wouldn't live long enough for it to be much to worry about.

"We're almost there, Brother Derek."

I cringed at the title. Listening to myself being called Derek for who knew how long was going to be bad enough, but Brother Derek? *Jesus fucking Christ.* The biggest danger might end up being me eating my own gun after being called that shit nonstop.

Everyone had called me Riptide—or Rip—for so long I almost hadn't responded when Jacob had called out to me when we'd met up. I was going to have to get over it.

My eyes narrowed as Jacob angled the truck onto a little two track that cut west toward the mountains. It was about half a mile south of where Sherry Holden's vehicle had been found deserted. We'd always stopped there and hiked back to the compound. We couldn't use their roads in and out of this place, but knowing where they were was going to be useful as fuck when the time to came to exterminate them.

The fence and buildings came into view. I leaned forward to peer up at the guards who were standing near the top of the fence. That scaffolding was new. Before they hadn't had the high ground like that, making it easier for us to spy on them. It just occurred to me that with every passing day their fortifications would get stronger. The longer I took in here the harder, and more dangerous, it would be for us to assault this compound and take these guys out.

We'd agreed—much to Lockout's displeasure—to stop watching the compound while I was here. We'd stopped sending men out here the morning we'd voted to send me in. There was too much risk if someone was caught. I was the newest member and it would cast too much suspicion on me. I was truly alone out here.

We got out of the truck once Jacob pulled through the gates—also new—and I pulled my duffel bags out of the back. I tossed them over my shoulder, looking around as I did.

What struck me first was the clothing. All the women were in dresses, or skirts and blouses, while the men were in what looked almost like old western wear. They were all heading together like a herd of cattle.

Where the fuck were these people shopping? Pioneers 'R Us?

"Brother Derek! Welcome!"

I turned and faced the man who was striding across the village. His arms were held out and there was a beaming smile on his face. I'd have to be a fucking idiot to miss the calculating look in his eyes, and I wasn't stupid. I took stock of him. Blond hair, blue eyes, about six-foot with a wiry frame. Nothing special. According to Butcher these guys weren't usually superior physically. Their talents were in their ability to bullshit people into believing anything they wanted.

"Thank you," I told him in a normal tone once he got close enough. I'd play the game, to a point. I wasn't a good enough actor to try to play the over the top, excited believer.

The flicker of awareness in Ethan's eyes told me I'd chosen correctly. Other Derek had mentioned that Chet would have told them a little about me. I wasn't about to act like the fucking coward other Derek was, but if I'd shown up giddy Ethan would have put a bullet in my head. The cool reservation I was projecting had just gotten me past the first test.

"Follow me," Ethan told me, the smile on his face turning malicious.

Great. Nothing like jumping directly into the fire inside the lion's den.

He led me to the middle of the compound. There was some kind of fucked up altar up on a stage and bleacher-like seating surrounding it in a half arc. The seats were packed.

Looked like everyone had shown up to see the new guy. The hairs on the back of my neck rose like they tended to do in dangerous situations. I didn't need my instincts to be screaming at me like this. I could see that this could be a potentially threatening scenario all on my own.

"I'll take those, Brother Derek," Jacob told me.

Letting him take my bags, I pointed to one. "Careful with that. It's got all my equipment in it." Judging by the clothes, I had a feeling that most of the items in my bags were destined for the trash. But I needed the computer and hard drives. They were my connection to The Order's finances, and my only connection to the outside world.

I followed Ethan up onto the stage. We stopped in the middle and I cast a look around. The last of the people had come into the area and were watching me. My eyes stopped on a pair of eyes as blue as my favorite cove back on the Long Beach Peninsula. My breath caught in my throat as I watched her speak to random women as she moved through the crowd toward the dais.

Graceful as a ballerina she stepped around people, avoiding all contact with men, but gifting the children with her heart stopping smile. Our eyes locked again, and my dick hardened. Her beauty was like a punch to the gut. This was her first time seeing me, but I'd been dreaming of her for weeks. Seeing her in front of me was the culmination of weeks' worth of preparation. Getting to the compound, meeting Ethan, seeing the other people in the community hadn't made it real. She did.

My lungs burned, forcing me to take the breath I hadn't realized I was holding. Sloane had slowed to a stop, looking almost as surprised as I was.

Her eyes were clear and bright and the look in them turned from confusion to animosity. I had to bite back a grin. It didn't bother me that she was suspicious as to why I was staring at her. Time had slowed, so I couldn't tell you how long I'd been watching her, but it was enough that the younger girls who'd come to stand near her were giggling and shooting blatant looks between her and I.

Here I stood, ready to take Sloane out of here, and she was looking at me like I was a pile of garbage and all I could do was smile at her courage and willfulness. I could understand the mistrust. Even though I knew I was leaving this place with her, I wasn't sure I could trust her yet. It would depend on how brainwashed she was. So far, I liked what I saw. In more ways than one.

Berry colored lips parted in shock as one of the girls whispered something to her. She shot the girl a chastising look, then ducked her head, breaking our eye contact. She didn't leave though, and every once in a while she peeked up from beneath her lashes to see if I was still watching her.

"Brothers and Sisters!"

I gave Ethan a disgruntled look as he bellowed directly into my fucking ear hole. It broke my focus on the beautiful woman nearby. As soon as he glanced over at me—probably feeling my urge to punch him in the side of the head—I pasted an innocent look on my face.

Fuck me, it's hard to act weak and intimidated.

"We're here today to welcome Brother Derek into the fold!"

Did he have to do everything at the decibel of a scream? Fucking hell. I moved slightly away from him just to preserve my damned sanity and so I wouldn't give into the temptation to end him here and now. I remembered what Butcher had said. Killing him would have disastrous effects. I sighed and crossed my arms over my chest, waiting for the show to end so I could figure out how to navigate this place. After getting just this glimpse of the way these people were living I was in a shitty mood.

"Brother Derek has joined us from the world of demons! He wants to walk the path of purity. Of morality. He's come to see the lie that the people of the Sky God tell and knows that the only way to salvation lies with The Order of The Earth!"

I bit the inside of my lip to keep from grinning at the pure fucking bullshit spewing from Ethan's mouth right now. We'd heard plenty of this when we were watching them. It wasn't new. It was different as hell hearing it in person though. And seeing the men in the crowd nodding and starting to call out in agreement. The women were silent, eyes downcast.

The men are a bunch of fucking nutjobs.

Except that I was one of those nutjobs now. I had to play along. More than playing along, I had to sell it to them. If I keep calling them wackos, even in my head, I was going to fuck up and get caught. I shut my eyes tight, focusing. Opening them, I looked over at Ethan like he was God incarnate. Which, I suppose, was the point.

Sell it. Your life, her *life, depends on it.*

"Brother Derek knows that the only way to heaven, to true enlightenment, lies within the Earth God. I alone can grant you eternal life!" Ethan turned toward me. It was like a hyena stalking toward a lion. He was a slimy, weaselly, piece of pond scum. But I had to put up with him, with the game, in order to obtain my objectives. If I didn't fully immerse myself into this role—if Ethan didn't believe it —I was fucked.

"Do you, Brother Derek, submit to the initiation?"

Say what?

"Yes," I said, tone eager, adding a pleading look to my face.

What fucking initiation? This is going to hurt.

Ethan searched my expression and though I didn't let my satisfaction show at his frustration when he found no reaction other than enthusiasm, I still felt it. He was using this to check my dedication, my loyalty.

If he asks me to suck his fucking Earth God dick, I'm killing him.

Unease slithered through me as Ethan's eyes shifted to satisfaction. "Then kneel. Put your hands upon your head. And prepare thyself to take the Earth God's gifts into thyself."

The. Fuck?

It took every ounce of willpower to kneel before this swine. The planking was hard beneath my knees, grounding me as I raised my hands to the back of my head.

Ethan moved behind me, but I kept my eyes forward, refusing to follow him. I kept the stupid, eager smile on my face. *The whole compound is watching you.* It went against every instinct I had, letting an enemy around to my six, but it was what I had to do.

The cheers of the crowd made my eyes narrow. I'd watched a documentary once where they'd reenacted a medieval hanging. The crowd had acted much like these people. Though here it was mostly the men interacting. Out of the corner of my eye I saw a trio of young boys with savage grins on their faces. They'd edged in closer to the stage to watch the show. I knew whatever was coming wasn't going to be good. For me at least.

A flash of blue caught my attention and I zeroed in on Sloane again as she shifted from foot to foot. Unease was radiating off her and it was enough to let me know that whatever was coming was going to be bad. Anger filled her eyes, but this time it seemed to be on my behalf.

"Hear unto me, my laws. Obey them and be rewarded. Break them and face my wrath!"

So. Fucking. Dramatic.

Sloane's plump lips twitched into a smile and I wondered if I'd just said that aloud? No. Ethan would have gone nuts if I had. He seemed to be waiting for something.

"I hear you!" I yelled. There were smiles from the crowd. Seemed to be the right answer.

Ethan continued. "No lying with children!"

The stupid smile I was wearing fell off my face and I almost turned around to face him. What the fuck had he just said? My muscles tensed, the question fleeing my mind when I heard something whistling through the air. Pain exploded over my back as the crack of a whip sounded near my ear. Fire licked over my skin as I felt my t-shirt shred beneath the tail of the weapon.

This motherfucker is whipping me.

Disbelief held me still through the first two commandments. I didn't even hear Ethan's words anymore as rage crept in. I was seeing red, ready to burn the fucking world for the disrespect, when I caught sight of Sloane again.

She watched, sadness filling her expression, as the whip cracked again and again across my back. These assholes didn't believe in ten commandments. No, that was too easy. There were twenty-fucking-one.

I focused in on her eyes, locked my gaze onto her. There was something more than sadness there. She was pleading with me. *Don't stop or you're dead.* It was written on her face. *Don't beg, don't run, don't stop, or Ethan will kill you.* I knew it as surely as if she were whispering the words directly to me.

The agony was causing black spots to dance on the edges of my vision. I'd be damned if I'd black out. I wouldn't give this fucker the satisfaction. I was going to have to ask someone what these commandments were later because, other than the first, I hadn't heard a damn thing.

Ethan stepped in front of me, signaling for me to rise. "Welcome to The Order, Brother Derek."

People cried out in congratulations, but I ignored everyone. Their voices were taking on a tinny quality, letting me know I was hitting the edges of my limit.

"I'll expect to see you tomorrow at nine a.m. for your introduction." He walked off, barking something as he did.

If his introduction was anything like the initiation I was going to end up losing my shit less than twenty-four hours into this plan. Hands grabbed me, steadying me.

"Easy."

The soft voice had me looking down. Sloane wrapped my arm over her shoulders, and I followed along as she brought me down off the stage. I was moving on autopilot. Even when I wasn't completely functional mentally, it was hard for me to take my eyes off her. She was so goddamn captivating, a momentary distraction from the agony.

"I've never seen anyone make it through that and stay conscious to the end," she said, giving me a quick peek before looking down at the ground again. "Most pass out. Others run, or beg. It's a good thing you didn't do that."

Her voice was soothing and it made me want to close my eyes. My tongue was thick inside my mouth, preventing me from speaking. I don't ever remember being this out of it. My back had gone mostly numb after the first few lashes, but I had a feeling he hadn't used a gentle touch. I didn't even want to think about what my back looked like.

We made it into a building and before I knew it I was face down on a bed. I didn't want to give in to the fight, but unconsciousness dragged me down.

CHAPTER 5

Sloane

I dipped the rag back into the bowl of water and gently separated the shredded pieces of Derek's shirt with my free hand. It was being held together solely by the collar, the rest a torn mess that was sticking to the blood seeping over his skin. His back was a crisscross of torn flesh. He'd bear these marks for the rest of his life. I knew, because I wore them as well. We all did. Though my marks decorated the majority of my body. Most people only endured one or two whippings other than their initiation. It was a favorite punishment of Ethan's. But since I stepped in regularly for others and received their punishment, I had more than most.

No one escaped the 'initiation'. Thankfully, Ethan waited until the children were eighteen to induct them into The Order officially, but otherwise the only non-scarred flesh here was his. I, of course, got my scars earlier than that. It had taken a lot of persuasion, and additional scars, to convince Ethan to wait until the kids were eighteen. It was one of precious few victories I'd had here. If you could consider it a victory.

I cut away Brother Derek's shirt and paused at the expanse of muscle I uncovered. My eyes widened and I looked down at him with renewed interest. He wasn't bulky like Bruce and Jacob, but he had muscle stacked on muscle nonetheless. I hadn't been expecting it. It had probably kept his injuries from being even worse.

Ignoring the funny fluttering feeling in my belly, I dabbed the wet cloth onto his back. The gasp tore from my throat when he jerked around and snagged my wrist, glaring at me. He'd gone from completely unconscious to…this. There was a feverish look in his eyes, so I was sure he wasn't fully aware of what was going on, but as soon as his gaze landed on me the anger on his face softened. He looked down at where he was holding my wrist, the dripping cloth dangling from my fingers.

I didn't like for most people to touch me. Throughout my life most touches had been filled with pain and anguish. But his touch? It had my pulse racing beneath my skin. That fluttering was back in full force. Why was I having this kind of reaction to him? I wasn't sure what my body was trying to tell me, other than to pay attention to the man in front of me, but I knew I'd never experienced it before. No man had made me feel more than anger or disgust. Yet here I was, sitting beside him, with some unknown emotion battering at me like a storm. It was building up inside of me and I was afraid to look too closely at what it might mean.

Brother Derek's fingers squeezed my wrist, reminding me that we were silently staring at each other. His hand was touching a large corded scar that wrapped around my wrist. It'd come from being tied up for countless hours while I awaited a severe punishment. I'd thought, at the time, it would be the end of me. Somehow, my mother had managed to talk Ethan down on the severity of the punishment. I never found out what she'd offered him that had changed his mind.

"I need to clean your wounds before I put the poultice on them, Brother Derek," I told him. My voice was soft, as though I were soothing a raging beast. I managed to project a calm demeanor even though my body was rioting. The grip on my wrist and the wild eyed look spoke to me of danger and death. The place between my legs grew damp, making my eyes widen as a flash of pleasure pierced my core.

Gasping, I pulled back, but Derek's hand tightened on mine. Every touch seemed to wring a direct response from within me. It was unusual. When I'd been a teenager, the other girls had spoken in whispers about what it felt like to pleasure themselves. They'd spoken of urges and desires and I'd remained quiet, because not once had I experienced what they spoke of. Was this…desire? I'd long since given up on ever hoping I'd enjoy having a man's hands on me.

But Derek didn't seem to be the usual kind of man Ethan allowed into his community. He hadn't responded to the initiation the way most did. Bruce and Jacob were the only two who seemed to know what they were doing. Bruce was only here to increase security after what had happened before. Ethan allowed him to stay because he was oafish and loyal, not smart enough to ever betray him.

Jacob was as loyal as they came and had proven it over and over before Ethan had allowed him into his inner circle. The man was terrifying, all dark looks and a watchful eye that assured you he'd kill you without remorse.

Brother Derek's thumb brushed over the pulse in my wrist. It was dancing as fast as a hummingbird's wings. I found it hard to breathe while he was looking at me. He'd stared at me during the initiation as well. After the first few strokes of the whip the smile he'd worn had faded and something new—and slightly terrifying—had emerged. I was unendingly curious about this new man and what his role here was to be. I was expecting a small, mousy man. That was the typical kind Ethan allowed in. I certainly didn't expect…this.

Even more unexpected was the way he was eliciting these feelings from inside of me. My nipples had hardened into points and were pressing against my blouse, almost as if they were begging for something. My core clenched, aching to be filled. I wasn't completely oblivious to the way between men and women. Those girls who'd been my friends had filled me in once they'd gotten married, but it'd sounded so awful I couldn't understand why my body seemed to be preparing me for the act in the way they'd explained.

Derek was a gorgeous man. That was plain to see. His hair was a mix of brown and gold and stopped down around a square, defined jaw. He was like the depictions of Greek Gods I'd read about once. Those icy blue eyes held me enthralled. My reaction to him was unusual, but it would be hard for women to resist his smile. I was sure of it. The fact that my body was responding to him now was inconvenient and unwelcomed.

Just because the man was good looking didn't mean I could trust him. He was joining Ethan's ranks. That meant he was the enemy. Still, as much as I said this to myself, I couldn't fight that I was drawn to him.

He let go of my wrist when I tugged again, shot me one more penetrating look, then laid back down. His eyes were open, though he didn't seem fully conscious. It would be better for him if he wasn't awake for this, but there wasn't much I could do.

Tucking aside my wayward reactions to him, I went back to gently cleaning his back. The whip had dragged over the stage between each strike, picking up dirt and debris, which was now lodged in Derek's wounds. It took far longer than I would have liked, but I finally had strips of clean cloth—slathered with the poultice—draped over his injuries.

It only took me a few additional moments to leave water on the nightstand near his bed for him. I'd come back and help him eat later tonight, but mostly he just needed rest. He wouldn't be comfortable for weeks to come, but he'd live.

Moving toward the door, I froze when his deep voice rumbled through the room.

"Thank you."

Glancing over my shoulder, I found him—head turned—watching me. I nodded at him as those new sensations flared to life again, then left his new home. I always volunteered to help those who'd been initiated. If I didn't know them well it gave me a chance to find out about them. To see if they'd be an ally or a foe. There were only three men here who I semi-trusted. They never engaged in any of the punishments and seemed to treat their families well. Most proved my initial fears correct—they were too far gone and brainwashed to be helped. Most gave away the reasons they were here quite quickly.

Rubbing my hand over my belly, I tried to ease it as it danced. It couldn't be possible that a new man could cause this kind of reaction from me and that he would end up being as awful as the men here. Right? Shaking my head, I prayed that it wasn't so. I liked to think my instincts were too sound to fall for something like that. Then again, I never expected the sensations that were currently washing through my system to ever show up. Not for me. There had to be a reason I was responding this way to the newest member of our community.

Ethan had begun gathering new followers within the last few years. At first he'd kept things small, it was easier to control a small group. Something had changed four years ago. Now there was an influx of new men entering the fold. With more men being brought on, Ethan had begun pulling in women as well.

The easiest way he'd found to keep women around—because who would choose this lifestyle if they weren't born into it—was to take in the vulnerable. He found homeless women and young girls and inducted them into the community. I couldn't necessarily blame them. He offered them a home, and protection from abuse. The scary thing was, they were genuine promises, to some degree. It was just that everything else that would follow wouldn't quite live up to the expectation.

I wondered if he told them when he first approached them that they'd end up imprisoned here? That they'd be married off almost immediately—as long as they were eighteen—and that their life would no longer be their own? I wondered if he were honest about it, how many of these women would choose to remain where they were versus come here? I feared too many would still come here. He knew how to find women that were desperate for an escape. He offered an escape from the drugs and forced prostitution, or so he promised. I don't think you could explain to them that this place was just a different kind of bad.

Our numbers were a little over one hundred now. Ethan was still quite picky about who he brought on, but we were growing. That was why Ethan chose the middle of the desert to start over new. He thought if we were out here then he'd be left alone to amass his empire. What he didn't let on to the others was that his shenanigans always drew attention. No matter how small the town, he would draw enough attention that we would have to leave. Out here, he thought he might be safe.

I rolled my eyes in disgust at him and made my way across the village to the little home that I shared with three other unmarried girls. They ranged between fifteen and seventeen. In a few years they would hit 'marrying age' and be moved into a home with their husbands. Men still outnumbered the women here, so many were waiting for the younger girls to age up.

Brother's Derek's handsome face chose that moment to flash through my mind. Worry that he was going to end up disappointing me had me promising myself that I wasn't going to get involved with that man. It didn't matter how handsome he was, or how he made me feel. It didn't matter that just a glance from him made my heart start to race, and caused a heat to simmer low in my belly.

It's a coincidence. The next time I see him it'll be different

Shaking my head at my bold-faced lie, I entered my house and stopped dead in my tracks as seven teenage girls' heads snapped in my direction. I was like a mouse being hunted by barn owls. "Girls," I greeted them, wondering what was going on.

"Sister Sloane," Beth Ann spoke up, eyes shining, "is it true you tended to Brother Derek?"

Irritation at their intrusion chased away the fog of pleasure Derek had left me with and I fought not to roll my eyes. I should have realized the handsome new stranger was the reason they were all perched in my house waiting on any piece of gossip.

Just wait until they see him with his shirt off.

"It's true," I told them, biting back the smile when they all giggled. "I assume you're all here to help me make dinner then?"

They jumped out of their chairs like the house was on fire. There were mumbled, breathless excuses tossed around as they rushed from my home, leaving only the three who lived here with me.

I gave Tilly, Janice, and Audrey a pointed look. "I expect any news I come home with to remain inside these walls."

"They came to us, Sloane," Audrey said with a shrug. "I didn't want to let them in, but Tilly thought that would just make them worse."

It probably would have. My girls were amazing. They were more like me than the others. They saw this place for what it was. Saw the men here as monsters. That also made it more dangerous for them.

"It was good of you to keep up the pretenses," I told them. "Never-"

"Let them see that you know," all three finished out my sentence for me with smiles.

My heart softened and threatened to melt inside my chest. I loved these girls as though they were my own. The three of them had different circumstances and had ended up living with me mostly because of their abusive fathers, but having them move in had brightened my world. They were first on my priority list of getting out of here. Them and Abigail. I sighed as I thought of the young girl. She was a spitfire. How her mouse of a mother and evil prick of a father had made such a sweet, inquisitive, bright child was beyond me.

"Help me make dinner," I requested, and all three girls stood.

"What are we having?" Janice asked.

"Roasted chicken. Brother Derek will have bone broth."

Tilly and Audrey shot each other amused looks. "He's quite handsome," Tilly stated.

"That's true," I said, taking a whole chicken and placing it on the cutting board. I began parting it out as they chittered together. It was always exciting for people here when anyone new came, but to have a relatively young, attractive, man join always sent the single women into a tizzy. Men under forty were rare. Handsome men…exceedingly rare. Ethan made sure of it.

"You're not at all affected by him?" Janice asked me, placing her hands on her hips. Her dark curls bounced as she cocked her head. "I'm pretty sure he has a dimple."

Tilly rolled her eyes, pulling her blonde hair back into a bun. "No he didn't."

"I love dimples," Audrey interjected. "I hope my husband has them." She shot me a look, realizing what she'd said. "On the outside, I mean," she clarified.

Stopping what I was doing, I turned and surveyed them all. "You're allowed to dream about your future husband, Audrey."

"You don't."

They were watching me with a look of hero worship, so I sighed. Guilt made me admit something to them I'd never told another person. "Yes, I do. I just don't tell anyone about it."

They gave each other looks of disbelief. Frowns marred their pretty faces. I didn't want them thinking there was something wrong with dreaming of finding a man who would be strong and brave and protect them from the world. I'd heard them whispering about these very things most nights.

"I want a man who is kind, but…dangerous."

All their brows shot up at my admission. "Dangerous?" they all breathed the word out.

I nodded. "To everyone but me. I'm so sick of feeling afraid. I want him to wrap me in his arms so I feel safe and slay any who would dare to harm our family."

"You want a man to murder?" Tilly asked, sounding confused. Even though we all knew this place was evil, that the ways Ethan taught us were…off, we still had been living these beliefs since we were old enough to know them. Murder went directly against the commandments.

Unless you're Ethan or Jacob.

Fear kept the words locked inside my throat. I needed to keep my cynicism in check around the girls. If they accidentally let anything I said slip, they'd be severely punished, if not outright killed. Ethan and his lap dog didn't have to follow the rules the same way we did. The hypocrisy never seemed to matter to them.

They did whatever they wanted, and Jacob followed every directive Ethan gave. The girls didn't know what I knew. They thought the worst that happened was the whippings and the beatings. The women tried to keep what really happened from the younger girls. Especially what happened to the older women. If I didn't get out of here soon I'd have to sit these three down and tell them what they could really expect from any husband they were given to. It wasn't going to be a pretty conversation. It wasn't a pretty life.

I'd come to realize that the night I bumped into Jacob carrying my mother's dead body out of our home. He hadn't bothered to explain. He'd just stared at me in that silent, scary way of his and growled at me that if I told anyone what I'd seen, I'd be joining her.

Confronting Ethan hadn't granted me any answers and had gained me fresh scars. It hadn't been until years later that I'd learned the truth, she'd been planning to get me away from this place. She'd had everything mapped out in the same little book I now had. Even though she'd believed in Ethan and this way of life, she knew that she couldn't let me grow up here.

The guilt from her death had plagued me for a long time. It still reared its ugly head from time to time, but I'd mostly come to the realization that my mother had loved me enough to take the risk. From that moment on I'd taken up her mission and was determined to see it through.

I shrugged, realizing the girls were waiting for my response. "As long as they're bad men? I'm fine with my husband murdering to protect me and our children."

The girls seemed to think about that as we all went back to our work. Audrey was chopping vegetables, Janice was making dough for bread, and Tilly was making an apple pie. Tilly had a talent for baking. We tasked her with making our desserts each night. It'd added a few pounds to my hips and thighs, but I wasn't complaining. There'd been instances before when the times had been so lean most living here had been skeletons. I filled out my five-five frame well. I wasn't waif thin, but I wasn't what one would consider voluptuous. I considered myself pretty average.

Even during good times, Ethan would withhold rations if his citizens were caught causing trouble. And I was a perpetual trouble maker.

A knock on the door had me frowning. "Just a moment!" I called out as I went to wash the chicken from my hands. Pulling open the door, I froze.

Ethan took that as an invitation to stroll into my house uninvited. He didn't think he needed an invitation. After all, God didn't wait for an invitation. Or so he thought. I was shocked he'd knocked.

"Girls," I told them, voice calm though I was panicking inside. Why was he here? "Why don't you go to your rooms and get started on your homework?"

They were gone before the words even finished forming. Ethan watched them scurry away, like a fat overindulged cat deciding if he wanted to have fun by chasing scared little mice.

Finally, his blue eyes settled on me. Fear caused me to take a few steps back, but I hid it by turning to the dinner preparations. I fought not to shake. It didn't matter that I knew he wasn't a god. Or that all of this was bullshit. He still commanded my life and could kill me with a snap of his fingers. No one here—other than me—questioned him. Even then, I was very deliberate as to how and when. I enjoyed breathing and wanted to keep doing it.

I tucked my hair behind my ears. My fingers itched to pull it back into a ponytail, but that was only allowed of the girls under eighteen. The rest of us had to wear it free, flowing down our backs. We wore dresses and skirts, because the men demanded it. When I got out of here I planned to cut my hair short. Into a pixie cut. I'd seen photos of it on the internet and the urge to control even just the tiniest piece of my life made me want to cut my thick hip-length hair as short as I could.

"Did Brother Derek say anything?"

"No, My Lord." I folded my hands together in front of me, refusing to show him anything but a calm, peaceful expression. The current beating I'd taken was still fresh in my mind, so I was doing what I could to pacify him. "Would you like something to drink, My Lord? To eat?"

What I wouldn't give to poison you.

As if Ethan could hear my inner thoughts, he scoffed. "No. Did he wake up?"

I hesitated. Lying here could come back on me, but if I mentioned that Derek had been awake nearly the entire time Ethan might take that as a sign that the other man was too strong. "No, My Lord. He passed out as soon as I got him home. I left him resting."

Ethan rubbed a hand over his jaw, deep in thought. "Okay." He walked over to my door and opened it. Pausing, he looked at me over his shoulder with a calculating look on his face.

Unease slithered down my spine. I didn't like the look. He was planning something. That didn't bode well for anyone.

Without another word he left the house. It was as though he'd sucked all the oxygen from the house while he'd been here. I wheezed out a breath and set a hand on the counter to steady myself.

The girls peeked their heads around the corner. "Is he gone?" Tilly whispered. She knew he was or they wouldn't have dared to ask.

I nodded and waved to them. We needed to finish dinner so I could go tend to my patient. I tried to shove Ethan's concerning behavior from my mind. Just like I tried to ignore the little jump of excitement at the thought of seeing Derek again.

CHAPTER 6

Riptide

My eyes opened the moment the front door did. I turned my head and watched to see who was walking into what, I assumed, was my house.

As soon as Sloane called out, the tenseness fled from my muscles. I didn't bother to answer, she'd see that I was awake soon enough.

Her steps faltered as soon as she came into view and saw me watching her. A hesitant smile spread over her face so I offered her one as well. I didn't want her to be afraid of me. It didn't matter that pain was making me a cranky son of a bitch. Looking at her I could forget that it hurt to even breathe. I wanted her to sit down and stay a while. This was my opportunity to speak with her.

"Hello."

"Hi," I replied, grimacing at how gravelly my voice sounded. "Thank you again for tending to me."

Her steps were hesitant as she came toward me. She was watching me like she expected me to pounce. If I wasn't feeling so shitty and it wouldn't scare the fuck out of her, I might. It didn't matter that my back ached like a sore tooth, I wanted her.

My wounds weren't deterring my cock, which was thickening against the bed. Images of her naked beneath me were sliding their way into my mind. I forced them out so I could focus on her.

"You're welcome." She set a basket down next to the bed. "I brought you some food and some pain medication."

One of my brows shot up. "Is that allowed?"

There was a slight hesitation as she reached down into her basket telling me that the next words she spoke weren't the truth. "Of course."

She twisted the cap off a bottle and shook two pills out into her hand before holding them out.

I stared at her graceful fingers, the soft skin of her hand. I wondered if it was soft everywhere. She wore a long sleeve blouse that buttoned up to her neck and covered her wrists. Her skirts swept the floors. Other than her hands and face nothing was uncovered. My gaze flicked up to hers. "I don't want to get you into trouble."

She shook her head, her long thick hair moving with the motion. It was a shade or two darker than my own. The late afternoon sun streamed in through the window, setting off strands of gold that streaked through it. "I already told you, it's allowed."

Deciding not to argue, I took the pills, enjoying the little spark that flared between us as our fingers touched. Her eyes widened, but I just smiled. I took the glass from her and downed the pills. Normally I wouldn't want to take anything that might fog up my brain, but that fucker had done a number on my back. If his plan was to drug me up before he killed me, then so be it. If he was using this angel to deceive me, then I'd happily be led to my death, as long as it was her leading.

"My name is Sister Sloane."

I blinked, realizing it was a good thing that she'd told me before I'd accidentally used her name. It would be a bit awkward to explain that I'd heard it weeks ago when we'd been spying on their camp. Not that I could actually tell her that.

"Nice to meet you Sloane. I'm Derek."

"Brother Derek," she said with a smile, then ducked her head as though expecting my anger.

Gritting my teeth together at the thought of her being worried about something as simple as correcting me, I nodded. "Brother Derek. Does that mean I need to call you Sister Sloane?"

"It's what's proper."

Brotherly and sisterly feelings were not how I thought of her, but I held my tongue. "What do you have there?" I craned my neck to see over the edge of the bed.

"I brought you soup."

My eyes searched her face. "Do you always care for the injured?" *Or are you feeling this connection between us, too?* From the moment I'd seen her it was like I'd been hit with a recognition. Like I'd known her all my life though I'd never seen her before. It was an odd feeling, but I was slowly coming to terms with it.

Having her seated here next to me...it felt like I was home. That was bullshit. Home was back in the city, with my brothers, but for some reason she was making this more bearable than I expected.

"Often. Although we have a few other women who help as well." She gave me a smile and set the bowl with a lid on the nightstand while she pulled out a spoon.

I watched quietly as she set up. Her motions were smooth and graceful. She watched what she was doing as well, but I saw her sneaking looks at me when she thought I wouldn't notice. I closed my eyes, giving her a break. It didn't seem to be within my control to stop staring at her.

"Open."

My eyes opened and I saw her holding a spoon. She blew softly on the liquid and I nearly groaned out loud. My mind jumped into the gutter and all I could think about was her wrapping those berry colored lips around my cock.

I wasn't in so much pain I couldn't feed myself, but I didn't tell her that. Spending more time with her was more of a necessity at this point. It would take more than my threadbare control to watch her walk away from me. Opening my mouth, I let her feed me. The spoon trembled in her fingers and the air around us sparked. There was no way she wasn't sensing what was between us. Hell, it was getting so hot in here I was afraid something might catch fire. Remarking on it now was sure to send her running in the opposite direction—based on the unsettled tells she was giving off—so I kept my mouth shut.

"What brought you here, Brother Derek?"

My smile slowly spread over my face. "Came out here to be with family."

"Oh? Who?"

"Chet Holden."

Her hand froze mid-way to my lips, and I wondered if I shouldn't have told her that. She would have found out soon enough. Better that it came from me. It wasn't like I wanted to claim Chet. He was a piece of shit, but I had to play the fucking game.

She shut down in a heartbeat. Gone was her smile and she refused to meet my gaze. It was like shutters slamming closed, doors locking, and she knocked down the connection simmering between us. Her opinion of Chet was very apparent. Suspicion was back in her gaze when she finally looked up at me.

At least she wasn't fond of Chet. In the long run, that's a good thing.

"I'll leave this here for you," she offered, setting a plate with a few slices of bread aside and the rest of the soup. Her cold tone made me flinch. She jerked her arm back, when I reached out to touch her, and stood. "I'm sorry, but I need to go."

"Thank you for dinner, Sister Sloane," I told her. The last thing I wanted was to make it worse. Hope that I could change her mind about me was all I had right now. If I pushed the issue I could kiss that opportunity goodbye.

Her eyes flicked to mine and she gave me a small nod before she hurried out of my home. The scent of mint filled the air around me, making me wish she'd stayed.

"Well, fuck. Thanks a lot, Chet, you fucking bastard," I muttered.

* * *

The next morning, I dragged myself off the bed, groaning as I went. My back wouldn't be healed fully for weeks, but I'd been 'summoned' by the great Earth God. I shook my head in disgust.

Gritting my teeth, I picked my bags up and opened them. I hissed out a curse as I saw all my clothes gone. I knew those assholes were going to do that.

I sighed, then went over to the dresser and opened a drawer. Grimacing at the clothes I found there, I pulled out what I'd need in order to go see Ethan.

Sitting on the bed, I managed to pull my underwear and pants on. I sat glaring at the button down shirt. The last thing I wanted to do was put that on. I still had on the strips that Sloane had placed on my back. They were dried to my skin. There wasn't enough time to shower and I wasn't getting them off any other way. Besides, they'd offer a layer of protection between my shredded skin and the shirt.

"What are you doing?" Sloane gasped as she hurried through the doorway.

"I'm supposed to meet Ethan in twenty minutes."

Her hands landed on my shoulder and arm, though gently, as she tried to urge me to lay back down. Concern knitted her brows together. "No one ever meets with him the day after. They usually see him after a week."

I studied her worried face, wondering if she'd already forgiven me for who my cousin was, or if she was just too distressed about me being up and about to think about it. My guess was the latter. Her face was close to mine as she continued to try to maneuver me into place. How would she respond if I kissed her right now?

She'll probably slap you.

Deciding to take a safer course, my hand lifted of its own accord and I cupped her cheek. She stilled, eyes darting to mine, surprise and desire darkening the blue. How many of those people were afforded a week of rest because Sloane stood up to Ethan for them. Possibly took a beating for them. All so they could heal?

"I'm fine," I insisted, enjoying how soft her skin was beneath my fingers. "We have a lot to discuss. Besides, I'm not one for laying around in bed."

"You need to rest," she countered, frowning at me. Gone was the coldness from last night. There was enough hesitation in her gaze that I knew she hadn't forgotten that I was 'Chet's cousin', but like me, she couldn't seem to help herself. I liked that.

"I will," I said, rubbing my thumb over her smooth cheek again. "After the meeting."

The movement seemed to remind her that I was touching her and of how close she was standing, because she backed away from me. I let my hand drop.

"I brought you breakfast." She motioned to the basket she used to bring the food over. Her hands were clasped together in front of her as though to keep herself from reaching for me.

That could be wishful thinking, so I didn't push my luck by trying to touch her again. It shouldn't be so hard to keep my hands to myself. Even now they twitched. The urge to place them on her hips and pull her to stand between my thighs was so strong I knew I needed a distraction.

Reaching over, I plucked a plate out of the basket and a fork. "Thank you." There were eggs, sausage, and pancakes. I made quick work of the food, famished, while she stood there wringing her hands.

"Your back is going to take longer to heal if you refuse to take the time to rest."

I grinned at her. "Worried about me, Angel?"

Her eyes narrowed, temper sparking in those gorgeous blue depths. "I'm not an angel."

Cocking my head, I studied her. "Is that considered offensive because Angels are a creation of the Sky God?" I didn't fully understand these people, their customs, or beliefs.

She shook her head. "No. But angels are free of sin."

One side of my mouth kicked up into a smirk. "And you're not?" I was implying sex, but the way her expression dropped told me she was thinking of something much less fun and possibly traumatizing. She was on the verge of tears.

"I'm sorry-" I started.

"It doesn't matter." Her heart was right there on her sleeve and I'd just been the one to rip it out of her chest.

The need to hold her and ask her what had brought the sadness to her eyes nearly overwhelmed me. Instead, I let the subject drop. She didn't know me and certainly wouldn't welcome comfort from me. Not yet.

Glancing at the clock on the nightstand, I sighed. Placing the now empty plate on the nightstand, I stood and picked up the shirt. Leaving her was the last thing I wanted to do, but I had to meet with Ethan.

"Wait." She hurried over to the dresser and pulled open a drawer. I suddenly knew who'd packed it full of the clothes I'd need. She pulled something out and I watched as she approached me.

"How many things do you do around here?"

Her eyes darted away from mine. She didn't answer my question, instead she held up the wrapping. "It's going to hurt going on and coming off, but it'll make it more comfortable while you're moving around and keep your shirt from irritating your skin more than needed."

I nodded. "Will you help me with it?"

Her cheeks pinkened, but she stepped closer. Her tits brushed against my upper abdomen when she reached around me. She was small compared to my own six-two frame, but had a strength of will that made me sure she could be a force to be reckoned with.

I inhaled her minty scent as she wrapped me in the bandage. I gritted my teeth as my wounds tugged and pain shot through my entire body. She was right, it hurt like hell, but it would be worth it later. I focused on her instead. She was bent in front of me as she secured the bandage at the front so I could easily release it later. When she was standing tall she was around five-five. Despite her height, she wasn't frail. Even her hideous clothes couldn't hide the curves she was packing and I was willing to bet under that shirt she had some muscle to her. You didn't live a life like this without building up some strength.

My fingers twitched at my side as I once again thought about grabbing her full hips and tugging her against my body. She was standing so close and her curves would feel like fucking heaven. I kept my hands to myself. There were still too many unknowns here for me to give in to the lust pounding through my system right now. I wanted to toss her onto the bed and burrow under her skirts, bury my face between her legs.

For all I knew that would get me hung. Or shot. Who the fuck knew. Plus, I still couldn't let my guard down around her. Not until I found out how deep into this lifestyle she was.

I let her help me shrug the shirt on and I buttoned it. I ignored the over vest and coat she held out to me. Tucking in this damn shirt was the most Ethan was getting from me today. I glared down at the boots on the floor.

Sloane appeared and I bit back my pride and let her help me put on socks and those fucking boots. In all reality I would be fine sleeping the day away today. My body was sluggish and achy. She was right, I shouldn't be up. It wasn't like I hadn't been through similar things during my time with the Green Berets. Not the beatings, though SERE school was close, but the exhaustion and muscle pain. You learned how to power through it.

"Thank you," I told her, holding out my hand and helping her rise from the floor. The bandage did help. Every move I made wasn't causing flames to lick over my skin any longer. "I have to go."

"Me too," she said, eyes darting to the clock.

"See you later?"

She gave a quick bob of her head then rushed out the door. No wonder she was always flitting about if she was helping tend to the sick and making sure people had the items they needed.

I stepped out onto my porch and watched her hurry across the compound. It was still early morning, but people were busy, bustling around. I watched them for a few minutes before making my way to Ethan's office.

CHAPTER 7

Riptide

The surprise on Ethan's face was almost worth the pain of walking over here. Almost.

Ethan looked down at his watch, but I was a few minutes early so he just motioned for me to sit with an evil grin. He knew exactly how painful that was going to be and was relishing it.

Evil fucker.

"Good morning, Brother Derek."

"Good morning, My Lord," I said between gritted teeth as I sat on the chair. My back protested the movement and was letting me know it. If I ever had to utter the words My Lord after I got out of here I pitied anyone around me.

"I would like to go over the finances and what your plans are for them. I'd also like you to get with your contacts to set up work crews to make the utilities we have out here permanent." He looked down at a sheet of paper. "If there's any chance of bribing someone at the permitting office to get it all done on the up and up, but behind closed doors, that would be ideal."

His list was impressively long and I knew I was going to have my work cut out for me. While I was here I'd actually have to get some of these things accomplished. Of course he wanted to see if he could get these projects permitted, and without inspections. It would make it harder to be thrown off State Lands if somehow he'd managed to gain the permits to build here. Arizona was finicky about squatters and often they ended up with more rights than the property owner. I knew thanks to helping out one of my brothers by renting his house for him while he was overseas. It'd been a clusterfuck to get the current renters—who'd refused to pay—out so I could get new people in. I wondered how the government would feel about being tied up by their own laws. It would serve them right.

I winced inwardly because somehow I'd just looped around to wanting to stick it to the government, just like Ethan. I tuned back in as Ethan continued listing shit off that he wanted me to do.

"My Lord…"

He paused, looking up at me.

"It's going to take me a few days to get my work station set up and for me to properly dig into your finances, once you give me full access, that is. Once you do, I'll be able to walk you through everything."

Ethan had only given Chet, and therefore other Derek, partial access to make sure he could do what Ethan was asking. Ethan certainly wasn't stupid. Letting one man, a man not even on the compound at the time, have full control of his money would be stupid. Giving me full access now was easier, after all he could just kill me if I stole any.

"Of course. In three days' time, then." He tapped a few buttons on his computer. Once his phone dinged, he looked at the authentication code and entered it. "There. Now you'll have the access you need." He paused, facing me and steepling his fingers together. "I'm sure I don't need to remind you of the commandments."

Someone sure as hell needed to. I shook my head.

"Good. Stealing from me would be a grave mistake."

I forced myself to give him a pleasant smile. "I wouldn't dream of it, My Lord. I want this to be my home."

His eyes narrowed as he studied my face. I refused to let the mask slip, only showing him a happy man eager to be here. It was only technically the second day and already this was taxing. Butcher hadn't been kidding about the difficulty in doing this. I was up for it, but I wouldn't have minded a beer with my brothers. It didn't matter that it was only nine a.m. I'd have plenty of takers.

"I'll show you around the town."

I was surprised he was taking the time out of his day to personally show me around, but I was sure it had something to do with keeping an eye on me. It was going to be a while before I gained his trust. After all, Chet was missing—dead, not that Ethan knew that yet, for all he knew he'd skipped town—and I had access to all the money. I was a stranger with an unusual amount of power. Ethan must hate that. In the meantime, I needed to start getting to know the others. Figuring out who here was going to be savable and who was a lost cause.

We walked out of his office and he started the tour. There were many more buildings here than when we'd first found the compound. They must be putting up one per day. I listened quietly as he spoke, soaking everything up. Knowing the layout was going to be beneficial when the time came. There would likely be that many more buildings by the time our club came for them.

That seemed to be part of Ethan's plan. Speed. Get the buildings up, get the utilities in, and get the permits. By the time someone got around to realizing that nothing should have been built and no permits should have been issued, it would be too late. He would be a 'real' church. They wouldn't be able to evict him. I wasn't sure about his past, but I'm betting he'd been run out of a few towns in his life. He was learning from his past mistakes.

I had three days to get a handle on these finances and I was eager to get to work. We'd been wondering how they were funding this lifestyle. Between my own expertise with computers and Rat, that shouldn't be too difficult. Okay, okay, it was because of Rat and only because of him I'd have a chance. He was going to remote into my terminal and make the magic happen.

I was decent with computers, but nowhere near his level. Static had already gotten me a list of names that I could contact for various jobs I'd need to get done. It'd been a shock to see that they hadn't destroyed my cell phone. Probably the only reason they hadn't was because I needed to be able to talk to other Derek's contacts in order to get Ethan what he wanted. That would work in my favor.

Of course, Ethan was keeping the phone on him, so I couldn't blatantly ask anyone for help. He would be reading all my texts and listening to all my calls, as well as checking the emails. He didn't even bother to give an excuse, just said it as if it were as natural as breathing. I wouldn't have any kind of contact with my brothers. Only with people who could help me get the to-do-list Ethan was giving me done. I wasn't about to try to send anything covert unless absolutely necessary. Too damn risky.

I walked slowly alongside Ethan, not letting him see my impatience to get started. His gaze had turned calculating. He had something on his mind.

"Two days from now will be your wedding day."

Shock almost tripped me up, but I managed to hold back what I'd initially thought. "Wedding day, My Lord?"

Ethan's grin stretched slowly over his face. "That's right."

Other Derek had mentioned something about getting a woman. I'd assumed he meant a fucking girlfriend. I should have realized it'd be more than that in this place. Hell, after looking at Derek, I realized it would have to be a wife bound to him by a cult. A girlfriend would run off.

"We have a young woman for you." He stuffed his hands in his pockets. The look on his face told me he was enjoying this, immensely. "She's…a bit of a handful," he explained. He cocked his head, giving me a hard look. "Starting Wednesday night, it'll be your job to keep her in line."

Shit. I knew what that meant. This was another test. Being the new guy they were giving me the woman everyone else had passed over because she was too much of a *handful.* These pussies saw a spitfire as a bad thing. *Of course they would.* Hell, I wouldn't mind this at all if it weren't for two things. One, married? I wasn't looking to get married. And two... Sloane's face entered my mind.

Gritting my teeth to help stop the anger from exploding out of me, I bit back my thoughts on his plans. I was going to need a damn mouth guard or I'd walk out of this place with no teeth.

We'd stopped next to a building, and my anger faded when I heard a familiar soft feminine voice. I peered through the window. My brows shot up when I saw Sloane at the head of the classroom, children listening to her lecture. She was the teacher here, too? Was the woman a saint?

It didn't matter what I wanted. I had to keep up appearances. It wasn't easy to paste a happy look on my face, but I managed. "Thank you, My Lord. I'm looking forward to the challenge."

He tossed me a look of confusion. I fully understood that any trouble my new 'wife' started was going to be made my problem. Physically, in most cases. Even crazy cult leaders don't enjoy beating women, much easier to beat men and let those men in turn discipline their women. Ethan was looking forward to punishing me in any way he could until I became an integrated part of this group. He had a sadistic side that needed to be kept fed. It wasn't hard to see. Who better to beat on than the new guy?

Biting back a sigh, I followed him back to his office. My back was a raw bundle of nerves at this point, but I didn't utter a single complaint. Showing weakness to him was like putting blood in the water around a shark.

He stopped by his door. "We're done for now. I'll introduce you to the men later. I expect you'll be ready to go over the finances in three days," he said. There was no mistaking the warning in his voice. "Wednesday at five p.m. you'll need to be up on the dais. I'll have Brother Jacob bring you something to wear."

I nodded and left. There was so much to do in such a short time I didn't give in to the urge to fall face first onto the bed. Downing a few of the painkillers Sloane had left for me, I started setting up my laptop and other equipment on the small desk that was in the spare room. It would double as my office. The home they'd provided me was small, but it wasn't like I needed much space. I was surprised they'd even bothered to give me my own area.

I shouldn't have been. It was a cult, not a literal torture chamber. These people had mostly, or at least partially, come from the real world. You needed certain basic luxuries or they would eventually doubt the power of their 'Earth God'. So a small, but semi-private space shouldn't be a surprise.

The time passed quickly and I quietly closed the lid to my laptop when I heard a knock on the door. Jacob shoved a hanger with neatly pressed clothes on it. Without saying anything, he left, hurrying off to whatever his next task was.

I hung the clothes in the closet and went back to work. By the time I raised my head again shadows had made their way across the floor as night crept in. Raking a hand through my hair, I stood and stretched, immediately regretting it when my back twinged.

Throwing myself into work had kept me from thinking about what was going to happen in two days. Rat was the only one I'd have a form of communication with, because it was going to take both his and his wife's enormous brains to help me pretend to be as smart as other Derek.

I tapped on the keyboard, opening up the app we installed on the computer. It was Rat's own invention and only worked as a direct line between us. We couldn't speak to each other, but it allowed him to see everything I was doing on the laptop and assist in making the shit happen that I needed to, like making shell corporations. I didn't know how to do that, but all I had to do was type into a search what I needed done and he'd take care of it for me. Anyone snooping on my computer wouldn't have a clue that I wasn't doing these things myself.

I quickly shut down the program as I heard another knock on my door.

Getting up, I opened it. My breath caught in my throat as Sloane's beautiful blue eyes locked onto me. I hadn't been expecting to see her again so soon. A grin slowly spread over my face. It wasn't a coincidence. Couldn't be. She could have found someone else to bring me food and check on me. She couldn't help this pull between us anymore than I could.

"You shouldn't be up," she admonished me, a frown marring her pretty features.

I leaned a shoulder against the doorframe. "Then why did you knock?"

Her cheeks blushed a delicate pink color and I found myself wanting to see how deep I could make her flush. I wanted to keep flirting with her. Instead, I stepped aside and let her inside.

She quickly dropped the basket of food on the table and spun when I walked up behind her. Panic was written all over her face and she all but jumped out of her skin. I wondered if she'd been told that I was being given a wife—not a phrase I ever thought I'd hear—in two days' time. Maybe that's why she was acting this way.

"I need to go."

She scurried past and I didn't stop her. It took all of my willpower not to grab her by the waist and pull her back against me. To take her lips with mine. She wasn't mine. A woman like her likely already belonged to another man. She was running home to a husband and children and I was left here aching just from the sight of her.

Shaking my head, I sat down to eat the meal she'd prepared and tried to reason out how to let her go. At least for now. Once we took over this compound and saved those we could, there might be a chance.

CHAPTER 8

Sloane

I dropped Derek's breakfast off with him the next morning, making sure not to linger for too long. For the first time in my life I felt drawn to a man, and was even flirting with him. It wasn't something I was accustomed to, wanting to spend time with a man, or having him return the attention.

It was probably just hope that made me think there was something different about him. I shook my head and continued on.

Abigail came running out of one of the alleys between the houses and ran directly to me, sobbing.

Crouching down, I hugged her close. She shook in my arms, crying so hard she couldn't tell me what was wrong. There was dirt streaking down her cheeks along with the tears. It was early morning and I knew her mother scrubbed her clean at the start of each day. Her brute of a father liked to say that cleanliness was next to godliness. I wasn't sure that meant what he was interpreting it as.

"What happened, Sweetheart?"

She clutched at me, looking over her shoulder.

My eyes lifted and I groaned. Swaggering across the street toward us were Jarrett, John, and Gary. Jarrett and John were brothers and were sixteen and seventeen, and Gary had just turned ten. All three of them had egos as big as Texas and their parents acted like the sun rose and set on them. They were spoiled and as mean as a porcupine who'd been cornered.

There were very few children here I didn't love, but these were three of them.

"Move along, Sister Sloane," Jarrett called out, a smug smile on his face.

I rose, glaring at them and took Abigail's hand, turning to lead her away. It was rare that I allowed them to boss me around, but I wasn't ready to start up trouble for myself yet. If I was injured, there would be no one to care for Brother Derek.

Abigail cried out as she was jerked backward out of my hold. I turned toward them, facing the little brats. "Let her go. She's got a tutoring session she's late for." It was a lie. We didn't have anything planned, but these little shits didn't know that.

"Not anymore," Gary said, piping up. He'd only started hanging out with the older boys since we'd moved here, but they'd already managed to poison him and had made him as mean as they were.

"What do you want with Abigail?"

"None of your business," Jarrett said with a laugh.

They knew better than to hurt her in any way that was sexual. Ethan didn't put up with that, not even from under-aged boys. But that didn't mean that they didn't enjoy hurting the girls. Tilly had come home a month ago with a black eye. When pressed she'd finally admitted that John had punched her. There'd been no reason for it, other than he'd wanted to. I wasn't about to leave this girl in their care.

All three of the boys were watching me with mean expressions on their faces. The older boys had been indoctrinated into their father's beliefs quickly and their mother was nothing but a doormat. The poor woman received weekly beatings from her husband. He believed that pounding on her would keep her in line.

In a way, he was right. He'd broken her spirit long ago. She was a quiet woman who balked at her own shadow and rarely left her home. It left her sons to roam around the village, causing trouble. Gary had worshiped the older boys for years now and he was turning out to be as mean as they were. Seeing as Barclay was his father, if he'd turned out any other way I'd have been shocked. Ethan loved all three of them. They were model children in his eyes. They would grow to be perfectly obedient and loyal like Bruce and Jacob. Three more bullies he could command and use to keep the rest of us in line.

I looked around, unsure how I was going to escape this predicament. They were still relatively young, but Jarrett and John were already taller than me. They were almost as big as full-grown men. Gary was smaller, but with the other two always close by that didn't matter. They outweighed me and were likely stronger than me. The teenagers and their younger friend knew it, too. They threw their size around, making the rest of the children's lives miserable.

A movement caught my eye and I called out. "Brother Graham!"

The man paused and came my way. He eyed his teenage sons as he approached. "Sister Sloane. What can I help you with?"

"Abigail and I were just on our way to a tutoring session," I told him. It was important that I was careful. Graham was just as mean as his sons and I didn't need four of them ganging up on me. "I saw Jarrett and John here and was wondering if you wanted me giving them extra lessons as well?"

Abigail had wisely kept her mouth shut during our entire exchange, and just stared at the ground, not speaking. She was so frightened her face was pale, and her lower lip quivered, but she remained quiet.

Graham's upper lip curled as he thought about my question. "No. What do they need more learnin' for? Ain't nothing you can teach them. Jarrett. Your mother needs your help at home. John go with him. Gary your pa was lookin' for you." Graham spit, the glob landing close to my foot. "Get goin', all of you."

I grabbed Abigail once again and hurried away as the boys began arguing with their father. That would end with them getting cuffed upside the head if not worse. It was a small price to pay for their attitudes. "Are you okay?" I asked her, moving with her toward her home.

"Yeah. Thank you Sister Sloane." She refused to look up at me.

"What was that all about?"

She shook her head, not wanting to answer me.

"Abigail," I said in a warning tone.

Before she had a chance to answer, her mother opened her front door. "There you are- Oh! Why are you all dirty?" Her mother looked at me in confusion.

"She tripped," I offered.

Her mother started scolding the girl, ushering her inside her home. I knew for a fact she would put her straight into a bathtub and scrub her clean again. I planned to corner Abigail later and figure out what those boys were up to. It wasn't likely to be good. I had a feeling —considering Tilly's black eye—it had something to do with hitting other children.

A few years ago another group of older boys—who were all now over eighteen and fully involved in Ethan's daily routine—had started up a 'game' where they assigned points each time one of them hit someone. The smaller the child, the higher the points. It had been impossible to end. Until one day, one of the kids punched a woman's baby. The brain swelling hadn't been stoppable. The baby had died and the boy had been whipped, then was allowed to go back to his life. He was now on Bruce's security team. It was no wonder none of us women felt safe here. Why women hardly ever stepped up, even for their children. Death was an everyday occurrence within The Order.

It wasn't that mothers hadn't taken punishments for their children. They had, but the more it happened the more depressed they became. At this point, most of them just tried to keep their heads down. I couldn't blame them. I would probably do the same if I had a husband who would beat then force himself on me daily.

I hurried over to the schoolhouse, ready to get my day started. It wasn't a surprise that Jarrett, John, and Gary weren't in attendance.

They picked and chose when they came and it was less and less lately. It didn't hurt my feelings. Trying to keep those kids under control was a headache. I preferred it when they didn't show up.

The day passed quickly and by the time I got home, I was over an hour later than normal. The situation with Abigail this morning had put me behind and I hadn't been able to catch up. The girls had gotten dinner started, so by the time I made my way over to Derek's home, I was only half an hour late.

My heart tripped in my chest at the prospect of seeing him again. It didn't seem to matter how much I scolded myself, excitement overcame me each time I caught sight of him. I knocked on his door and waited with my basket of food. As soon as it opened, I offered him a hesitant smile. Straight white teeth flashed as he grinned at me.

"Hello again, Sister Sloane."

"Hi. I brought dinner," I told him, hefting my basket.

He stepped aside and I walked past him. My body brushed against his and my cheeks flushed. There were feelings and urges roiling around inside of me that I'd never encountered before. They were all connected to him. I was curious to find out what they were, though I knew I'd never have that chance. The risk wasn't worth it. It was hard for me to keep in mind that this man had joined Ethan's ranks when he smiled at me. Hard for me to remember that he was Chet Holden's cousin.

That was enough to cool the fever that was overtaking my body. Chet Holden had been a slimy, mean, asshole. Could it be possible that Derek wasn't like that? Maybe. Was I willing to take the chance? Sighing inwardly, I admitted that I wasn't sure. I couldn't seem to temper my response to the gorgeous man standing in front of me. I wasn't sure if I should trust my instincts about him or what I knew of his family. My emotions played tug-o-war with me at night. They were easy to forget during the busy daylight hours. And I had no problem setting my reservations aside when I was near Derek. But in the darkness of the night, I worried I was making a mistake by continuing to help him.

"Are you planning on cooking for me forever?" he asked as I set a plate on his table.

I shook my head. "No, only for a few more days. Then you should be able to handle it yourself." In truth he was up and around much quicker than any others had ever been. I shouldn't continue to bring him anything. Should put as much distance between us as possible. Even thinking that way made my heart hurt. What was wrong with me? I didn't even know this man. Not seeing him at the start and close of the day shouldn't have any impact on my life.

Frustration at myself mounting, I began unpacking the basket. This was all too confusing. I wished he'd never come here. Then I could continue on with my escape plan with no doubt plaguing me.

"Did you bring a plate for yourself?"

Looking up, I caught his gaze. "It wouldn't be proper for me to eat with you."

"Your husband wouldn't like it?" he prompted.

I set out the rest of the food I'd brought for him, ignoring his question. It was important that I learned as much about him as I could, but it was best if he didn't find out anything about me. He was a big man so I'd brought enough for two, even though I wouldn't be eating with him. As soon as it was set out, I nodded at him. "Goodnight, Brother Derek."

"Wait-"

I didn't turn back around, just quickly escaped out his front door. My urges made it impossible for me to spend much time near him without it feeling like I would combust. I couldn't trust myself. I certainly didn't trust him.

My pace didn't slow until I got into my home. I slammed the door shut and leaned back against it, trying to catch my breath and calm my racing heart. The girls looked up from their seats at the table.

"Was someone chasing you?" Audrey asked, looking worried.

"No," I told her. "I thought I heard something." The lie not only protected my pride, but it also meant the girls wouldn't go sneaking around at night.

The girls weren't very rebellious, that trait had mostly been beaten out of us. But every once in a while their mischievous sides would emerge. I did my best to keep them as safe as I could.

Sighing, I sat down at the table. I was getting tired of always having to protect everyone else. Not so much that I'd stop doing it. That wasn't something I could ever do. But I needed to get out of here. We all did. I kept getting the feeling that something was coming. Things were going to come to a head. I didn't know how, where, or when, just that it would be soon. I could only hope that I and the other women and the children would come out on the right side of whatever it was.

CHAPTER 9

Riptide

My eyes scanned the crowd, noting any male of fighting age and his physical conditioning. The good thing for us was most of these men looked more like other Derek, scrawny and unlikely to be much of a fight when the time came. That didn't mean they couldn't be dangerous. All zealots were. But there were only about twenty men who seemed to be in the rotation guarding the compound. Jacob and Bruce were notable exceptions. They looked like they came straight from 'Goons R Us', equipped with a shared brain, limited vocabulary, and ill-fitting suits. They were the security detail. I tucked all this information away.

Everyone was gathering for my wedding. My. Wedding. Jesus. My mouth was as dry as the desert surrounding the village. Nerves tightened my muscles, preparing me if I chose to run. Not that it was an option. It wasn't time yet. It'd only been a few days and I still had so much to learn before we could launch our attack. Going back to studying the surrounding faces, I tried to ignore the nervous sweat rolling down my spine.

There were plenty of men who got married long before twenty-eight, but it hadn't ever been something I thought about. It'd been easy to enjoy the company of women over the years, but one had never caught my eye enough to want to keep her. Now barely seventy-two hours after getting here I was being assigned one.

I placed my finger between my collar and my neck and pulled. The suit fit perfectly. No one would be able to explain why this damn button down felt like a noose. I glanced around again, looking for the somehow familiar flash of blue. My eyes narrowed when I didn't find her.

"Make yourself ready, Brother Derek."

The look I shot at Ethan was probably less than friendly. I'd never thought of myself as someone who gave away their emotions easily. There were times I wondered if I had more than one or two, usually happy and relaxed. But in this situation, I found myself having to force a neutral expression more often than not.

I wasn't like Hush and Hellfire, the strong, silent, usually grumpy type. Believe it or not, I was more like Butcher and Toxic—though no one wanted to compare themselves to those two assholes—quick to smile and joke around. Not here, though.

Granted I'd only been here for a few days, but damn was I turning into a sullen, pissed off dick in this place. Being myself could get me killed. Not to mention fuck up any opportunity for those who were stuck here.

I hadn't even gotten started on my true reason for being here since I had a deadline for those finances and my back was fucked up. Music from a stereo nearby started up and everyone in the bleachers stood up.

Steeling myself, I faced the aisle they'd made with some kind of runner placed in the dirt and met the eyes of my bride as she slowly walked toward me. My jaw clenched as I bit back the shock pounding through me. It couldn't be.

Blazing blue all but spat at me from twenty feet away as Sloane walked herself down the aisle. It took everything in me to keep my jaw from dropping. I glanced over at Ethan, but he was giving Sloane a warning look.

Holy shit. Sloane was the trouble maker. She was going to be my wife. I probably should have guessed, but I'd just assumed that she was already married. I thought back to the first time I saw her, when she had stopped a child from getting beaten. The pieces started to come together, and for a moment I had a glimmer of hope about her.

Relief hit me like a ton of bricks and I quit sweating like a holy man outside of a brothel. Suddenly, this didn't seem like it was going to be so bad. I still didn't know if I could trust her, but at least I wasn't being saddled with some woman I wasn't interested in.

Hopefully she doesn't earn you too many beatings.

She marched up to my side and as one we both faced Ethan. Fury was pulsing off her in waves. Her hands were strangling the stems of the bouquet she was holding and I had a feeling she was wishing they were wrapped around my throat.

Ethan started shouting to the crowd. It didn't seem to matter to him that he was mic'd up this time. Feedback from the speakers nearby blared and he lowered his volume a bit as we all winced.

"You could have warned me last night," Sloane hissed at me, still looking straight forward.

Turning my head slightly, I studied her angry pinched face. "I had no idea." Guilt mixed with the relief as I tried to sort through my emotions. I couldn't force myself to feel too badly about this situation because in the end…I got her. She was my prize. Was it fucked up? Probably. But I was hoping I could win her over.

"He didn't tell you that you were getting married?"

"Well, yeah, he did. But not to who."

Ethan's eyes narrowed on us, a warning to shut up, as he continued talking to the crowd.

Sloane's head snapped in my direction and she glared. Her eyes sparked, bright and beautiful, but she didn't speak. She didn't need to. Her eyes were saying all she needed to. She was hoping I'd drop dead.

Too bad for her I was feeling healthy as a horse, though still sore from the whipping.

"...The love that these two share is blessed by your Earth God…"

Sloane's lip curled up in disgust at Ethan's words, but then she went back to berating me, just at a lower pitch so Ethan wouldn't notice. My lips twitched. I would be as pissed as her at being forced into this if I wasn't here for another reason entirely. Her anger was justified. That didn't mean that I didn't find her completely gorgeous. Relief once again flooded me. At least it was her. She might not want me, but that would be temporary. I'd change her mind.

We repeated the vows that Ethan forced on us. Exchanged the rings that The Order bought. Everything here came from him. He didn't allow for any form of self-expression. By the time the ceremony was over, Sloane's hand was in mine and I'd given her a peck on the cheek. I'd wanted to kiss her properly, but I was still playing a role. I'd wait until we had some privacy to show Sloane the man she'd agreed, well technically been forced, to marry.

We were whisked off to a bigger building that served as a hall. People must have been busy all day preparing for this while I'd been neck deep in numbers. There was food, a large cake, dancing, singing, and it seemed that most of the people living here used this as an opportunity to cut loose and have a good time. It made me wonder if they did this often or if their lives were filled with long stretches of boredom interrupted only by fear or the occasional happy moment.

The women and children all approached our table and while I was treated with nothing but respect it was easy to see that Sloane was dearly loved. It eased something within my chest to see the others hugging and whispering with her. They looked genuinely pleased for her.

She was a de facto leader of the women and children. No wonder Ethan needed to keep her under control. They all admired her. Beat her too often and you alienate your own people. Let her defy you… you lose credibility. What a predicament we had here.

It'd taken about an hour, but she finally relaxed next to me. She leaned against me as though she was too exhausted to keep the ramrod straight positioning she'd held until then.

I picked up the wine glass someone kept topping off. I'd have given my left nut for an ice cold beer, but made do with the wine. Still, I didn't drink much of it. I noticed my wife, *my wife!*, had hardly touched the dinner set before her, but I didn't insist she eat. The last thing I wanted was for her to shut down again.

Her slim fingers shook as she picked up her own glass and took a small sip. I wasn't sure if it was fear, anger, or nerves.

Reaching over, I placed my hand on her thigh. "Want to get out of here?"

Her eyes widened as she looked over at me. "We haven't even had cake yet."

"Do you want cake?" I asked her, searching her eyes.

"Not really." There was a spark of relief there.

"Let's go."

I rose and held out my hand for her. My fingers wrapped around hers and I pulled her to her feet. We began walking toward the door.

"Brother Derek. A moment."

There I went, grinding my teeth again. I leaned in close and whispered to her. "Wait here." Turning, I put a smile on my face and walked over to where Ethan and Jacob were speaking with Bruce. The huge man watched me with suspicion. He'd be one I'd need to keep an eye on and clearly he thought the same as me.

"Thank you for everything tonight, My Lord." It fucking stung to have to thank him for shit, but I did it.

"You're welcome. Since tomorrow is technically your honeymoon, I'll give you one extra day on the finances. We'll meet Friday morning at eight a.m."

"Yes, My Lord."

"Sign this."

Taking the paper he handed me, I read it with a frown. It was a legitimate marriage license. Jacob must have somehow gotten it from Tucson. How he'd managed to bribe someone there to give over this form without me or Sloane present was a mystery. I signed the bottom, noting that Sloane's signature was already there. "When did she sign?"

"When I told her this morning that today was her wedding day." The smile that spread over his face was smug. "Oh, and Brother Derek."

I arched a brow in question, pausing as I'd been about to leave.

"I expect to see evidence of the consummation tomorrow."

My brain stuttered as I tried to figure out what the fuck he meant by that. "What?"

"The sheets," Jacob added, that ever present glower on his face. "I'll be over in the morning to collect them."

"The...sheets." My mind finally caught up. I looked over my shoulder at Sloane and realized that meant she was a virgin. "I'll see you in the morning," I told Jacob, before walking away from them.

I was all twisted up inside as I took Sloane by the hand and all but dragged her back to my place. My dick was hard—not something I was especially proud of—but the idea that no one else had touched her was sexy as hell. But I also hadn't been with a virgin since Mary Beth Hallbecker and that had been my junior year of high school. I hadn't planned to...consummate...shit. This poor woman didn't know me from Adam and here we were expected to not only have sex—my cock throbbed, reminding me that it was in favor of that outcome—but to show the evidence of it. *Fucking barbarians.*

"What's the matter?" Sloane huffed as she tried to keep up with me as my long legs ate up the distance between the hall and my new home.

I slowed slightly so she wasn't struggling to stay beside me in her long white gown. "Sorry. Just needed some space."

Her worried blue eyes watched me speculatively. "What did Ethan want?"

My jaw flexed and I shook my head. "Don't worry about him."

She gave a bitter laugh as we entered my house. "I wish I had that luxury. I've been worrying about him for my whole life."

Looking down at her, I gave into the impulse that'd been riding me all night and tucked one long curl behind her ear. My fingertips trailed down her neck. Her silky smooth skin was cool to the touch despite the relatively warm night.

"Why aren't you married?"

"I am," she whispered.

"Before now," I clarified with a shake of my head. "I figured-"

"No one wanted me." Her lips twisted into a small grin. "Apparently I'm a bit of a troublemaker."

"Apparently." My own grin widened.

"You...don't seem worried about that. Ethan will-"

"Leave Ethan to me. You and I will figure out what works for us."

Her brows drew together. I reached out and brushed my thumb over the crease there.

"Why did you agree to marry me? Why did you sign the license?" I asked.

"He threatened to hurt people I cared about," she admitted. "I had three teenagers living with me. He told me that if I didn't marry you he'd make sure they were given to the most awful men here."

Rage bubbled inside my gut. "What a fucking douche bag," I snarled.

Her eyebrows shot up, shock covering her face. "You're not what I expected," she whispered.

"What did you expect?"

"Chet."

A snort of disgust was out before I could stop it. "My cousin and I have nothing in common." Ducking my head, I locked eyes with her. "Nothing."

She gave me a hopeful smile. "Could you help me with this?" She turned and gave me her back. There were at least thirty little buttons marching down her back.

I started at the top and with each patch of skin that was revealed I grew harder. The scars on her skin didn't bother me, and they certainly didn't lessen my arousal. I only wished I could have been here to prevent her from getting them. There wasn't anything I could do now except make sure no one ever touched her again. No one but me, anyway. My finger brushed lightly over her skin.

Biting back the groan of appreciation at my wife's beauty, I finished up the task as quickly as my fumbling fingers would allow. I was going to have to talk to her about the expectations for tonight. Giving her time and space to get to know me would have been ideal, but I wasn't sure how to do that and produce the required 'proof'.

She turned again, a look of curiosity on her face. "Why is my married name not Holden?"

Butcher had convinced us that going with the truth as much as possible was the best option so I'd used my real last name. After checking with other Derek and realizing that Ethan hadn't done a background check on him yet—he'd done it the day he'd called me, according to Rat—we'd had enough time to have Rat switch my identity with other Derek's.

"Chet's mother and mine are sisters."

"Derek Skore." She tilted her head. "Mrs. Sloane Skore."

I grinned at her. "Has a nice ring to it." Something occurred to me. I knew so little about her. "How old are you?"

"Twenty-two."

Relief eased the tightness in my chest. It would be my luck that Ethan would do something fucked up like give me a child-bride. I was glad that wasn't an issue. I would have guessed Sloane was older based off her sensible personality.

"How old are you?" she returned the question.

"Twenty-eight."

She gave me a smile, then headed off to the bedroom to change out of her gown. Sometime after the ceremony some of the men had moved over the majority of her belongings and left them in my house. Everything was boxed up neatly and I had a feeling that was what she'd been doing all day today. I wondered if her talk with Ethan had been as much of a surprise to her as it had been for me. Judging by her anger at the ceremony, I'd say yes.

I unbuttoned the first few buttons of my shirt and stripped off my suit coat. My back was aching, but it was beginning to scab over in a few places. Some of the deeper slashes were going to take a while, but I had nothing but time.

Grabbing a bottle of whiskey off the table—it was filled with gifts for the newlyweds—I tried not to be irritated over the fact that these people walked in and out of my space as they pleased. That was the reason I kept the laptop locked up when I was gone. Sitting down, being mindful of my back, I poured a glass of the liquor and waited on my new wife.

CHAPTER 10

Sloane

I sat down on the bed and drew in a shaky breath. Ethan had come to me this morning and as soon as I saw it was him walking through my door I knew something was wrong. Still, no one could have prepared me for him telling me that I'd be getting married. I just assumed I'd dodged that bullet.

It hadn't taken me long to convince one of the older, single women—Mae—to move in with my girls. They'd be safe with her watching over them. It was one less thing for me to worry about.

My hands shook as I peeled my dress off my shoulders. It pooled around my waist and I sat there naked. Something told me that my new husband was respectful enough to give me time to dress. And even if he wasn't, it didn't matter. He was going to see my body tonight anyway. It belonged to him now.

It made me wonder how he'd feel about getting damaged goods. My hand smoothed over my forearm and the various marks and scars stood out against my skin. When Derek went to touch me he'd find the same on my legs, belly, chest, and back. Even the nape of my neck. Only my hands, feet, and face were spared. I hated my scars. Even though most of them weren't red any longer and a few had even faded, I still knew where each was. They were ugly.

How would he feel about all the scars that littered my body? The last thing I wanted was for that beautiful man to find me unattractive. There wasn't anything I could do about it, though. I was his.

Tears welled up in my eyes. Being married was going to make it that much harder to execute my plan. I'd have to get all my goodies out of my house because it didn't belong to me anymore. Someone else would end up moving in there. My girls would be moved somewhere else and wouldn't have my protection anymore. Even if Derek would be okay with them living with us, our new home didn't have the space for three teenagers.

I couldn't express my deep hatred for Ethan right now. A wedding was supposed to be a blessing, supposed to be the happiest day of a woman's life. Not only was him shoving this on me a roadblock to my escape, but it was a bigger chain around my freedom while I was stuck here.

I wasn't exactly sad to have been married to Derek. At least it was him and I had a chance of having a husband who wasn't as awful as the other men here. As far as I could tell—and it wasn't much since I'd only met him a few days ago—he seemed like a good man. But then again, good men didn't join cults.

The tears dripping down my cheeks were just because of the changes. It was overwhelming. Everything was going to be different. It worried me. I scrubbed my cheeks, drying the tears, and stood. I shoved my tight fitting dress off my hips and went to hang it in the closet. Digging through the boxes of my things that had been moved over here, I found pajamas and climbed into them. They weren't what anyone would call sexy, just a pair of cotton pants and a long sleeve t-shirt. I didn't own lingerie and even if I did, I wasn't sure I would want to wear it tonight.

Derek may be my new husband, but I didn't know him. Didn't know if I could trust him. That didn't mean I could avoid my duty as a wife. At least not tonight. I either gave myself over willingly, or…well, willingly was the best option.

I stepped out of the bedroom and paused when I saw him drinking whiskey. A knot tightened in my stomach. I'd be finding out sooner rather than later what sort of drunk my husband was. I brushed my cheek as I thought about the type my father was. There'd been plenty of bruises throughout the years from him.

He hooked a foot around the chair next to him and dragged it out. "Have a seat."

Sinking into the chair, I watched him warily from my peripheral. My chest was tight, making it hard to breath. A piece of me was brimming with excitement. I was about to find out what all the fuss was about. But I was also a little terrified. What if it hurt? Curling my hands together, I waited. I wasn't sure what to say.

"I'm sorry I didn't tell you that Ethan had mentioned getting married," he said, draining the glass. He poured two more glasses and set one in front of me.

I shook my head, but he pushed it closer. "Have some. It'll steady your nerves," he told me, draining his again. "I honestly had no idea it would be you. He didn't mention who I'd be marrying."

"You didn't ask?" I brought the glass up and took a small sip. A shudder wracked my body as the taste burned its way down my throat. I wasn't used to drinking much more than an occasional glass of wine.

"Would it have mattered if I had and wasn't happy with his answer?"

I blinked at him, then shook my head. Understanding drained away the last dredges of anger. He was as stuck as I was. "You wouldn't have had a choice in the matter."

"Just like you didn't," he replied. He sighed. "I'd like to give you a chance to get to know me-"

"We can't," I whispered, staring down into the glass.

"What do you mean?"

"If he doesn't see the evidence that we…consummated the marriage-" I swallowed hard, fear creeping in. "A couple tried to wait once. They were both young and she wasn't ready to sleep with her new husband. The punishment Ethan handed down..." I looked up and met his eyes. "He received far worse than she did, but I wouldn't want either of us to go through that."

Derek sighed again. "I had a feeling that would be the case." He narrowed his eyes. "We can take it at your pace. I assume you're a virgin."

My cheeks heated and I knew without looking they were bright red as I nodded. Was it that obvious?

"Have you ever done anything?"

"I kissed one of the boys once."

"Where?"

"Behind one of the sheds we had in the town I grew up in."

"No... I mean, kissed him where?"

"Oh," I muttered, blush deepening, "on the lips." I peeked up and found him watching me with a serious look on his face. Embarrassment made it hard to speak. These kinds of topics weren't appropriate. But, then again, he was my husband now. We both needed to make peace with that.

I hadn't wanted to get married, but now I was. As long as Derek was kind to me I would be the best wife I could be. At least until it was time to leave.

"Tongue?"

I shook my head, focusing back on the moment. He was probably thinking there was something wrong with me that no man had ever wanted to touch me. "It's forbidden for the men to touch the young girls."

"Thank fuck for that."

His words made me relax a little. There were still men here who would try if it weren't for the rules. I was happy to know my husband wasn't like that. "And by the time I came of age, I'd already shown myself to be a trouble maker. So no one ever showed any interest and I soon just became another woman they weren't supposed to touch."

He nodded and poured another drink. I didn't have to explain what trouble maker meant, I could see the understanding in his eyes. I leaned forward, hesitating when those shocking blue eyes of his landed on me, then I pulled the glass from his hand.

He didn't argue when I stood and put them inside the sink. I heard his chair scrape backward and tensed as he walked up behind me. I didn't turn to face him, just stared down at the sink.

"We still don't have to do this," he offered. "I could open up a wound on my back and that would be enough proof."

I shook my head as I turned. "No." Panic flared up at the thought of trying to pretend. "I don't want you to do that. It's not good for your wounds. Plus…I can't trust that Ethan wouldn't somehow find out."

"What did he do to them?"

"He nearly killed Ben and he snapped Lacey's femur. She still walks with a limp." I swallowed hard and licked my lips. "You're my husband," I whispered. Closing the distance between us, I laid my hand on his chest. We'd do this tonight and then if I found out later that he wasn't what I was hoping, I could always stop sleeping with him then.

"I could tell him it was my fault. That I drank too much whiskey and couldn't…"

I stopped him by placing my finger over his lips. What irony, that the nicest thing a man was willing to do for me was to not sleep with me. The double irony was that for the first time in my life I felt desire. And it was for him. I looked into his deep blue eyes. Without saying a word, I told him it was okay.

Nerves fluttered in my belly as his hands slid up my arms, over my neck. The shirt sleeves had stopped him from feeling my scars on my arms, but as soon as he touched my neck he froze. The time was here.

"I try to hide them," I admitted.

"The scars?" he asked, looking down at my skin.

I nodded, miserably waiting for his opinion. My breathing was fast and erratic. It shouldn't matter what he thought, but it did.

His eyes narrowed as he pushed up my sleeves, one at a time, and traced his fingertips over the marks on my forearms. "Why do you have so many?"

Ducking my head to avoid his intense stare, I looked down at the floor. "I'm a troublemaker, remember?"

"Why do I get the impression you got many of these scars by taking punishments for others?"

My head snapped up and I stared at him in shock. How had he known that? Had someone been talking about me? If so, who? The women would have told me. Most of them were loyal to me, even in their desolate states.

Derek nodded as though I'd just confirmed his question. "Your scars are a testament to your strength of character, Sloane."

I didn't respond, not willing to believe him. At least not yet.

He seemed to understand that I was anxious to move forward. To get this over with. Many of the women had told me of their wedding nights. I didn't know much of sex, but if their experiences were the norm, this wouldn't be pleasant. He shifted until he was cupping my face. I looked up at him and my breath caught as he lowered his head.

His kiss was warm and gentle at first. Just a meeting of mouths. His lips were softer than I thought they'd be. He released my cheeks and his arms slid around me, pulling me closer to him as he deepened the kiss.

I parted my lips for him and the rush of desire that filled me when his tongue brushed mine surprised me. This man had managed to get my heart racing more than once since we'd met a few days ago, but kissing him was doing more than that to my body. I was pressed against all the hard planes of his muscles and something clenched low down in my belly when I felt his erection prod me.

That one brief kiss with Billy behind the woodshed had been my only experience and I'd thought it would remain that way. Now that Derek was kissing me, I was so glad it wasn't. His lips were eliciting all sorts of pleasant sensations. He chased away the nerves as he changed the angle of our lips.

Clinging to him, I leaned into his body, desperate for more. My body had never been more alive. Nerve endings tingled as his fingertips brushed over me. My lips were swollen and sensitive, but I never wanted him to stop.

The kiss took on a more determined note as he pressed me back against the counter. This wasn't the kind of kiss I'd gotten before. That had been a quick pecking of lips and then hours of paranoia that we'd been seen.

This was the kiss of a man. A man who knew what he was doing. Derek's hand slid up under my shirt and gripped my hip. His thumb dipped down below the waistband of my pants and my eyes popped open. I hadn't even realized I'd closed them. Turning my head, I broke the kiss, dragging in ragged breaths. It was hard to pinpoint the different sensations and feelings that were zipping through me. He'd balled me up into one huge cluster of need.

No wonder people want to do this so much.

Derek didn't let me breaking the kiss deter him. His mouth trailed down over my neck, causing goosebumps to appear on my skin. Who knew someone licking over your neck would feel so good?

During the few times I'd managed to get on the computers I'd been able to learn a few things from the outside world. Things they didn't teach us. I'd watched a porn video once. It had been so…loud and fast and…awful. I hadn't dared to look again. In fact, I'd only made it partially through that one. Enough to know a few things. So I wasn't going into this completely blind.

"C-can we go into the bedroom?" I asked. My legs were shaking and I wasn't sure I could hold myself up much longer.

Without a word, he raised his head, took my hand, and led me into the room we'd be sharing from now on. As he closed the door, I disentangled my fingers from his and sat on the bed. I watched as he approached me. Squeezing my hands into fists, I continued to stare as he reached behind him and pulled his shirt off over his head.

My eyes roamed over his body and I sucked in a little breath. He had muscles everywhere. There were tattoos that covered both arms from shoulder down to his wrists. My fingers itched to trace the ink that ran over his skin. Aside from his, I'd never seen tattoos in person before, only a few pictures on the computer. My eyes drifted lower.

His abs were well defined and made me want to rub my hands over them. He was very different, physically, than the men here. It wasn't the first time I'd seen him shirtless, but before I'd been worried about caring for him and hadn't had the time to enjoy the view.

He was watching me, his blue eyes intense and focused completely on me. It made me shiver with delight. There was a hunger there that even I could recognize. He nudged my thighs apart and stepped in between them.

My eyes kept darting away from him, then it was like they were drawn back, like moths to flame. I didn't want to be rude and stare, but he was the most gorgeous man I'd ever seen. He was forcing my body to feel things I'd never really known. He'd only kissed me for a few minutes and my panties were damp.

"Do you want to touch me, Sloane?"

My eyes shot up to his. I didn't know what to say.

A smile spread over his face. "I don't have to call you Sister Sloane in our bedroom, do I?"

I choked on a laugh. "No. Sloane is fine…Derek."

He grimaced. "In our home I'd rather you call me, D. Or Rip."

"Rip?"

"It's my middle name," he explained. He leaned forward and encircled my wrists with his hands, dragging them forward.

I gasped when my fingers flattened out over the abs I'd been longing to touch. His skin was hot and smooth. He released my wrists, but I left my hands where he'd placed them. He didn't make any mention of the scars on my wrists, though I knew he'd felt them against his fingers.

"Go ahead and touch me, Sloane. I've been waiting to feel your hands on me."

Swallowing, I smoothed my hands over the ridges of muscles. The courage to ask him why he'd been imagining me touching him never appeared, so I kept my mouth shut. He had a light dusting of hair that started low on his belly and led down beneath the slacks he was wearing. My finger traced it downward until it hit his waistband.

A deep groan sounded, causing me to jerk my hand back. I looked up at him, but he was watching me with hooded eyes.

"You're going to fucking kill me."

That made me blink. I opened my mouth to ask him if I'd done something wrong, but all I could do was gasp when he moved onto the bed, straddling my thighs as he wrapped a hand around my throat. Was he going to hurt me?

He pushed gently against my throat and I laid back for him. He went back to trailing his lips over my neck and collarbone. His hand wasn't squeezing, but I still had a hard time breathing. It had more to do with what his tongue was doing than with his fingers. At least that was true until his free hand shoved my shirt up.

I couldn't contain the squeal when his fingers brushed over my sides. Jerking away from the soft touch, I grabbed his wrist with both hands.

His chuckle vibrated against my skin. "Ticklish?"

I glared up at him as he tickled my side again. "Stop that," I snapped, trying to squirm away again. There was nowhere for me to go, though. His knees were on either side of my thighs, and he had me pinned down by the throat. The fact that he was being gentle with me was the only reason I wasn't panicking. Having a man pin me to a hard surface by the throat wasn't new to me. What *was* new was the heat that was coursing through my body.

His dominant position on top of me was turning me on. It was strange and new, but I didn't ask him to stop. I sort of liked it. Just not the tickling. He'd made me forget all about the scars. About finding myself ugly because of them. He made me feel beautiful and desirable.

"Okay. I won't do that again," he murmured as he raised his head and took my lips again. This time he dove into a deep kiss.

The moan was dragged out of my chest only to be swallowed up by his mouth. Embarrassment seeped in. I wasn't sure if I should be making any noise. The lady in the video had made more than her fair share, but I couldn't figure out why at the time. If this was what she'd been feeling, maybe I understood now.

My eyes snapped open when Derek's—Rip's—fingers pinched my nipple. I hadn't realized until that moment that it was a hard little bead. The stinging ache felt so good that I gasped and turned my head again, breaking his kiss.

His lips followed mine and he slid his hand up a little higher until he was gripping my jaw. He wasn't allowing me to escape him, but between his tongue dancing with mine and his fingers moving over my breasts and nipples, I couldn't breathe. There was too much pleasure. If I made it out of this without drowning in it, I'd be lucky.

CHAPTER 11

Sloane

"Rip," I moaned into his mouth, testing out the new name he'd requested I use. It felt right to call him that.

This time he broke the kiss, but he didn't ask me what I wanted. He released me, flung his leg over me until he was kneeling beside me.

"What are-"

I squealed again as he grabbed the comforter and jerked it out from under my body, then tossed it into the corner. Then he took me by the shoulder and hip and physically placed my body into the middle of the bed. A wince made its way over his face and I realized he'd probably hurt his back. He kept moving though, so I didn't bring it up. The men around here didn't like being questioned. Especially not about a weakness of theirs. I'd learned that the hard way.

All that was beneath me now was the white sheets. The fact that he had the strength to move me the way he had was impressive. He was already back to straddling me, and his hands quickly divested me of my shirt. My arms moved, trying to cover my scars from his view. There were too many to ever hope to keep them from him.

His eyes snapped up to mine, an unreadable expression on his face. "Don't hide from me," he growled. "You're fucking beautiful."

He forced my hands down by my sides, staring down at me. His gaze roamed over the scars that were visible to him in this position. Heat grew in his eyes as they raised to my breasts. He wasn't pitying me as far as I could tell, just enjoying looking at his new wife.

It made me relax beneath him. I wriggled under him, not understanding the ache that was taking over my body. My eyes rolled back into my head when he leaned down and took one of my tender tips into his mouth. His tongue brushed over my nipple and he sucked hard.

"Rip!" I gasped, arching into his mouth. Whatever it was he was doing to me, I didn't want it to stop. His name turned into an unintelligible groan. The pleasure was too intense to hold inside.

He switched sides and raked his teeth over my other nipple, causing me to cry out again. "Fuck you're so sweet and soft," he said, voice muffled by the kisses he was giving me.

"Please." I had no idea what I was begging for, but I had no doubt that he knew.

"Are you aching for me, Angel?"

I nodded, my breathing coming in deep pants. He had my hands pinned, my legs were between his, there was nowhere for me to go. Yet, I longed to move. I didn't want to get away from him, but the urge to rock my hips was strong.

"Leave your hands there," he ordered as he let them go. He moved down my body, spreading my legs so he could lie between them.

My eyes widened when his face came to rest just above the juncture of my thighs. "Rip, wait."

"Not happening, Angel," he told me with a grin. "I've waited too long for this."

Too long for what? We'd only known each other for a couple days. What was he talking about?

He didn't give me a chance to voice the questions. His head dipped down as he tugged my pants down and off. His mouth closed over me and all I could do was try to breathe.

I wasn't sure if his mouth was making my panties wet or if it was me, but either way I was wishing he'd take my clothes off completely. The thoughts made me freeze. The breath was stuck inside my chest. Who was having these kinds of thoughts? I'd never had them before, but all it took was Derek's hands and mouth on me and I was acting wanton.

"Quit it."

I looked down and found him giving me a hard look. "What?"

"I can hear you over analyzing from here, Angel. Knock it off. Everything that happens between us is natural. It's what husbands and wives do."

Muscles I hadn't realized had locked up began to relax. I melted beneath him.

"That's better, Baby." He didn't give me a chance to try to cover myself. His mouth dropped down again. "I plan on eating this pussy every day for the rest of our lives."

There was no holding back, my hips bucked against him as he sucked on my clit. His tongue would dip down and lap up the wetness I knew was spilling from my body, before he went back to teasing my tender bundle of nerves. He had me hurtling toward something. It was taking over my body, my mind. There was no chance that I could stop it now.

"Rip," I gasped, fisting the covers in my hands. "Please. Don't."

"You better be telling me don't stop, Sweetheart, because I'm not planning on listening to anything else." He hadn't even raised his lips from my flesh, just spoke against it and went back to rocking me to my foundation.

I didn't want him to stop, but the intensity of the pleasure building inside of me was frightening. He was going to tear me apart and I wasn't entirely sure he'd be able to piece me back together again. I had a feeling that after meeting him, nothing was ever going to be the same.

There wasn't time to worry about it because I reached the crest and screamed as my body broke apart. Shaking overtook me as I was drenched in bliss. My body bowed up as I writhed underneath him. He didn't stop sucking and I swear the cascading sensations he was creating were going to kill me.

I didn't die, though. Slowly, I came down from the high he'd created within my body and I moaned as his tongue stroked over me. I was tender and sensitive.

He seemed to realize this and moved up my body. My eyes were closed, enjoying the last of the pleasure as it lingered. I heard a zipper and opened them. My eyes widened as I stared down at him as he took off the slacks and underwear. There was no way that would fit.

My gaze darted up to his and I shook my head, trying to scoot away from him.

"Where are you going, Angel?" he asked, amusement clear in his tone.

"You- I- We can't."

"Oh, we can," he breathed against my lips.

His tongue invaded my mouth and I tasted myself on it. A thrill shot through me. This was all so new and I didn't know if what I was feeling was normal, or if I was the strange one.

"It won't fit," I said when he finally released me from his drugging kisses.

His chuckle was deep and filled with male satisfaction. "Trust me, Sloane. It'll fit."

I frowned at him, not completely sure. My body jerked when his hand reached between us and one of his fingers brushed against my core. My hands went to the front of his shoulders to steady myself—though I don't know why since I was pinned between him and the bed—as he slid one long finger inside of me.

"Fuck, you're tight."

"See?" I huffed.

He laughed again. He pulled his finger from my body and shifted until his length was pressing against me. His hands cupped my cheeks and he stared into my eyes as he pressed forward.

My mouth dropped open. The stretching of my body was intense, but I breathed through it. He stopped and I frowned.

"This next part's going to hurt, Angel. Only for a minute," he promised. "Then I'm going to make you fly again."

I tensed, but he'd already thrust forward. Crying out, I dug my nails into his chest. I was careful not to reach around and touch his back. The pain was a bright flash, but it soon eased and I realized he was buried completely within my body. He was kissing my face, his fingers on my nipples, tugging and pinching.

As soon as I relaxed beneath him, he started kissing me again. It didn't take him long to build that ache back up inside of me. How could he have me here again when he'd pleasured me so fully before?

"Hang on to me, Sloane," he murmured in my ear.

I gasped as he pulled out of my body and then slid back inside. There wasn't any pain, just ecstasy. I was wet, ready for him, as he eased in and out of my body.

"So fucking tight and wet," he groaned. His face was buried in my neck as he picked up the pace.

My legs wrapped around his back—forgetting all about his injuries—I hung on as he sent my body spinning into a vortex of pleasure. "Rip!" I called out. That feeling was upon me again and even though I knew once I reached the end it would feel amazing it was still so new and scary. I was free falling and he had all the control. I could feel him dragging out of me, then shoving back inside and if he didn't go faster I was going to go crazy. "Faster," I gasped.

"Dirty girl," he said, but it sounded like praise. He picked up the pace and I groaned.

The friction was so fucking delicious. Every sensation was bombarding me and I didn't know how to process it all. He gave an extra hard thrust, then rolled his hips, and I splintered. The move had rubbed his pelvis over my clit. My orgasm hit me with the speed of a freight train. My cries sounded strangled and I was sure I'd end up losing my voice after tonight. I didn't care about anything but the waves of pleasure he'd created.

He buried himself inside of me and groaned low and deep. The feel of his cum filling me tipped me into another small orgasm. I felt myself pulsing around him.

He held his weight off my body, but his head was down and I could hear his harsh panting in my ear. I was pleased that he'd found his release because he'd wrecked me. It was a good thing he was my husband because I'd never be able to sleep with another man without thinking of him. He'd ruined me and I wasn't all that upset about it.

He rolled onto his side, then tucked me up against him. "Did I hurt you?"

I was facing away from him, so I couldn't see his face. Shaking my head, I smiled. There'd been one momentary blip of pain, but he'd seared it away with pleasure.

His lips brushed over my head and I relaxed in his arms. We were lying there in the aftermath when suddenly he swore.

I stiffened in his arms. "What's wrong?"

"I didn't use a condom."

My frown was deep as I looked at him over my shoulder. "Why would you?"

He looked like he was considering how to answer my question.

"We're married. Ethan wouldn't allow contraceptives here anyway. The more babies, the more followers."

His frown matched mine now. He moved his hand down to my belly. "...a baby."

I didn't comment because I wasn't sure how he was feeling. He sounded like he was in shock. There was also wonder in his voice. Cuddling back into him, I shut my eyes. The long day was catching up to me and I was ready for it to be over.

CHAPTER 12

Riptide

I laid in the dark, listening to Sloane's breathing evening out. Getting married was a big enough shock to my system, but to realize that if I kept having sex with her the odds of her getting pregnant were high was overwhelming. Who knew what kind of fucked up things Ethan would do in the future to ensure that the couples he chose continue to have sex. Like Sloane said, he needed us to reproduce. It was the preferred method for him to get his minions.

Rubbing a hand over my face, I tried to accept that. Even if Ethan didn't require some kind of proof, I wasn't sure I'd be able to keep my hands off her. Not after the responsiveness she'd shown me. My dick was already hardening, just thinking about her spread out beneath me, trusting me to treat her right. Judging by the things she'd told me, she hadn't had much love or affection in her life. I wanted to change that. To show her how good it could be between us.

But a baby? It wasn't like I had anything against them. They were cute little buggers. I just never expected that I'd be having them so soon. There wasn't any sort of timeline I was following. Have a wife by twenty-eight. Kids by thirty. Nothing like that, but no one had ever made me feel like I needed those things. Until now.

My heart had leapt inside my chest when Sloane had so casually remarked that Ethan wanted the couples having kids. It made sense. That didn't mean it hadn't put a bit of fear into me either.

She had no idea who I really was. What I was doing here. How would she feel once she found out almost everything she knew about me was a lie? *Everything but my feelings for her.* Another realization hit me. At some point the charade would be over and we'd go back to the real world. Would she stay with me?

The thought of what her reaction might be unsettled me. I put my arm around her waist, pulling her back more securely against my body. Something about her made this place easier to swallow. If it had been some other woman I wasn't sure I'd be as calm as I was now. As it was all I could do was wait and see how this would all play out. I'd explain to her that I'd infiltrated her life in order to help her and the others. It would hopefully be enough to convince her not to hate me.

In the meantime, I planned to enjoy my time with her. I buried my nose in her hair, enjoying the minty scent that clung to her. We could take our time to get to know each other, but I was going to have to keep my hands to myself. If I knocked her up that would irrevocably tie us together. I didn't mind so much, but she might once she found out the truth.

She murmured in her sleep, her hand coming up to rest on my forearm. She seemed to need to touch me as much as I did her. I let my eyes close, but it was a long time before sleep finally claimed me.

* * *

THE NEXT MORNING, I groaned as sunlight woke me up. Even as a kid, I'd been an early riser. Getting out onto the water right as the sun was rising ensured you caught the best waves. I missed living near the ocean, but my parents had already moved to Tucson by the time I'd finished my service. Between that and my club being here it'd only been natural for me to stay. I traveled a few times a year to visit my beloved ocean and that worked well for me.

Sloane shifted in front of me, rubbing her pert little ass against my morning wood. She'd slept the whole night wrapped in my arms. My staring must have woken her, because she stretched and yawned.

I put a few inches between us. My cock was already fucking throbbing and ready for another round.

She rolled and gave me a shy smile as she tucked her hand between her cheek and the pillow. Her beauty hit me like a punch to the throat, making it hard to breathe. I couldn't believe she was mine. She might not appreciate the marks that adorned her body, but I hadn't lied to her yesterday, I considered them marks of her courage. After seeing her help that little girl and agree to take a punishment for her, and then understanding what Ethan and his cronies did to people here, I'd known where her scars had come from. She had a lot to learn about me, but right now I was fully content with her being my wife.

Will she stay yours?

"What are your plans for today?" she asked.

"It's our honeymoon," I told her with a grin. "Maybe we could go into town. Find something to do together."

The smile slipped off her face. She bit her full lower lip and shook her head. "Ethan doesn't allow anyone except Bruce or Jacob to go into town."

That explained why we never saw anyone leaving to go get supplies in the city. Between the spider web of little tire tracks and trails they had out here and the fact that only two people ever left, we had no hope of catching them unless we just got incredibly lucky. From what we could tell they varied the way they traveled in and out.

"Alright. What would you like to do?" I asked, giving in to temptation and trailing the backs of my fingers over her cheek.

Something softened in her eyes and I enjoyed having her look at me like that. I hoped it wouldn't take me long to get the feel for this place or for my new bride.

"I'd like to unpack my things."

"It's your home now. You're welcome to do whatever you'd like with it." It belonged to her more than it did me. "Then maybe you could show me what it is you do during the days."

Her eyes widened in surprise. "I teach, most days."

"That sounds fun." Not really. I didn't have the patience to teach other people things. That was better suited to other men. I could work in teams with people, figure out what motivated them to give everything they could to whatever cause was needed, but actually sitting down and teaching them how to properly complete a task? No thanks.

I knew for a fact I'd end up being like my own father. The man loved me more than life itself and I felt the same for him and my mother, but neither of us had wanted him to help with my homework as a kid. I'd learned that lesson early on when I'd sat there wide eyed while he'd bellowed at me, 'It's two plus two! What does that equal? Two plus two!' As if yelling it at me would make me understand it any quicker or keep him from yanking his hair out.

"What?"

I blinked as I realized I was chuckling out loud. "Sorry. I was just thinking back to my father trying to help me with my homework. It's definitely best if someone else takes the teaching jobs instead of me."

Her smile brightened. "Your dad isn't the patient sort?"

"He is with a lot of things. Not math, though."

She cocked her head. "Ethan brought you here to take care of the finances, right?"

I nodded, realizing the mistake I'd made.

"Wouldn't that mean you're exceptional at math?" Her frown would be adorable as she reasoned out her question if she hadn't about caught me in a lie. Math had never really been my friend.

"My dad's not, but I am." Lie. Rat was. I couldn't create programs or apps, or do much more than add and fucking subtract. My biggest skill was a knack for figuring out different types of technology. I could use and repurpose things for tasks no one thought they'd be used for, but I couldn't build them. It'd helped me a lot in the military. It was even helpful to the club, but that was about it.

It didn't really matter. I'd left the military, but hadn't needed to get a job. I devoted my time to my club. Somehow, this surfer kid had figured out way back in the day to dump a few paychecks into the stock market. I'd made an investment with a fledgling technology company that had skyrocketed a few short years later and made me incredibly wealthy.

You wouldn't know it to look at me since I still only wore jeans, t-shirts, dirty work boots, and my cut. But I'd bought my parent's home and signed over the title to them. I'd paid for my sisters' homes as well.

Mostly, I reinvested the money. My luck had held out and most of the time I just ended up making more. Most days I ran The Bunker. The club's bar gave me something to do when Priest had everything locked down with the club. I pitched in with Lockout to pay Priest a salary that allowed him to be ready and available to his kids, but got most of the day to day things done for the club.

I fucking loved our bar. Everything from running it to working behind the counter. It gave me a sense of fulfillment and it helped me keep an eye on things that were happening within the city. Most people would look at me and write me off as soon as they found out I was the manager of a bar. Add in being in a motorcycle club and they'd turn their noses up so quickly they'd never find out I was one of the richest men in the city. Not that I let that slip to many people.

Attitudes sure changed when others found out you had money. I wasn't about to put up with the nasty changes. Only a select few of my brothers knew about my wealth, and of course, my family. I was a pretty private guy. I liked to focus on making sure our club members had what they needed and stay out of the limelight.

That was why it'd surprised my folks when I'd told them I was going to be the VP for the club. Dad had been in an MC back in the day. He'd loved the lifestyle, but a workplace accident had broken his back, preventing him from riding. It'd broken his heart. He'd retired from his club and they still treated him like family. I'd had a legacy spot available to me and if I hadn't met Lockout, I'd have taken it.

Even though I'd ridden everything from a surfboard, to a skateboard, to a BMX bike growing up, a motorcycle was the first motorized vehicle I'd driven. Showing up to school on the back of a Harley sure hadn't hurt my reputation with the ladies. I pretty much loved anything that allowed me to go as fast as possible, but bikes would always be my first love as far as vehicles were concerned.

"I'd love to show you my classroom," Sloane told me. The light pink flush on her face made it easy to see that she was pleased that her husband was showing interest in her.

Little did she know that I wanted to know everything about her. I wanted her to share her deepest secrets with me. "I need about thirty minutes to get some work done, and then I'll be yours for the rest of the day," I promised her.

"I'll get started putting some of my things away while you work." She slid off the bed and turned to face me. Her eyes widened and dropped down.

I'd rolled onto my back and my hard-on was tenting the blanket. Shrugging, I gave her a wicked smile. "That's what happens when a man wakes up with his sexy wife rubbing her ass on him."

Her face flushed pink and her jaw dropped open, causing me to laugh at the shocked look on her face. "I'm going to have so much fun teasing you." Shaking my head, I got up and started to dress.

Her soft touch on my back had me pausing before pulling my shirt on. My eyes closed as she lightly traced the unbroken skin across my back.

"I should put more poultice on this. I don't want it to fester."

"Tonight," I told her. I let the shirt drop down, covering my back and turned. Catching her wrist, I pulled her hand up and nibbled on her knuckles. "You can fuss over me then."

She gave me an unamused look, and shook her head, but she left it alone.

I set my laptop up on my desk in the back room and logged into the different programs that allowed me to view Ethan's finances. It only took a few clicks to see that Rat had done everything I'd requested. He'd already created three different shell companies and transferred money to them.

These shell companies were decoys. We'd be able to funnel the cult's money through them and have it laundered before being returned back to Ethan available to use. It would take a lot of work for anyone to realize these companies weren't fully functioning businesses. We weren't on anyone's radar yet, according to other Derek, and it was safe to set these shells up to enable the cult access to their money.

Ethan hadn't mentioned where he was receiving his money from, but the need to have it laundered told me it wasn't on the up and up. That was one of the things I needed to find out. Who was funding Ethan?

I hurried through my work and was pleased with everything that had been done so far. It would allow me to report back to Ethan and actually have something to show for it. Now I could enjoy the rest of the day with my new wife.

That made me pause. *My* work. *My* wife. It had been two days and I was already getting blurry about my real mission. I reminded myself that the honeymoon was temporary. Yet, I was still going to enjoy it.

CHAPTER 13

Sloane

I peeked into the office where my new husband was working. His head was down, shaggy hair concealing the side of his face while he tapped away on his computer.

This was the perfect time to go collect my things from the hidey hole I had in my house. I needed to get it out of there before they assigned the house to someone else and I couldn't get to it.

It was easy to slip quietly from my new home and I kept my head down as I hurried across the compound. I had an empty container with a lid that would hold the things I'd squirreled away over the years. It would probably take me a few trips. I just hoped no one would notice. If they did, I'd just claim that I'd forgotten some things.

The house was quiet and empty when I got there. Even though I knew Mae and the girls wouldn't mind me coming to get the rest of my things, I didn't want them to see what I had. It would put them in danger. If Ethan ever found my stash anyone who knew about it would be punished. Or worse. My thoughts strayed to my mother. I wasn't about to let that happen to my girls.

Unlike the others, my girls had a tendency to think and ask questions. They were too smart for their own good, so I'd just never told them about my plans. I couldn't bear to watch them punished. Beaten. All because of what I was doing.

I used my body to move my former bed away from the wall. There was the shelf I'd built that was hidden by the frame. I loaded the most important things first and then placed clothes on top—in case anyone looked inside—before putting the lid back on. One more trip would do it. I might have been able to fit it all in this tub—it was fairly large—but then I would have trouble hiding it.

As soon as I stepped out of the house, I heard crying. My heart clenched in my chest. I cast a look back toward Rip's house and nibbled on my lip. It would be in my—and my new husband's—best interest if I minded my own business. Whoever was in distress certainly wasn't mine to worry about, or so the different men of this community had tried to tell me over the years. But I couldn't leave them to their fate. I didn't have it in me to ignore someone who was hurt or in trouble.

I dropped my tote on the side of the house and made my way through the little back alleys between the houses until I found what I was looking for. Leaving my tote of goods was an itching worry in the back of my mind, but as soon as I found Mae struggling in the dirt beneath one of the single men here in the cult, anger snapped inside of me.

With a warrior's cry, I launched myself at his back. I didn't even know who it was, but it didn't matter. Mae's desperate eyes had met mine and I'd seen the plea for help.

The man let out a startled cry and he shoved to his feet, toting me around like a rag doll on his back. I scratched his face with the nails of my free hand while I held on with the other. He was like a bucking bronco.

"Run!" I gasped at Mae.

Her eyes widened and she struggled to get to her feet. Her blouse was ripped down the front and she had bruises from her cheeks down to her waist.

The man turned his head and snarled at me and my heart dropped to see that it was Barclay. He was as mean as a rattlesnake and almost as dumb. "You stupid, bitch! It's my right!"

I ducked my head down against his back when he reached behind him. He still managed to grab a hold of my hair and soon dragged me down off his back. Pain splintered through my skull. I wasn't a fighter. Wasn't strong. My desperation to keep these women safe was the only thing that allowed me to fight back.

He shoved me, sending me sprawling into Mae, knocking us both to the ground with twin cries of pain.

"I'll do whatever the fuck I want with her!" he bellowed.

Inching backward in a crabwalk, I tried to keep Mae behind me. "She doesn't want anything to do with you, Barclay." My voice shook a little. It was hard to stay calm when there was murder there in his eyes.

A small crowd was forming. I saw Tilly help Mae up and then disappear with her. At least they were safe. A boot landed against my ribs, causing the breath to whoosh out of my body. Agony blurred my vision and I curled in on myself. I'd be lucky if Barclay didn't kill me.

Out of the corner of my eye I saw his leg cock back again and I curled in tighter on myself. After he kicked me—if I was able—I was going to hit him in a man's sensitive area and run. It was my only chance. It would mean I'd end up getting a formal beating from Ethan later, but at least with that it would be regulated. He wouldn't kill me. At least not in front of the others. He never took the women's beatings as far as he did the men's.

My eyes popped open when I heard the roar of a pissed off animal. What kind of beast would have gotten past the fence and into our compound?

The kick never came. The animal was Rip. He'd tackled Barclay mid-kick and was sitting on top of him raining down punches like he wanted to drive the other man into the ground like a stake.

Janice and Audrey ran over and helped me get to my feet. "I got him as soon as we saw Barclay throw you off his back," Audrey told me, motioning to my out-of-control husband.

"We have to stop him," I gasped, my ribs throbbing with every shaky step I took. My hand landed on Rip's shoulder and I yelled, "Stop! Please!"

The glare he shot at me withered my soul, but as soon as he realized it was me the look softened. He was holding the front of Barclay's shirt, fist held back, about to bring it down on the other man's face again.

"They'll kill you if you kill him," Janice said quickly when I couldn't catch my breath.

"He shouldn't have touched my wife."

"She attacked me!"

I glared down at Barclay and pushed past the pain from my ribs. "You attacked Mae!"

"It's my right to sleep with her," Barclay argued.

Rip's lip lifted in disgust at the man's words. "Why the fuck do you think you have a right to sleep with someone who doesn't want you?"

"The older women are ours," Barclay explained. His hands were up, as though to shield his face. Rip had just beaten the hell out of him easily enough. We all knew his hands wouldn't protect anything if Rip decided to keep going. "Ethan lets us have them."

"What do you mean?" If I thought Rip looked like a wild animal before, he looked rabid and murderous now. Barclay's confession was making things worse.

"Ethan lets us have the older women who aren't married," he said again.

Rip looked at me for more of an explanation. "He's right," I said with a sigh. "The women who aren't married, but are over a certain age are given to the single men and widowers of the community to… satisfy them. It keeps them away from the young girls." Barclay's wife had died in childbirth. I wasn't sure if it was a mercy, or not, considering she'd been married to such an awful man.

"Even if they don't want to sleep with them?" Rip asked.

I bit my lip. It was one of the awful realities of living here. Those poor women were raped to keep the young unmarried girls and the married women safe. "Yes," I whispered.

Rip's eyes narrowed on my face as he digested that news. If he was anything like me, it would fester and rot in his gut.

"It's not right," Audrey said, voice and eyes fierce.

"It's not," I agreed. "I always help hide the women away when they need it. Or interfere like I did today."

"Trouble making bitch," Barclay muttered.

Rip dragged the man up until their faces nearly touched. "You say anything like that to my wife again and I'll fucking bury you."

"What's going on here?"

Barclay winced, though I wasn't sure if it was from Rip's threat or Ethan's booming voice. A large crowd had gathered now and I looked around in desperation. I didn't want Rip to get into trouble because of me. Yet, here we were.

Someone nearby was speaking to Ethan. I couldn't hear what they were saying, but judging by the hand gestures, they were explaining what had happened. I didn't bother to go tell my side. By now I'd learned that no one would listen, especially not Ethan.

I held out my hand for Rip to take and warmth filled me when he did. I didn't know if I could trust him fully, but for the first time in my life, I felt safe. This wild animal wouldn't hurt me. He'd protected me.

Rip stood up, leaving Barclay in the dirt. The other man's face was a mass of bruises and blood. I didn't feel sorry for him in the least.

"You attacked Brother Barclay?" Ethan wasn't asking, he was accusing me.

"She was helping another woman of our community," Rip cut in.

I remained quiet, but knew that wasn't going to appease Ethan. Sure enough, anger clouded Ethan's face.

"You may be new to our rules, Brother Derek, but I assure you, Sister Sloane knows each and every rule she broke here today. Sister Sloane, why don't you inform your husband of them. Now."

Rip wrapped his arm around my shoulder, pulling me into the

warmth and safety of his body. It didn't matter that my heart hurt nearly as much as my ribs, I forced myself to answer. "I disobeyed a man of the community. I spoke back to him. I attacked him."

"There are probably a few more in there," Ethan stated, "but you get the idea, Brother Derek." Ethan circled us like a shark.

My head turned, following the movement. I didn't like letting him get behind me. That was when he liked to attack the most. I wanted to see the punishment coming. Out of the corner of my eye, I saw Barclay with a huge bloody grin on his face.

"Sister Sloane will take her punishment and then we won't speak of this anymore."

"No."

My eyes widened and I tensed in Rip's hold. He couldn't say no. Could he?

Ethan stopped in front of us, his eyes narrowed dangerously. "What did you say, Brother Derek?"

My husband was calmer now, but looking into his eyes I could see he was no less dangerous than a minute before. He was cold and calculating. His next words were very deliberate. "I'll take my wife's punishment. You said it was my responsibility to keep her under control. I'll take her punishment."

A slow smile crept over Ethan's face. "You're already going to have your own punishment for breaking the rules, Brother Derek. There's no need for you to take-"

"I'll take her punishment as well, My Lord." Rip insisted, staring straight ahead.

"So be it. Go to the dais." Ethan walked away without another word. It was easy to see he was pissed, which meant this was going to be an especially hard punishment.

"No," I whispered, clutching Rip's shirt. "You can't. Your back."

He grabbed my hands, pulling them off his shirt. He looked down at me and there was softness there in his eyes again. "Go home, Sloane. There's no reason for you to watch this." He dropped my hands and strode away toward the stage in the middle of our little town.

Janice and Audrey hurried over to me and wrapped their arms around me. Tilly ran up. "I didn't know where to hide Sister Mae, but Brother Derek said to leave her at your house." She looked at all our dismayed faces. "What's happening?"

CHAPTER 14

Riptide

I didn't look around while I walked to the dais. My back was an aching mass of nerves thanks to the beating I gave that piece of shit a few minutes ago. If I saw that asshole Barclay's—who named their fucking kid that—smug face, I'd end up finishing what I started, pain or no pain. Fury raged inside of me over the fact that he'd even touched Sloane. I wanted to rip his balls off and shove them down his throat.

Not to mention the fact that he'd laid there and tried to justify the fact that he'd tried to rape a woman. Butcher had prepared me for the things I might find once I got here, but it hadn't mattered. Until you saw these things actually happening there was no way to steel yourself against the horrors these people lived with.

The fact that Ethan was 'punishing' me for helping my wife and punishing her for stopping a rape was…insane. There was no rationalizing this shit. The people here who bought into all this bullshit were crazy, pure and simple.

Was it good that Ethan protected the younger women? Yes. But at the cost of the older women? How the fuck could you make that okay? You couldn't. The mental gymnastics of this place were hard to keep up with.

There was a massive circle that'd been created between the bleachers and the stage. It looked like paint. I frowned at it, but then met Ethan's steely gaze. I'd questioned him in front of the others. Stupid, but there'd been no other choice. The last thing I was going to allow was for Sloane to be punished for anything. No one would ever lay a hand on her again without me killing them for it.

I watched seven men begin to strip out of their shirts as Ethan started up his usual booming speech. My eyes narrowed as I saw Bruce and Jacob were among the men. My focus was completely on them, so I wasn't really paying attention to Ethan. I didn't give a shit right now about what he had to say.

The seven men stepped into the circle and I didn't need Ethan's words to know they were my punishment. Of course they had to pick the seven biggest fuckers here. Bruce and Jacob were much bigger than the others, but being outnumbered seven to one meant that it didn't matter the size of the other five. I was going to get my ass kicked.

My muscles tensed when a hand landed on my shoulder. I glared at Sloane. "I told you to go home. I don't want you watching this."

She returned my look, putting her hands on her hips. "I came to warn you. You can't fight back."

"What?" I asked.

"If you fight back, Ethan will just keep adding men until you can't anymore." She pointed to where a group of men were standing near the seven who would be entering the circle first. "They'll beat you until you're either unconscious or dead."

"They're going to do that anyway," I muttered, frustrated by this whole process.

Sloane shook her head. "Ethan will stop it before then if you just take it." She hesitated, then pressed in close to me. I wrapped my arm around her shoulder, glad that she was taking comfort in me. It would be understandable if she was standoffish with me, but she seemed to understand that I wouldn't hurt her. "It's not too late. I can take my part of the punishment."

"Not happening, Wife." I leaned down and brushed a kiss over her lips. "Now go home." I swatted her playfully on the ass to get her moving.

"I should stay. Help you get home afterward-"

"Go," I ordered. She didn't know me well, yet, but if I knew my angel, she'd try to help me in some way and end up seeing Ethan's punishment anyway. "I'll get myself home." Or I'd lie in the dirt and rot.

She nibbled her lower lip, but finally gave me a nod and hurried away.

The tension slid out of my muscles. I didn't want her to watch me being beaten for two reasons, if I was being honest. One was to protect her. The other was for my damn ego. I wasn't a useless man. Fighting came second nature to me and I usually gave as good as I got. Having her watch me lay there while I got pounded on would be a huge blow to my already bruised pride.

Everything Ethan did in this community was to beat down his people. He didn't want them having thoughts of their own, let alone acting on them. He wanted them to be mindless drones. It was easier to control them that way. If people thought they could question him, then his rule as the 'Earth God' was over.

Ethan called my name and pointed toward the ring. Sighing, I stripped off my shirt and stepped inside. My hands tightened into fists as the seven men circled me. There was glee in most of their eyes, though Jacob looked like he'd rather be anywhere else right now. Bruce was grinning at me as his fist plowed into my face, sending my blood down into the dirt.

With every punch and kick I took from these pieces of shit, I plotted my revenge. The day was going to come soon, when I'd have my own crew to back me up and I was going to make each and every one of them regret taking part in this today.

I ended up down on the ground, a sea of faces blocking out the sky as they whaled on me. Sound was muffled until all I could hear was the heavy breathing from my attackers and grunts that fell from my own lips.

Someone kicked me in the back and pain lanced through me. Another responded by kicking me in the stomach. My ribs groaned with each hit. I focused on the dirt. If I looked up at them they'd read the hatred in my gaze and know that I hadn't learned whatever fucked up message Ethan was sending. Then this would just keep going.

Finally, Ethan bellowed out for them to stop. He couldn't let them kill me. He still needed me. I held the access to his money. He walked over to me and I had to smother the fury inside of me before I could meet his eyes. He nodded decisively and waved the others away. "That concludes both punishments, Brother Derek."

It had better. Every inch of me was bruised or cut. I shoved to my feet, swaying a little as my head spun, but I refused the offers of help from some of the others who'd been in the crowd. I needed them to know I wasn't broken. It would be important later when we came for them.

I made it back to the house they'd given me and shoved my way inside. Sloane's worried expression turned to horror as she looked at me, but I didn't stop to comfort her. I stumbled my way to the bed and fell forward.

* * *

GROANING, I pried my eyes open and looked around the room. The sun was shining brightly and it forced me to squint. Someone had landed a hard kick to my head that I was pretty sure had resulted in a concussion. Sleeping wasn't a great idea if that were the case, but it wasn't like I'd had a choice. I'd blacked out. At least I'd managed to get into the bed before doing so. Sleeping on the floor hadn't appealed to me and there was no way Sloane would have been able to lift me.

"You're awake." She came directly to my side and held out a glass of water.

Grunting, I forced my body to roll so I was on my back. It wasn't possible to catalog all the various aches and pains. I took the glass, then the pills she held. "How long was I out?"

"All night. Most of the day today." There was worry on her face, but she didn't ask anything. She somehow seemed to realize her husband was a pissy patient.

I didn't like being sick or injured and usually lashed out at everyone around me when I was. "Thanks," I told her, downing the pain meds. "Missed a meeting with Ethan."

"He stopped by. I let him see you to prove that you weren't faking."

Snorting, I shook my head. "Faking. After having to take a beating like that?"

"He knew you weren't going anywhere, but he likes to see the aftermath of his handiwork. It'll help soothe his temper." She sat next to me on the bed. "If I was worried about what he'd do to you, I wouldn't have let him in."

"It's fine." I looked down and realized the top sheet was missing.

Sloane followed my gaze and a blush stained her cheeks. "Jacob came for it not long after…" She stood up. "I'll get you something to eat. Rest. Ethan will come back once he thinks you've had enough time to recover."

I nodded and stared up at the ceiling. Fuck, I missed my brothers. Being in here was going to fuck with my head if I wasn't careful. It was crazy how only a few days ago I was so confident that this would be an easy mission to complete. Now I wasn't so sure.

It was imperative that I begin to learn who here was worth rescuing and who was a lost cause. I had seven names in the lost cause category already. The sooner I got us out of here, the better.

CHAPTER 15

Sloane

A few days later, I was heading back to my classroom. I'd taken the time off to nurse my new husband back to health. It was the least I could do since he'd taken my share of that beating.

Everyone had been busy that night either watching my husband get punished or hiding. The beatings usually riled up the single men, so most of the older women hid in their homes with the doors barricaded anytime a punishment took place. It didn't always save them, but it worked enough that they always tried.

The streets had been empty, leaving me with enough time—and no witnesses—so I was able to easily move the rest of my stash over into Rip's home. It was imperative that no one know what I'd stolen or where I kept it.

My heart had broken seeing Rip when he'd come back that night. He still wore the bruises, but had been out of bed the next day, refusing to lay there and rest. He would rather deal with the pain than lay around.

He'd left early this morning to meet with Ethan. I kept my eyes down as I walked. The last thing I needed was to cause more trouble for Rip. Now that I was married, Ethan would use my husband in order to make me behave. It was one thing when I did something that I knew would earn me a punishment, but to do something knowing someone else would take it for me? That would, by default, have me behaving.

That will please Ethan.

I made a face at that thought and opened the door to my classroom. I had about thirty minutes before it would be filled with students and I needed to set up my materials.

As soon as I'd gotten back to my new home, I'd checked on Mae. She'd insisted she was fine and had gone back to the row of houses where the unmarried older women lived. She'd given me a hug and apologized for getting me and my man in trouble. I told her no woman should have to apologize for what happened to her.

I sighed as I sat down behind my small desk. Pulling a small piece of paper out, I studied it. On here was the tally of all the items I'd stolen from The Order. I had everything I needed except money. There wasn't nearly enough of that.

We were hardly ever given cash. Everything here was bartered. I taught everyone's children, so they built me a house, dropped off extra food, etc. Ethan gave us all rations, but I would get extras thanks to my position. To get out of here we would need more than food. We needed a way to the real world, and a way to stay there.

Like I'd told Rip, Jacob and Bruce were the only two allowed to go into the city to pick up supplies. Ethan claimed it was safer that way. I knew the truth.

He doesn't want any of us finding out this way of life is bullshit.

My head snapped up at the thought and I looked around, worried that I may have said it out loud and that someone might have overheard. When I saw that I was still alone, I relaxed. We couldn't even think a curse word without worrying that we'd be overheard and hit for it. That was the life the women and children here led.

The men had it better, but only marginally. In all honesty, this wasn't a place for anyone. Ethan was the only one here who had control and free will. The rest of us were his slaves. Bruce and Jacob enjoyed being Ethan's slaves. They were sadists, they loved to hurt people. Ethan afforded them that opportunity as often as possible. Jacob was less vocal about it. Bruce liked to crow and get involved with every punishment he could. But out of the two of them Jacob was the more dangerous one. He was the one Ethan went to the majority of the time when he needed someone disposed of in the middle of the night.

I was pretty sure I was the only one here who knew about that part of Jacob other than those in Ethan's inner circle. There were very few he trusted. Jacob and Bruce were two who had that trust.

I frowned down at my tally, trying to figure out how to get more money. That was the only thing holding me back. We weren't going to have an easy time getting jobs, and Ethan would be searching for us so we'd need to lie low for a while. That meant we had to have enough finances to find a place to stay and for food.

"Hi, Sister Sloane!" Amara said as she came through the door. She gave me a wide smile.

"Good morning, Amara. Have a seat." I taught three separate classes for the different aged children. This morning I was working with my mid-range class.

As students began to fill the seats, I hid away my tally sheet and focused on them. We laughed together as I taught them the various subjects I had on my syllabus. If Ethan ever figured out where I'd learned most of what I was teaching, he'd kill me. I planned on being out of here long before that happened.

The hours passed quickly and soon I set the children free to go complete their daily chores. My heart leapt inside my chest as I realized that I had someone to go home to. Rip was proving to be an intelligent, caring man and I enjoyed our time together.

I started supper as soon as I got home, surprised that he wasn't back yet. I wasn't sure what he and Ethan were speaking about today, but I hoped there wasn't any more trouble. That was the last thing my husband needed.

He didn't know it yet, but the community was buzzing with gossip about him. Everyone was quite impressed with not only the way he'd handled himself during the whipping and the beating, but that he'd stepped up and taken my punishment as well. Not to mention that he was up and moving around after only a few days. His ability to withstand pain was what was impressive to me.

Ethan, of course, managed to spin that to his benefit. He crowed about Derek being a fine example, taking responsibility for his failures. Not complaining, arguing, or begging. Ethan was enough of a bastard to take full advantage of that. It wasn't all bad though. The women were all half in love with Rip already. The kids had quizzed me about my new husband with a form of hero worship in their eyes.

It was all incredibly dangerous. The more the people admired him, the angrier Ethan would get. Ethan would get away with this beating, but over time it would be a problem as Rip's reputation began to grow. If it got bad enough he'd see Rip as a threat to his leadership. That was never good.

The door opened and I smiled at Rip. "Hello."

"Hey, Angel." He came over and brushed his knuckles over my cheek.

I dropped my eyes as pleasure coursed through me. He was very demonstrative and I loved that. I just wasn't used to it anymore. Receiving a soft touch wasn't something I'd had in a long time. My mother died when I was nine years old. She'd been the only one who'd cared about me. There was no doubt in my mind that Ethan had her killed. That had made stomaching being here all the more difficult for me, but I'd had no choice.

At the time, I'd been too young and by the time I was old enough I'd decided I wouldn't leave the innocents here to suffer while I escaped. Some days I wondered if I'd made the right decision. Then the guilt for letting those intrusive thoughts into my mind would pull my mood into the dark depths for the remainder of the day. If I escaped, Ethan would think I had help and he'd kill anyone who he suspected of assisting me. That alone was enough to keep me here for now.

There was only one person in The Order that I tip-toed around, and that was Jacob. At first glance he seemed like the quiet shadow who followed Ethan around. Once I'd figured out he was a killer, controlled only by Ethan, I grew a newfound fear of the man. That fear led to a form of respect. I wasn't stupid and I didn't want to end up in a shallow grave that no one would ever find.

Ethan was smart to never do any killing himself. It kept his hands clean enough that the people here didn't blame him. He had his lackeys do the killing for him. There were always plenty of people willing to do his dirty deeds.

"Smells good."

I looked back up at Rip and smiled. "Thank you."

"Is that bread?" he asked, motioning to the dough I was rolling out.

"It's for a pie crust."

Interest sparked in his eyes and a smile formed on his handsome face. "Pie, huh? Any chance it's apple?"

"It is," I confirmed.

He groaned and my eyes widened as heat shot straight between my thighs at the sexy male sound of appreciation. My eyes dropped to his mouth as he licked his lips.

"I love apple pie."

"Good," I breathed. Clearing my throat, I looked back down at my dough. What was wrong with me? We'd only slept together on the night of our wedding, but over the last few days this persistent ache had built up inside of me. It was like an itch I couldn't find so that it could be scratched. That ache flared brighter as Rip moved in closer to me.

"Something wrong, Baby?" he asked.

I blinked and stared harder at the dough, fighting not to look over at him. His body was pressing against my back and his voice had gotten raspier. Did he somehow know what he was doing to me? No, that wasn't possible... Was it?

Shaking my head, I used my rolling pin to continue working. "Of course not. Go wash up. Dinner will be ready soon."

Rip's chuckle was dark and wicked and my eyes darted toward his retreating back as he went to do as I'd ordered.

I huffed out a breath and leaned forward against the counter. Why couldn't I seem to pull myself together? Was this why the other women refused to leave their men? Maybe. But I couldn't understand how they could feel this way for men who hurt them, physically, mentally, and emotionally, over and over again.

The only reason I was beginning to open up to Rip was because he'd proven to me that he was willing to protect me. None of the other husbands had ever taken a beating for their wives. They usually handed out an extra one once she'd healed enough after the public punishment. I couldn't imagine he'd hurt me after he'd refused to let others do so.

I wasn't planning on completely dropping my guard. Not yet, but something deep inside me was telling me that I could trust this man. I really wanted to. It'd been so long since I'd had someone I could lean on.

Rip came back out just as I was finishing up the lattice work on top of the pie. I placed it on a cooking sheet and inside the oven, then dished our plates. As I turned, I bumped into my husband. "Oh."

"Here, I'll take those." He pulled the plates from my hands. "Go sit. I'll get us something to drink."

I stood there, staring at him like he was a three headed monster. It went on long enough that he shot me an amused look. "What? Do I have something on my shirt?" He looked down and studied it. "Maybe I should take it off?"

Shaking my head, my only response was a squeak as I moved woodenly toward the table and sat. He'd already set our plates down next to each other and was currently pouring us lemonade into glasses.

Rip sat down and set my glass next to my plate. "So what was with your response?" The teasing had gone out of his tone and now he watched me with a steady gaze.

"I'm not used to…"

"Anyone helping you?" he prompted when I didn't finish.

"Especially not men. Not in the kitchen."

He nodded. "I get that. Well, I'm not like the men you know."

That was the truth. I smiled at him shyly. "I'm starting to realize that."

We ate in silence for a few minutes and then he began asking me about my day. My heart fluttered in my chest as he gave me his undivided attention. If I wasn't careful I was going to fall madly in love with my husband.

What a world I live in, where love is a dangerous thing.

He asked me questions as we ate. Innocent questions that there wasn't any danger in answering. It was just a way for us to get to know one another.

"If there was one place you could visit, where would you go?"

I set my fork down and focused on him. "The ocean." My voice sounded wistful, even to myself.

"Which ocean?" he asked, amusement in his tone.

"I don't care which."

"Have you never seen the ocean?" he asked me, frowning.

I shook my head, eyes shifting down to my plate. How I must seem to him.

"I grew up next to the Pacific Ocean, over in Washington State," he offered.

The excitement building in my chest had the questions pouring out before I could stop myself. "Is it beautiful? Is the water warm, or cold? Could you bring me there one day?" I froze after the last question left my lips. Desperately, I wanted to grab a hold of it and stuff it back inside my mouth. I couldn't give anyone—not even Rip—the idea that I was planning on leaving.

He didn't mention anything about my slip up, instead he laughed, then answered the first two questions. "Maybe one day we'll go," he said in a vague tone.

Ethan would never allow it. I didn't say anything about it out loud, but I knew it was nothing but a dream. One that would never come true if I didn't get out of here.

We were getting ready for bed later and I froze in the doorway of the bathroom. I'd gone in to change into my pajamas. It didn't matter that we were married, I hardly knew this man and couldn't bring myself to strip naked in front of him yet.

He was in nothing but underwear as he prepared himself for bed. I wasn't sure what drew his attention, but he looked over at me and grinned. "Hope you don't mind. It's too damn hot to wear those flannel pants to bed." His hand went to his chest and he rubbed one of his pecs.

All the moisture in my mouth dried up as my eyes followed the movement. Was he trying to kill me? Had anyone internally combusted before?

"That...that's fine. It's your home." My voice was more breathless than I liked, but there was no helping it. Not while this sexy man paraded half naked in front of me. Somehow I'd gone from blissfully ignorant about sex to not being able to think about anything else.

Each night I'd dreamed of him touching and licking me. I'd woken up hot and aching. He hadn't made any further moves on me. Not surprising really considering his injuries. That didn't mean that I didn't want him to initiate something.

He came over and brushed his lips softly over mine. "Good night, Angel." With that, he turned and got into bed. With his eyes closed, he asked, "Could you hit the light when you're ready?"

I huffed out an irritated breath. My lips were tingling and my nipples were hard little beads beneath my shirt. Why wasn't he doing more than pecking me on the lips? Had he decided he didn't want me after all? I paused on my way toward the light switch, horror flooding me as a thought struck.

Maybe he hadn't liked what we'd done together? Or maybe he was still in too much pain? He'd refused to take any more medication, claiming he didn't like how it dulled his mind.

"What are you doing?"

I glanced over my shoulder and found him studying me. "Nothing. Sorry." Hitting the switch, I quickly approached the bed. I froze as I realized I was going to have to climb over him to get to the side he'd left open against the wall. "Um..."

"Don't be shy," he said. His arms were tucked behind his head, pillowing it as he watched me in the moon-bathed room.

I started to climb over him, then gasped as his large hands spanned my hips. He didn't make any other move, but now I was motionless above him, straddling his hips.

"We'll have to try this one day," he purred at me. "I think I'd like to watch you bouncing on my cock."

My gasp was loud as his filthy words painted a very vivid picture in my mind. His hands tightened on my hips, but then he released me.

"Let's get some sleep, Angel."

I laid down beside him, nipples and clit throbbing, frustration mounting. My breathing was fast and erratic and I had to fight back the urge to rub myself against him like an animal in heat. Turning to face the wall, I forced myself to calm down. If he didn't want to sleep together, then there wasn't much I could do about it.

Rip had slammed into my life like a rogue wave hitting an unsuspecting ship. I was worried about what would happen when I finally had enough supplies to leave. Would he come with me? Would I be able to trust him not to turn me over to Ethan? If I went without him would I be able to survive?

My heart hurt at the thought of leaving him behind. We'd been married for mere days and he'd already changed me at the core. What was going to happen when I had months to fall in love with him? Sighing, I closed my eyes and shoved the thoughts to the back of my mind. I'd deal with whatever came. I always did.

CHAPTER 16

Riptide

The weeks had passed quickly and I'd begun to figure this place out more and more. There hadn't been any more trouble, so my bruises and wounds had healed. My back was going to be scarred for life, much like my wife's. I hated that Ethan had marred her beautiful skin, but not because I found it ugly. It proved what a strong woman she was. I hated it because every scar was an indication of the abuse she'd suffered.

She had scars all over her body, of varying sizes, and I'd been studying them over the last couple weeks. Every time she flashed skin, I cataloged the marks. I knew better than to comment on them, even though they didn't detract from her beauty in the slightest. *She* thought they did. For me they made her even sexier. Each one accentuated a curve, like a toned muscle. Only they screamed of more than a physical strength, but a strength of will. Each spoke to me and I had the urge to trace each scar with fingertips and tongue.

I rolled over and bit back the groan that built inside my chest. I was waiting for her to come to me. The last thing I wanted was to force myself on her—especially after finding out that happened often to the women here—I wanted her to show me some sign that she wanted to sleep with me again. I tried to remind myself that we had no condoms, no birth control. That this marriage wasn't real and would end soon, and we'd have the real world to deal with. Yet I couldn't imagine going home without her as my wife. Despite the fact that I knew I'd be killing Ethan, reality was still completely warped.

I refocused on the beauty next to me and tried to calm myself. My dick was no help in that. I was hard and throbbing, my morning wood raging out of control because of the gorgeous angel sleeping next to me.

Pushing out of bed, I went into the bathroom to get ready for my day. It was strange. If it wasn't for a few things here and there I could almost forget that we were living out in the middle of the desert. Having amenities out here made it much more bearable.

I walked out of the bathroom and got dressed. When I turned I found my wife watching me with sleepy eyes. "I might not be around today."

Her brows pulled low and she propped herself up on an elbow. Her little t-shirt she wore to bed was pushed up, exposing the soft skin of her stomach. It took all my control not to say fuck it to my plans and go back to bed with her.

"Where are you going?"

"I have a few things I need to do in the city."

Sloane's eyes widened. "Do...do you think Ethan will let you go?" Her voice was breathless and it sounded so sexy I had to adjust my hardening dick.

"He won't have much choice. He tasked me with getting permits for this place. I need to meet with the inspector in order to do that. I won't be alone, Mumbo and Jumbo will be with me," I told her with a grin as I sat on the edge of the bed. Giving into the need to touch her, I slid my hand under the blanket that covered her lower half and let my fingers drift over her calf.

I'd slowly started letting Sloane in on a few things here and there.

This was the first time I'd spoken with her about what I was doing for Ethan. I'd also been touching her—innocently enough even though I wanted more—getting her used to my touch. We flirted each time we were together. I was doing my best to win her over, but I knew I was the one who was going to have to make the first move as far as getting her to trust me. The easiest way to do that was to give her information and hope she'd reciprocate.

"I'm also in charge of The Order's finances."

Her eyes widened even more, her mouth making a sexy little 'o'. "I would have never imagined that he'd let someone he didn't know have that kind of access."

"Again, he didn't have much choice. What they need done, none of them can do. It takes a particular set of skills to manage money in… the ways Ethan needs it managed."

She nibbled her full lower lip as she thought about that. It was a habit of hers, one that drove me insane. I wanted to be the one nibbling on her.

"Sloane…"

She cocked her head and waited for me to ask my question. She somehow just seemed to understand me, better than most people did. She didn't push, didn't try to force anything with me, just accepted what I was willing to give. I'd been testing her in small ways since after the incident with Mae. Nothing had set off alarm bells, so it was time for me to see if she could be trusted with more.

It was a risk. If she told anyone about what I was doing, I'd be in deep shit. Somewhere deep inside, I knew she'd never betray my confidence. So I continued.

"Do you know where The Order gets their money from?"

She hesitated, studying me in the same way I'd been watching her just a few moments prior. She was coming to some kind of decision, just as I had. "They require any new man who joins to pay for the privilege," she admitted.

My brows shot up. That actually made sense given the large amounts that were deposited into the bank account Ethan had set up. "That's it? That's a lot of money to only come from new members."

"That's it. Ethan never wanted us to interact with the public, so that didn't allow for us to have businesses or sell items. He charges an exorbitant amount for these men to join The Order. He makes the price high for a few reasons. He refuses to allow many people in. He'd rather have our members born into the lifestyle. He makes those from the outside sell everything they own and come in with the clothes on their back and all their money. Complete devotion and reliance on The Order."

"Makes sense. That makes them easier to control," I said thoughtfully.

"Exactly. And it also means that the men who are able to pay are stuck here."

"And with the help of my skills, the money can grow and continue to fund the lifestyle you all live."

"What do you mean by 'your skills'?" she asked.

"I was an investment banker. Still am," I corrected, even though the lie was bitter on my tongue. I couldn't tell her everything yet. All I could do was hope she'd forgive me once I was able to. "I've been investing the money and making it grow. I also move that money when I need to pay for inspectors and stuff." I had to be careful here. Other Derek did all that, all to get into this place and get his own wife. The last thing I wanted was to lie to her, but if Ethan heard that I'd been telling my wife anything other than my cover story, it'd be my ass.

She nodded, scooting a little closer to me. My hand was still caressing her, but the shifting had my fingers moving higher up her leg until I was brushing her thigh.

She peeked up at me through her lashes. "I thought maybe you were mad at me."

That had the motion of my hand pausing before I started up again. "Why would I be?"

"Because of the punishments."

"I think you were incredibly brave in helping Mae," I told her firmly. "No one should have the right Ethan has given those men."

"It isn't much better for the wives," she commented, then relented, "most of the wives." She fidgeted with the blanket that was still covering her legs. "If you aren't mad at me…then why…"

She refused to look up at me, so I grasped her chin gently and forced her eyes up to mine. I rubbed my thumb over the curve of her jaw, then dropped my hand. Our gazes remained locked.

"Then why…what, Angel?"

Pink was creeping over her neck as she tried to gather the courage to speak. I had a feeling I knew where this was going, but I needed her to say it. The control had to be in her hands, even if it was difficult for her. Otherwise it would be too easy for her to look back at this time and say that I'd handled things badly. I was doing everything that I could to do things the right way. Or as right as they could be given the situation.

"Why haven't we…had…se-" She shook her head and huffed out a breath of frustration.

"Sex?"

She nodded, biting her lip. "I thought maybe you didn't want to."

"Oh believe me, Sloane. I want to, but I've been waiting for you to be ready." That was true, but I was also trying to be careful so I didn't get her pregnant. She was going to despise me if I got her knocked up and took the choice out of her hands at the end of this. I wouldn't leave behind a child. She would be stuck with me in her life even if she decided she didn't want me.

She gave me a look of disbelief. "I've been ready!" She looked mortified that she'd just blurted that out. Her face turned a dull shade of red.

I chuckled and then groaned. "Of course you'd tell me this now. When I have to go." My emotions were all tangled up and she was driving me insane. I shouldn't touch her. It would be better to give her some excuse and keep my hands to myself. I just couldn't seem to do that.

She started to move, then hesitated, before straddling my thighs. I straightened out my legs on the bed so as not to impede her movements. "Maybe tonight we could do that?"

I fisted my hand in her hair, jerking her head back so I could kiss her. Our tongues danced long enough that she started grinding against me. My dick was throbbing and leaking pre-cum into my underwear. I tightened my hand, not letting her move when I pulled away from the kiss.

My lips were still on hers as I muttered, "You're driving me crazy, Angel. Tonight I'm going to fuck you until you scream."

Her gasp was adorable. She was still so innocent and I couldn't wait for all the ways I could corrupt her.

"But for now, I have to go."

I kissed the tip of her nose, then set her aside. Adjusting my dick as I stood, I moved toward the door. I paused in the doorway and looked back at her over my shoulder. "How did you know how Ethan made his money?"

A guilty look flooded her face and her eyes darted away from me. My angel wasn't very good at lying.

"You're hiding something," I said, thinking out loud. "You're going to tell me what it is when I get back. Don't worry, whenever you confide in me, those secrets will never be told to anyone else," I promised her.

She didn't say anything, so I left. It only took a few minutes before I was knocking on Ethan's door. "Good morning, My Lord."

"Brother Derek. What can I help you with?" His head was down as he studied documents laid out in front of him on the desk.

I wondered what he did all day. Every time I came in here he always looked busy, but what did he do? I had a feeling Sloane might know. It was time for both of us to do a little opening up.

"I need to head into Tucson."

That got Ethan's attention. His head snapped up and he shot me a hard look. "Why?"

"I've been in contact with an inspector that's willing to push our permits through, sight unseen, but he's insisting on meeting. And on being paid." I sat down across from Ethan. "He's supposed to text this morning with the meeting place and time."

A muscle bunched in Ethan's jaw. He wasn't pleased with this announcement. "There's no other way? You can't just wire him the money?"

"None that I've found. He's the only one my contact was able to find that was willing to take a bribe and do what we want. But he wants cash. Nothing to be traced back to him. The guy is paranoid. If I don't go myself, he'll think he's being set up by the cops." I took the phone that Ethan handed over after reading through the texts.

"Jacob will go with you," he said. I was surprised it was only Jacob. I figured Bruce would be there, too. It was clear by his tone he wasn't pleased about this, but like I'd told Sloane. There wasn't much he could do about it.

"Thank you, My Lord."

"He set the meeting for an hour and a half from now. You'll need to leave immediately in order to make it. What is the price he's set?"

"Ten thousand."

Ethan's lips thinned. He looked like he'd sucked on a lemon. I'd have laughed if it wouldn't have disastrous results. He nudged the phone toward me on the desk. "I'll have Jacob secure the cash and meet you at the truck."

If I had set up a wire transfer, I would never leave the compound. By making this a cash drop, it gave me the perfect reason to go to town myself. There was no way Ethan would let me go any other way. So this was my only shot. It also meant I had access to the phone without his prying eyes.

Before I knew it, I was back inside Jacob's truck heading back to Tucson. If only I was leaving for good. I frowned and realized I was at the point now where I wouldn't go anywhere permanently without Sloane.

Taking the phone out, I shot a quick text with the address and time to Lockout. I quickly deleted the text after it was sent because Jacob was giving me shifty looks.

"What are you doing?"

"Confirming with my contact that we'll meet him at his designated time and location."

Jacob grunted in response, but he didn't argue. There wasn't much he could do about it. That was the theme of the day and I hoped my luck continued to hold out.

CHAPTER 17

Riptide

I slurped my milkshake loudly and grinned to myself when Jacob shot me an irritated look. The man hardly ever spoke. It was becoming my mission in life to annoy the shit out of him.

As soon as my watch read ten-thirty, I saw a balding man in a wrinkled suit hurry into the outdoor seating area. His eyes landed on me and when our gazes locked he nodded and came over.

"Derek Skore?"

"That's me. I take it you're Marvin?"

He nodded and looked around like he was afraid we were being watched. He set a briefcase down on the table and flicked the clasps open. "I have the paperwork here." Another darting look around, then he licked his lips and held out the documents.

"Why so nervous, Marvin?" I asked as I looked over the permits. Marvin was competent enough that I wasn't worried that he was fucking me over. Static would have made sure he knew better than that. He was the one who'd given me Marvin's information. Once other Derek had mentioned that he had contacts and handled these kinds of things, I'd collected the information from everyone I knew.

"I've never… Never mind. It's nothing." He fiddled with briefcase on the table. It had a false bottom in it. He lifted it up and slid it to me so I could place the money inside.

I had the cash wrapped in paper. I removed it from my bag and placed it inside his briefcase. There were people walking past on the sidewalk, but no one was paying me any attention. I'd already scouted the restaurant and there weren't any security cameras out here on the patio. There shouldn't be any witnesses of our exchange.

He snapped the case shut and frowned at me. "I used a different inspector's name and back dated the paperwork. Jim died last year. When you get caught, don't breathe a word that I helped you."

I arched a brow at him. "Do I look stupid enough to do that, Marvin?" When he didn't answer fast enough, I leaned forward and pinned him with a dark look. "Or maybe you think I'm some kind of fucking rat. Is that it?"

"No, no, no, no, no." He shook his head, placing his briefcase protectively in his lap. He stood up and moved away. "I-" He gave up on whatever he was going to say and bolted.

Jacob and I gave each other an amused look.

"You know some interesting people, Brother Derek."

I chuckled, but I was barely listening. The rough and rugged sound of multiple motorcycles pulling into the parking area had caught my attention. I grinned at the waitress as she dropped our food off.

"We should get back."

"Relax, Jacob," I told him, slapping him on the back. "Food just got here. It would look suspicious if we just took off. Besides, then we wouldn't get our lunch." I picked up my burger and took a huge bite.

Jacob scowled at me, but picked up a French Fry and bit into it. "Fine, but we're leaving as soon as we finish."

"No problem," I told him, burger stuffed in my cheek like a chipmunk.

We were only a few bites in when black leather caught my eye. I couldn't believe how strong the urge was to go over and wrap them all up in a hug. Lockout, Hush, Butcher, and Toxic all strolled toward our table as if they had all the time in the world and nowhere to be. Fuck. I'd even hug Butcher at this point. I missed my brothers.

Anticipation raced through me as they got closer, but I kept my eyes down on my food. Letting Jacob catch me looking at them would give away what was about to happen.

Toxic bumped into our table as he tried to squeeze into the table next to us. We were the only people outside on the patio, so Jacob gave a hefty sigh of irritation. The stainless steel and wire mesh table rocked, spilling our sodas and my milkshake all over.

"What the fuck is your problem?" Butcher snarled at me, before I even had a chance to say anything.

My laugh was incredulous. Leave it up to Butcher. *"My* problem?" I asked, casting a disbelieving look at Jacob. "Your friend ran into *our* table."

"And your fucking coke is all over my boot," Butcher growled. There was a sparkle there in his hazel eyes. He was enjoying this. Asshole.

"Sounds like a you problem," I commented.

"Brother Derek," Jacob cautioned.

"Brother Derek? What the fuck are you? Amish?" Toxic asked, getting in on the game.

Lockout's lips twitched, but he and Hush stood back and let the two younger members pick the fight.

"None of your fucking business," I said, shoving to my feet.

"I'm going to make you lick all the soda off my boot, you pansy ass mother fucker," Butcher threatened. He reached over the table and suddenly I was flying through the air.

I winced right before I landed on the table closest to Lockout and Hush. So much for going a few days without having bruises. We were going to have to make this look real. I couldn't risk sending too many texts. The one I was able to send was a risk to begin with.

I hit the ground with a jarring thud as I rolled off the table. Lockout hauled me up by the front of my shirt. There was an apology in his eyes as he cocked his arm back. His fist plowed directly into my face and I felt my nose break and gush blood.

That fucker. He knows better than to mess with my face. It's too pretty for this shit. Those assholes had already broken my nose a few weeks ago. Now this.

He shoved me back into Hush, who hooked his arms around mine, preventing me from retaliating. A quick glance over was all we needed to see that Butcher and Toxic were keeping Jacob busy. I quickly relayed everything I'd learned.

"You have a month, Rip," Lockout muttered. He threw a punch into my side and I grunted in pain. "Four weeks from today, and we're coming to get you. Anyone who's innocent can come with us. We're killing the rest." Another punch caught me in the ribs and caused stars to dance in front of my eyes.

"Got it," I mumbled, before breaking away from Hush and launching my elbow back into his stomach. He let me go with a bellow of pain and I hit Lockout with a jab cross combo.

Lockout smiled at me as blood dripped down his face from where I split the skin on his cheek. "We fucking miss you. You'd better keep your ass safe in there."

"Cops!" Hush shouted and he grabbed Lockout and started to pull him away. "Be careful, Rip." With that he motioned to the others and all four of them jumped the small wrought iron railing that fenced off the outdoor patio from the sidewalk. A moment later I heard bikes roar to life and head out.

I went over to Jacob and helped him up. He was fuming, but he brushed off his clothes as though it didn't matter. If there was one thing Ethan taught his people, it was how to take a beating. Something about Jacob told me there was a lot I had to learn. He'd held his own. Butcher had a black eye and Toxic's lip had been bleeding by the time they'd taken off. The man could fight.

"Sorry," I told him. "Didn't realize those assholes would jump us that way." The bruises on his face—and those I couldn't see on his body—made me grin to myself. He deserved far more and I'd be taking my revenge on him in a month.

"Let's get out of here before those police officers come out here." Jacob hopped over the railing the same way the others had. I pulled out some cash that Ethan had given me for the trip and dropped the bills on the table next to ours. Luckily, I'd folded the permits and put them in my back pocket before Marvin had even left. It would have sucked to get this far and have them be ruined.

Jacob was quiet the whole ride back and I was grateful for it. Seeing the guys had been a brief high, but now I was feeling pretty fucking low. I wanted to take Sloane and run. Fuck the cult. Fuck Ethan. Fuck everyone but her.

I knew I couldn't do it. There were women and children here who needed to get rescued just as badly. I thought of Tilly, Janice, Audrey, and Mae. They were the first on my list of people we'd be walking out of the desert with. I hoped it would get a whole lot longer.

We went directly to Ethan's office once we got back and I handed over the permits and the cell phone.

"Trouble?"

"Some fucking bikers jumped us," I told him.

His eyes flicked over to Jacob, who just shrugged. "They started a fight. We held our own. They took off when some cops showed up for lunch and we did the same."

Ethan nodded then glanced down at the documents in his hands. His smile slowly spread as he realized they were permits not only for the land and the buildings, but for the utilities, too. Honestly, we probably hadn't paid Marvin enough for the miracles he'd worked, but ten thousand was what he'd asked for so that was all we gave.

"Good work, Brother Derek."

"Thank you, My Lord."

"Everything is going well with the shell corporations?" he asked.

I nodded. "Everything is on schedule. The money is already trickling in. Another week or so and you'll have access to a good chunk of it and won't need to worry about anyone tracing where it came from.

Sloane hadn't mentioned it, but considering Ethan needed the money laundered I had a feeling most of the men paying The Order had gotten it by less than legal means. Most of them were probably like Chet. Corporate CEO types who'd embezzled from their companies.

"Good. I look forward to your next progress report. Good night."

He always managed to dismiss people in a way that felt insulting. I gave him a silent acknowledgement and left. It wasn't very late, certainly wasn't evening yet, so I headed back to the house. Sloane would still be working with the kids for another hour or so.

I settled in at my desk with my laptop and dove into the work that awaited me there. My head snapped up an hour later when my wife came through the door.

As much as I wanted to throw her over my shoulder and take her straight to our bed, I knew she'd be irritated if I threw off her routine. Sloane was a woman who valued a never changing regime. She would make us dinner, and some kind of delicious dessert, then we'd eat before we settled in for the night.

I decided to let her have her routine while I asked her some of the difficult questions I needed answered. I locked up my laptop, then walked into the kitchen.

She was already at the sink, apron around her waist as she peeled potatoes. She seemed lost in her own thoughts and didn't realize I was home. Pleasure at seeing her standing there overwhelmed me. She was all mine. It was me she was waiting on and it made me realize how fucking lucky I was.

I crept up behind her and wrapped my arms around her. My chuckle spilled from my chest along with a grunt when she elbowed me in the gut with a squeal of surprise.

"You have good aim, Wife."

She gasped and spun in my arms, hands covering her mouth. "I'm so sorry! I didn't know you were-" She broke off, eyes narrowing on my face. "Rip, what happened?"

I'd forgotten about my nose. It'd hurt like a bitch when I reset it on the drive home, but now it was barely aching. "We ran into some trouble in town today. It wasn't a big deal."

She put her hands on my cheeks, turning my face this way and that while she studied my nose. "It's broken."

"I reset it."

She patted my cheek and turned back to her preparations. There wasn't anything to be done for a broken nose once it was reset and she knew it. "What happened?"

I told her about the fight and she laughed. "I'd have liked to see those guys beating up Jacob. I just wish they hadn't done the same to you."

"No one beat me up," I growled into her neck.

She laughed, but tilted her head so I could trail my lips over her skin. Her hands shook a little as I nibbled my way from her neck to her ear. She gave a little moan as I sucked on the lobe of her ear. Before I could do anything else, she leaned to the side in my arms, breaking the contact between my mouth and her ear. "Out," she said with a smile.

I groaned and dropped my head down onto her shoulder. "You're torturing me, Angel."

"Well unless you don't want dinner, you need to leave me to it. I can't concentrate when your hands are on me."

"Just my hands?" I asked, tone wicked.

"Or your mouth," she admitted.

I released her and went to sit at the table. "It's better this way," I told her. "We have other things to talk about."

CHAPTER 18

Sloane

My hands shook as I peeled the potatoes for tonight's dinner. All day the knowledge that he had questions he wanted answers to had been plaguing me. There was a part of me that wanted to trust him and tell him everything I knew and what I'd done. But it was terrifying. If I confessed everything and he ran to Ethan it would cost me my life. Ethan would have me killed for stealing from and betraying him.

My eyes had strayed to my clock multiple times each hour, waiting for Ethan to walk in and drag me off. He never did. As far as I could tell, Rip hadn't told his boss anything. Ethan would hate it if he knew I knew his secrets.

Taking a deep breath, I let the words tumble out. I kept my gaze on my knife as I cut vegetables. Seeing a disappointed look on Rip's face would crush me. I'd rather not see it. This was my test for my new husband. It was risky because if he failed and told Ethan, I would pay.

But he had to know. And he hadn't let me be beaten before. Everything inside of me was screaming that I could trust him.

"I know how Ethan makes money because I spy on him," I admitted. A quick peek over my shoulder—I was a glutton for punishment—showed that he looked surprised, but there wasn't any disappointment on his features. I blew out a breath of relief before I continued. "I break into his office at night and go through his paperwork." *In for a penny, in for a pound.* "Read his mail. Things like that."

Rip's mouth was hanging open now and I couldn't help but laugh. I smothered it with my hand, but a few giggles slipped out.

He stood up and came toward me. "And here I thought you were an angel," he said with a shake of his head. "You're a sinful little thief is what you are."

I gave a delicate shrug, but leaned back against his chest when he wrapped his arms around me. Who would have thought that I could feel so comfortable with a man? That I'd find one who seemed to have feelings for me like I did him?

"The devil was once an angel," I informed him in a self-righteous tone. I'd read enough of The Bible that Ethan liked to mock to know the story.

He grinned at the teasing. "I guess you'll have to be my little devil when you've been a bad girl." Goose bumps raised on my skin. "And my angel when you've been a good girl."

He spun us away from the counter and pinned me against the wall. I gasped as his hands roamed underneath my apron.

"Rip, I have to make-"

He turned me in his arms and kissed me, ending my objections. His hands were in my hair now, holding me in place so he could ravish me with his mouth. The man turned my legs to jelly. My thoughts into mush. And sparked to life desire faster than I could blink. I moaned into his mouth.

He had us moving again and I was bent over the kitchen table before I knew what was happening. My eyes widened on the bare wall in front of me as he rucked up my skirt and his fingers found my already dripping core.

"Rip! We're in the kitchen."

"I know you're a classy lady, Sloane," he said, groaning when he slid a finger inside me. "But you're my wife and I'm going to dirty you up a bit. When you're in our home, with me, you're going to be my filthy girl. I want to fuck you in all the ways I've been imagining since I first saw you."

There were no words. I didn't know how to respond to all of that, but my pulse spiked as he said these things to me. I think I liked his dirty talk. That he seemed to find me beautiful even though I had scars all over. There was lust in his eyes when he looked at me. I knew he wasn't faking it.

His body covered my back and the table beneath us groaned under our combined weight. He didn't seem to care. He was too busy whispering dirty things in my ears while his fingers brought me closer and closer to orgasm.

"I want you to come for me, Sloane. Prove to me that you're mine. That you'll always be mine. I fucking love seeing you turn into a dirty girl. My dirty girl."

His words were shocking, and enticing. My thighs shook as my body coiled tighter. I was just about to come, when he pulled his finger out of me and stopped rubbing my clit. Huffing out a breath in irritation, I shot him a glare over my shoulder.

His grin spread across his face. "Something wrong, Angel?"

"Don't stop."

"Don't stop what?"

My glare intensified. He couldn't make me say it. The words were too shameful. What we were doing was shameful, wasn't it? But oh, it felt so good. How could something that created these sensations be shameful? Maybe that was just another thing I'd been lied to about my entire life. It felt right, being here with Rip. We were husband and wife. I let the building shame slide away.

"Tell me that you want me to fuck you, Angel."

"I-I want you to fuck me, Rip."

He shuddered, the vibrations pouring into me from where we touched. "That's so goddamned hot."

I bit my lip as my core clenched. I was empty and now that I knew exactly what I was missing I wanted him to fill me up and make me feel the way he had before.

"Please, Rip."

"One more, Baby. Tell me you want me to slide my cock into that tight little pussy."

I shook my head, then laid my forehead down on the table. My breaths were coming quickly and I wanted this more than anything, so I whispered the words he asked for.

My pussy stretched around his hard length as he took control of my body. I didn't care. I was giving it willingly. Control was the last thing I wanted right now. Crying out as he bottomed out inside of me, my pussy clamped down on him.

"You keep that up, Little Devil and this is going to be a very short ride."

It wasn't like I'd done it on purpose. He just had me so worked up, I couldn't seem to help myself. He still had me pinned to the table with his weight, but my hips were grinding back against him as much as I was able to move.

I need more.

"Okay, Angel. I'll give you everything you need."

My eyes opened and I wondered if I'd said that out loud? I didn't think so. He was just reading the desperation of my movements. My eyes rolled back as he dragged himself from my body, then thrust back in. My hips hit the table and the little bite of pain somehow made this all feel that much better. I didn't know how he could read me so easily, but he just seemed to know what I needed.

My moans were low and tortured as he fucked me. The table creaked and groaned. He was growling and continuing to speak dirty, delicious things to me.

He finally rose up off of me and I shoved myself up onto my elbows, hanging my head as the bliss washed over me with every roll of his hips. His dick was rubbing a spot deep inside me that was going to make me hit a high note when I came. I just knew it.

Everything inside me was coiling tighter and my entire world centered around him. His hands were on my hips, holding me still so he could power into my body. The sounds echoing through our kitchen were obscene. There was no way I was that wet. Right?

I dropped back down so my chest was flat against the wooden surface of the table. I couldn't focus enough to hold myself up. All my concentration was taken up by rocking my hips back into him. It made a smacking sound that was increasing my pleasure and I wondered if he enjoyed it too.

"Fuck, Angel. You feel so damn good." He leaned over me so he could growl into my ear. "I'm going to make you come so hard you won't ever think of another man again. You'll beg me to fuck you every night and come apart in my arms. You're mine and I'm not fucking letting you go."

Letting me go?

I flinched a little at his words. Did he somehow know about my plan to leave here? Would he come with me if I told him? I wasn't quite ready to spill all my secrets so I bit the insides of my lips. All he had to do was start asking me questions and I'd sing like a canary right now. I was too open. Too vulnerable to him.

His weight left me again, but his hand snaked around, underneath my body and he started rubbing my clit in time to his thrusts.

That was all it took to send me straight to the heavens. With a strangled cry, I did exactly as he predicted and came harder than before.

His fingers bit into the flesh on my hips as he pumped into me. "So good. That sweet little pussy milking me is more than I can take, Angel." His shout as he came was somehow satisfying to me.

I liked hearing how much he enjoyed my body, because I enjoyed his, too. I was still innocent to the ways of sex and men, but I had a feeling Rip would happily teach me what he knew. I was ready for that.

He collapsed onto my back and I closed my eyes, enjoying the feel of his weight pressing down on me. There was a sense of connection between us and I didn't want it to end.

Eventually, it had to and Rip scooped me up into his arms and carried me to our bedroom. I buried my face in his neck and inhaled his scent. It was a fresh scent that I'd never smelled before and I wondered what it was.

Before I could ask, he set me down and disappeared inside the bathroom. I heard the tub running and stepped inside with him. We were both still fully clothed, but somehow that just made what we did even hotter. What was wrong with me? My pussy pulsed, sending a flood of wetness down to coat my thighs. It was his essence mixed with mine. My cheeks heated with the realization.

He turned toward me, a determined glint in his eyes. "You take a bath. I'll handle dinner." He didn't wait for my response, just began undressing me with a skill and speed that was shocking.

When I was naked in front of him, his eyes roved over me and I wondered if he was going to make love to me again. Instead, he pulled me close for a bruising kiss before turning me and giving my naked ass a slap. "Into the bath, Angel."

I squealed in surprise and took a step forward. A nice long soak before dinner sounded amazing, so I stepped in and sank to my chin in the hot water.

My body buzzed pleasantly from its release and something in my chest loosened the slightest bit. I'd told him a few secrets now and he hadn't run to Ethan with them. I hoped with all my heart that I could trust this man. *My* man.

If I made it through the next couple of days without being found out, maybe I could trust him with the rest of my secrets. There was still so much about me he didn't know.

Will he feel differently toward me once he knows who I am? What I plan to do?

Sighing, I closed my eyes and banished the thoughts from my mind. There was no point in worrying myself sick until I knew I could trust him with all of my truths. If Rip was half the man I was beginning to suspect he was, he wouldn't judge me too harshly. I hoped he'd continue to want to protect me. Maybe even love me.

CHAPTER 19

Riptide

The time Lock had allotted me was passing too quickly. Irritation and worry were my constant companions. It'd already been two weeks since I'd seen my brothers and while I was making some headway on my list of names, it wasn't enough.

All of the men I'd spoken to were already on the 'can't save' side—not a surprise since most of them paid to be in here—but some were born into this and I had to do my due diligence. If they didn't want to be in this life any more than the women or children, we'd do what we could to help them.

I had a feeling most of the names on the 'can save' portion of my list were going to be women and young children. That was fine by me, but the problem was I couldn't get any of them to speak to me long enough to gauge how they felt about living under Ethan's rule. Most of them saw me coming and either turned and went the other direction, or flat out slammed doors in my face.

It wasn't all that surprising. The men here didn't exactly treat them well. Suspicion of new men coming into The Order probably kept them safe. Still, I had to try. And in a way that wouldn't raise any suspicion.

Ultimately, I was going to need Sloane's help. She knew everyone here. I was convinced more and more each day that she didn't want to be here, that she didn't buy into this. I just needed to know for sure.

Needed to know she really loved me. Not being brainwashed by a cult would be a plus, but ultimately, I needed to know that this was real.

I stepped out of the house. My work was completed for the day and ready for Rat to step in and work his magic with, leaving me to get back to why I was really here. I considered stopping in to see Sloane.

We were growing closer each day and no matter how many times I tried to talk sense into myself and keep my hands to myself, I ended up fucking her until we were both seeing stars. Leaving her alone wasn't something I could do. I was ready to just throw in the towel.

Not only was she beautiful, but she was smart, caring, and funny. She'd told me a joke last night that'd had me laughing for a solid ten minutes. I enjoyed seeing her laugh. She got to the point where she couldn't breathe and tears would run down her cheeks. It was my mission in life to bring her to that point at least once a week, if not more.

I paused as two people went running by. Cocking my head, I followed behind at a slower pace. Jacob's truck was parked in front of one of the houses and he was carrying a woman out.

People were circled around, watching. "What's going on?" I asked one of the men standing nearby. I thought his name might be Mitch, but I didn't bother to address him by name just in case it wasn't.

"Darren beat Sarah almost to death." The soft voice came from slightly behind me, but I'd know it anywhere. Mitch just nodded in agreement.

I held up my arm and Sloane ducked underneath and pressed against my side. Pleasure curled around me. Knowing that she came to me for safety and comfort was everything I wanted. Wrapping my arm around her was the most natural thing in the world now. We'd grown so close in such a short amount of time. A fucked up place like this helped you bond.

"Is Ethan going to let that stand?" I asked, glancing over to make sure Mitch wasn't listening. He'd already pressed forward along with the rest of the crowd to see everything they could. Sloane and I stayed where we were.

"No. He'll have Darren beaten to the same degree Sarah was."

I smiled. "Good. He deserves it." There'd been a few times while I'd been living within The Order that I'd actually agreed with some of their crazy rules…and the punishments handed down for them. "No man should beat a woman."

"Oh… No. I mean, no they shouldn't, but that's not the problem."

I cast her a confused look. The sad expression on her face made my gut twist. I didn't need her to explain to know this would get worse. She did anyway.

"Husbands are allowed to beat their wives." My jaw clenched in anger, but I didn't interrupt her. "The problem is that Jacob is going to have to take Sarah to the hospital if she's going to live. It casts too much attention on The Order." She gave me a grimace that passed for a wry smile. "That's unacceptable."

I sighed and scrubbed a hand over my face. Darren still deserved the punishment that he'd get, but hearing that the husbands had free rein to abuse their wives made me wish my brothers were coming to bail us all out tomorrow, whether I was ready or not.

"What will they do to him?"

"They're going to beat him nearly to death."

"Won't that mean two people in the hospital?" I shook my head. "These rules rarely make sense."

"It doesn't matter. Ethan handed them down and he enforces compliance," she said, her voice lowered. "Darren won't be given a hospital. If he lives, things will go back to normal. If he dies…so be it…according to Ethan."

No wonder the people here walked around like drones. If they so much as look sideways at one of Ethan's contradictory laws, they're beaten or killed. There wasn't anyone they could go to for help. Except maybe Sloane.

Over the last month, I'd heard more and more stories about what made my wife a trouble maker. She'd been helping anyone she could and taking the punishments for years. It explained all the scars on her beautiful body.

We followed the crowd as they made their way to the stage. I watched with a clenched jaw and fists as men doled out Ethan's punishment for Darren. Looking down, I studied Sloane's face as she watched. There was zero doubt about it, I needed to get her out of here, one way or another.

After the spectacle was over, I asked Sloane, "What now?"

"They'll dump him in his house and it's up to him whether he wants to fight to survive."

"Will you help him?" I asked, remembering the way she'd tended me after my initiation.

"No," she said, voice hard as stone. "This isn't the first time Darren has seriously harmed Sarah. It's just the first time she's had to go to a hospital." She peeked up at me. "Would you be disappointed if I told you that I hope he dies?" The guilt flashed over her face as she said the words.

"No," I replied, tugging her into a full on embrace. "I'd say we were thinking the same thing."

The tension melted out of her body. It was time. She'd confessed her secrets to me. It was time to tell her the truth. Doing so had worry clawing at my insides. I didn't want to lose her, but she deserved to know who I really was. On top of that, I needed her help to finish finding out who was salvageable here. She'd be instrumental in getting these people out of here when my club came.

We'd rain down destruction and death and we'd need someone we could trust to get the women and children to safety until we could take them from this Godforsaken shithole.

"I have another class," Sloane said, leaning up onto her tip-toes to give me a kiss. "I'll see you tonight." She tossed me a smile over her shoulder as she walked away.

Following her to the schoolhouse was an everyday occurrence, though she didn't know it. I blended in with the crowd and watched her walk along. Women and children called out and spoke with her as she went. She was the one ray of light in this gloomy life. No wonder the men hated her the way they did. She opposed everything they stood for. She was pure goodness and selflessness. I hadn't heard a mean word come from her mouth unless it was for the abusers who hurt her friends here.

I waited until she went back inside the building she conducted her classes in, then headed home. Speaking with her should help me gain ground on my list. I just hoped it didn't set me back too far with her.

There wasn't much choice. I needed to tell her everything. Even if I didn't need her help, I would do the same thing. That didn't mean I was looking forward to it. Maybe if I hadn't been a dumbass who'd fallen in love with his wife this would be easier.

I froze, hand on the doorknob to my home, as that realization struck me. This wasn't lust—though there was plenty of that—or infatuation. I'd fallen head over boots in love with Sloane.

"How is that even possible?" I muttered as I walked into my house. "It's been a month."

She'd pulled me in much like I'd seen her do with so many others here. Her caring and kindness were infectious and I couldn't fight against it. Every time she'd smiled up at me in that shy way, my footing had slipped a little more. When she'd started trusting me, knowing I'd take care of her, protect her, I'd stumbled a little more.

In a place like this it didn't take long for feelings to grow roots and flourish because we'd been leaning on each other. Whether we realized it or not, it was what we'd been doing. Feelings were elevated at a quicker rate because at any moment either of us could have been found out and killed.

I wondered if she felt the same for me. The only way to find out would be to tell her. It all circled back around to admitting the truth to my wife.

Tonight. I'd admit to her who I was and why I was here. I'd appeal for her help. And I'd let her know that I loved her. Hopefully, she'd forgive me for deceiving her and trust me when I told her that my love for her was real.

Shaking my head, I sat down at the desk and began checking over Rat's work. I shoved all thoughts and feelings out of my mind and focused on the numbers on the screen.

CHAPTER 20

Riptide

"Brother Derek, come with me. I have a special task for you," Ethan said to me. I looked up from my computer. He was standing in the doorway, hands pressed together, fingers steepled steadily in front of his chest. He was wearing his ceremonial robe. I hadn't seen him wear it since the day I was initiated.

This can't be good. Clearly he was dressed for another special event. An event that I was about to take part in. "Of course, Eth…My Lord." I stood up, dropping my laptop into a drawer and locking it before moving away from the desk. It took all of my self-control to shove aside the anger and indignation that this fucker had just walked into my house, unannounced. Like he owned the fucking place. That made me pause. He did own the damn place.

Ethan led me outside to the center of the compound, to the altar and bleachers where we'd just been that morning. The sun was beginning to sink down below the horizon. Sloane would be getting out of class soon, and instead of our usual routine of making dinner together, I was stuck here. Instead of having that conversation with her, I was here watching Ethan warily.

Jacob and Bruce were standing to the side of the altar, and kneeling between them was Ross. I'd spoken to Ross a few weeks ago. A name hadn't gone on the 'can't save' side of my list so fucking quickly. The man was a slimy little rat and I knew it from the moment I'd met him. He'd made that inner instinct inside of me hum. He was *not* a good man.

Ross had a panicked look on his face. I was hit with both a feeling of satisfaction and unease. Ross creeped me out from the day I met him, but I wasn't sure what was going on. The only times I'd seen Ethan use this stage—other than on Sunday for their version of church—was for initiations, punishments, and the occasional wedding. It was a one-size-fits-all spot.

Ethan walked up the small steps to the altar. I stopped at the bottom and waited. A crowd was gathering, it looked like everyone, except a few perimeter guards, were slowly filling up the bleachers.

"Brother Derek, if you would," Ethan said, reaching out his arm and indicating that I should stand next to him.

Taking my place, I looked behind him at Ross. He had a split lip and his eyes were darting around, trying to find anyone who would look at him for more than a second.

This isn't good.

My eyes scanned the crowd. Most wore blank expressions, though a few looked like they might be awake and watched on with mild curiosity. No one seemed to know what was happening. I scanned around again, looking for Sloane. My gaze was caught on the woman and child who'd come up onto the stage. Right in front of us stood Molly and her mother, Tina. Molly looked scared and ashamed, Tina however, was furious. Her eyes were locked onto Ross.

Something horrible entered my mind. A thought that I couldn't shake. Suddenly I knew what was happening, why I was up here, and what would happen next. Disgust with Ross roiled inside of me. If what I suspected was true, Ross deserved what he was about to get.

"Everybody settle down, take your seats. I've called you from your duties for a reason." Ethan began pacing the stage, assuming his normal movements for when he was preaching. His words were calm, measured. Normally when he was up here he was practically screaming for all to hear. Not today. The crowd could sense it too. They were so silent you could hear a mouse fart. Ethan didn't need to scream in his usual way. His eyes kept flicking back to Molly. I had a feeling he was keeping this calm for her sake. It was alarming, considering where this was going.

"We live in a place of peace. I provide you protections from this world, from the corruption and immorality of the human demons that fill the cities and streets." He pointed back toward the direction of the city. We were too far out to actually see much more than the glow of lights as night began to fall. "I do this because you are chosen. I do this because your Sky God failed you, because you, the chosen, my chosen ones, have been deemed worthy of a better life. I, your Earth God, have taken you from the impurity and given you a better life."

It took everything inside of me to silence the snort of derision that threatened to come out. He thought this was a better life? Where husbands beat their wives and children and he and those he deemed fit punished everyone? Ethan ruled with a heavy hand and like Butcher had warned me, the contradictions I found here were mind boggling.

"I don't ask much in return from you, just love and devotion to me. But in order to do that it means you need to have love and devotion for each other. If you disrespect each other, you disrespect me."

"Do I allow for violence between the devout?" he asked

"No!" was the unanimous shout from the crowd.

Other than when you beat Sloane, but I guess that doesn't count.

"Do I allow harm to come to any of you?"

"No!"

I finally found Sloane, standing in the crowd, her face was impassive but her eyes were screaming *bullshit!*

I'd been here long enough now to know that everything he was spewing was fake. He was fine with violence and harm as long as it followed his fucked up rules. I stayed quiet, wondering what my part in all this was going to be. I didn't have anything to do with Ross and I hardly knew Molly and Tina. Sloane had introduced me to them during my second week here, but that was all the interaction we'd had.

"Good, good. I needed to make sure you understood. I need to make sure that everyone here understands." He walked over to Ross and looked down at him. His preacher-smile vanished and he sneered down at the man, and just for a second I could swear I saw fangs in Ethan's grin. "Brother Ross has forgotten himself here. He has forgotten his place, rejected morality, and wishes to return to the world of demons."

The noise that came from the crowd was unlike anything I had ever heard in my life. Somewhere between a yelling, "booo", and a guttural growl. They were in sync, a possessed hymn.

If I were a dog my hackles would be up. There was a frisson of energy coming off the crowd in waves and it sparked over my skin and sent unnerving tingles down my spine. This was the freakiest thing I had ever seen in my life. I looked down at Sloane again, making sure that she was okay. If she needed me, I'd be off this stage in a heartbeat.

She risked a glance towards me, her way of saying she wasn't a part of this. Seeing that she was fine and wasn't likely to get pulled into whatever Ethan had going on had relief slithering through me. It mixed with the unease that was pulsing inside of me. No matter what Ethan had going on here tonight, as long as it didn't touch Sloane, I could handle it. Somehow she was still vibrant and full of life. She didn't allow the violence and corruption to touch her. I wanted to keep it that way.

"Brother Ross has forsaken his vows. He has violated our most precious of laws. Do *not* hurt the children! He has taken it upon himself to give in to the ways of the demons." Ethan looked sorrowfully at Molly. He actually looked genuine, he really was sorry that this happened to her, under his protection. That genuineness took me by surprise. "We will not, we do not tolerate such acts in the Order. Such immorality will not stand!"

There were cheers and agreements bellowed from the crowd. I understood it. I agreed with it. And that scared the fucking hell out of me. More than once I'd found myself agreeing with some of the things Ethan has done. None had struck a chord inside of me like this, though. It made the unease deepen.

Ethan walked over to me. "Brother Derek, you have taken the vows. Now it is time to prove your devotion to us." He opened his robe and removed a pistol, placing it in my hands. "Show the children that they are safe here. Show them that no harm will be tolerated."

My feet felt like they were stuck in cement. I made my way over to Ross, fighting my heavy feet across the length of the stage. The mix of emotions threatened to pull me through the floor. Sure, I'd killed men before. Always in combat, or for the safety of others, and always a known enemy. I had no sympathy for Ross. If I or any of my brothers had rolled up on him, doing what he had done, we would have killed him on the spot. No questions, no guilt.

But this was different. This was a public execution. In front of civilians, in front of children. Their watchful eyes were boring into my back as I made my way over to where Ross was kneeling. The part that was eating away at me was in spite of how public it was, this didn't bother me. The thought of killing him didn't bother me. None of it bothered me. *That* was the problem. I agreed whole-heartedly with Ethan and his punishment. That was a slippery fucking slope for me. I didn't want to live in a world where I agreed with Ethan, yet here I was.

Ross's chest was shuddering as he took in huge gulping swallows of air. Tears were streaking down his face, but he wasn't begging. His hands were behind his head, finality had finally chased the panic from his eyes. He knew he had fucked up. These were his own laws he'd broken. I was just being asked to uphold his punishment.

I was thankful that his guilt wasn't in question. Tina's eyes were all the proof I needed. But if anyone required more they'd only need to look at Molly. Her head was down as though she couldn't stand to look at anyone around her. The fact that they were forcing her to stand up in front of everyone, in front of her abuser, announcing what had been done to her was horrific in itself. Add into that having him executed in front of her. No wonder the people here were beyond fucked up.

No. It was easy to see that this little girl had been violated. If I had to take Ethan's word alone of this man's guilt, I doubted I would do what was being asked of me. I'd been trying to stay out of the public punishments. There were plenty of men who enjoyed participating. Whether I agreed with why the punishment was happening or not, I'd held back. Ethan clearly hadn't liked that. This was his way of remedying that. Ross's punishment was being meted out and I was being pulled further into the fold. I could feel it. Each day the horror of this place dulled. I could easily see how these people stayed. It just became their way of life and it didn't seem wrong anymore.

This was a warning to the entire group. Granted, the message—don't abuse the kids—was one that I fully supported, but it didn't matter. Once I started killing for him, he had me. After I did this, what would Ethan ask of me next? Would the next one be as obviously guilty as Ross? It wasn't like I had much of a choice either way.

This was how prisoners of war got converted to the enemy's side. One small concession at a time. Each concession made the next one easier. Today's concession was easy. What would tomorrow's be?

I was in front of Ross now. The fact that he wasn't pleading for his life surprised me. Part of me wondered if he wanted this, though given his crime I wasn't about to wonder for too long. He'd crossed a line that was unforgivable. For all of us. I looked over at Ethan, he gave me a slight nod. My gaze flicked back to Ross—I was careful not to look at anyone else—raised the pistol, and fired.

* * *

I SPLASHED cold water onto my face and rubbed at my eyes. Opening them, I looked into the mirror. "What the fuck have you gotten yourself into?" This wasn't the first time I'd asked myself this since getting here. It was the first time I was this scared.

Staring at my own reflection, I watched the water slowly running down my face. I kept watching myself, waiting for some sort of explanation from the man staring back at me. No answer was coming. Time would tell whether the things I did here would rival what I'd done in the service of my country, or for my club.

Killing wasn't the problem. Especially men like Ross. It was the invasive thoughts and memories that crept in during the dead of night that were the issue. No matter the reasons for why we did the things we did, there were still consequences. The price I would pay for my actions here would be worth it if I could rescue some of these people from this existence.

I stepped away, walked out of the bathroom and sat on my bed, untying my boots. Butcher had warned me about this. That they would have a perverse sense of justice and rules, and in some cases they might be things you would agree with. Shooting a pedophile was always an easy one. It never occurred to me that I would be in a situation where I wouldn't be allies with a pedo killer. After all, they were protecting kids. Ethan was protecting kids. Right?

Shaking my head, I tried to make it make sense. They were fine with beating the children into submission, but anything else was grounds for what happened today. They should all be taken out back and shot just for the beatings alone, but they were right in the other ways. I blew out a breath, shoulders sagging. I hadn't been here long enough to wrap my mind around all of this. I just hoped I didn't end up as fucked as the rest of these people by the time I got my ass out of here.

"They killed Sherry Holden," I whispered to myself, dropping my head down and spearing my fingers into my hair. "They were going to kill Caitlyn. He might have been protecting Molly today, but tomorrow he could kill her, kill any of them, for any reason he damn well chooses."

Coming in here I'd figured I could pretend my way through it easily enough. That there was no way any part of this Jonestown wanna-be group could sway me. I certainly wasn't about to see Ethan as a living God. But killing Ross was way too easy to justify, and worse, it still felt good. Felt right. That was the slippery slope I was standing on. How much of a nudge did I need to end up joining Ethan down at the bottom?

I needed to get us out of here. Only two more weeks. The longer I stayed the more I would kill my own soul in the process. I needed to get Sloane out. As if by mental command, she stepped inside our bedroom. She glided gracefully across the room and sat next to me.

"Are you okay?" She wrapped her arms around me, tucking her body against mine.

Raising my head, I looked over at her. I cupped her cheek. Her soft skin was always so inviting. Looking into her eyes I knew that I could trust her. I'd already figured it out prior to this, but now I just *knew*. Not just trust with the plan to escape, to help me get her out of here. I could really *trust* in her. I could hand her my soul, I could be open with her, and dare I admit it, vulnerable. I don't think in my life I've ever trusted anyone the way I knew that I could trust her.

"I'm fine," I reassured her. "But there's something we need to talk about."

A confused smile crossed her face. Smiling was her normal response. I knew without asking, it was a way for her to hide all the anger and guilt she felt from living with Ethan.

I leaned forward and kissed her. If it was the last one I'd get after I bared all my secrets to her, then I was going to make it worth it. We were both breathing hard by the time I pulled back. Grabbing her hand, I brought her to the kitchen and sat down at the table. This was going to take a while and I didn't want to watch her pull away from me if that was her inclination. Sitting across from her gave her some space to process while I told her my truths.

CHAPTER 21

Sloane

"I'm getting you out of here. All of you. The kids, the women, anyone that can be saved."

My breath caught in my throat. Every fiber of my being froze, too afraid to hope. Had I just imagined him saying those words to me? If he wasn't sitting there watching me with patient blue eyes, I would have pinched myself. This had to be a dream. Hearing the man I'd fallen in love with saying those words to me was a dream come true.

He was waiting to see what I'd say to the bomb he'd dropped. If he thought I was going to fight him on this, I was about to surprise him.

"I have supplies."

He blinked slowly at me, clearly not expecting that. "What?"

I stood up in a rush, my skirts swirling around my legs as I moved into the bedroom and knelt down. He watched with interest as I pried up a floor board at the side of our bed with my fingernails. Inside was my treasure trove. Showing this to him was the biggest risk I'd taken yet. Any of the secrets I'd told him before could have gotten me killed.

This was worse because if he told Ethan it would decimate my plan to escape. I'd rather die than stay here with no hope to flee in the future. This was my hope. And now *he* was that hope.

He hadn't told Ethan—as far as I was aware—about anything else I'd confided to him. I knew the man I'd married was trustworthy. Or I wouldn't have ever showed him my items.

The hollow space was filled with…years' worth of things. Money, USB drives, clothes, shoes. I'd managed to squirrel away all manner of things that I—and the others—would need in order to escape Ethan.

Rip's eyes narrowed on the stash of pencils I'd rubber banded together. Their points had been sharpened to an extreme tip and I fidgeted as he turned his gaze on me.

"Tell me you weren't planning on going up against armed guards with pencils?"

Heat seared my cheeks. "It was the only weapon I could get my hands on. And they're better than nothing," I whispered.

His eyes softened and he cupped my cheek, brushing his thumb over it. He loved to touch me and I wasn't going to lie, I loved that he did as well.

"I'm here now. You won't have to go against the guards at all."

It was amazing to me how—in such a relatively short amount of time—I'd come to know my husband. I trusted him to keep me safe. He'd keep the others safe, too. He crouched down next to me, eyeing my things—avoiding my anxious gaze. I was worried that he'd find fault with my efforts.

"You amaze me." My head snapped up and I looked over at him, my heart lodged in my throat. "The strength and courage it must have taken for you to break free of the chains that Ethan has placed around everyone living here is immeasurable. And somehow you've managed to keep from getting pulled into it all. Not just that, but to maintain the façade while planning to escape."

Tears welled in my eyes at his praise. I didn't know how much another person being proud of me would affect me. I couldn't speak for a moment, I just sniffed and looked away.

"You took all this yourself?" he asked, changing the subject. His voice was low and gravelly.

"It's taken me years," I admitted, doubt creeping into my tone. "It's always been my plan to escape from here. I just couldn't go alone and leave everyone else to their fates."

"It's fucking impressive as hell, Sloane."

I looked down as he grabbed my hands, forcing me to drop the floorboard as he interlaced our fingers together.

"You're the most amazing woman I've ever met." His hand lifted and he brushed his knuckles over my cheek.

It didn't matter that the tears I'd been trying to hold back had broken free and were streaming down my face. No one had spoken to me with such kindness, not since my mother died. Not until him. It was so nice. So genuine. He gave me such hope for the future.

"I wish I could do more," I squeaked out, voice husky from fighting back the sobs that worked their way up from my chest.

Standing, he pulled me up with him, then swept me into his arms. He sat down on the bed, with me in his lap. I took comfort in him and buried my face in his chest. "You've done more than enough. I'll take it from here."

"How?" I breathed, pulling back so I could look up into his face. "How is a single man going to get so many of us out of here? They'll kill you."

A pained expression crossed his face. "That's the other thing I need to talk to you about, Angel."

I brushed the tears from my cheeks and tried to focus on what he was telling me. The look on his face was making me nervous and I didn't want to tune out and over analyze before he had a chance to tell me whatever it was he needed to.

"First, I want you to know something." He was back to cupping my cheeks, forcing me to stare into his gorgeous eyes. "I love you. I've loved you since the moment I saw you."

My eyes widened and I gasped. I already knew I was in love with him, but I'd never expected him to have fallen for me. And for him to tell me was a shock. The men here didn't act like they loved their wives, let alone verbalize it. Happiness flooded me down to my bones.

"I love you, too, Rip."

Something flickered there in his eyes. "I sure hope you still feel that way after I tell you everything, Sloane." He dropped his hands from my face and wrapped his arms around my waist, almost as if he was holding me to him so I couldn't escape. I didn't want to go anywhere, so I sat and waited to see what his secrets were.

"I'm not the Derek that Ethan was expecting," he admitted.

My brows drew together, unsure of what he meant, but I didn't interrupt.

"I'm a biker. The old lady… girlfriend of one of the club members, is a Search and Rescue contractor and she noticed people going missing out here in the desert who she couldn't find. She brought us in to help figure out what was going on. We ended up finding men burying Sherry Holden-"

I gasped and slapped my hand on his chest, making him pause, eyes filling with tears again. "Sherry's dead?" I asked, voice wavering.

He nodded slowly, watching me closely.

"I helped her and Caitlyn escape," I told him, eyes closing. "I feared… What about Caitlyn?" My voice cracked as that sweet little girl's face flashed through my mind.

His hand slid around the back of my neck and squeezed. I took comfort in the touch. "Caitlyn's alive." The relief was instantaneous and would have knocked me over if I wasn't sitting down. "We got there in time to rescue her and she was adopted by one of our members."

He went on to explain that his club was all former military and that they helped people in their city. Whenever the cops couldn't step in, they did to make sure the city stayed safe.

I wasn't really sure exactly what a motorcycle club was, but this wasn't the time to ask those kinds of questions. Just like I wanted to ask what he'd done in the military. Getting to know the man I'd married wasn't the top of the priority list even though I wanted it to be. There was one thing I couldn't go forward without knowing.

"So what's your real name?" Fear and worry were coursing through me after he told me the rest. He'd been planted here, by his club, to find out who could be saved and who couldn't. He'd never planned to marry me. Did that mean he'd divorce me once this was over? My heart throbbed with sadness at the thought.

"It's really Derek Skore. Riptide is my road name." When I frowned, he explained, "We give each other nicknames when we join the club."

"Why Riptide?"

"I was on leave back when I was still in the military. Went home to Ilwaco and I was doing some surfing. Ended up saving a kid who was getting pulled out in a riptide. That stretch of ocean is known for them. My next deployment my brothers ended up finding out about it and the name stuck."

There was some of that story I didn't understand, but the idea of seeing the ocean was so exciting. If I managed to get out of here, I wanted to go. It'd always been a dream of mine to see an ocean, any ocean.

"Sloane, I know this is a lot to take in, but I need your help. You know everyone here. Would you be able to help me with who we can get out of here and who we can't trust?"

I shoved all my feelings to the back of my mind. It didn't matter that he'd lied to me, that he wasn't who he said he was. We could deal with that later. As much as I wanted to scream, to cry, to ask so many things, I had to focus. Too many were going to be depending on us for their safety. He was going to help us get out of here. Our ticket to freedom. I couldn't really get mad at him for not being forthcoming with me because I'd done the same with him. Since he'd admitted the truth to me it was time for me to do the same.

"Of course I will, Rip..." I nibbled on my lower lip. "Is there something else I should call you?"

He shook his head, his shaggy hair swinging into his eyes. He'd need a haircut soon unless he was planning on letting it grow longer. I'd been shocked that Ethan hadn't insisted on shaving it down into a buzz cut when he got here. I knew now that Ethan hadn't wanted to rock the boat too much while he was getting to know Rip. He couldn't afford the man to back out of their deal because of something like a haircut. Too much money at stake.

"I told you the truth that night. I prefer D or Rip. Either is fine."

Nodding, I plucked at my skirts. "I'm more than willing to help you, and so grateful you and your club are going to get us out of here. I...I have something else to tell-"

He broke my words off with a kiss and I couldn't help but melt into him with a moan. Our mouths fused together and my mind melted under the intensity of his kiss.

"Sorry," he said, pulling back. "I just...Sloane, I meant what I said. I love you. Marrying you might not have been in my plans, at least not like this, but there's a part of me that is fucking glad it happened." He raked a hand through his hair, looking sheepish. "I know I've been lying to you, but starting now I'll make it up to you."

The knot in my chest eased and I smiled at him. "I actually understand. You didn't know who you could trust coming in here. Thank you for giving me that trust, Rip."

The secret I needed to tell him was important, but I was so scared of how he'd react. There was time enough later to confide in him. It wouldn't hurt to wait a little longer. Then I'd tell him the only thing I had left to hide. The only thing that caused me shame anymore.

"I want to continue this once we get all of you out of here."

My heart leapt with excitement and hope and I nodded. "I do, too."

Relief flashed over his face. "We have a lot to do and not much time to complete it. We need a meeting place that you can send everyone to on the night this is going to go down. I'll have one of my brothers lead you out of here and back to where we'll have our vehicles. I don't want you here when the fighting goes down."

"I want to help," I insisted.

"You *will* be helping," he said, tucking a piece of my hair behind my ear. His tender touch melted my heart. "They are going to be looking to you to guide them. They won't know my brothers and are going to be scared. They'll need you. Otherwise we're going to have a dozen bikers trying to herd scared women and children, worse than trying to herd cats. It'll put them into too much danger when we'll have Ethan and his men to deal with."

I nodded. He had a point. It terrified me, thinking of him going up against Ethan and the others. It wasn't that I didn't think he was strong enough to defeat them. I knew he could. I was just used to Ethan being the most powerful man around and him having all the control. "Don't underestimate them," I told him, searching his gaze to make sure he was taking this seriously. "They're ruthless."

His grin was so sexy it made my belly clench with lust. "Trust me, Angel, they have no idea who *they're* going up against."

He wrapped me up in a hug and I let him, relaxing into his hold. He'd told me a lot already, but there was so much more to learn about him. Did he really want me to stay married to him? Or would he change his mind once we were out of here and in what he kept referring to as the real world?

I tried to set the worries aside as we began planning. There was enough to do without worrying about what would happen then. We had to make it out of here in one piece first.

CHAPTER 22

Riptide

Today was the day. Or tonight would be. My nerves were bunched so tight if one more thing was piled onto my plate, I'd snap like an overstretched rubber band. It was always like this before an op. I would triple check the equipment, make sure everyone's gear was working. I could handle the stress of combat. What I couldn't handle was if one of my men was hurt because of something easily preventable. In this case, I was worried about Sloane and the others. They had no training, I would be asking a lot of them.

If we failed tonight, they'd end up paying the price. Me and my brothers would lose our lives, but the women and children who were all set and ready to run from this place would be forced back into this life and they'd pay every day for the deception they'd participated in.

I was already looking forward to taking down Ethan, but knowing what was at stake for them would ensure that we won. Nothing else was acceptable. I looked around as I walked down the street, doing a mental inventory.

Tonight, I'd meet my brothers outside the walls and lead them into an attack on The Order. Excitement fired inside my blood. I was ready for this. Ethan deserved what he was going to get. So did the other men here.

Despite the doubts that had occasionally plagued me while I'd been here and the horrific shit I'd seen Ethan put his people through, I was glad I'd come. Not only because the people here were about to be free, but because of my angel. I'd meant every word when I'd told her I loved her and wanted to continue this once we got back home. I wanted my club to be her new family, my home to be hers.

My eyes passed over Jacob and Bruce, who were standing next to the large fence that surrounded the compound. They looked relaxed. No one suspected a thing.

Sloane had helped me pinpoint the people who'd be walking out of this alive and she'd approached each of them. She'd warned them to pack a small bag of things for themselves and their children. Everything else would be left behind. She'd promised them that me and my club would help take care of them once we got to Tucson.

Getting to know me more over the last few weeks made it easier for them to trust her words. It astounded me that she hadn't gotten angry with me when I'd told her who I really was and why I was here. None of her people had gotten mad either.

I guess when you've been under the thumb of a dictator who doesn't hesitate to kill for disobedience, you'll take any savior you can get.

Mae had used that word. Savior. That, I certainly wasn't, but to them it was true. I sighed and tried to focus. There were only a few hours left before this went down.

Sloane met me out on the street, falling in step beside me. "Everything's ready," she said in a low voice.

"Angel." I waited until she looked over at me. "I need you to follow the plan tonight."

She nodded. "I will, Rip. I'll see you once you've finished."

I stopped and pulled her into my arms, giving her a long kiss. A group of girls walking past giggled at us, but kept going. I smiled down at her. "I'm a lucky fucking man."

* * *

A WHISTLE CUT through the dark and I adjusted my direction. My heart was racing knowing I'd see my brothers again. Knowing that everything would end tonight. It was dark, the moon wouldn't rise until later, making it hard to walk without running into cacti. There was no way I was turning on a flashlight, though. That would be too fucking obvious. The dark would help us in the long run.

By the time I saw the shadow darting toward me it was too late to maneuver away from it. The body hit me at full speed and I grunted as we tumbled down to the dirt. I landed on a stray prickly pear paddle. It was impossible to fall in this desert without hitting some kind of cactus. I bit down and howled low in pain as the spines jabbed into my back.

"That's what you fucking deserve for making us worry," Butcher said from where he was sitting on my chest. His fist connected with my jaw, making the world light up under what Butcher would consider a love tap.

"Get off him, you asshole," Toxic muttered, pulling Butcher off me.

One of these days I needed to send Toxic a fucking gift. He was the only one who was able to keep Butcher under control and the duty always fell to him. Control was a strong word. When it came to Butcher it was more like point and release. He completed his task without ever fucking complaining, though. The two had quickly become friends and Toxic was often Butcher's voice of reason.

It would be goddamned weird to send another man flowers. What did you get for a man that said, 'Thanks for keeping the psychopath entertained and out of trouble?' A fruit basket maybe? A dog collar? Who knew what kind of freaky shit those two liked. They were like two peas in a pod.

Toxic reached out and pulled me to my feet. His arms crushed me in an embrace before he handed me off to the others. There were a lot of painful back slaps and more punches as we all reunited. It was to be expected and there was a huge grin on my face.

"Good to see that you're alive," Lockout said with a chuckle. "Is everything ready?"

Hush handed me a rifle and I nodded. I gave the magazine a tug and checked that a round had been chambered. Didn't want to get in the middle of the gun fight and miss my chance at revenge on some of the men in the compound.

We were standing close enough in a circle that they could see me. "It is. We have forty-eight women and children, and three men—a total of fifty-one—who are all staged up in a building waiting on us."

Looking around, relief washed over me. The majority of my club had come. There were men everywhere, waiting to go into battle with us because we'd asked it of them. Even Static was here. I clapped a hand on his shoulder, silently thanking him for coming to help me.

"Good," Lockout said. "The quicker we get this done, the better. Dash, George, Static, and Smokehouse. You're in charge of getting the fifty-one we need to rescue back to the vehicles."

Smoke's jaw dropped. "What?"

Dash and George were both members, but they were older and didn't have as much to do with these types of operations anymore. They also had children, we always took that into consideration. They'd always come out to help and show their support, but if we could keep them out of the direct line of fire, we did.

"It's a lot of people, Smoke. Some are bound to stumble and get lost, and with fifty-one of 'em, they won't be quiet. I need you to keep it all together." Lockout's glare was easy to discern even in the darkness.

Smoke hesitated for a second before responding, "Wherever you need me, Prez."

Smart. Going against Lockout's orders was a good way to get your ass handed to you and get fucking demoted. Smoke was disappointed that he wasn't going to get to play, but Lockout was trusting those four to keep the innocents in all of this safe. It was the most important job of them all. Smokehouse knew he was being trusted with the biggest responsibility tonight. He'd do his job.

Static just nodded when Lockout met his gaze. He was here as support for the club. He'd been out of the life for a long time now, so Lockout wasn't about to toss him in the middle of things. Not when he wasn't officially a part of our club…yet. I had a feeling that wasn't going to last long. The yearning there in Static's eyes told me he was tired of living life straight and pure. He missed this shit. Missed us.

"Once they're out of the village," Lockout continued, "we start our assault. Smoke and his team will assume a guard position at the fence while the women and kids escape. Hellfire, Ricochet and Priest," He motioned to them, the trio stood and headed off into the desert, "They will take a position on the North of the compound, when you hear gunfire start your attack. The rest of us will move in from the south. The three of them will keep the cultists pinned while we sweep through." He looked over at me. "I assume the leftover men don't deserve mercy?"

"Fuck no, they don't," I replied. "Kill them all. You'll want to be careful with Ethan, Jacob, and Bruce. They're going to be the most difficult to kill." I described what the three men looked like. "I'd prefer to take out Ethan myself," I requested.

"As long as it doesn't put anyone in danger, that's acceptable. You certainly deserve it after what I'm sure you had to put up with in here." Lockout said with a nod. "Let's get going. Rip, you lead."

There hadn't been any time to relay what I'd gone through during my time with The Order. There'd be plenty of time for that later. They were all going to be in for a surprise once they realized I had a wife.

We moved along as quietly as we could until the fence surrounding the compound came into view. We doubled back and everyone crouched down.

Whispering, I told Lockout, "It's best if a couple of us sneak in, get everyone out and send them on their way before all this kicks off. Get Smoke and his team in place, give me three to get the rest out."

"Sounds like a good plan. Hush, Butcher, and Toxic you three come with me and Rip. Smoke, you're in charge until I get back."

Smoke nodded, clapping a hand on my back for good luck. I returned the gesture. I couldn't wait to fucking crack a beer with my brothers and tell them about this wild ride. I'd missed every one of the fuckers.

Lock and the other three fell into line behind me. We slipped through a hole I'd made in the back half of the fence a few days ago. Smoke and his team were waiting there to help the people who'd be coming back through. The hole was closest to the building that all the women and children were hiding inside. I didn't want a huge line of people sneaking through the compound at night, so I'd made sure we had a place to escape nearby.

As soon as my brothers were through, we moved around to the door of the building. The lights were out inside, only a few candles spread out along the walls battled against the darkness.

"Rip!" Sloane whispered, rushing forward.

My arms wrapped around her. "Is everyone here?" I asked in a low voice.

"Yes. Everyone is here and ready," she replied. Her eyes strayed toward my brothers. "We don't have a lot of time. Mae and I managed to convince Ethan to lead the men in a late night sermon while she would do the same for the kids. All the men are gathered at the altar."

"Brilliant," I told her. Turning, I found my brothers all wearing shit-eating grins. I gave them an unamused look. This wasn't the time for them to start giving me shit about the woman in my arms and that looked like what they were about to do. "Save it for later," I snapped at them.

Lockout chuckled and repeated the order. They didn't dare disobey him.

"We're going to lead you out of the compound," I said, raising my voice just enough that everyone could hear me. "Then four of our people are going to take you to the vehicles. You'll wait there quietly for us and we'll get you out of here safely. Got it?"

Heads nodded and some murmured in agreement. They were ready to get the fuck out of this hellhole and so was I.

"Follow us. Stay silent." I took the lead, heading back toward the hole in the fence. Pausing before I left the shadow of the building, I scanned the streets and along the fence, looking for any of the guards. No one was around thanks to Sloane and Mae's plan.

As one large group we crept over to the fence. Lockout and Hush took up positions on either side of the hole and started directing people as they ducked through. It was all done in a very low murmur, but still my nerves were fraying at the ends. If we were caught here and now, too many people would die in the crossfire. The men were gathered on the other side of the compound, but all we needed was one guard to spot us and we were fucked.

Soon enough we were all on the other side of the fence. I grabbed Smoke by the cut and tugged him close. My voice was a low growl of warning. "Take care of them."

"Of course, Rip," he responded.

I knew that even though he wasn't happy to be on what he'd consider babysitting duty, he'd do his damndest to make sure they were all safe. He wouldn't fuck around with the lives of innocent people.

Kissing Sloane, I watched as they all walked off into the darkness, toward safety. Face hardening into a cold mask, I turned back toward the compound. It was time to demolish The Order. They'd be nothing but a smear of blood out here in the desert by the time we were done with them.

CHAPTER 23

Riptide

With the last woman through the fence, I pivoted on the ball of my foot and brought my rifle up. A calmness settled over me. How quickly the old training came back. The gun was a comforting weight tucked up against my shoulder. With Lockout to my left, and Hush, Butcher, and Toxic behind me, we started moving toward the altar. They formed up in a 'V' behind me, a wedge moving through the alley ways. This allowed us to move together, but not have to worry about accidentally shooting each other in the back.

About one hundred meters from the fence I threw my left arm up with a fist. Silently, they stopped behind me, waiting for my cue to move again. Keith was one of the guards still on patrol and he was walking along the fence, looking bored. Too bad the sorry fucker was about to die without knowing what hit him. Even with all the men at the altar, I knew there would be a few perimeter guards. It was important to take them out so that there wasn't anyone running in behind us once we got to the middle of town.

If we could neutralize him and any others without being given away, we could trap all the men at once. It would be like shooting fish in a barrel. It was the best case scenario for us considering the men outnumbered us three to one.

I motioned for Lockout to come closer. Without words, I indicated he needed to sling his rifle and draw his knife. My president gave me a feral grin when he caught on to what we were about to do. He didn't mind following my lead since I was the one who knew the layout and the people. That's what made Lockout such a great leader. Unlike Ethan, he trusted his people and did whatever was best for our safety and success, even if it meant putting one of us temporarily in charge. It wasn't a danger to his pride to follow for a change.

We crept up on Keith, slinking alongside the houses. I waited until he turned his back, then leapt from the shadows. My arms wrapped around his neck, cutting off his air before he could scream. Lockout's knife was in his gut before he knew he was under attack. His hands clawed at my arms even as blood dripped down his body. Holding him immobile, I waited until his body went limp in my arms. I dragged him back toward the shadows, hoping to leave him somewhere he wouldn't be discovered. We were only halfway to the safety the houses provided when everything went to hell.

"Hey! You there! Stop!" The man's shouts were followed by gun fire. We'd been spotted by another guard, and he decided shooting us was best. Stupid fucker. The fact that he didn't stop to think who else might be in the line of fire—he didn't know the women and children were gone—was a clear indicator that he wasn't well trained. Not to mention the fact that he was spraying rounds everywhere, rather than making any direct hits. The last one was lucky for us because it meant he was more likely to miss us.

I dropped the body and dove for cover as bullets whizzed past my head. Even bad shots could get lucky and I didn't feel like adding a bullet wound to the list of injuries I'd sustained while here. Butcher, Toxic, and Hush answered with gunfire of their own, dropping the guard in his tracks. I came up with my rifle at the ready. "Let's go.

They'll be heading for the armory." We'd lost the element of surprise, but that didn't mean we didn't have a job to do.

I picked up the pace, rifle still butted up against my shoulder, ready to use if I needed it. We were closing in on the center of town and I had no clue how many men would be waiting for us. The altar would come into view any minute. With our cover blown, thanks to the guard, I knew we'd be outnumbered. It played into our favor that most of the men who'd lived on the compound weren't trained like we were. They were good at beating on women, but that was about it. That's why I wasn't going to feel an ounce of guilt when we killed them.

A few men ran towards us, they were unarmed and cut down with ease. "The armory is on the other side." I pointed toward the building where they kept their weapons. We ran toward it, hoping to get there before they had a chance to load up. That hope was quickly decimated.

Three men came around the end of the stage and opened fire. I dropped behind the bleachers and let three rounds rip off, suppressing fire to give my guys a chance to find cover. Wood splintered next to my face as their bullets once again zipped past me. I snapped off three more. We had each other pinned. That was okay, my guys would be maneuvering to flank them. It was my job to keep them distracted. I was damn good at my job.

Popping up again, I fired, then ducked back down. Hearing the bullets scream by overhead, I waited them out as they returned fire. More gunfire split the night air, followed by a shout of pain. I stood up, glad when I wasn't shot at again. Lockout and Toxic were jogging up on my left, Butcher and Hush came in low to my right. "Well, which way now, lover boy?" Butcher asked with a smirk.

We heard more gunfire from the north. Priest, Hellfire and Ricochet had started their attack. I ran forward, the four of them falling into our original wedge formation. "Come on!" I yelled. It was too late to cut them off from the armory, but we might be able to pin them there. Meet up with the others.

Trap them in an armory. I shook my head at the thought. It was a terrible tactic and would make for a nasty standoff. Wasn't much we could do about it at this point, though. Other than kill them as quickly as we could.

I peeked around the last corner to the armory just in time to see men taking up positions in the street around it. "Fuck," I muttered. I motioned to Hush for another magazine. Dropping the empty one from my rifle, I slammed the fresh magazine into place. Looking up at the four of them, I relayed the plan. They were all watching me, waiting for instruction. I'd be doing the same if any of them had been placed in charge. That was what I loved about my brothers. We all set egos aside and worked together.

"Hush, Butcher, Toxic, you three pin them down here. These houses are empty and should give you good cover. Lock and I will slip around to the right and come out the window of that house," I motioned over my shoulder, "and hit them from the side. Roll them up real quick." They nodded, and we headed for our positions.

Speed and stealth were the only things on our side for now and we needed to use them to our advantage. They had the numbers to overwhelm us if we let them. This was our battle to lose, but only if we were stupid enough to fuck up. We weren't stupid and we wouldn't lose. I'd make sure of that. Ethan and his piece of shit minions were dying tonight. Jury was out on whether they knew it yet or not. Ethan was arrogant enough to think they'd be able to take us out. I knew he was wrong.

Lockout on my heels, I kicked in the front door and ran through the house. When I came to the bedroom window I raised my rifle to smash it and paused. I could see Jacob and Bruce ushering Ethan out of the armory.

"Fuck! The bastard is getting away." I looked at Lockout desperately, I couldn't leave them hanging, but the urge to go after Ethan was overwhelming. He gave me a nod of confirmation. He would have my back no matter what I chose to do. Relief clogged my throat as I leapt through the window, rolling up onto my feet and firing as I stood. I charged the guards in the street. Despite the dark I could see their eyes turn into giant white saucers as Lockout and I busted right through them, causing them to scatter in fear. I watched them run off into the night, choosing life rather than pitting themselves against us.

We'd deviated from the plan, but the others rolled with it. We met up at the side of the house we'd just come from.

"Ethan is getting away, you four keep going until that armory is cleared out." Before Lockout could say no I took off in the direction that Ethan was headed. The last thing I was going to do was leave my brothers behind with less back up. I'd go after Ethan myself. The other four were elite fucking killers. They could handle an armory full of terrible shots and weak men. Bullets kicked at my feet as the bastards tried to cut me down. They were hoping to kill me before I could reach their leader. Hopefully I was giving the guys a needed distraction to move in.

The sound of gunfire fell away, more of a low echo as I moved away from the armory. Jacob, Bruce, and Ethan would be heading for the trucks. Had to be. It only made sense that they would take the precious Earth God away from the fight. It wasn't like any of the cowards would stay and fight themselves. Certainly not Ethan. He would rather sacrifice all the men's lives than put his own on the line. For all he knew he was sacrificing the women and children as well. I doubted they'd figured out in the middle of the fight that they were gone.

I turned towards the vehicles and picked up my pace. My lungs heaved as I ran through the night. I'd gotten out of shape living here the last couple months. Working out everyday was something I was used to in my normal routine. There hadn't been a chance for that here, not without drawing attention.

Skidding to a stop, I watched as Ricochet, Hellfire, and Priest came running out of the darkness. We met up and I quickly relayed where the others were.

* * *

MOTIONING as we ducked behind a building, I pointed out the six men as they made their way toward the vehicles. Ethan had his typical guards, Bruce and Jacob, as well as a trio of others trailing behind. I couldn't tell who they were in the darkness, nor did I care. My focus was that slimy fucker who was trying to make his escape. It was time to cut the head off the snake. Anything less meant Ethan would disappear and start a new cult. We couldn't allow that to happen.

"Lead the way, Rip," Hellfire told me in a low voice. "We've got your back."

The others nodded in agreement, so I made a beeline for the men, hellbent on stopping their escape. They were maybe two hundred yards away, but we had to hurry or they'd end up getting into Jacob's truck and we'd be fucked.

I didn't need to keep a close eye on my guys. Didn't need to see their faces to distinguish my brothers from each other as we moved through the shadows. Their movements alone were enough to differentiate so that I knew who was where, as we ran toward our targets. Getting separated and coming back together as we took out stray guards and men wasn't a hindrance. We'd trained and fought together enough that we knew each other no matter the circumstances.

The darkness had been lit up with a glow by a few burning buildings, but it was still making it harder on Ethan and his crew as they stumbled along. They weren't used to slinking around in the inky blackness. Weren't used to fighting for their lives. Ethan's panic was beginning to overtake him. His head darted around as he searched the night for signs of us. The only reason he'd made it this far was Jacob and Bruce.

We came to a stop as close as we dared, Ricochet and Hellfire veering off to our left, leaving me and Priest covering the right side. Walking directly to them would be too dangerous. Bruce was no slouch when it came to his weapon, not like the other men here. Something told me Jacob was just as deadly.

Ricochet and Hellfire were taking aim at Ethan. I could see them just on the other side of a stack of crates. Someone had started up Jacob's truck and the headlights bathed them with golden light. I ground my teeth together as the trio of extra guards broke off and made their way toward my brothers. My feet felt like lead weights as I moved, trying to intercept them before they had a chance to get my brothers in their sights.

Watching as though it were playing in slow motion as I ran forward, Ricochet turned toward them, then hesitated. I tried to raise my rifle, it was heavy in my hands. I wasn't fast enough. Didn't have enough time. My heart raced as I called out to my brother, fear icing the blood in my veins.

Ricochet watched them, unmoving. What the fuck was he doing?

Move. Fight. Do something! I mentally screamed it at him, not willing to shout out loud because I needed all my breath to get to him in time. I still knew I'd be too late.

They began to fire. One of the crates splintering next to Ricochet seemed to snap him out of his trance, but not in time. One of the rounds struck Hellfire, he tumbled back and fell. My voice was hoarse as I yelled Hell's name. Ricochet moved forward, fury on his face as he shot round after round. He kept firing until the trio were down, blood staining the ground, illuminated by the glow of the headlights.

I closed the rest of the distance, running past the bodies straight to Hellfire. Skidding on the ground on my knees, I slid to a stop near his prone body. He turned his head, tensing until he saw that it was me. "I'm good, I'm good," he growled, clutching his shoulder. Pain was etched into his features, but he was breathing.

Kneeling next to him, I did a quick survey. Relief rolled over me. He'd live. "Like hell you are," I said anyway, "another inch and it would be through your heart."

"But it's not, I'm good, just…" He was cut off by Ricochet.

"Not again, God dammit, not again!" The words were like the howl of a wounded animal, echoing through the compound.

I turned to see Ricochet standing over the bodies. He was looking from them to Hellfire and back. Priest had been running to him, but his gait slowed and he stared down at the gunmen, horror etched on his face. He glanced over at our grief stricken brother as he stood over the bodies, unsure how to help him.

"Go help them," Hell gasped. He struggled into a seated position, but otherwise seemed fine. Picking up his weapon and putting it into his hands, I left him behind the cover of the crates and ran toward the others.

Now that I was closer, my suspicion was confirmed. There was only one reason Ricochet would be losing control like he was. He was pacing back and forth, agitation clear in his body language as he broke down.

There'd been a reason I'd recognized the trio of gunmen as I started over. They were kids. The fact that Ethan and the others had them out here was evil, pure and simple. They shouldn't have been here. They should have been with Sloane and the others. Should still be innocent in the ways of the world. Ethan had turned them early, made them his child soldiers.

My heart sank, breaking for Ricochet. None of us ever wanted to hurt children, but it had been a case of them or us. They would have happily killed us where we stood. Unfortunately, it'd been Ricochet to pull the trigger. This wasn't the first time for him and it wasn't going to help his already fucked up mental state that this happened.

I wanted to pull him into a hug, show him that he wasn't alone in this. Desire to turn back the clocks and make it so that I was the one who'd been standing there instead of him nearly overwhelmed me. I'd do anything to help Ricochet out, but first I had to get to him.

We approached slow and cautious. Ricochet had a habit of losing himself in the past when he went berserker and I knew it was coming. The last thing I wanted was for him to attack us. I reached out a hand even though we were too far away and called his name. He didn't respond.

Sloane had warned me not to go to these particular kids to try to convince them to come with us. She'd told me they were already too far gone to save, that they'd turn us over to Ethan in a heartbeat. The three kids idolized Jacob, according to her, and seeing them out here confirmed that she'd been right. Two were teenagers—brothers named John and Jarrett—and the third was Barclay's son. Gary had barely turned ten years old. Kids carrying rifles were no less dangerous than adults, as Hellfire's wounds would attest to. That wasn't going to matter to Ricochet. Not after everything he'd been through.

Priest and I were still moving toward him when Ricochet screamed into the night sky, a broken, horrific sound, then took off after Ethan.

"Shit!" I yelled, fear coursing through me. If we lost Ricochet, I wouldn't be able to forgive myself. The kid deserved a fucking break and I'd just led him directly into his own worst nightmare. Fury and fear were thick in my chest as I tried to call him back. "Ricochet wait!"

"Shit. Poor kid," Priest said, sadness filling his eyes. Ricochet was the youngest of us and we all were protective of him. He'd been hurting for so long now, it was slowly eating away at us all. We just wanted to help him. Make him realize he wasn't alone. That we'd die for him. Priest started to take off after him.

Grabbing his shoulder, I hauled him to a stop. "We can't leave Hell alone. Not injured. Stay with him. I'll take care of Ricochet."

Everything slowed as I looked over at our injured brother. I hated to leave him, but Ricochet had just gone into berserker mode. If I didn't get to him…well, I had to get to him. There was no other alternative. Him losing control this badly had only happened one other time, and it was why he'd been discharged at only twenty-four years old, but he'd been slowly losing control more and more lately. He'd finally snapped tonight. What'd happened back then hadn't been his fault, so he'd been honorably discharged, but it'd halted his career and fucked his mind up. He was still dealing with the fallout.

We all were. We did everything we could to help him, but nothing seemed to work. It fucking killed me to watch him battle his demons every day. I'd take them away if I could, beat back the pain and sadness for him.

Priest and I split and I ran after Ricochet. My ears were ringing, whether from all the gunfire or the worry that I wouldn't make it to my brother in time. I knew if I found him, I'd find Ethan. I didn't blame Ricochet, I was bitter and pissed off and I hadn't even been the one to end the lives of those kids. Ethan had brought them out here hoping they'd be enough of a decoy to give him time to get away. Hiding behind kids was the lowest form of cowardice. It would have fucking worked, too, if we'd been able to tell in the darkness that they were fucking kids.

Jacob had turned those truck lights on to help us see who it was, but the headlights had backlit them. It'd reduced them to nothing but moving shadows. Ricochet and Hellfire had been blinded and unable to recognize them for what they were when they started shooting. Though I wondered if somehow Ricochet had caught a glimpse of them and that was why he'd hesitated. Hellfire being shot had spurred him to act, the consequences be damned.

By the time I caught up enough to see them, Ethan was already getting into another truck with Jacob. Bruce was climbing into the back with his rifle. The truck's engine roared as Jacob stomped on the gas. Ricochet had dropped his rifle. What the fuck was he doing? Trying to get himself killed? Fear for him coursed through my veins and I forced my legs to move faster, trying to get there in time to help my brother.

Running full speed—fuck, the kid was fast—Ricochet launched himself into the back and slammed into Bruce. Dust and rocks sprayed everywhere, pelting me as I ran behind them, as Jacob gunned it and fishtailed across the road. A loud thud in the dust revealed Ricochet and Bruce, rolling around on the ground. Bruce's gun was nowhere in sight, so I left Ricochet to deal with the man while I ran after Jacob and Ethan.

The truck was disappearing into the blackness. If I didn't hurry they'd be gone. Stopping, I let out a quick, hard breath to steady myself. Rifle raised, I fired. I kept firing until the truck swayed and slammed into a cactus. Letting out the breath I'd held while firing, I panted as I watched for movement from the truck. There was nothing but dust floating in the air. Turning my attention away from the truck, I focused on my brother.

Even if they survived and escaped, I could pursue them on foot now that the truck was out of commission. Right now, I had to help Ricochet. Jacob and Bruce were the only real fighters in the cult. They were monsters of men, and now, seeing Bruce fight, I knew for sure that they'd been trained. Ricochet was unfazed by the man fighting back against him. He was operating on rage and anguish.

Bruce drove his fist into Ricochet's face, causing him to stumble back. He raised both arms over his head and smashed them down on Ricochet's shoulders like the Hulk smashing a car. Ricochet dropped to his knees with the blow.

Ricochet wasn't a small man by any means, but Bruce still towered over him. Ricochet rocketed up, throwing a series of blows into Bruce's stomach, doubling him over. He locked his arms over Bruce's head and began driving his knee into his face. He looked like he was intent on driving his knee through Bruce's head.

Bruce collapsed under the onslaught to his face. Ricochet dropped on top of him and dropped punch after punch into Bruce's face and body, trying to incapacitate the man.

The whole event from when Ricochet had launched himself into the truck to right now had been a mere handful of seconds. Slowing as I approached my brother, I looked down at what was left of Bruce's face, which at this point was the back of a skull. The face was unrecognizable as human any longer. He'd literally beaten the man to death. There was blood, gore, and what I was pretty sure was brain matter splattered down the front of Ricochet. I cautiously touched his shoulder. He popped up, fists raised.

"Hey, hey, hey, it's just me. We're good. You got 'em." I held my hands in front of me defensively. My sides ached and I was taking deep gulps of air as I caught my breath.

His eyes were wide, a mix of rage and panic. His fists were just balls of blood, and I could see more than one of his fingers were twisted and broken. Punching through a man's skull would do that to a person.

"He's dead," I said, trying to soothe him. Horror at the situation was settling in. Ricochet had killed a kid in self-defense, then brutalized a man in the name of revenge. I couldn't blame him for that, but I knew the events that happened tonight were going to have consequences for him. Regret for my part in Ricochet's torment weighed heavily on me. And though I promised myself I'd do everything I could for him, I knew it wasn't going to be enough.

"Bruce is dead. Hellfire needs you, okay? I need you to go back and see to his wounds." My voice shook as I tried to reach my friend. He was wrapped up in a mist of rage and misery. Had been that way for a while. I just wanted my friend to smile and be able to let what had happened go. He deserved everything good. He was an amazing fucking kid. He was the best brother we could ask for, despite how much he hurt every day.

That snapped him out of it. He stared at me, looking dazed. Now that the adrenaline and fury were melting off him, he was left wondering what the fuck had happened.

"I need you to go find Priest. Help him take care of Hell," I told him again. He needed something to distract him right now and as much as I wanted to protect him, I had to find Ethan and Jacob. I had to end this. Then I'd help Ricochet.

"Hellfire, right. I got it, I got him," he stammered as he turned and stumbled off toward where we'd left the others. I hated fucking leaving him to go back alone. Not in the state he'd just been in. He was back in the real world now, but I knew exactly what'd happened. Only the officers knew Ricochet's story. He hadn't wanted the whole club to know, so we'd kept it quiet, but we'd needed to know so we could keep an eye on the kid.

When this night was over, we'd be having a long conversation with Lockout about this. This wasn't the first time Ricochet had lost it. And he was getting worse. Much worse. That was tomorrow's problem. Right now, I had to find Ethan.

CHAPTER 24

Sloane

With the last of the children coming through the fence Rip stuck his head through. "You've got this, Angel. Take care of them, but most importantly, take care of you." He winked at me, then covered the opening. He'd only been gone for moments, yet I wished he was with us now. I knew that he had to be with the rest of his people. Had to fight Ethan and the others.

My heart sank. I wished it was someone else. I didn't want him in danger, and I didn't want him away from us. Not that I would say a word. This was who he was, a born leader and protector. He needed to do this.

I could understand that, so I focused on what I needed to do. My people needed me to be strong for them. Most of them were terrified, eyes wide and barely holding back tears. But they were here and that was the first step toward being brave and making new lives for ourselves.

"Let's go, I need you to sort of move up and down the line, keep everyone together," Smokehouse told me. "They're all scared and could bolt at any moment. They know you and trust you. Static will be at the front leading them out, I'll be the last in line. But you, just move up and down and talk to them, reassure them. Okay?"

"I can do that," I told him, giving him a smile. It made sense. To get this far only to have everyone scatter into the desert would be a tragedy. They might get lost or killed. Having this job would keep me busy enough that I wouldn't worry. Well, worry more.

"Everyone listen up, my name is Static, this is Dash, George, and Smokehouse. We're getting you out of here. Follow me in a single line. Dash and George will be in the middle and Smokehouse will bring up the rear. It's dark, we're going to move slowly so no one gets lost, but don't wander off. Stay with us and you'll be safe."

Everyone was blinking at him owlishly in the dark, but one thing my people were good at was taking direction. There was a low murmur of agreement and the men began to line everyone up.

I walked up next to him. "You can trust these men. Like I told you all before, they are friends of Derek. I'll be right here with all of you." That seemed to ease some of the tension. "Keep an eye on each other. We have to watch out for one another now, okay?" Heads nodded at me. I turned and patted Static's forearm. "They're ready."

Static turned and headed off into the desert. I stayed where I was, patting shoulders and murmuring words of encouragement to everyone as they walked past. Everything was going fine until we heard the first gun shots.

My heart skipped a beat in my chest and I turned towards the noise, Rip at the front of my thoughts. Fear and worry clogged my throat and as illogical as it was, I wanted to run right back through that hole. I couldn't fight. I didn't know how to use a weapon even if I had one. Yet, I wanted to somehow help him.

You are helping him. By keeping everyone calm and moving them out, he knew he didn't have to worry about us. I knew it was true. I just couldn't convince myself that I shouldn't be by his side.

Smokehouse moved in close to me. His hands dug into my shoulders, forcing my eyes to dart to his. He'd read the anguish and mixed feelings on my features. "Hey, they're professionals. They've got this. Done it a hundred times. Go up there and reassure your people."

"Okay," I said woodenly, turning and heading up the line. I knew Smokehouse was right, and that I needed to comfort everyone, but I was also glad for the distraction. Maybe that's why he told me to do it. As much for myself as for them. "It's okay, we knew this was coming. We just keep moving away from the village and we'll be fine."

Now that we were moving, taking steps away from the place where most of us had been enslaved for years, if not our whole lives, determination was beginning to creep over the women's faces. Nate, Daniel, and Ben were helping women and kids pick their way past the cactus and carry their meager possessions. We hadn't taken much. It would have been too suspicious. We each had a bag with a couple of changes of clothes and that was it.

I hurried my steps, trying to get all the way to the front. I stopped when I saw Static, and decided that right here was a good place. I could see everyone again as they passed me, and I could look down the line for anyone that was panicking.

There was even more gunfire now. Coming from all over the village. I never asked how many of Rip's brothers were coming. It sounded like he brought a whole army. The fact that these men were putting themselves into danger for us was mind blowing for me. The men who were fathers and husbands to the people walking past me couldn't even be bothered to care about their wives and children. They didn't really care if they lived or died, other than the inconvenience that it would bring when there was no one to bring them dinner and slake their lust on.

But these strangers were putting themselves into harm's way to help us. There was no incentive for them to do so. I paused at that. Derek knew us, and they knew Derek. Riptide. What must it be like to have friends and family that simply trusted you when you needed help? To have no reason other than your friend asked for you to do something for him? Rip asked them, and they all came. That type of love and loyalty, it's something I'd never known. Until now.

These were good, decent men. They would have our loyalty and gratitude forever. Knowing all this made it easy for us to follow them, even when the darkness swallowed us up and we weren't sure where this ended. We'd figure it out along the way and Rip would help us. These men would help us and best of all, we'd finally help ourselves.

I looked down the line and could see everyone starting to falter. Panic would take hold soon. I kept doing my best to reassure them. We were so close to being free. We were closer now than I ever imagined we would be. I realized we were closer to ruin, too. We had to keep it together.

Smokehouse came jogging up to me. He pulled me aside and whispered into my ear. "Listen, a few men have left the compound. They'll be heading towards us any minute now. I'm going to take Dash and deal with them before they get here. I need you to stay with the group. It's going to get loud, and they'll want to scatter."

My tongue was stuck to the roof of my mouth, drier than the desert. I tried to speak, but nothing was coming out. He touched my arm gently. "Hey, I'm not going to let them get to us. They won't hurt anyone. But the group needs to stay together. Rip told me how strong you are. You've got this."

He turned, and with Dash in tow, took off into the dark. *Rip believes in you.* That thought had me moving. *He trusts in me. I won't let him down.*

George passed me, taking up Smokehouse's position at the back of the group. Static had slowed down enough to give him time to get back there and me time for a little pep talk. He couldn't stop completely, not with our enemies bearing down on us, but he gave me a few precious moments.

"Don't be frightened, just keep moving. Stay on the trail, stay in line," I called out, just loud enough for everyone to hear me. My tone shifted from gentle to more authoritative. I never knew I had that tone. Even in my classroom, I lead with gentleness and kindness. My people had enough anger and meanness directed toward them on a daily basis. Not that I was being mean, just firm. They needed it right now to hold themselves together.

Gunshots echoed across the desert. They sounded like they were right next to us. "Smokehouse is there, he's dealing with it. Don't panic, just keep going. They'll keep us safe."

Everyone's pace quickened. I could feel the panic nearing a breaking point. I hoped that that was the end of it, but the gun shots kept coming. I trusted Smokehouse. He was Derek's brother. But there was just so much gunfire. How many men were he and Dash fighting? Panic was threatening to overtake me, and if I let go, the whole group would break.

They would scatter, trample each other. Some would run back to the village. They might get shot. Ethan would kill us all for defying him. Going back only led to pain, despair, and death. They couldn't go back.

You've got this, Angel, Derek's voice echoed in my head. My heart rate came down. I wasn't going to panic. I wasn't going to break. Taking a stranglehold on my fear, I refused to let it loose. "Keep it together everyone. Those gunshots mean our rescuers are fighting. That's the sound of our liberation. They're fighting for us. You can't give up on us before they do! Keep moving. Don't panic. We're almost free!"

There was that determination etched on the women's faces once more. They'd heard me and knew they had to keep moving. Relief was white hot. We were going to make it out of this.

"Sister Sloane! Sister Sloane." June came running up to me.

"Honey, I need you to stay in line."

"But, it's Tilly, Janice, and Audrey."

My heart sank as a new wave of terror threatened to take hold. I didn't dare let my imagination run wild. "What happened?" I asked, grabbing June by the shoulders.

"Abigail got scared when the gunshots started. She ran off. The girls went after her. They said they could get her and catch back up before anyone knew she was gone. She ran back toward the village."

Dammit. They would be the ones, too. They were my little shadows. I would be reckless enough to run after someone. So of course they would, too. Especially poor Abigail. She and her older sister, Trina were here with us, but her mother had refused to come. She was so far gone she thought that if she took enough beatings from her husband, Dennis, that the great Earth God would grant her immortality. It was sad, but in the end, I hadn't been able to convince her that she was brainwashed.

I *had* managed to talk enough sense into her to get her to agree to let the girls come with us, but she'd stayed. Abigail was running back to her mother because she was scared. She was a bright, inquisitive child, but she was still only seven years old.

"Thank you, get back in line. I'll handle this." I pushed her toward the line of people, marching like a line of ants, and looked up. Smokehouse and Dash were still gone. I couldn't leave my girls, but I couldn't leave the group either. "Mae!" I shout whispered. A tap on my shoulder almost had me jump out of my skin. I turned around.

"What do you need?" Mae was there.

"Some of the girls ran off. I'm going to get them. Keep everyone in line, keep them moving. Tell Smokehouse as soon as you see him." Static and George had to keep this group moving. We couldn't afford to stop, and I couldn't distract them. Once Smokehouse and Dash got back, if I hadn't returned, they could come find me, but until then, it was up to me to get the four girls.

"Okay." I could tell she was worried, we all were. But she would keep them moving. The gunshots were further away now. We were getting away from the village and it sounded like Smokehouse was almost done. At least I hoped.

"Sister Sloane," a tear filled voice sobbed through the darkness. I turned to Trina. There wasn't time, but I couldn't leave her like this.

"It's okay, Trina. I need you to stay with the group. I'm going to get Abigail. It'll be fine. We'll be back before you know it."

"I'm supposed to take care of her," she said sadly.

"And you will." It was a big ask of a seventeen-year-old girl, but it had been that or leave Abigail behind with her mother. I had no idea if any of the women who'd refused to come with us were even alive right now. There was so much noise coming from the compound there was no telling what was going on. I knew Rip and his brothers would never harm them, but that didn't mean Ethan's men wouldn't.

They weren't above killing their own wives and kids. "I'll be back. Stay here with Mae. Okay?"

Trina nodded and fell back into line. I let out a sigh of relief. The last thing I needed was another girl out there running around in the dark. I bit my lip, knowing that all the guys were going to be pissed at me, especially Rip. But I couldn't allow my girls to be hurt. They were my responsibility, I promised to keep them safe. I gave Mae a hopeful hug, then ran back toward the village.

CHAPTER 25

Riptide

With Ricochet heading back to guard Hellfire I could turn my attention back to Ethan. The truck was still where it'd crashed. I could see the headlights shining against the cactus. I was ready to take off after the men who'd bailed from it, but the gunfire behind me forced me to put Ethan aside for a minute.

I ran back towards the armory, moving through a parallel alley for cover. I found Lockout not far from where I had left him. "What's our status?" I asked him, taking a knee next to him.

He was kneeling at the corner of a house, using the wall for cover but giving him a clear view of the armory. "They've dug in around the building. They have more ammo than we do, they're ready for a standoff." He gave me a grim look. "Are all the civilians out?"

"There are a few wives who refused to leave. I don't know where they are, but I'm sure their husbands have them hiding somewhere out in the desert." At least that's what I wanted to hope.

"If they're not waitin' to put a bullet in us," Hush said with a grim look on his face.

"Hush, Toxic, go search the surrounding homes. I don't want to be responsible for killing women who are just trying to hide, but be careful. Who knows how involved they are."

"There are only a handful." I gave them directions to the houses the women lived in. If they were hiding anywhere inside the village it would be in their homes. It'd nearly fucking killed me to leave them behind. I'd told Sloane that I'd just drag them out of here. Force them to leave with us when the time came. She'd only shaken her head, sadness in her eyes. Forcing them would give our plan away. It'd come down to being unable to sacrifice them all for the sake of a few.

Butcher had warned us about this. We came here prepared to execute all the fanatics. We hadn't been fully prepared to deal with having women and children turning against us as well as the men.

He told us how this could become another Waco or Jonestown. Jonestown would have been preferable. They took themselves out. Lockout needed to be sure that there were no hostages before he did the next part.

"Ethan is still out in the desert. I have to go after him before he escapes. There's no one left in there," I pointed to the armory, "no one left to be saved anyway."

I waited until Toxic and Hush came back. There wasn't time to spare, but I wasn't going to leave Lockout down two men. Our brothers came around the corner and I could tell by the grim looks on their faces it wasn't good news. "Did you find them?"

"Yeah, we searched all the homes," Hush responded, "but they were all in one."

"The fuckers murdered them," Toxic spat out. "They stayed and were loyal and for that they got a bullet between the eyes."

My heart dropped. I knew somehow I was going to have to tell Sloane what had happened. It would break her heart, but she deserved the truth. She'd tried to convince more than a few of those women to come with us and they'd refused. They hadn't given us up, though, and they could have. They'd given everyone else a chance to run. For that I'd always be grateful to them.

"I have to go," I told them. "Ethan's not getting away with this." There was no doubt in my mind he'd given that order.

Lockout nodded, fired a few shots towards the armory, then sprinted over to Butcher. I didn't have time to see this through. Lock and the others would handle it. That's why they were here. To watch my back and help take care of shit when I couldn't be in two places at once.

I was already jogging down the alley toward Ethan's truck. I'd only made it just outside the perimeter fence when I heard the screams. The area in front of me lit up nearly as bright as day. I glanced over my shoulder to see twenty foot flames erupting out of the armory. Smaller, human sized flames ran out the sides.

I don't know how Butcher did it, I would ask later, but I knew this was his and Toxic's handiwork. Toxic was a bit of a fire bug and Butcher was an expert in demolition. Explosions started as the flames reached the ammunition. Soon the whole village would burn to the ground. We were so close to the end.

Continuing up to the truck, I kept a close eye on my surroundings. Who knew where these fuckers were and I didn't want to get ambushed. As expected, the truck was empty. I circled around it looking for signs of which way they went. I looked out to the desert, I could see the glow from the city lights out in the distance. It was miles away, tens of miles, but the only thing to navigate off of. It also happened to be the same direction as where we had stashed our vehicles.

Damn. I hadn't thought about that. We parked so that we would have the quickest route out of here. It never occurred to me that if anyone escaped, they would head that way, using the city lights to navigate off of. All other directions were pitch black and led further into the desert. Right now it was an obvious mistake, but there wasn't much I could do about it. I took off running toward our vehicles.

Fuck! I was kicking myself the whole way. He didn't need to know where we were parked. Just by heading toward the lights he would likely hear or intercept the women. Ethan and Jacob were probably still armed. I didn't see any weapons in the truck. Now that the village was on fire, who knew what kind of a state Ethan was in.

I skidded to a stop and held my breath. I was already panting but I needed to hear clearly. My chest ached from all the running. Who knew a couple months of not working out religiously would cause me to be so out of shape?

Nighttime in the desert was excellent for carrying sound. I could hear feet shuffling and the kicking of rocks. I took off in that direction. My lungs burned, but I forced my body to keep moving. Nothing was going to stop me from finishing this.

My imagination was threatening to run wild. I pushed those thoughts to the back of my mind and kept running. I stopped again, listening. There was more shuffling and female voices. Scared voices. My feet were moving before my brain could even send the command. I was running, breakneck, through the desert now. I had to get to Ethan and Jacob before they got to the women and children. Before they got to Sloane.

Sharp stabbing pains jabbed at my shins as I plowed straight through every type of cactus out here. I ignored the feeling of death by a thousand pin pricks, all that mattered was getting to those voices. I tried to reassure myself, I told her to stay with the group, stay with Smokehouse and Static. There was no way she was close enough for Ethan to get her. The group should be nearly to the vehicles by now. I should be able to get to Ethan before he got to her.

But I knew my wife. Fear and pride pierced my heart. If anyone had wandered off from the group, Sloane would be there to find them. There was no way she would leave her people behind. I loved her for that, though right now it was the one trait of hers that filled me with the most fear.

I prayed as I ran that I was wrong, but I knew what I was about to run into. The moon was starting to crest over the mountains, illuminating my path. It was a small break, but at least someone was looking out for me. I picked up my pace. I could hear the voices over my breathing and stomping. They were scared. Ethan was near.

I was going so fast I almost collided with the girls. I grasped one by the shoulders, both to slow myself down and to keep her from bolting. "It's me, it's Derek," I huffed before she had a chance to scream.

Tilly, bless her, got right to the point. Mostly. "He has Miss Sloane. We were looking for Abigail. Ethan had her and was going to take her, and us, and then Sister Sloane was there and she told Ethan to take her instead and to let us go and-" She broke off on a sob as Janice, Audrey, and Abigail circled around, offering comfort.

Tilly was doing her best, but I just didn't have time for all the details. I squeezed gently on her shoulders, making her pause. As gently but urgently as I could I asked "Where are they?"

Tilly opened her mouth and froze, stopping herself from rambling. "That way." She pointed towards the lights in the distance.

"Thank you." I turned toward the mountains to the east, where our vehicles were parked. "Do you see that peak there?" I asked, pointing.

"Yes," Audrey was the one who answered this time.

"That's where the group is. Walk toward that peak, until you hit the road, then take a right and follow it. You'll find the vehicles and the group. Stay together and go." I was sending them a bit out of the way, but that was so that they wouldn't accidentally run into Ethan and Jacob again. It was too dangerous, so instead I was sending them east, then south, versus straight south on the line Ethan had gone. That was the way I was going, though. I took off running south, hoping to catch up with the monsters who had my wife.

Stabbing pain coursed through my side, but I didn't slow down. I didn't try to assess the situation. I leaned into my run and went full bore. Nothing was going to keep me from getting to Sloane in time. She was mine and if either man thought they'd have a chance to hurt her, they'd find out they were dead wrong.

When I came up on them, I spotted Jacob holding Sloane by the arm, trying to drag her away. Ethan was yelling frantically. He knew just how fucked they were. Not only was their village gone—most of his people slaughtered or had willingly left him—but I had all his fucking money. He had nothing left. Nothing except the only thing in this world that mattered to me.

That was all I was able to see before I rocketed into the air and tackled Jacob like a human missile. We landed in a mess of tumbling limbs, rolling over our rifles, rocks and cactus. I was poked, stabbed and hit by so many things I couldn't tell where on my body I was hurting. Everywhere would suffice for now. My move had tossed Sloane away from us and to the ground herself, but at least she was out of Jacob's hands.

There was shouting and pleading coming from Ethan. It was all indistinguishable. I was a little busy trading blows with Jacob to focus on much else. I had to even the odds before I faced Ethan. Then I was going to prove that the Earth God was nothing but a fucking liar and a scam artist, even if only to myself and Sloane since no one else was around to see him die.

Jacob was every bit the walking mountain that Bruce had been. He relied on his size and strength, but he had no underlying skill. He simply leaned into his strength to make up for it. He'd intimidated the people of The Order with his size and his scowl. They'd all been terrified of him, but the only people he'd hurt and killed had mostly been willing to go to their own deaths. It made for an easy murder when your victim was halfway accepting of it.

Jacob expected to be fighting Brother Derek. It was there in his eyes, triumph. He still believed that I was the useless computer nerd who he'd picked up on that first day and brought out here. Idiot. He was about to find out differently. Not only was I trained for this, but I wrestled with men his size on an almost nightly basis. My brothers were just as big, and had actual technique. He stood no chance against me even though he had a few inches and about twenty pounds on me in size.

We rolled across the sage brush, stopping with me on my back. A rock stabbed into my shoulder blade while Jacob leaned back, fists locked together and raised over his head. He was going to bring them down onto my face.

I bucked at the hips, causing him to lose balance and fall forward. I drove my fist straight into his throat, crushing his trachea. He rolled to the side, grasping his neck, desperately trying to choke out a breath. I twisted and wrapped my right arm around his neck, left arm bracing the back of his head.

A gunshot rang through the air. Fear locked my breath in my chest. I looked up at Ethan, he was holding a pistol pointed to the sky. He held Sloane in his other hand. Relief that he hadn't shot her was the only thing I had a chance to feel before I shoved it down. Emotions in battle got people killed. Before he could say anything I stood, and with a twist of my arms broke Jacob's neck. I let the body fall limp and lifeless at my feet as I faced Ethan.

He stared back at me, his face fully deranged now. Killing Jacob certainly didn't help his state, but I couldn't deal with both of them. My brothers would have heard the gunshot; they'd be on their way.

That was little comfort as right now was the most dangerous moment for Sloane and they weren't going to make it in time. Ethan was alone. His backup was dead. It was just him, Sloane, and I. He could do anything. It was up to me to keep Sloane alive. I was willing to lay down my life to make sure of it.

Ethan looked at Jacobs' body, then looked back to his village as it burned. He was realizing what I already knew. It was over. There was nothing left for him. His eyes darkened with malice. That was why he was so dangerous at this moment. There was nothing left for him to live for. He could easily decide to kill Sloane, just for the hell of it. Just to hurt me, the man who'd brought down his entire operation. To hurt her, the thorn in his side for so many years.

"Let her go Ethan, you have nowhere left to go."

"Nowhere to go? I am your God! You do not order me!" He shook Sloane's arm, causing her to stumble slightly. "Betrayed by my own daughter! This will not stand! The earth shall be soaked with the blood of the betrayers!"

Daughter? That hit me like a sledgehammer. I opened my mouth, but nothing came out.

Ethan kept ranting. "This is your fault Brother Derek! You were tasked with keeping her in line. You were supposed to put an end to her blasphemes and her free spirit. This is on you Derek. Your failures brought this on!"

Sloane's his daughter. So many things clicked into place, but I forced them all aside. It was a lot to take in. Why hadn't she told me before? *You know why. She hates Ethan.* Probably didn't want me to be disappointed that she was related to him. As if I could ever be disappointed in her. I shoved that aside, too. There wasn't time to examine how I was feeling about that bit of news.

All that mattered was disarming him. If he thought there was no way out, he would kill her. In that moment I knew it didn't matter who her father was. I loved her and no one was going to ever hurt her again.

My gaze met Sloane's and I saw the apology there in her beautiful blue eyes. The same eyes her father had. How had I never noticed? Maybe on some deeper level I always knew. Why else would Ethan have kept her around despite the trouble she'd caused? I doubted it was because he loved her. It was more likely that she'd grown up with most of the people in The Order and the women wouldn't have taken her murder as easily as they had others.

There was no way for me to relay to her that she had nothing to apologize for. It wasn't her fault that her father was a raving lunatic. She'd done everything in her power to atone for his sins over the years. She never should have had to take that burden on, yet she had. If anything, the truth only made me more proud of her. Few people would have fought back the way she had. Few had. She'd been the only one to stand up for the innocents. Now she had me to stand for her.

I just had to figure out how to get her away from him. Ethan was holding the gun, but it was pointed down toward the ground as he spewed nonsense about being the Earth God. The guy really did believe his own bullshit. It was amazing to witness. Somehow he'd bought into his own lies and thought he was some divine power.

A small movement caught my eye. Sloane shifted her body slowly toward Ethan. My brows drew low and I scowled at her. I gave her a slow shake of my head. Every movement we made was deliberate and slow, so as not to catch Ethan's attention.

Before I could do anything to stop her, I watched as Sloane took her shot. I couldn't allow my worry for her to paralyze me. My muscles bunched, preparing to take advantage of the opportunity she was about to give me. I'd give anything for there to be another way, but my wife wasn't a wilting flower. She wasn't about to stand by and do nothing while her father killed us. Just like she hadn't stood by and allowed them to take four young girls as hostages. She'd been more useful to him against me, and she knew it, so without hesitation she'd traded herself. She knew full well that he could kill her at any time. And still she'd done the right thing.

There was no way for me to explain the pride and love I had for her right now. All I could do was wait, and watch, as she swung her leg back, then kicked forward with all her might. She aimed for the backs of Ethan's knees, crumpling them forward when her shin landed against them.

Lunging forward, I hit him on the way down, sending us both sprawling into the dirt. I had lost my rifle in the fight with Jacob. All I could do now was wait for an opening. Besides, I didn't want his death to be that easy. I wanted to look into his eyes as the life drained out of them.

We rolled as we fought over the gun he had in his hands. I needed to get his pistol away from him before he managed to put a round in my gut. Until I disarmed him, I had to be careful. Letting go of his wrist—leaving only my left hand wrapped around it and keeping him from leveling that gun into my face—I landed a blow into his side.

Ethan wheezed in pain, but his grip didn't falter. He knew once he lost that gun, it was over. He was pinned beneath me and I was willing to do whatever it took to come out on top in this fight. Ethan wasn't a trained fighter, but the coward was a fucking snake. A desperate snake, and desperation could give men ridiculous strength.

I didn't see what his other hand was doing until it was too late. He took a handful of sand and tossed it in my face. Grit entered my eyes, making them burn and water. Everything was blurry and the piece of shit managed a punch to my jaw.

He wriggled out from under me while I was trying to rub the dirt from my eyes. I blinked hard a few times and looked up. He was standing over me, a wicked grin on his face as he started to bring the gun up.

"No!"

We both looked over right as Sloane swung a mesquite tree branch into Ethan's face. The resounding crack of the wood slamming into him made me grin. Once again I was up and moving.

This time I managed to knock the gun from his grasp as I took him down to the ground for the second time that night. My hands were wrapped firmly around his neck while he sputtered and clawed at my wrists.

The more he struggled, the harder I clamped down. "Shouldn't an Earth God be able to smite me for doing this, Ethan?" I taunted him. His eyes bulged in response. Looking over my shoulder, I saw Sloane standing there, watching. "I can't leave him alive," I told her, hesitation in my tone. Was she going to blame me for killing her father?

Anger slid into her gaze. "I want you to kill him," she told me. "He means nothing to me."

I turned my attention back to the man who'd hurt her so many times over the years. "You're lucky I don't have the time to torture you to death. You deserve to have your fingers, toes, and dick sliced off for daring to injure my wife. I should bleed you out, let the desert sand soak up your useless lifeforce before leaving you out here to fucking rot." I leaned in close and growled into his ear as he began to die. "I wonder, if you'd known that it would come to this, back when you hurt Sloane for the first time, would you have ever *dared* to touch what belongs to me?"

Pulling away, I did exactly what I'd wanted to for so long. Ethan's lips moved, but he was lying still. His life faded before me, but I still kept my grip strong around his neck for a few minutes more. I wanted to make sure the asshole was really dead. Last thing I needed was him popping back up like a fucking jack-in-the-box.

"He's dead, Rip."

I glanced over my shoulder and found my brothers from the village standing there. Lockout had been the one to address me. Both

Butcher and Toxic were standing on either side of Sloane, silently offering their protection to her.

Hush came over and held out a hand, pulling me to my feet. "We sent Ricochet and Priest back to the vehicles with Hellfire."

"We need to find the girls," Sloane said, finally speaking up.

"The girls?" Toxic asked her. "Which girls?"

"I ran into them on the way here," I told her, kicking sand over Ethan's motionless body. It wasn't to hide him. We'd end up bringing all the bodies to our friend with the funeral home. We didn't need the cops finding a massacre out here. No, I just did that as a sign of disrespect to the Earth God who'd made his daughter's life hell for her whole life. "I directed them back to the vehicles, so we should head there first."

Walking over, I pulled Sloane into my arms. She sank into my embrace, fitting perfectly against me.

"I'm so sorry I didn't tell you that Ethan was my father," she whispered. "I tried so many times."

"It's okay, Angel. I understand why that would have been hard to admit. It doesn't matter anymore."

We started walking back toward the vehicles, my arm draped over her shoulders.

"Thank you so much. Thank all of you," she said a little louder, "for everything you've done for us tonight. It couldn't have been easy, but we'll forever be in your debt."

"There's no debts with us, Angel," I replied. "We'll help everyone get settled and learn how to live life the way the rest of us heathens do." I grinned down at her and enjoyed her laugh as it echoed through the darkness.

We had a lot to figure out now that we weren't stuck inside The Order, but she and her people being free was a good place to begin. We'd figure everything out from here. I'd half expected to die tonight, certainly would have for her, but now we'd get to move forward together.

CHAPTER 26

Sloane

Everything was a bit of a blur. Derek's brothers had brought out large cars and were shuttling everyone out of the desert. My girls had already made it back to the area where the vehicles were parked and Static and Smokehouse had them wait until I got back before sending them into the city. Running forward, I fell to my knees hugging each of them close in turn. They were crying and babbling. We were a pile of tears and limbs. Before long, Rip helped us up and sent the girls on ahead.

"Go," I told them with a tearful smile. "I'll be right behind you." Embracing them each one last time, I watched as the car bounced over the dirt road until it was out of sight.

I insisted on staying until the last of the women and children were taken from here. It ended up being me, Ben, Daniel, and Nate—the only three men who were salvageable from that place—and Rip's crew.

We quietly climbed into the different vehicles. Rip was sitting next to me, but he hadn't spoken to me much. It could be that he'd just been busy and he was preoccupied, but I was feeling incredibly insecure. He found out my last secret in a way I hadn't ever planned for. I'd tried to tell him before all of this kicked off. He'd interrupted me with a kiss and it had been easier to let it go than to insist that I tell him. I was regretting that decision now. I should have had more courage because Rip finding out this way was my fault. It didn't need to be such a shock for him if I'd done things right. I wished I could go back and tell him when I had the chance.

It was me and three of his brothers in the SUV. It wasn't necessarily the best place for the conversation, but I didn't want the uncomfortable tension to keep escalating.

"I'm so sorry I didn't tell you I was Ethan's daughter before," I said in a low voice.

His eyes flashed over to me and he gave me an abrupt nod. "We'll talk about it later, Sloane."

I slumped down in the seat, staring at my hands that were folded in my lap. We were free. I should be riding that high, but the shock and disappointment I'd seen on Rip's face when he'd found out the truth prevented it. I was already so unsure of where we stood. We'd told each other that we loved one another and that we wanted to continue what we had outside of the compound. Would he still want that now that he knew I was related to a madman?

The drive took longer than I expected, and by the time the SUV stopped, I was ready to get out and stretch. I frowned as I looked around. "Where is everyone?"

"Static has a place where we were able to take everyone for the night. We don't have enough space for them all here," Rip told me.

"Okay. Thank you so much for helping us." I reached out and squeezed his arm. Before he could say anything else, I turned and walked toward where one of his brothers was loading Daniel, Nate, Ben, and the last of the women into the van.

A firm hand gripped my upper arm and pulled me to a stop. "Where are you going, Sloane?"

I faced him and gave him a smile. His eyes were narrowed on my face, but he didn't look angry. "I'm going to where my people are."

He shook his head. "You're my wife. You're staying here with me."

I watched in shock as he dipped before me and then gasped as my world was turned upside down. Literally. "Rip!" I was hanging over his shoulder as he stalked toward the building he'd called the clubhouse. Others chuckled and called out as we passed and all I could do was hang there and glare at his back.

The world righted itself as soon as we stepped into the clubhouse. There were five women standing there with wide eyes and their mouths hanging open.

"Ladies," Rip said by way of greeting. "This is my wife, Sloane. Could you keep her company and explain a few things about the club while I go help the others settle everyone in?"

I didn't think it was possible but their eyes got wider as they nodded mutely. Then it was like a crack formed in the dam and they rushed forward, all speaking at once. Suddenly both Rip and I were being hugged.

"We're so glad you're okay," a tall, dark-haired woman told him as she hugged him. She turned to me and gave me a beautiful smile. "Hi, I'm Seek."

She wrapped me up in a tight embrace and my eyes closed as I sank against her. It wasn't typical for me to take comfort in a stranger but something told me these were good women and I was so emotionally and physically exhausted, I didn't have the energy to deny myself.

They swept me upstairs faster than I could react. They were so full of energy that I wasn't sure if I was walking or being carried along. I went with them, shooting a look over my shoulder at Rip. My anxiety increased at the thought of leaving his side.

"I'll be back, Angel," Rip called out. He gave me a reassuring smile, waited until I nodded, then he turned and walked out.

We ended up settling inside an apartment upstairs and I perched on the edge of a recliner as all the women stared at me. I gave them a wan smile.

"Sorry," a woman with brown curly hair said. "We don't mean to stare. It's just we weren't expecting Riptide to come back with a wife!"

Laughing, I relaxed a little. "I don't think it was what he expected either," I admitted. "Could you tell me your names again, please?" They'd been a storm of voices and movement downstairs and I wasn't sure I had things correct.

"I'm Jenny," the lady with curls told me. "Priest is my old man."

Blinking, I opened my mouth to ask what that meant exactly. Another lady beat me to it.

"An old man is like a boyfriend or a husband in the club," she told me. "I'm Kit."

"Who's your old man?" I asked.

She laughed, tossing her mane of dark hair. "No one. My brother is in the club and we basically grew up here when our dad was a member so Lockout—the president—allows me to stick around."

"She's not a sweet butt, though," one of the two blonde women said. "Oh, I'm Tory."

My jaw worked as I repeated the words she'd said. This was an entirely different world than the one I was used to.

"There's a lot to learn," the second blonde said, "but you'll get the hang of it soon enough. I'm Daisha."

"And I'm Suzie," the last woman, a red-head, said, introducing herself.

"Sloane," I told them with a smile. My head was spinning, but their welcoming smiles had set me at ease.

"You lived at the compound?" Seek asked, curiosity in her eyes.

"I did." Something brushed against my arm and I started so hard, I jumped in my chair.

"Sorry! Auron, Jecht, come."

I looked over at Seek as she called her two dogs over. One went directly to her while the other brushed himself against my legs. Ethan hadn't allowed us to keep animals. He said they were dirty and immoral. One of the kids had found a stray that'd had puppies and snuck one home. Ethan had ordered the animal be killed. He'd been furious when he couldn't find it to kill it.

He'd suspected me all along, but hadn't been able to prove it. That didn't mean that he hadn't whipped me for the offense anyway. But the dog had lived. I'd snuck into a nearby town and found a mother with her young boys at a grocery store. They'd happily taken the pup.

I rubbed the back of my neck where the tail of the whip had left a deep scar. The marks along my body were memories of growing up within The Order. They ensured I'd never forget the lessons Ethan taught me. Maybe one day I could put them behind me. "May I?" I gestured to the dog at my feet. He was staring up at me with a lolling tongue and kind, intelligent eyes.

"Of course. Jecht is still pretty young and he doesn't know his manners as well, but he is sweet as pie," Seek told me with a smile.

My hands sank into his soft fur and I scratched behind his ears. Everyone watched me quietly as I leaned forward and buried my face in his scruff. He whined and pressed closer to me. Somehow this animal knew to give me comfort. Maybe I'd get a dog now that I had a new life. A being that would love me unconditionally and wouldn't care where I came from.

Overwhelmed, I breathed in deep, trying to push back the fear and worry. Everything was different and I was going to have to learn to live a completely new way. Later, I'd be excited about that, but for now it was frightening.

Arms went around me and I looked up and was startled to realize all the women were squatting down, circled around me and Jecht. Their arms were on each other's shoulders as they huddled around me.

"I know you don't know us yet," Kit told me, a soft look in her eyes, "but we're family."

"That's the whole point of the motorcycle club," Suzie said.

"Anytime you need anything, we'll all be here for you," Daisha continued.

"Everyone. Even the men. But us women stick together," Jenny said, wrapping an arm around my waist. "We'll help you adjust and learn how to live in this new lifestyle."

"I would love that," I told them with tears in my eyes. If only I was sure that Rip wanted to keep me. We still hadn't gotten to speak since he found out who I was. What if he decided to cast me aside? It would be easy for him to do. They already had the rest of my people somewhere here in the city.

"Would you like something to eat? Or drink?" Seek asked.

I shook my head, then paused. "It's a weird request, but…"

"Anything," Seek insisted. "What is it?"

"Could I take a shower?" Dirt was caked to my skin, sand inside my clothes, and I felt bedraggled compared to these gorgeous women.

"Of course!"

"It's just…I don't have my bag. It has my clothes and things in it. It's still in the SUV. Rip didn't let me grab it before…"

"Don't worry," she told me, patting my knee as I trailed off. "You'll get used to the guys."

"Are they all like that?" I asked. It was so different from the Rip I knew from The Order. "I never would have guessed he'd just toss me over a shoulder like that."

"Oh yeah," they all said in unison, then laughed.

"They all have a little barbarian in them," Jenny said with a snort of amusement. "But they'd never hurt their old ladies. In fact, they'd kill for us."

"And our kids," Suzie said with a small smile.

"Do you all have kids?"

"I don't," Kit piped up.

Everyone else just nodded, except for Seek. She smiled and placed a hand on her belly. My eyes widened as I realized she must have recently found out she was pregnant.

"Come on," she said, before I could say anything to her. "You can borrow some of my clothes."

They dragged me into her bedroom and to her closet. They began pulling out clothing at a rate that made me dizzy. Back home I'd had four skirts and five blouses. The amount of clothing this woman had was making my head spin.

"Don't you have anything girlier?" Kit asked, flicking through the clothes hanging there. They all looked back at my skirt and blouse.

"We didn't have a lot of options for clothes," I told them, tugging self-consciously at my skirt. Ethan had been very strict on what could be worn. Just another form of control he'd exerted over all of us.

"Sorry," Seek said with an apologetic laugh. "I don't really wear dresses."

"Try these on," Jenny suggested, handing me a pair of jeans while Kit handed me a shirt.

I shook my head, fear crawling through my chest. Pants weren't allowed. They were a sure fire way to get yourself a beating. "I couldn't."

The women glanced between each other, understanding and something close to pity there. It shook me out of my fear. I wasn't under Ethan's thumb anymore and I didn't want anyone to pity me.

Taking the clothes, I disappeared into her bathroom. I wasn't ready for anyone to see my scars. Looking in the mirror, I stared at the woman there. My hair was dirty and limp and I had dirt smeared across my face, but the long sleeve shirt clung to my curves and the jeans accentuated my small hips, though I had to roll up the bottoms of the pants. Seek was quite a bit taller than me. I'd seen clothes like this when passing through new towns, but never on myself.

"Do they fit?" someone called through the door.

I opened it and they all smiled and gave me compliments. Seek set me up with a towel and everything I'd need for the shower I wanted. They left me alone to bathe.

The warm water was revitalizing. The exhaustion, the fear, the shame, swirled down the drain along with the dirt on my skin. A sense of hope and wonderment was beginning to rise inside of me. The Order was done. I was a free woman.

By the time I joined them in the living room again, I felt like a new woman. I hadn't bothered to put on my panties or bra. They were dirty, so I'd just rolled them up in my skirt and set them aside. It felt weird to have nothing on under my borrowed clothes, but I'd make sure to launder them before returning them to Seek.

Someone shoved a glass of wine in my hand and we all sat around talking and laughing. I knew without a doubt that I was going to end up being good friends with these women.

"Where are your children?" I asked.

"Over in Jenny's apartment," Suzie said. "Sylvia is watching over them. She's a friend of ours."

I was glad to have some time with the women. They began teaching me about this lifestyle they lived. It sounded like it was centered around family. Could I dare to hope that I'd ended up with the one man who could give me everything I'd ever longed for? A family of my own—children—but also a group of people like this who loved and cared for me? It was everything I'd ever dreamed of. Suddenly the thought of not only losing Rip, but all this as well, was a heavy weight in my chest.

The wine relaxed the rest of me as we spoke and soon I'd fallen asleep in my chair. Warm arms lifted me and I knew by the fresh scent that it was Rip. I cuddled into his chest without bothering to open my eyes.

"I said help her settle in, not get her drunk." Rip's tone was filled with amusement.

"It was their fault," Seek said, and I knew without looking she was passing blame to the other women. When no one spoke up I had a feeling they were all passed out as well.

"Sure it was. Thanks for tonight," he told her.

"Anytime, Rip. It's so good to have you home."

"Good to be home. Lock said we'll have church tomorrow, around eleven, to go over everything."

"Goodnight. Take care of her."

"You know I will," he said and I felt his lips brush the top of my head. I let sleep pull me back under, safe and protected in his arms.

CHAPTER 27

Riptide

I woke early the next morning, wrapped around Sloane. Burying my face in her soft hair, I let out a sigh. I left our bed, careful not to wake her.

No one was around downstairs, so I went behind the bar and grabbed myself a couple beers. Popping the top on the first, I took a long pull as I sat down at a nearby table. I groaned with pleasure as the taste hit my tongue. I'd fucking missed beer. I didn't consider myself an alcoholic, but after going a couple months without drinking it, I'd built up a craving.

I wasn't sure how long I'd been sitting there when Hush took the seat next to me.

"You realize it's seven a.m., don't you?" he asked with amusement written all over his face.

"Yup." I took a swig of the beer then gave him a wicked grin. I offered the second bottle to him.

He shook his head, with a mournful look at the beer. "Seek can't drink, so I'm also not drinkin'. In solidarity."

My brows drew together. "Why can't Seek..." It hit me and I sat forward. "She's pregnant?"

Hush grinned and nodded. "Found out a few weeks ago."

"Congratulations you old bastard," I told him with a laugh.

"We're drinking?" Butcher asked, walking up. Without waiting for an answer he went behind the bar and came back with a bottle without a label and glasses.

"What's that?" I asked. With Butcher you always had to be suspicious.

"Moonshine," Toxic said, sitting down on the other side of me, leaving Butcher to sit across the table. "Got it as payment for a favor."

Hush narrowed his eyes on the bottle. "You mean someone made that themselves and you're planning on drinkin' it?"

"We already drank the other three bottles...and lived," Butcher replied. His tone suggested he was offended that we thought he'd serve us bad alcohol.

He slid a glass toward me. I shrugged and downed it. The liquid burned my esophagus on the way down and I coughed hard, wondering if I'd have any stomach lining left after this. "Fuck me."

"Good right?" Toxic asked with a grin.

"Not sure good's the word," Hush wheezed. He'd tried to decline the shot, but Butcher and Toxic were persistent about their alcohol.

Butcher refilled our glasses. "Why we down here getting drunk?"

"I was just having a beer," I said, defending myself. "Had no intention of getting drunk."

Butcher's expression was blank as he tried to make sense of my words. When he couldn't, he just took another swig of the moonshine.

"Well, now we are," Toxic said, saluting me with his glass.

"Why're you down here instead of upstairs with that pretty wife of yours?" Hush asked, tone sly.

"Just needed to think a bit."

"'Bout?" He made a face, then downed his second shot.

I explained how I'd ended up with a wife. They were all watching in rapt fascination, though Butcher had resorted to taking pulls straight from his bottle at this point.

"So what's the problem?" Hush asked, shooting Butcher a dark look when he lifted the bottle again. "Lockout's goin' to fuckin' kill you. We have church soon."

Butcher just shrugged. Lockout was used to him and would deal with him like he always did.

"Is it fair of me to tie her to me?" I asked. It was the question that had been rattling around in my brain since last night.

"Has nothing to do with her being that fuck stain's kid?" Toxic asked, taking the bottle from Butcher so he could pour himself another shot. "You looked like someone nailed you in the balls when you found out."

"It's insane to think someone as pure and kind as Sloane came from that warped, evil bastard. But no. I don't care about that."

Hush leaned back, folding his arms behind his head as he watched me. "So, you're thinkin' you'll be the hero and set her free now that she's out of that fucked up place?"

I shrugged. That was what I was considering. "She's been so sheltered. What if she wants to live life instead of being stuck with a man that her piece of shit father forced her to marry?"

"Somethin' I've learned about women is that it's best to talk directly to them, before assumin' you know what they want."

Butcher snorted. "Like they're going to tell you what they really want?"

"Most of 'em want you to know them well enough that you can guess what they want without asking," Toxic said in agreement with Butcher. "If you're not a mind reader, then you don't love her."

Hush shook his head. "You two shut the fuck up. No one needs to be takin' your advice on datin' and women. That'll be a fuckin' disaster."

Both men nodded as though that was a certainty. There weren't any hurt feelings. I wasn't sure either of them had emotions, so it wasn't easy to get a rise out of them.

"I remember someone comin' at me and givin' me a gash in my

cheek when I was being a stubborn dick and tryin' to stay away from Seek," Hush continued on after Butcher and Toxic went back to drinking. Something flashed there in his eyes, warning me about what was about to happen.

"Aw fuck, Hush. Don't-" That was as far as I got before he'd hurtled out of his chair, taking me backward on my own.

We crashed into the ground, the chair breaking apart beneath my back. Buying furniture around here was a constant because we broke so much of it. A fist planted itself in my gut and I huffed out a pained breath.

Hush had about twenty pounds on me, but I was faster than the old man. We rolled, exchanging punches as the other two called out encouragement. They were taking bets on who would win.

My ears rang as Hush's haymaker landed against the side of my head. "Knock it off, you dick!"

"Nope," he said with a grunt as I managed a hit to his sternum. "Not until I beat it into your head that you've finally found yourself a good woman. It'd be a fuckin' mistake to walk away now."

We both knew that this was between friends. I wasn't his VP right now and that meant there were no rules. It was the same as before, when I'd started a fight with him when he'd needed it beaten into him that Seek was his salvation. He wasn't going to hold back now that I needed to be taught a lesson.

"Oh, my!"

Sloane's dismayed voice worked its way into my brain and I glanced over at her. She was standing there next to Jenny, her hands covering her mouth.

"Don't worry," Jenny said, patting her on the back. "They do this all the time. They don't have the vocabulary to talk it out like adults." She shot us a satisfied smile at her dig.

"Stop," I growled at Hush, eyes still on my wife. The fear sweeping over her face made me realize how this looked to her.

Tears started rushing down Sloane's cheeks. Worry filled Jenny's face as she tried to console her.

"Hush," I snarled. "Fucking stop." I managed to bring my knee up from my position beneath him and catch him in the nuts. It was a cheap shot, but my angel was breaking down and I had to get to her. I rolled onto my hands and knees, shaking the disorientation away from Hush's hits. "Sloane, it's okay."

"Why-" she started, her voice cracking as she broke the sentence off. "You...you have punishments here?"

My heart broke into a million pieces at the fear and anguish on her face. "No, Baby," I told her, shoving to my feet. I froze as she backed up a few steps, shaking her head. Fear was written all over her face. It killed me to see it.

Jenny looked back and forth between us, but stayed next to her. She didn't know what was going on, but the fact that she was choosing to stay nearby and protect Sloane was something I'd thank her for later. Jenny rubbed soothing circles on Sloane's back, trying to calm her.

"Punishments?" Hush asked, getting to his own feet. He was probably pissed about the ball shot, but he could see that Sloane was terrified, so he didn't say anything about it.

Even Butcher and Toxic had gotten to their feet, though they were silent. That was a rare thing for them. No one except for me understood what was going on, but they were all worried about the sweet woman in front of me. It hadn't taken long for her to work her magic on them. They all were falling in love with her. It was her gift. Anyone who met her—anyone who wasn't an evil asshole—saw how kind her heart was and wanted everything good for her. My brothers were no exception. They'd gotten a first-hand look at how she'd been treated in The Order and now they wanted to make sure she didn't feel a moment of fear again in her lifetime. She'd already endured enough.

"There's no punishments here, Angel."

Her eyes darted back and forth between me and Hush. I could see the disbelief in the blue depths. She didn't believe me. Didn't know if she could trust me. That twisted the knife in my heart. I wanted to be her safe harbor. The one she could run to when she was scared. Instead, she was backing away from me.

"What the fuck's going on?" Lockout boomed, making Sloane jump. She was about to dart away like a frightened bunny.

I held up my hand, making Lockout and Priest come to a stop nearby as they took in the scene before them. "Hush is my friend, Angel. My brother. We beat advice into each other's heads sometimes, but we'd never really hurt each other."

Her eyes dipped to where I could feel blood dripping down over my neck, uncertainty flickering over her face.

No one spoke, letting me handle this. They only had a small idea of where her fear was coming from, but I knew exactly why she was so scared. What she'd been through.

"We don't hand out punishments here. At least not whippings and beatings," I reassured her.

Jenny gasped, her hands covering her mouth at the horror of the thought of Sloane being whipped. Many of my brothers had been there the day she'd taken a beating for Abigail, so it wasn't as shocking to them.

"No one here will ever raise a hand to you," I promised her. "Not without me killing them for it." I could assure her of this because none of my brothers would ever dare to hurt one of our women. Even if it *was* something they wanted to do—and none of them were that kind of man—they wouldn't out of respect.

Sloane's shoulders sagged and she finally took a step toward me. That was all I needed. She was in my arms within seconds, sobbing against my chest.

"I'm sorry," she whispered, burying her face against my cut.

"Never apologize, Angel."

"I'm the one who should be sayin' I'm sorry," Hush said, shoving his hands in pockets, looking contrite. "I was just returnin' a favor I owed him." The smile he gave me was more a baring of teeth.

Flipping him off, I chuckled. "He didn't mean to scare you."

Sloane's cheeks pinkened as she looked up at me. "I didn't mean to cause a scene."

"It's going to take time to learn how things work around here," Lockout told her, approaching slowly. No one wanted to set her off again, but she seemed fine now. The panic that had been in her eyes was gone. I tightened my arms around her, as much for myself as for her. "These guys get into fights all the time-"

"Like you don't join in," Butcher told Lockout with a laugh.

"*We* fight all the time, but Rip's right. We don't hit women. There are no physical punishments here," Lockout continued, ignoring Butcher. "It's how we play. We fight each other, but never seriously hurt each other."

Sloane nodded. It hadn't taken her long to figure out Lockout was in charge. Since it was the way she was raised, she fell into taking what he said as truth. He was our leader, so she trusted him. I didn't take it personally. He was my president. It was best if she understood the chain of command. It would make things easier as she began to understand life here with the club. I could see there in her eyes that she instinctively trusted Lock. It made me relax. I wanted her to trust my brothers. They would protect her with their lives and she needed to understand she could come to any of us if she had a problem.

"We're going to have church early," Lockout said, changing the subject. "Just the officers and their old ladies."

Everyone left Sloane and me there, so I could finish calming her down. Lockout was including Seek, Jenny, and Sloane, for two reasons. Seek was the one who began all this and needed the closure. He also wanted Seek and Jenny to understand what Sloane had been through, so they could help her adjust to life here. She would need the women as we moved forward.

I'd only given Lock the brief highlights of my time with The Order the night before. The rest I'd tell them all as we sat around our church table.

"Are you okay?" I asked her.

She nodded. "I'm sorry if I embarrassed you," she replied softly, wiping her cheeks.

I gripped her chin in my fingers, forcing her to meet my eyes. "You didn't. There wasn't any way for you to know what was going on when you saw that. I'm sorry for worrying you. I never want you to be scared of me, or my brothers. I'll do my best to explain things like this before they have a chance to worry you."

"Now that you've explained it, I understand."

"You can go to any of these men if you have a problem and they'll help you. They'll treat you with love and respect. Never doubt that."

She nodded and rested against my chest again. There was a long conversation we needed to have, but first we needed to get church over with. It was going to be difficult for her to hear my account and help explain the way she'd lived. It was easy for those who didn't experience it to judge, but I knew my family wouldn't. She didn't know them well enough yet to understand that, though. Tension radiated off her body.

There were a lot of conversations I needed to have today. First was church. Then I'd have to speak to Lockout and the others—without the women present—about Ricochet. Hellfire was off getting sewn up, but being well taken care of by a friend of ours. Not that he'd been thrilled to be taken to Doc, no one ever was, but he was going to be fine. I didn't want to leave my talk with Sloane until last, but the others were higher up on the priority list right now. She was safe here with me and we'd talk as soon as there was time. It was the best I could do.

"Come on. Let's get this over with." I wrapped my arm over her shoulders and led her back to our meeting room. We took our seats and I took her hand, lacing our fingers together, offering silent comfort, as we waited for the rest of the officers to settle in.

CHAPTER 28

Sloane

Rip's hand tightened on mine as people shuffled in and took their seats. My stomach twisted as I thought of Rip telling them about what'd happened while he was with The Order. I wasn't sure how they'd take what he had to say.

He'd warned me that he'd let them know everything that'd happened. They'd earned the right to know by getting me and the others out of there. I'd be forever grateful to them, but that didn't mean I wasn't anxious about their reactions.

Everyone looked over at Lockout as he began to speak. This man was a natural born leader. The easiest way to tell was that he led other leaders. Rip and every one of his brothers that I'd met so far were powerful men in their own right. They weren't the weak-willed men who Ethan had surrounded himself with. They were confident and exuded strength, yet they followed a chain of command. One that put Lockout at the top.

After seeing Static lead us out, and Smokehouse defend us while escaping, I knew that any of these men could step up and lead as necessary. The men in The Order were just sheep and bullies. They did as they were told. They could never have done what these men did. They wouldn't have wanted to, either. They'd enjoyed keeping their women and children under their thumbs.

I'd found out last night, from the other women, that Rip was second in command. It didn't surprise me. I wasn't sure how he'd managed to fool Ethan and the others for as long as he had, but I'd begun figuring out right away that he wasn't the usual kind of man Ethan allowed into The Order. That's why finding out that he was also in charge of all these men didn't come as a shock. He'd shown me what a good person he was and how he took care of what was his.

"Welcome home Rip, and welcome to the family, Sloane."

I smiled at Lockout and dipped my head. Back in what had been my home the only time everyone's eyes were on me was when I was doing something they'd considered wrong, or in front of my students. I wasn't sure how to deal with the friendly looks instead of scrutiny. There was hope that feeling that way would fade, but for now I would do my best not to offend anyone or embarrass my husband in his home.

Lockout had continued to talk, but I was only half paying attention. My nerves were dancing around like errant children past their bedtime. It made it hard to listen. At least until Rip started to speak.

His deep voice caught my attention and I watched him as he recounted his time with The Order. Every once in a while I would glance around, then immediately wished I wouldn't have. The men all wore grim expressions and both Seek and Jenny looked horrified.

Would they consider me too damaged from my time living with lunatics to be worth saving? I swallowed hard and pulled my hand from Rip's. I folded them in my lap, staring down at them as I tried to ease the worry and shame. From the corner of my eye I saw him look my way and frown, but he didn't stop.

"They actually *whipped* you?" Seek asked, anger sparking in her tone.

When Rip didn't answer her, I looked up. She was staring directly at me, her expression dark. I swallowed, eyes darting around. Everyone was staring at me. Gathering my courage, I nodded. "Yes."

"Just for the initiation, or…" Jenny let her question trail off.

"Anytime Ethan decided I had sinned," I told her, straightening my shoulders and holding my chin high. The thought of these people pitying or thinking badly of me hurt my heart. I wanted their respect. But I wasn't the kind of woman to cower. I hadn't for Ethan or his people and I wouldn't here either.

Rip's arm dropped over my shoulders and he gave me an understanding smile that looked like it was laced with pride.

It didn't matter how scary this was, I would face it head on and do so with pride and courage.

"I want to kill them. With my bare hands," Seek announced. She was seething mad, but it broke the tension in the room.

The men all laughed and even I chuckled a little. Hush pulled her closer so she was leaning on him. "Sorry, Babe. We already killed 'em as dead as they could be."

Seek grumbled. "Should have ripped their balls off first, then killed them."

A couple of guys shifted in discomfort at the mental imagery as she began detailing how she'd have done it.

"You're savage," Hush said with a laugh. "Knew there was a reason I loved you."

Every fiber of my being sighed, *awww*, at his declaration. "You're so cute."

When they all looked at me, my eyes widened. I hadn't meant to say the last thought aloud. Clearing my throat delicately, I gave them an apologetic smile. "Sorry."

"Don't be," Seek said with a laugh. "And thank you."

"You're cute, too, Angel," Rip said into my ear as he tucked my hair behind it.

My cheeks heated, but pleasure at his compliment built inside me. The man had a way of making me feel special. I hadn't ever seen him do the same with any other woman—though I'd really only seen him around married women—but I liked to think it was because he wanted to see me smile.

The meeting continued on and I listened quietly as the rest of the men told the women how the assault on the compound went. I used the time to watch each person around the table. The women had explained that these men were officers or enforcers and that meant they held higher standing within the club. They'd also explained that as old ladies they didn't deal with club business.

That was fine by me. I didn't want to be involved in another organization, no matter how innocent. I just wanted to be left to live my life on my terms and no one else's. There were going to be rules here, if Rip decided to keep me. I could live by rules as long as they weren't oppressive and didn't come with punishments that'd be permanently scarred onto my body. Compared to that, everything else was easy. A quick glance over at Rip's face showed that he was listening intently to another man who I was sure was named Butcher.

I wasn't always great with remembering names, but was excellent at faces and body language. Another man spoke up, explaining his part in the attack from last night.

Butcher's hazel eyes met mine and I quickly looked down. I hadn't realized I'd been staring for too long. Everyone around the table was relaxed, except for him. I'd been trying to puzzle out why he was so tense. The feel of eyes on me had me glancing up again only to find him still watching me with calculating eyes. He gave me a respectful nod and focused on Lockout.

We'd come to some kind of silent agreement. One that acknowledged that both of us had skeletons in our closets that made us unable to fully relax in a room full of people. Even people that were considered family. It made me feel an instant connection to him and I wondered if there was a chance that we could be friends.

Would Rip allow me to have a man as a friend?

I frowned at the thought. Freedom was still so new, but I wondered if I'd ever be able to live without seeking permission for ordinary, everyday decisions most people made without even thinking? I sure hoped so.

Chairs scraping startled me, and I jumped as everyone stood up and began to leave.

"Hey. You okay?"

I looked over into Rip's worried blue eyes. Nodding, I gave him a small smile. "My mind wandered and the sound startled me. I'm fine."

He nodded slowly. "I know it couldn't have been easy to have to go through all that."

"It's okay. It was my life."

"Was, Angel. Now you get to make something completely different going forward."

We stood and began heading out toward the main area of the club. I froze in the hallway as I saw a little girl dart through the bikers, making her way toward the man called Priest. She and three other little girls wrapped themselves around his legs.

"What's going on?" Rip's hand smoothed over my head, a soothing gesture, but I often wondered if he even realized how much he touched me.

I'd never ask because I wouldn't want him to stop. His touch gave me more comfort than he'd ever know. I hadn't spoken much during that meeting and they hadn't asked me to, but Rip had made the last couple months of life with The Order almost bearable. At one point, I'd thought to myself that as long as I had him by my side that I could possibly even live out the remainder of my life in that messed up place. I was glad we didn't have to, but that's how much he'd changed everything by showing up. One day, I'd tell him how grateful I was to him.

I didn't even realize I was moving until Rip called out my name. As soon as she heard it, Caitlyn whirled around. Her eyes widened and she raced toward me.

Dropping down to my knees, I caught her in my arms. We wrapped around each other in a deep hug. We hadn't known each other very long, but from the moment she and her mother had gotten to the compound I'd taken them under my wing.

Both Rip and Priest squatted down near us, giving each other pointed looks as Caitlyn sobbed in my arms.

"She's okay," I told them. "Hi, Squirrel." I smiled down at her and she returned it with tear stained cheeks.

"I didn't know if I'd see you again," she told me.

"Here I am. And I'm so happy to see that you're okay."

"You know each other from the compound?" Priest asked, even though he knew the answer. He was giving Caitlyn a chance to tell him herself.

A quick look showed that everyone was listening, but they weren't crowding closer. I appreciated that. It was going to be hard for me to be in some of these situations for a while yet.

Caitlyn nodded and took the hand he held out, though she stayed comfortably wrapped in my arms. "Sloane helped me."

"Caitlyn-"

She was already continuing, not paying attention to me. "The mean man told my... Chet that it was his choice whether to-" Her face screwed up as she tried to come up with the word.

Rip's hand went to my back and he scooted closer until I could see his face. His eyes narrowed as he looked at me, but spoke to her. "Initiate you?" he offered.

Caitlyn smiled. "That's it. Initiate me. Chet said yes that he wanted both mommy and me to understand what that place was." She looked up at me and I squeezed her until she gave a happy squeal. "Sloane yelled at the mean man and Chet. Mommy sent me away with some of the other girls."

A muscle flexed in Rip's jaw. "Did you take her initiation?" he asked me in a low voice.

I could feel everyone watching me, but I didn't want the girl to know what we were talking about. It'd been hard enough to keep the girl from realizing what had happened to Sherry, let alone that I'd taken her whipping for her.

"No one would let that happen to a girl that young," I finally said when Rip kept watching me with an expectant gaze.

"Everyone was," he said, clearly angry, "except for you."

"There's an age limit for a reason," I said, my eyes flashed up to his then over to Priest's. "Chet Holden was a fucking asshole."

A huge smile spread over Priest's face. "I agree one hundred percent. What does that mean?" he asked, looking between Rip and I. "That you took her initiation for her?"

Jenny stepped forward and picked Caitlyn up, distracting her and the other girls as they left the room. It wasn't hard to pick up on the fact that this wasn't a conversation to be had in front of children.

"Nothing," I said, rising and brushing off my skirts. Their floors were so neat you could eat a meal off them. It made me wonder who cleaned this place each day. Back at the compound it'd been impossible to keep the desert sand out of my home. I was fussing with my skirts to avoid the question. I hadn't done what I did for recognition.

"It means Ethan gave Chet the option of having his kid whipped along with his wife and he chose to do it. Sloane stepped in and took Caitlyn's whipping so she wouldn't have to endure it," Rip said, his face a mask of cold fury.

I flinched when a low angry murmur started up in the crowd around us. Reaching out, I touched Rip's arm, unsure exactly what he was angry at. Ethan and Chet for sure, but was he also mad at me for bringing more harm to myself? He laid that fear to rest by pulling me into his arms. Resting against his body, I was able to relax again.

"You're fucking kidding me," Priest bit out, looking at Rip as if he'd grown another head.

"No. I'm not. That's how they initiate everyone in there."

"Usually they wait until the children turn eighteen," I told him, "but it hadn't always been that way so Ethan had…experience…whipping children."

Toxic was standing nearby and he scrubbed a hand over his face, his expression a mix of anger and horror. "I agree with Seek. I wish we could go back and fucking kill them all over again."

Butcher watched me with almost a sad look in his eyes. "This must be overwhelming for you. Getting out of there. Being brought here. Having to learn a whole new set of rules to live by." He stepped in closer and stuck his face into mine.

I leaned harder back against Rip, a little uncomfortable at the intensity in the other man's eyes.

Rip's arms tightened around me. "Back off, Butcher."

"I just want Sloane here to know," he said, staring so hard into my eyes I swore he could see my soul, "that no one will ever do what they did to her again. I'll fucking dismember them if they try."

Muscles that had tensed up when he'd gotten close, melted like butter. He was making a declaration of protection for me and it was so incredibly kind. Tears filled my eyes. Before Riptide no one, other than my mother, had cared enough about me to want to protect me. The only people in The Order who had cared had been weaker than me. I'd been their protector. No one ever offered that to me until the day Rip demanded he take a beating for me.

Now his family was piling around me, each of them vowing to keep me safe. There was no holding back the tears.

"You'd have to get to them before me, Butcher," Rip said, but he held out a hand and they shook.

Seek smiled at me and wrapped her arms around me and Rip. "See?" she whispered, making me smile. "This is family. We'll do anything we can to keep you safe and happy."

Eventually, everyone started filing out of the area, until we were left with just Priest and Lockout. Rip still had his arms protectively around me and I was so grateful for the comfort. My back was to his chest and it felt like he was the only thing holding me up after that emotional display of his family accepting me fully.

"Thank you," Priest said, voice gruff. "Caitlyn is my daughter now and I couldn't love her any more than I do. Knowing what you did for her... I'm in your debt."

"There's no debt owed," I told him. "I would never have allowed that to happen to her. I'm so happy to see that she has such a loving family now. Sherry would be happy, too."

Priest gave Rip a questioning look, then leaned forward and kissed my cheek. He left without another word, going upstairs to his family.

Lockout gave me a smile. "You've got an entire motorcycle club full of champions now, Sloane. We're so glad to have you as a part of our family."

He left before I could say anything. Not that I would have voiced my worries about whether Rip would want to remain married to me. That was a conversation that needed to happen between just the two of us.

CHAPTER 29

Riptide

"How are they settling in?" I asked Static. He, Lockout, and I were watching the women bring the boxes of clothes we'd brought over inside.

The three men and more of our brothers were carrying the furniture into the different apartments. In preparation for this very day I'd tasked Static with finding and purchasing an apartment complex in the hopes that we'd be able to save enough people to fill it up. I'd cut him a check before I'd gone into the cult and he hadn't let me down. The money was nothing to me. Not when we needed somewhere safe to keep the families and this would do perfectly. It was a large building, but there were still only thirty apartments so many families had to double up. They didn't seem to mind. There were smiling faces everywhere.

"Good," Static replied. "They're in much better spirits than I would have expected."

"You didn't see where they came from," I told him with a grim look. "Anywhere other than under Ethan's thumb is a good place. Where'd you guys get all the furniture?"

"Friend of mine owns a donation center. She gave us everything she had," Static said. "We'll get the rest from a Goodwill or something."

"Give me a few more days," Lockout told him, "and we'll have the money we need to get them everything they could ever want."

I grinned over at my president. Rat was helping us with that. By the end of the week the money Ethan had been waiting on would be freshly laundered and would then be given to the survivors of The Order. Rat had agreed to continue working with the money on their behalf. There was enough for this group of people to live comfortably on for as long as they needed to. We would help them to get a proper education and find jobs.

"Rat is taking care of all of their legal documents."

"They didn't have any?" Static asked me with a frown.

"They did. Surprisingly, Ethan obtained birth certificates, marriage licenses, the works, for each of them. But I wasn't able to get them out of his office before it burned. They'll need copies of everything if they're going to get driver's licenses and other documents," I told them.

We fell silent, watching the bustle of everyone working. I smiled when I saw Sloane flitting back and forth, a baby in her arms, as she checked in with everyone. She'd begged to come along and I'd told her that she could come see them anytime she wanted. They all needed each other right now, but she was their rock. I had mulled over the idea of letting her stay here with them. I probably should have, for their sake. But there was no way I was letting her out of my sight. It may be selfish, but I wanted her nearby. It was as much for myself as to keep her safe.

As soon as she'd stepped out of the car women had crowded around, hugging her. Kids had gone from quiet and unsure to smiling and laughing. They'd watched her for years, fighting back against Ethan's systematic oppression of everyone around them. She was the sole person who had stood up against him. She'd fought for most of the people in this group, at one point or another. She bore the marks as proof. She found them ugly, but I saw them as badges of her courage, strength, and the depth of her kind heart.

"Well, I better get back to the office," Static said. His lips twisted in a wry grin. "As always, it was fun."

Lockout chuckled and we shook his hand. "We appreciate all your help out there, Brother. Don't be a stranger."

Static lifted his hand in a wave of acknowledgment of Lock's words as he walked away.

"Think he'll reconsider joining?" I asked.

"Oh yeah. Last night just whet his appetite. He's bored to death playing the law-abiding citizen," Lock said with a grin. "He'll be back."

"Speaking of getting back... How's Hell doing?"

"Good," Hush said, walking up from behind us and answering the question himself. "Cranky as fuck, but he's all stitched up. Pissed off that the doc told him he had to stay in bed for the next week."

"Can you make sure he does that?" Lockout asked him.

Hush nodded and stuck his hands in his jeans. "Where's the kid?"

I sighed and rubbed the back of my neck. It'd only taken about twenty minutes to explain to Lock and the others what had happened with Ricochet last night. I was fucking worried about him.

"He's visiting his sister," Lockout said, his face grim. "We need to have a talk with him. Things have gotten too far out of control. I know he wanted to handle shit on his own, but we're past that now. We'll deal with it soon, but for now I thought it might be best for him to be around some family. I reached out to her and asked if she could spend a few days with him. Once we're done getting the women settled, we'll talk with him."

"Think that's for the best," Hush said with a nod. "By the way..."

We looked over at him as he hesitated. His face had turned a dull red. "What's up, Old Man?" I asked.

He glared at me. "Well, I was going to ask you to be my Groomsman, but not now, asshole."

My mouth dropped open. "What the fuck? Seriously? Hell yeah, I'll stand up there with you."

"Nope. You fucked it up."

"Oh come on, Hush," I said as he walked off. He flipped me the bird and both Lockout and I laughed. "Can't believe he didn't ask you," I said.

"Who says he didn't? I get to be the best man." Lockout gave me a smug grin.

"Aw, what the fuck? You?" I complained. "I'd look so much better standing there next to him. Maybe that's why he doesn't want me as his best man. Has to have a less attractive man at his side when he marries his old lady."

"Fuck you," Lockout said with a chuckle.

"When's the wedding?" We walked forward to start helping with the rest of the unloading.

"Four months. Seek wanted to get married before she has the baby, but insisted she needed time to plan."

"I'm happy for the bastard. She's good for him."

"Speaking of women who are good for men…"

I followed Lock's gaze as it landed on Sloane. "Don't start."

"Gonna assume the reason you and Hush were beating on each other this morning had something to do with that?"

Sighing, I shook my head. "Just trying to wrap my head around what the best move is."

"I'd say it's whatever makes you both happy." He paused and gave me a piercing look. "Don't let a sense of obligation or guilt make you lose the best thing that's ever happened to you. You're too fucking smart for that, Rip." With that he walked away, leaving me to stew with his words.

I stepped over and lifted the other end of a couch and helped Toxic haul it up the stairs to a second floor apartment.

Before long, I was sweating and followed my brothers' lead, setting my cut and t-shirt inside one of the cages while I went back to hauling shit.

"What in the actual fuck, Riptide?" I paused and looked over at Toxic. He hadn't picked up the other half of the mattress we'd been preparing to move. He was glaring at me.

"What?" I asked, frowning as more of my brothers came to circle around me.

"What the fuck happened to your back, Rip?" Toxic spat.

I'd forgotten about that. My eyes strayed over and I found Sloane, frozen as she watched us. She gave me a sad smile then turned to speak with another one of the women. She knew it wasn't her place to interfere in this.

"Sorry, forgot all about it," I admitted. "This," I looked at Hush, "is why Sloane lost it this morning. Remember how I told you Ethan whipped people during initiation?"

"You told us," Priest said, "I guess I didn't think about it happening to you."

Butcher shook his head. "Fuck, he did a number on you. No wonder you were so gung ho to kill him."

"That's only a part of it. You were right, Butcher. The shit he and his men did in there was beyond fucked up. Worse, there were times I worried I might be starting to think like them."

Something in his eyes softened. "I get that. Really do. Best thing to remember is you're not like them."

"Despite the shit we do," Toxic told me, "those fuckwads are evil pieces of shit. I wouldn't piss on 'em if they were on fire."

I chuckled and clapped my hand on his shoulder. "Couldn't have said it better myself. Now, can we finish moving the rest of this furniture or do you need to stand around and talk about your feelings, Toxic?"

He snorted and flipped me off, heading back over to his side of the mattress.

I grabbed my end and found ocean blue eyes watching me again. The smile on Sloane's face was a punch in the gut. Lockout's words rang in my head and suddenly I knew he was right. I was too much of an asshole to be altruistic. Sloane already had my entire goddamned heart. The last thing I wanted to do was let her go. I'd just have to figure out a way to make her want to stay, if that was where her head was at.

It took another couple hours before we had all the furniture where it belonged and the trucks returned. Everyone was sweaty and tired, but the happy smiles on the women's faces were worth it. They'd been through enough that we were all eager to make things as easy on them as we could.

We'd all put our shirts and cuts back on and most of the guys had already headed back to the clubhouse. I was waiting for my wife. She'd done one last round to make sure everyone had what they'd needed. She, Seek, and Jenny had taken a few of the other women and gone grocery shopping for everyone.

I was happy to see the women getting along. It would shock me if someone didn't end up liking her. The only people who hadn't had been Ethan and his minions, for obvious reasons.

Sloane walked toward me, her hips swaying. She didn't even realize how incredibly beautiful she was.

"Hey there, Angel." I pulled her into my arms and dropped a kiss on her soft lips. Her cheeks pinkened and it made me wonder if she'd ever stop blushing when I kissed her in public. I secretly hoped not. There wasn't a single thing I didn't love about her. "Have you ever ridden a motorcycle?"

She shook her head and gave my bike a wary look. "It looks dangerous."

I laughed and hugged her close. "You spent your life standing up against a madman. Helped your people flee through the desert in the middle of the night. Went to save four young girls from that same madman...and you're worried about a motorcycle?"

Her smile spread over her face. "Well, when you say it like that it sounds a bit silly."

I kissed her forehead. "Come on." Leading her over, I pulled an extra helmet from beneath my seat. I put it on her, taking my time while adjusting the chin strap, enjoying the way her breathing hitched when the backs of my fingers brushed the delicate skin on her throat.

Her eyes followed me as I climbed on, then I turned and patted the back seat. "This spot belongs to you," I told her. She didn't realize the significance of that at this point, but that seat would always be hers.

She climbed on, tucking her skirts around her legs, then wrapping her arms around me. Her tits were plastered against my back and I couldn't help the grin that broke out when she squealed as I accelerated away from the curb.

"This is amazing!" she yelled into my ear as the wind whipped past us.

I'd had a feeling she'd love it. She'd been deprived of so many things and there wasn't anything as freeing as racing down the highway on the back of a motorcycle.

By the time I pulled into the clubhouse parking lot Sloane had relaxed and had a huge smile on her face.

"Come on, Angel," I told her. It was time for us to prioritize ourselves and have that talk. She'd had a lot thrown at her in the last couple days, but I wanted to set her mind at ease about us. I also wanted to ensure that my angel wanted to stay with me as well.

CHAPTER 30

Sloane

Most everyone living at the clubhouse had disappeared into their apartments after a long day of helping my people move fully into their own homes. I was so grateful to everyone for their help. The fact that they would take the time out of their own weekends to assist strangers just spoke to the kindness of their hearts. Most of them were huge, tattooed, and dangerous looking, yet I'd watched them pick up a child and work with them on their hip or toss them into the air only to catch them safely while the kid laughed up a storm.

I'd never seen men interact with children this way. The men who'd been a part of The Order considered it women's work to entertain the kids and wouldn't have ever babysat, let alone watched their own children.

My heart was so full it was in danger of bursting. There was only one thing left that I wasn't so sure about. If the determined expression on Rip's face was any indication, we were about to hash that out right now.

We stepped into the apartment he lived in. It was a two bedroom, two bath, and spacious enough for the both of us. We sat down on the couch and my heart was racing in my chest. This was the time he was going to tell me that he didn't want a damaged woman who'd been raised in a cult. My jaw set with stubborn pride, I began to make my plans. There was room enough for me at the apartments with the others.

Riptide's fingers gripped my jaw and turned my face toward him. "I can tell you're already overanalyzing this, Angel."

My lips trembled with worry, but then I forced it down. "If you're going to kick me out, I need to start making plans."

His eyes narrowed on me. "That's what you think this is?"

"You didn't come into The Order planning to take a wife."

"That's true."

My heart paused a beat then sank. "It's not fair of me to force you to stay with me."

A smile grew on his face. "Do you really think you could force me to do anything I didn't want to, Sloane?"

"Maybe not physically," I conceded. "I don't need you to feel sorry for me, Rip. I'm a big girl. I can take care of myself."

"That's also very true," he said, sliding the sleeve of my shirt up. When I tried to tug it back down, he gently shoved my hands away. His fingers rubbed against my scars. "These are proof of that fact. You take care of everyone around you, Sloane. Isn't it time you take what *you* want for yourself?"

My eyes dropped away from his. He was the only thing I truly wanted—now that I had my freedom—but how could I ask that of him.

"Look. I think that we're both suffering from the same thing here. At least that's what I'm hoping." He smiled at me when I glanced back up. "I had this idea that you were just gaining your freedom and that you wouldn't want to stay with me because I'd been forced on you."

My brows drew together. "That's not it at all."

He nodded. "Just like I don't want to let you go, even though I hadn't been planning on getting married when I went undercover." He hesitated, then admitted, "I saw you before you even knew I existed." Shock made me mute, unable to ask him any questions in the moment as he explained that he'd seen me the day I'd saved Abigail from a punishment. He and his brothers had been there, hiding, watching "It fucking killed me not to be able to help you. I knew then that you were special. Now you're my wife. You're mine. I love you and I don't want you to go anywhere without me."

I sucked in a breath, searching his expression. There was nothing but honesty and openness there. "You truly want to stay married to me?"

"No."

Shaking my head at the contradiction, I watched in bewilderment as he knelt down between my thighs.

"I want to know if you'll marry me again Sloane Renee Skore? There was no way for me to know, until I met you, what my life was missing. Now that I do, you can't take it away from me." He gave me a charming smile. "The power's in your hands, Angel. You can reduce me to a broken man, or you can agree to be mine forever." I opened my mouth, but he reached up and silenced me with a finger on my lips. "Before you answer, I need you to know that if you say yes, you're agreeing to everything."

"Everything?"

"A lifetime with me. Kids. Maybe a dog. One of those mangy, scroungy looking mutts from the local shelter." He cocked his head as he said the words, then nodded as though that was exactly what he wanted. "I want everything from you. All your love. All your devotion. Your loyalty. And I'll give all of mine in return."

He was wavering before me through the sheen of tears filling my eyes. "Yes," I told him, voice strong even though emotion was ripping through me. "I want all that, too. With you. I promise to give you everything I have." Without waiting for him to say anything, I launched myself down into his arms, tackling him to the ground.

His laughter cracked through the air. "Damn woman. You know

how to take a man down." He rolled until I was underneath him, his hand cradling the back of my head. "Cut me off at the knees the first time I saw you."

I sighed with happiness as he lowered his lips to mine. The kiss was soft and celebratory, but it didn't take long for him to deepen it. Desire crept in and soon we were tearing at each other's clothing.

This time I didn't give him a chance to reduce me to a melted puddle. Each time we'd made love he'd been the one to explore my body. It was my turn.

Tossing a leg over his hips, I pinned him to the ground. His smile told me he was allowing me to hold him down, because I had no hope against him physically.

I shoved his shirt up, running my palms over his smooth tanned muscles. "I never knew a man's body could be like this until you came along."

"Like what, Angel?"

Giving him a pointed look, I tossed my hair back. I'd decided against cutting it. Rip had given me all the freedom I needed and I actually really liked the length. "So…sexy." It still embarrassed me to speak this way, but Rip liked hearing me talk while we were together in the bedroom. He was always whispering his plans and what he wanted to do with me. Always asking me to tell him what I wanted.

Not wanting to give him a chance to keep asking questions, I leaned down and licked his nipple. His groan was deep and masculine. I enjoyed hearing him while he took his pleasure. Something I'd never thought to ever enjoy.

I still wasn't very experienced at sex, but he was teaching me. It was enjoyable for me when he raked his teeth lightly over my nipples, so I did the same to him.

"Fuck, Baby. That feels good."

I lapped at him, my hands exploring his body. When my right hand reached his waistband, I hesitated.

"Take them off."

Focusing on his belt, I took it off, then pulled off his boots. It didn't take long before I had him completely naked. He was lying on the floor, head pillowed on his arms, dick proudly jutting away from his body. He had no shame. Nor should he. I hadn't seen any naked men before him—the porn didn't count since it'd mostly shown the woman—but I couldn't imagine there was a more gorgeous man out there.

"I want-" Licking my lips nervously, I broke off, unsure of how to tell him.

"What?"

"To make you feel good."

"You always make me feel good, Little Devil." There was a wicked look in his eyes, so I was pretty sure he knew what I was asking. As usual he was going to make me say the words.

"I want to make you feel the way you do for me."

"When I eat your pussy?"

My face went up in flames. The vocabulary he was exposing me to was raunchy and yet sexy at the same time. I nodded my head.

"You want to suck my cock? Wrap those pretty little lips around it and swallow it?"

I blinked. That didn't sound right. Is that what women did for men? "I...don't know."

He chuckled. "That's what it's called, Baby. Come here." He got up and sat on the couch, throwing a little pillow between his feet.

I stood and walked over, settling with my knees on the pillow. "Will you help me?" It was embarrassing to have to ask him to teach me how to do this, but the heat flaring there in his eyes told me he didn't mind.

"Fuck yeah, I will. Use your tongue and lick me." His voice had gone husky and deep. I knew it was an indication of how turned on he was.

Lowering my head, I licked the head of his dick. He'd laughed at me when I'd called it a penis once before and asked me to refer to it as his cock, or dick. He'd given me a wide grin and added, "Or Big Derek."

It'd taken me a few minutes to understand the reference. I didn't think I'd be calling it that last thing anytime soon. His joking around had broken the awkwardness I'd been feeling at the time. He was really good at relaxing the mood.

"Wrap your lips around my cock and suck on it," he directed. His head dropped back onto the couch and his eyes closed as I did what he asked. "Fuck, Baby. Your mouth feels so damn good."

I knew I liked it when he…ate my pussy—it was hard to even think the words without blushing—so I could only imagine how much he was enjoying this.

"Move your mouth up and down along the shaft." He groaned, then stiffened. "Watch the teeth, Angel. Some men like that, but I'm less into pain than pleasure."

I wrapped my lips over my teeth so I wouldn't accidentally graze him as I bobbed up and down on his dick. The mushroom shaped head hit the back of my throat when I got a little too ambitious and I pulled back, gagging.

Rip smiled down at me. "We'll get you deep throating one of these days, no need to do it on your first day sucking cock."

I had no idea what he was talking about, but he'd stood up and lifted me into his arms. He carried me into the bedroom and laid me down before crawling between my thighs. "I wasn't finished," I told him. He usually kept going until I was orgasming.

"Trust me, Baby, I'll come all over that tongue one of these days, but if I do it today then the fun is over. I want to fuck you." He quit arguing at that point and reduced me to nothing but moans using his tongue and fingers.

I hadn't realized men could only come once. Well, I hadn't known —before him—that I could come more than once. Or what coming was. The thoughts fractured as he forced my orgasm on me. I wasn't going to complain. My body quaked from the pleasure as he crawled over me.

He was pressing into me before I had a chance to catch my breath. I locked my heels behind his back, holding him close to me. It was amazing how connected I felt to him when we were pressed together, him invading my body. I never wanted it to end. We could just stay here together, forever.

He began moving and suddenly I was wishing it would end. The friction of his dick thrusting inside of me was building me back up. I was frantic, nails digging into his back as I begged him to make me come.

"That's it. What a good fucking girl. Beg me. Fuck me back. Come all over my cock."

My breath was ripped away as I followed his command and broke apart again.

He let out a tormented sound as my pussy rippled around his length. "Fuck, Sloane. I can't wait to marry you." He started thrusting harder. "Again. To fuck you every day. To make you mine in every way."

His groan was low and tormented as he thrust into me one last time and held still. His chest was heaving as he enjoyed his own orgasm. I watched the exquisite agony pass over his face, happy I could give that to him. Even happier he did it for me. It wasn't going to be hard to be married to this man.

"I love you," I told him, brushing my lips over his as he lowered down.

"I love you, too, Sloane," he said, then rested his head between my breasts.

We'd hardly caught our breath, when Rip hopped up to his feet. I watched him curiously as he searched around for his clothes.

"Guess I should have started with this," he said, pulling a box from the inside of his cut.

I sat up, stretching languid muscles. It hadn't taken him very long to convince me that he not only didn't mind my scars, but that he found them beautiful in their own way.

They're a part of you and I love you, is how he'd explained it. That plus him appreciating that each mark was a time where I'd stood up to Ethan, taking my life in my hands—usually in service of another—made them badges of honor in his eyes. It made my heart melt into a pile of goo. It was hard to feel self-conscious about them in his presence.

I gasped as Rip walked back over and flipped the top on the box. A huge diamond winked at me, reflecting the light. The white gold band on either side of the center stone was twisted into a representation of a dolphin.

"I hope you like it," he said, sitting back down beside me. "I wanted to put a little bit of me into it and the ocean is like a second home for me."

"I love it," I told him, awe filling my tone. "I've never seen the ocean, but I swear I've been dreaming of it my entire life." I looked at it in wonder. "We didn't have anything other than basic rings, no other real jewelry in The Order."

He looked startled. I wasn't sure which piece of information prompted the response, but he pulled me into his arms then pulled the bare gold band off my finger, replacing it with his. "Did you want to keep these?" he asked, pulling his band off.

"No," I told him firmly. "I don't want anything Ethan gave us. I'll get you my own ring as soon as I get a job."

He stilled behind me. "You can get a job if you really want to, Angel, but I'd rather you didn't."

I turned in his arms and stared up into his handsome face. "Why not?"

"The thought of letting you out of my sight for eight to twelve hours a day…" His throat bobbed as he swallowed. "It kind of makes me feel overly protective. I'll do my best to keep it under control, but I can't guarantee anything."

"How am I supposed to support myself if I don't get a job?"

He snorted then tugged me closer, until our bodies were pressed as close as they could be. "I'll support you. What's mine is yours and though I don't tell many people this, I have more than enough."

Worry infused me. It wasn't that I didn't want my husband to take care of me. It was just hard.

"I get it," he said, making me wonder if I'd said any of my fears aloud. "You just came from a place where everything was forced on you. You had no rights to exercise your own choices. But I'm promising you now, you're free to make them with me. I may not always like them, but I'll do my best to respect them."

I turned in his arms, my thighs straddling his and kissed him. "Thank you." Somehow he'd managed to understand exactly how I felt, what I needed. "I'm not in a hurry to get a job. If something finds me, speaks to me, then maybe I'll pursue it."

He nodded and pulled my head down again for another searing kiss. "I can live with that."

"I have a favor to ask."

"What's that, Angel?"

"I was serious when I said I didn't want to keep anything Ethan gave." I motioned to the clothes that were spread on the ground from where we'd thrown them. "Can I buy some new clothes?"

"Absolutely. I'll take you shopping tomorrow. I'll also work on getting you added to my accounts as soon as Rat finishes with all the documents. He's making you a driver's license as well."

My eyes widened. "But I don't know how to drive."

"Don't worry, I'll teach you."

I squealed as he stood with me in his arms. "What are you doing? Put me down!"

"Never," he said with a salacious grin. "We're going to bed, Angel, so we can keep celebrating."

I buried my face in his neck, hiding my smile from him. How was it possible that this gorgeous, perfect man had infiltrated my life and stolen my heart? I promised both of us, silently, that I'd do anything it took to keep him happy and well-loved for the entirety of our lives.

CHAPTER 31

Riptide

"I don't know about this one," Sloane said, stepping out of a dressing room. She tugged on the short sleeves of the t-shirt, trying to cover a large scar on her bicep. It was old and white, but still visible. Smaller scars crisscrossed her arms down to her wrists, where thick raised skin encircled both.

Standing, I went to her and rubbed my thumbs over both of her wrists. One day I was going to have her explain why she'd received each mark. When she was ready. "It's up to you, but I think it looks great on you."

It was a plain maroon shirt that fell just below the waist of the jeans she had on. Nothing flashy or ostentatious—that's not something my angel would choose—but it made her eyes pop and complemented her skin tone. When I'd started to go toward the dresses she'd stopped me and marched over to this area. This was how the other old ladies tended to dress on any given day, though they'd occasionally wear dresses as well.

I smiled at her desire to fit in with the others. She had no idea she was already wrapping them around her finger. I was pretty sure Butcher was half in love with her already. Not that I was worried he'd try anything. It was more of the kind of love I'd seen him show his sisters.

No one would expect the crazy bastard to have a soft spot for anyone, but once you saw him with his sisters you knew there was a heart buried somewhere in that demented chest of his. Despite the trouble he liked to dig up, he was fucking loyal to the core to his family. We were his family so he treated us as such. He was a damn fine brother to have. Not to mention a fucking menace on the battlefield. It eased the worry inside of me that she had him—and by default, Toxic—looking out for her when I wasn't able to.

"Once you're done, I have a surprise for you," I told her.

She looked up at me, surprise and pleasure flashing over her face. "I'm done," she insisted. She returned to the dressing room and held out two pairs of jeans, four t-shirts, and a pair of sneakers. We'd already gone lingerie shopping—pulling her into the dressing room and fucking her against the mirror had been an enjoyable part of the experience—so she was set there.

My eyes narrowed on her items. "Sloane." I softened my voice for the next part because worry flashed over her face. "You need more than this. I'll bring you back another day and we'll keep adding to your collection," I promised her. "I'd stay longer today and have you get more, but then we'll be late."

"I don't need more," she insisted.

"Soon enough you'll learn that needing more and wanting more are basically the same," I told her with a chuckle. "The other women will help you spend some of your money, too."

I led her to the checkout counter and handed over my credit card. She watched with a frown on her face as it was swiped and I signed the sales slip.

As we walked away with her items in a bag, except the jeans and maroon shirt she was still wearing, she asked, "That's all it takes to buy things here?"

I explained credit and debit cards as we drove across the city. Pulling into a driveway, I shut off the engine.

"It feels like there's so much to learn."

"You'll get there," I told her.

She looked through the windshield up at the house. "Where are we?"

"You'll see." I was a bit nervous at what her reaction was going to be, but I didn't want to ruin the surprise either. If I knew my angel, I had a feeling this was about to go really well.

We got out of the car and I wrapped my arm around her shoulders. I shoved open the door to the house and called out, "Anyone home?"

It only took a few seconds before the horde descended. I stepped backward, leaving Sloane to fend off my family on her own.

"Derek! You're home!" My mother froze in the doorway that led to the kitchen as she spotted us. Her hands came together at her chest. "Oh my God, is this Sloane?"

My wife cast a wide-eyed worried look at me over her shoulder. I nodded encouragingly to her. "It is. Sloane, this is my mom, Peggy. My father, Dirk, and my sisters, Sally, Stacy, and Stephanie. I'll let them introduce their husbands and minions." Between the three of them my sisters had seven kids.

One of Stephanie's triplets flung himself into my arms. I picked him up and scowled into his face. "How have you gotten bigger in only a few months, Seth?"

He giggled and shook his head at me like I was the biggest disappointment. "I'm not Seth, Uncle Rip. I'm Sawyer."

I frowned at him. "Are you sure? I'm pretty sure that's Sawyer." I pointed at one of his brothers.

He giggled again. "That's Sam. You're really bad at this, Uncle Rip."

Tickling him mercilessly, I cast a glance over and grinned when I saw my mother hugging Sloane close. They were talking together as they embraced. My family had been shocked when I'd called and told them that I was home and had come back with a wife. It'd pacified my mom when I told her we were getting remarried and she'd be invited to that ceremony.

Both Dad and Mom had known that I was going to infiltrate the cult. I'd cleared it with Lockout prior to going undercover within The Order. If I'd been killed I hadn't wanted them not knowing why. But we'd kept it from my sisters. They'd only known that I was off on club business.

Mom came over and hugged me close as my sisters took their turns welcoming Sloane to the family. "She's wonderful, Derek."

"Thanks, Mom. I knew you'd love her."

"How did you manage to get a woman so pretty and sweet?" Dad asked with a shit-eating grin on his face.

I chuckled and responded, "It was an arranged marriage."

Dad crowed and slapped his leg as he laughed. "That's the only way a sorry shit like you would manage it."

"Fuck off," I said, joining in his laughter.

He grabbed onto me as soon as Mom let go and put me into a headlock.

"You're asking for it," I growled, fighting back against him. I struggled hard enough not to hurt Dad's ego, but not so much I injured him. The last thing I needed was his back flaring up on him. Mom would ream both our asses if we allowed that to happen.

"You're not strong enough to whip your old man," Dad said laughing, rubbing his knuckles painfully against my scalp.

"No horseplay in the house," Mom called out.

It was too late. Dad dragged me out the back door to the backyard, followed by my three brothers-in-law, and six nephews as everyone started up play fights with each other.

Sloane's mouth was hanging open as she, my mother, sisters, and single niece watched from the sliding glass door. "Do they do this a lot?" she asked.

"Yes," was the resounding response. "Come on," Mom told her. "Let's let the men 'bond' while we go catch up with some drinks in the kitchen.

Dad still had his arm slung around my shoulders, but we weren't struggling against each other anymore. "Good to have you home, Son."

"Thanks, Dad."

"Everything go okay undercover?" His worried blue eyes met mine.

"There were a few hiccups, but nothing I didn't handle." At some point I'd have to tell him and Mom about my new scars. I didn't want them to be surprised by them like my brothers had been. But that was a conversation for another day.

"The scars on your wife-"

"She's sensitive about them," I told Dad, giving him a pointed look.

"Wouldn't dream of saying a thing about them…to her. They do that to her in there?"

"Yeah," I said with a sigh. "Her own fucking father gave her most of them. He was the cult leader."

"That's fucked up."

"Agreed."

"She must be pretty wary of men."

"Believe it or not, she isn't." I smiled with pride. "She's got a hell of an instinct about people and she trusts her gut. Took to my brothers instantly."

"Good. We'll do our best to help heal any internal scars. She's a part of our family now."

I tossed my arm over his shoulders. My dad was all about family. Coming from an MC background himself had made him loyal to a fault. "Damn right she is." We walked back inside and paused in the doorway to the kitchen.

Sloane was smiling and talking with the others, her arms behind her back, fingers laced together to keep them in position. Her laughter floated through the air and I couldn't help but smile.

I just wished I could make her understand that no one was judging her for those scars on her arms. Even if my family didn't know why she had them—each one had been earned protecting others—they still wouldn't hold them against her.

Soon enough everyone had piled into the kitchen. We were standing around talking, eating lunch, and enjoying each other's company. I'd considered having Sloane meet only my parents at first, but this way my sisters and their families could take some of the pressure off her. She was chatting easily with everyone around her and it made the knot of nervousness in my gut loosen with each hour.

"Before you go," Dad said, a few hours later. "I just wanted to officially welcome you to our family." He stepped forward and placed a kiss on Sloane's cheek.

"What the hell?" Nick asked. "We never got a kiss for joining the family." My other brothers-in-law nodded in agreement, mock disappointment written all over their faces.

"None of you are as pretty as she is," Dad replied with a laugh. That got everyone going.

Mom stepped forward and hugged Sloane. "I hope that you'll consider our family yours. We're here for you, no matter what. Even when our son is being a dipshit."

Sloane barked out a laugh, then covered her mouth looking horrified.

"Don't worry, Angel," I told her, "that's part of being in this family, learning to take insults."

"You give as good as you get," Stephanie told me, hands on her hips.

"True."

Sloane smiled at Mom. "Thank you so much for including me. I'm thrilled to be joining your family."

We said our goodbyes and headed back to the clubhouse. Glancing over at her, I frowned when I saw the sadness on her face. "What's wrong, Sloane?"

She gave me a soft smile. "Nothing. Really. It's just…that's what a family should be like."

"It is."

"What I had wasn't anything close to that. Maybe if my mom had lived…"

Reaching over, I squeezed her hand. "Well, now you have it. Whether you want it or not," I joked.

She held my hand the entire way back, and stared quietly out the window. I didn't force her to talk. There were a lot of things she was going to have to work through. I knew enough to give her space to do that.

CHAPTER 32

Riptide

A few days later, we were all standing around, talking and laughing with our MC family. Lockout had planned a barbecue. There wasn't anything quite like having everyone here and spending time with them all. The only one missing was Ricochet. Something that wasn't lost on us.

Word had gotten around that I'd proposed to Sloane, so the women were admiring her ring. As soon as they dropped her hand, she resumed her way of standing that hid her arms. She refused to cover them up, but it was very clear to me that she was still uncomfortable.

Sighing, I took a drink from my beer. I wasn't sure how to help her over this hurdle.

"Why's she standing like that?" Butcher asked.

I glanced over at him, then looked back at my wife. "She's self-conscious of the scars on her arms."

He took a thoughtful pull from his own beer bottle, handed it to Toxic, turned and left.

"Where the hell's he going?" I asked.

Toxic shrugged and started drinking from both bottles in his hands. "Who knows."

"Toxic…" I asked, eyeing Butcher's back as he left. What I was about to ask felt wrong. I knew Butcher. Knew how he was, so I was sure that he didn't have eyes for my woman, but still…

"She's incredibly kind and sweet," Toxic told me, understanding there in his eyes. We all knew each other so well I didn't even have to ask my question aloud. He already knew. "But it's more than that for him. There were so many innocent women and children he wasn't able to save during his time with his task force. There were, well, some that had to be put down. Much the way Ricochet did. Butcher didn't have many wins on that task force." Toxic shrugged. "Sloane might be the first real victory. She's kind of become the embodiment of those he couldn't save. Despite everything that's happened to her, she is still kind to people. She's smart. Brave. He's drawn to her." He took a swig from the bottle then realized what he'd said and choked on the beer. "Not drawn like that," he wheezed.

"I know that," I told him, pounding him on the back harder than I needed to. "I just needed to understand why there seemed to be this connection for him. It makes perfect sense."

"If it bothers you, he'd gladly stay away."

"I hope he—and you—won't. She can use all the friends she can get." I told him. With that, I walked away. Hearing it from Toxic was as good as hearing it from Butcher himself. I was a possessive man, and even though I knew, deep down, that my brother would never feel that way toward my wife, I'd needed to hear it. Call me a selfish piece of shit. I needed to know she was mine and that I could trust her with the others. Now I did.

Hellfire looked up from where he was sitting in a camp chair. "Rip."

"How you feeling, Brother?"

"Fine. Ready to get back to work."

"I'm sure you are," I told him with a chuckle. None of us did well when we were injured or sick. We weren't used to being laid up.

"Have you spoken with Ricochet?" he asked, worry knitting his brows together.

"Lock has. He's spending time with his sister and her kids. We're all going to have a talk with him once he gets back. We're going to figure out how to set him straight."

Hellfire nodded, then a grin broke out on his face. "If it isn't the little mama."

I looked over and smiled as Seek came up. She sat down next to him and patted her still flat stomach. "I don't even feel pregnant," she said with a grimace.

"We'll check back in a few months," I told her with a laugh. "See how you feel then."

She stuck her tongue out at me. "Hopefully it'll be smooth sailing the whole time."

"Hopefully," I agreed.

"Where did Butcher disappear to?" she asked, jerking her head.

We looked over and watched him come back into view. He'd been gone for about twenty minutes. "Not sure."

He was carrying something in his hand. As he passed, Toxic fell into step beside him. The men approached Sloane and Butcher thrust whatever he was holding at her.

"What's that?" Seek asked, voicing my own question.

All three of us got up and headed over just in time to hear Sloane's confused question. "Thank you, Butcher...but what are they?"

I grinned when I saw what she was holding. "Why the fuck didn't I think of that?" I asked in a low voice. Seek gave me a confused look.

Butcher took the pieces of material back from Sloane. "May I touch you?" he asked in a gruff voice, motioning to her arms.

Sloane's eyes darted to me, asking permission. She didn't need it, but I nodded anyway. She held out her arm, nerves causing her to shake a little.

Butcher was overly gentle as he slid the stretchy cloth over her arm. He did the same with the second and then stopped to admire his handy work.

Sloane stared down at her arms in shock and delight. Butcher had found some of the fabric sleeves that go over your arms, making it look like a sleeve of tattoos. He'd found a pair that had beautiful butterflies and flowers all over them. They suited Sloane.

She looked up at him and swallowed hard, tears forming in her eyes. With these pieces of fabric on, she could still wear the clothes she wanted to, but no longer had to worry about anyone staring at her scars. For all they knew she had full sleeve tattoos that went from her wrists, all the way up her arms until they disappeared under her shirt.

"Thank you," she told him, her voice wavering. Then she did something that had all of us biting back laughter. She hugged Butcher.

The stunned look on his face said he didn't know quite what to do with her gesture. He glanced over at me and again, I nodded. Slowly his arms wrapped around her and he hugged her back.

Their reactions to each other made me feel like an asshole for having to ask about Butcher's intentions, even if it was just to understand. Toxic gave me an understanding glance.

There'd been no need for me to worry. Butcher would never betray one of us in that way. And Sloane wouldn't do that to me either. She already knew she was mine. I planned on proving it to her for the rest of our lives.

They broke apart and I swear Butcher was blushing, but everyone wandered away, giving us space.

"Thank you," I told him, shaking his hand. "I never even considered getting those for her. They're the perfect solution."

"At least until she wants to get the real thing," Toxic said in agreement.

The idea of my wife getting full sleeves of tattoos on both arms was intriguing. My dick hardened beneath my jeans at the thought. I was on board, if she wanted to. Mostly, I just wanted her to see her scars the way that I did. That was a hard ask since she'd borne the pain and humiliation of receiving each of them.

Butcher grabbed his beer out of Toxic's hand, then scowled at the empty bottle. He snagged the second one and then muttered, "You finished both of them? Fucking asshole." The two strode away, heading toward the cooler of beers, arguing about what it meant to leave a man's beer in another man's care.

Sloane laughed and shook her head. "They're funny."

"They're something alright," I admitted. "Do you like them?" I asked, motioning to her arms.

"I do! They're pretty." She smiled at me and brushed a hand over the sleeves. "I-" She hesitated, looking nervous.

"What is it, Angel?"

"I don't know what the rules are here?"

"Rules for what?"

"Am I allowed to be friends with other men?" She peeked up at me through her lashes, searching for any sign of anger on my part.

Anything she offered my brothers was going to be pure friendship. I'd known that from the beginning. That was why I'd needed to double check Butcher's intentions. Even though I'd been mostly sure prior to talking to Toxic, I had to find out. That's why the guilt of questioning him only lasted for mere moments. Neither Butcher, nor Toxic, would ever hold that against me.

"They're your family," I told her. "You're welcome to be friends with any of my MC brothers, or my brothers-in-law." I swallowed some beer before I told her the next part. "I can't tell you who you can or can't be friends with, Angel, but I'm not the kind of man who shares well."

Her eyes flashed fully up to mine, a knitted brow accompanying her confused look. "I'm not sure what you mean."

"Any man who isn't our family that you become friends with is going to end up getting the shit kicked out of him."

Her mouth dropped open, forming a little 'o'. "Why?"

"Because I know what men want," I growled at her, tugging her body against mine. "And they won't get it from you. You're *mine*. They can fuck off and find another friend."

She bit the insides of her lips, making my eyes narrow on her. She was doing her best to hold back either a grin or laughter. "Are you mad at some theoretical man before I've even met him?"

"There'll be no meeting him. Also, yes."

This time she did laugh, ignoring the glower I gave her. "Okay, okay," she said between peals of laughter. "I won't have any male friends except family members. Better?"

I gave a satisfied hum of a sound, then bent my head, lips pressing to her neck. "Better."

"Rip," she said, sounding embarrassed.

No one within The Order had given public displays of affection. I wasn't sure if that was because it'd been against the rules—I hadn't really learned all of Ethan's stupid laws—or if it was because there really wasn't any affection to be had. Either way, she'd get used to it here.

Both of my arms wrapped around her. "What?" I asked, tongue stroking her soft skin.

"There are people around." She sounded so scandalized, I couldn't help but grin.

"They can look somewhere else then."

"Actually, I had something I wanted to talk to you about." Now she sounded nervous.

The tone made my muscles tense. I looked up at her. "What's that?"

"Um...I wanted to know if I could spend a few days this week over at the apartments?" She wasn't struggling to get out of my arms, but she was brushing her hand over my arm. It was more of a fidgeting motion than anything.

She knew I had no problem with her spending time with her people. Which made me wonder what this was. "Why?"

"A few of the women have asked me to speak with their children. They're having a hard time coping." She wouldn't meet my eyes. "I'm not sure I'm the best one to help them, but their mothers can't seem to get the kids to talk to them."

All the tension bled out of me. She wasn't nervous to tell me. She was nervous that she'd somehow fail the children if she took on this task. "I think that's a great idea."

"You do?" Those beautiful ocean blue eyes were watching me, full of hope and love.

"I do. I'm sure Jenny would be willing to go and help you, too. She's probably had some training and knows how to talk to kids. I'm sure there are more than a few of the women who would benefit from speaking to you as well. Maybe if you like it," I said, thinking out loud, "you could take some courses at Pima Community College or the U of A and become a certified counselor."

She stood there, blinking up at me, tears filling her eyes instead of responding. It made me worry that I'd said something wrong. "Only if you want to, of course."

"I think I would," she told me in a choked voice.

"It would be the perfect thing for you," I offered, a bit hesitant since she seemed so upset. "You're built to help others. It's ingrained in who you are. I'm sure you got that from your mother-"

That did it. She was suddenly pressed against my chest, sobbing. My arms tightened around her and I glanced over and found both Butcher and Toxic scowling at me. I shrugged at them, as if their opinion mattered. They were experts at making women cry. They continued to stand close by, studying us.

Great. My wife has her own pair of guard dogs.

"Sloane. Why are you crying?"

"You've made me so happy!" The words were in direct conflict with her sobs as she spoke them.

I'd never fully understand women or their ability to cry when they were happy. The last time I'd cried was when I was ten and I broke my fucking leg skateboarding. Well, and when my dog died, but that doesn't count. Clearing my throat, I rubbed a soothing hand over her back until the sobs had died down to sniffles.

"Can you help me get into school?" There was a single tear drop hanging off her lower lashes on her right eye.

Wiping it away, I looked down into her sweet face. "You can have anything and everything you want," I vowed, meaning it with every fiber of my being.

"Anything?" she breathed, looking astonished.

"Anything within my power to give you."

She smiled at me. "I want to go to college."

"Done. I'll have Rat cook up some transcripts for you so it's easy for us to enroll you."

"And I want babies."

I froze. Those words were like a punch to the solar plexus. Mostly because I'd finally decided that was what I wanted, too. A little girl with her looks and charm. A son who I could pass on my love of bikes and surfing to. Hell, I'd do the same with my daughter.

A devilish grin spread over my face. "You want babies?"

"Yes," she answered, hesitating at the look on my face.

"That's no problem."

She squealed as I dipped and flung her up and over my shoulder. "Rip! Put me down," she shouted, laughter punctuating each word.

"Nope."

"Where the hell are you two goin'?" Hush bellowed from across the grassy area we meticulously maintained throughout the year. It was the perfect place for kids to play, though it was a bitch to keep alive in the hot summers.

"Don't you dare," she gasped.

I did it anyway. "My wife wants babies," I shouted back. Sloane groaned and shifted. I was positive she was covering her face. "So we're off to make babies."

Lockout, Hush, and the others all chuckled while the women giggled.

"You're in so much trouble," Sloane grumbled.

"Am I?" I asked, playfully slapping her ass.

She shrieked and hit my back in retaliation. "You can't tell everyone that!"

"Why?"

"Because they're going to know what we're doing," she huffed.

"Angel, they already know what we're doing. What we've been doing," I told her. "Speaking of, I'm surprised you're not already knocked up considering how many times we fucked before."

She gasped at my language, making me chuckle. I'd watered down the cussing while I'd been inside The Order. She was getting the full view of the man her husband was, now that we were home. She never complained, though I knew I shocked her often.

She cleared her throat, but didn't speak. Jostling her on my shoulder, I silently prompted her to speak.

"Fine," she mumbled. "There was a tea I made for the women when they didn't want to get pregnant. It wasn't perfect, but it made it harder to get pregnant."

My stride slowed as I thought about that. "Why did any of them have kids with those guys then?"

"It would be too suspicious if none of us ever fell pregnant," she admitted, "but also, the women often wanted their babies. They wanted a being that would actually love them."

"Makes sense," I replied. Sadness swept over me as I thought about that. They'd been so desperate for love and affection that they'd gotten pregnant even in those horrific circumstances. I couldn't blame them. Certainly wouldn't judge them for their choices.

Once we'd reached the clubhouse, I swung Sloane down and pressed her against the building. Cupping her cheeks in my hands, I kissed her. "Anything you want. Forever," I promised her.

"The thing I want the most..." she said once I stopped kissing her, "is you."

"That, you'll always have."

CHAPTER 33

Sloane

*L*aughing, I got out of the car along with the other old ladies and Kit. They'd become some of my best friends over the last month and a half. I was adjusting to life outside of The Order and helping my people to reach the same level of peace within their own lives.

This new world was strange for us, but I had so many people who were willing to help me. That loved me. The women who were married or dating the men of the motorcycle club. The men themselves. Rip's family. All of them had stepped up and I'd gone from alone—except for a psycho father who would as soon kill me as look at me—to a huge family who would do anything to make me happy. It was an overwhelming amount of support. I don't know what I did to deserve it, but I was eternally grateful for it.

I had a man—one who was going to be my husband, again, in a little over a week—who would die for me. How had I gotten this lucky? Was this karma finally paying me back after all these years?

The things I'd done inside The Order I'd never done with the hope of gaining anything. But that didn't mean that I wasn't coming to realize that I'd helped so many. This family of mine. My husband. They were absolutely rewards in my eyes.

I had everything I'd ever wanted. Everything. I just hadn't had a chance to tell Rip the good news yet. I cast an affectionate look at Seek, who was beginning to round out in her pregnancy. She was beautiful and glowing. Knowing I was pregnant with Rip's baby made me so happy I wanted to shout it from the rooftops. I'd found out early this morning, but had a full day planned with the girls and Rip's mom and sisters. I'd figured I'd better keep the news to myself until I could tell him. I'd been dreaming about babies all day, though. Since we both had brown hair—though his was a shade lighter than mine—and blue eyes, there wasn't much guesswork as to what the baby might look like.

Laughter and screaming hit us as soon as we rounded the corner. My mouth dropped open—so did all the other women's—and we all froze at the melee that was happening in front of us.

Priest's daughters, Gabby, Taylor, Cassie, and Caitlyn were running around the yard area, chasing Butcher and Toxic. At first glance I'd thought it was sweet that the men were playing with the girls. Then I'd realized what was happening.

"Butcher!" I gasped in horror.

He stumbled to a stop in front of me, looking sheepish. At least until something whizzed past him. His head snapped to the side and he pinned Cassie with a glare. "Hey! No shooting while I'm talking."

They were playing laser tag—something Rip and the others had introduced me to a few weeks ago—only instead of using lasers they were using...roman candles. They were shooting fireworks at each other!

"Your fault you stopped, Uncle Butcher," she sang out. A blue fire ball shot out from the end of her candle, pegging Butcher in the leg. Her giggles trailed behind her as she raced away.

"The game is paused," Butcher roared at them, rubbing his leg and muttering. All the little girls froze. "You'd think I wouldn't have to fucking say it," he told them.

All four of the girls wore devilish grins. None of them were appalled at his language or gruff tone. They knew him too well for that. He was completely wrapped around their fingers. Even I had caught onto his game. He liked to pretend that he didn't like kids, that babies scared him—okay, that last one might actually be true since he ran from Tory's youngest each time she brought the baby around—but he was so good with them. At least for Butcher he was.

"Butcher. Language," I told him with a sigh. I'd already resigned myself to the fact that raising children here meant they were going to have colorful language. These men couldn't go more than a few sentences without cursing. But they were loyal, brave, and loved their family. My children would be cared for, protected, and they'd grow up to be as fierce as their father and 'uncles'. I loved the idea of that. What I didn't love, but accepted, was that they would all be explosives experts.

"What the fuck is going on here?" Priest asked, eyeing his daughters as he walked out the door.

"You're the one who left Butcher and Toxic in charge of them," Seek pointed out. She'd gone and gotten all the guys. Now they piled around, grinning as they saw what was happening. "This is on you."

The girls took that opportunity to nail Toxic. He yelped and shook at his clothes as four flares shot out and hit him. "He said the game is paused, you fucking heathens!" he bellowed.

The girls hid their laughter behind their hands, trying to look innocent. The smoking firework sticks they held gave them away.

Toxic pinned Priest with a dark look. "Those girls are bloodthirsty."

"Please tell me you're not fucking shooting my kids with fireworks?" Priest growled at the other men. His tired tone told me this was not an unexpected development.

"Oh don't get your panties in a fucking bunch," Toxic muttered, shaking his cut again to make sure there were no embers inside it.

"Butcher's so drunk he's mostly hitting himself." Toxic pointed with his Roman Candle. "Look, he's holding the damn thing backward."

It was true. The opening to his firework was pointing toward the man. The burn marks on the front of his shirt were a testament to this.

"Keeps hitting himself in the gut, but your little sharpshooters here are keeping us so damn busy avoiding their shots he hadn't noticed yet. Little shits can run and shoot at the same time. Who taught them how to serpentine so well?"

Toxic let out a loud laugh as Butcher peered blearily down at his Roman Candle. "Well why the fuck didn't you say something?" he muttered, turning it around.

I knew for a fact that there was no way either man would hit one of those little girls. Not on purpose, and something else I'd learned from these men was that they didn't do anything by accident. They were letting the girls hit them with fireworks with no intention of ever retaliating.

Those things had to hurt, though I wouldn't know from experience. "Come on ladies," I told the women. We'd just come from dropping off Rip's mom and sisters after a day of wedding dress shopping.

We all turned to go inside when something screamed past me. I gasped as the firework kept going then burst about twenty feet in front of me where it exploded in a rush of color. Spinning around, I stared open-mouthed at Riptide. "Did you just shoot that at me?"

"No," he said, slowly hiding the candle behind his back. Another fireball erupted from it, straight into the air. His grin was huge and what he would reference as shit-eating.

It was a gross phrase if you asked me, but it fit the moment. I put my hands on my hips. "Derek Samuel Skore," I told him in my most authoritative tone. A lot had changed in the last month and a half, including me. It was easy to be brave when you knew the people surrounding you would never harm a hair on your head. I'd seen Rip shoot plenty of times now. The man didn't miss. He hadn't been trying to actually hit me or he would have. Which he'd never do and we both knew it. "If you hit me with that and harm our baby, I'm going to throttle you."

Everyone blinked at me as that news settled in. I'd planned to tell him alone first, but something told me he'd love that I made the announcement this way.

Rip let out a whoop of excitement and rushed toward me. He threw the firework on the ground, the last shots skipped across the parking lot, making Butcher and Toxic jump and run as they zipped past their feet. He lifted me into the air, his biceps bulging as he did. "Seriously?" he asked, looking so hopeful it almost made me cry.

"It's true," I told him, holding onto his shoulders as he spun me around. Happy faces flashed by, then he was crushing me in a hug so tight I worried I might pop.

"We're going to be pregnant together?" Seek asked, shoving her way into our embrace, then giving me her own hug.

Rip chuckled and backed up so my friends could embrace me. "Guess I only get half a second to hug my wife," he complained, rubbing the scruff that was growing in on his jaw.

None of the women were listening. They were all chattering happily, then the men started passing me around for hugs. Eventually, I was given back to my husband, who tucked me up under his arm as we all went back inside.

Roman Candle tag was put on hold for Butcher, Toxic, and the girls, but I could hear them giggling as their dad told them how proud he was for them kicking the crap out of the other bikers.

All the guys who were at the clubhouse sat down and had a drink, in celebration, with Rip and I. Of course, I had a glass of apple cider. Hush had picked some up for Seek so she wouldn't feel left out when celebrations happened.

I smiled as the men all pounded Rip on the back. Lockout looked like a proud grandpa—even though he wasn't that much older than my husband—and that feeling filled me again. The one that told me that despite all odds of ever finding it, I was finally home.

CHAPTER 34

Riptide

Holding out my hand, I smiled up at Sloane as she picked her way down the rocks. She was being careful, but little did she know that I'd never let her fall. I knew this path through the boulders like the back of my hand. The way down to my cove was written on my soul.

She kept glancing up and gasping at the view as we went and it etched the truth I'd known from the minute I'd seen her deep into the core of my being. She was my soulmate. I'd never shown this cove to another person. Beard's Hollow Cove was near The Cape Disappointment State Park. There were a few homes scattered on the public land nearby, but this was the only house close to the cove itself. The woods were so thick, that if you didn't walk by you wouldn't know about it. Since it was private property, no one ever wandered this way. There was a beach open to the public, but the rocks secluded this tiny section of sand away from the world.

The only one who knew of its existence, besides me, was the old man who'd lived in the house at the top of the bluff. As soon as my investments had meted out enough money, I'd shown up on his doorstep, cash offer and a contract in hand.

We'd talked for hours and he'd told me about how he'd bought this house for his wife. She'd been the love of his life and he'd lost her eight years prior. He'd seen me sneaking onto their little slice of shoreline since I was a kid, but he'd never busted me. I'd been surfing on the beach nearby and had paddled around the rocks. It was the only reason I knew the cove existed. From that point on I'd used the spot as my own personal haven. He and his wife had laughed together as they'd watched me surf and snorkel in the water. They'd been impressed at my tenacity. Swimming in the Pacific Ocean, this far north, wasn't for the weak-hearted. Even with a heavy wetsuit on, the water was still cold.

He sold me his home that day, saying that he knew no one else would love it the way I did. It was only my vacation home now, but I hired a staff to keep it well maintained. It received the love and care that its prior owners had put into it daily.

My feet hit the sand and I walked, hand in hand with the woman I was going to remarry tomorrow, toward the water. She'd told me—when we'd lived out in the desert, under the oppressive rule of a lunatic—that she dreamed of the ocean. Now it lay before her, waves crashing into rock and shore alike.

Her eyes filled with tears as her feet were engulfed by cold salty water. "It's everything I dreamed," she told me. Pleasure and happiness filled her expression. I wanted to put that look on her face every day for the rest of our lives.

We'd gotten in late last night and stayed in our home. I had every intention of christening every room of the house with her…later. "I'll leave it up to you," I told her. "We can go anywhere in the world that you want for our honeymoon. Or we can stay right here."

"I choose here," she replied with zero hesitation.

Laughing at her enthusiasm, I hugged her close, then let her go so she could explore. Watching her take in every inch of the cove, hearing her exclamations of delight when she found the tidepools, it made me fall more deeply in love with her. I couldn't wait to do this one day with our child.

The hours passed so quickly, I lost all track of time until a shout caught my attention. Lockout and the others were waiting at the top of the bluff, looking down at us. They'd come a day early to help us set everything up. The cove would be where our ceremony took place, with the picturesque Pacific Ocean as our backdrop, while the reception would be up on the grass in our backyard. I owned five acres out here and we wouldn't need to worry about disturbing the neighbors.

I helped Sloane scramble up the cliff. There was a dirt path to follow, but it zig zagged its way to the top and I wasn't about to let her fall. One day, I planned to make a wooden path with rails down to the bottom. Until then, I enjoyed helping. I placed my hand on Sloane's ass to steady her and gave her an innocent look when she glanced over her shoulder at me.

She shook her head, but kept going. Everyone was waiting up top for us. My parents, sisters and their families, and our whole MC family. All except one.

I glanced over at Lockout. "I thought Ricochet was supposed to be home today?"

Lockout put a hand on my shoulder and squeezed. "I talked to him this morning. He's going to stay with his sister for a few more weeks. This is hitting him hard, Rip."

"I know. That's why he should be here. That way we can help him." Guilt was eating away at me. I'd been the one to bring Ricochet into that situation. Knowing he was hurting, and that it was partially my fault, made me want to do whatever was necessary to help him.

"It's not that simple. Once he comes home he's going to have to truly face what he did. This time and before. That isn't going to be easy. We're not kicking him out. We're not abandoning him. But it's time to hold him accountable, time for him to face this."

"You and I both know he's sitting in his sister's guest bedroom blaming himself already, Lock."

"True, but I didn't think it was right to drag him home yet. He's thrilled for you and said to tell you he's sorry he's missing this-"

I nodded in understanding. "But it's too hard for him to be here, doing this, right now. I get it. I'm just fucking worried about him."

"Me too, Brother. Me too." Lockout sighed. "Enough of this. We have a shit ton of work to do to get this place ready for your wedding."

* * *

THE NEXT MORNING, the sun rose, battling against the fog and mist. The fog should burn off before Sloane and I said our vows. As long as it didn't rain, we'd deal with whatever the weather did. The forecast was calling for cool temperatures, but no storms. This area typically received more than seventy inches of rain a year. It wasn't the best time to be doing an outside wedding on the beach, but I wasn't willing to wait for summer. I was remarrying her now.

Hellfire stumbled into the kitchen, grunted a good morning to me, and all but dove at the coffee pot. We'd stayed up most of the night drinking. We'd watched as the women and girls all pampered each other. Priest's girls had waited long enough for Uncle Butcher and Uncle Toxic to get drunk enough before slyly talking them into face masks and toe nail polish. Both men were now sporting pink toes and neither seemed to give two shits. Not that any of us would have turned those cute kids down. Priest had four little hellions on his hands. Smart and wicked. They were going to make all of our lives hell when they hit their teenage years.

The rest of the guys started waking up and coming downstairs. Butcher groaned as he walked in. "Who punched me in the fucking face last night?"

"The bourbon," Smokehouse replied in a helpful tone.

"The women up?" I asked.

"Like we're going to risk asking that and waking them up," Hellfire said. "Do you have any idea how mean women can be when you interrupt their sleep?"

That had everyone laughing. Hush walked down the stairs. "They're awake. I heard Seek in the bathroom."

"Heard her?" Smoke asked.

"She's been gettin' mornin' sickness for the last few weeks," he said with a sympathetic grimace.

"That sucks. Being pregnant doesn't sound fun," Smoke declared. "Not sure why women want that shit."

"They get a baby from it," Lockout told him. He leaned down, hands on the table, and leveled Smokehouse with a look. "Whatever you're thinking, Smoke, don't say it. Don't bring that kind of karma down on your head, Brother."

Smokehouse seemed to consider his words, then shrugged and did what he always did, shot off at the mouth. "I'm never having kids. I'll just dote on all yours."

I met Lockout's amused gaze and shook my head. My thoughts used to run pretty much in line with Smokehouse's, look where that had gotten me. About to marry my wife—for the second time—and a kid on the way. Smokehouse wasn't much older than me, but he led that bachelor lifestyle.

There'd been no plans for me to settle down. It hadn't even been on my radar. Then suddenly I found myself planted inside a cult, being forced to marry the most beautiful woman I'd ever seen. Smokehouse's day would come. And thanks to his dismissal of Lockout's warning it would probably come at just as unlikely a time for him. Hopefully without the cult.

Mom came downstairs and cooked us all breakfast, then brought the women's portions upstairs. Some of the guys helped her carry the plates up.

I'd been banned from everywhere except one of the guest bedrooms we were using to get ready and the kitchen. Kicked out of my own damn bedroom because no one wanted me to see the bride before the ceremony. I didn't bother to point out that we'd done this before.

The time flew and next thing I knew I was in a pair of cargo shorts and a button down shirt—thank God my angel hadn't required I wear a suit—along with my groomsmen, waiting along the top of the bluff. It was as though the weather gods were answering our prayers. It was only around fifty degrees, but the wind had died down. The air was completely still. Most everyone, except the wedding party, was wearing jackets, but we'd decided we could deal with the cold long enough to let everyone see our wedding attire. It wasn't too bad out here as long as that wind stayed away.

All the guests were making their way down with our help. We made the trip multiple times to help the women and kids. When it was time, I made my way down once more, Gabby clinging to my back. The girls were old enough to walk, but when they'd begged Priest for piggyback rides, I'd offered myself up as tribute since he couldn't carry all four at once. There was literally not one thing I wouldn't do for those girls.

Lockout had hidden all the booze last night before most of us had passed out. That wouldn't stop Butcher and Toxic from sniffing it out, but it gave us time to get through the ceremony before they were hammered. The last thing we needed was anyone falling down the steep cliff that led down to the cove.

I waited patiently as the bridesmaids and my bride made their way down. Once they were on the sand, I nodded at Gabby who hit play on my phone. It was hooked up to speakers and the wedding march echoed amongst the rocks of the cove.

Kit, Jenny, and Seek walked over the sand with Hellfire, Hush, and Lockout. Their seafoam green dresses drifted behind them as they walked forward. The women looked gorgeous and I couldn't believe what a difference this day was turning out to be, compared to the first time I'd married Sloane.

Everyone was wearing matching grins. Mine was gone along with my breath. It was hard to breathe when love was trying to strangle you. All I could do was stare at the woman walking toward me. She was in a simple, flowy white dress that was perfect for a beach wedding and was sandwiched between Butcher and Toxic.

Both men had on shirts that were complete eye sores, which of course was the point. If they had to ditch their cuts, they made everyone pay. Butcher's had flamingos on it and Toxic's had pineapples. Upside down pineapples. I was going to have to ask him later if he had any idea what that signified. I hoped he didn't. I was terrified he might.

Sloane's smile was radiant as she walked toward me. The sun was shining down on us, warming the sand, and I had everyone I cared about in one place. Almost everyone. Ricochet flashed through my mind. Somehow I was going to have to figure out a way to help that kid, but not today. Today I needed to marry the most perfect woman I'd ever met. I was a lucky fucking asshole and I knew it.

The trio stopped in front of the arch we'd hauled down here last night then Mom, Dad, Sloane, and I had spent hours decorating with flowers. I'd declined help from anyone else as it gave the four of us a chance for time to ourselves before the wedding. Everyone else had taken that opportunity to start up the party. They'd been drunk off their asses before dinner had even started.

Priest started up his speech. He'd married some friends of ours over in Austin a few years back. Years ago we thought it would be fitting to make him an ordained minister. It started as a joke, making Priest a priest. Little had he known then that it meant the rest of us were going to insist he perform weddings for all of us down the road. In Butcher's case, likely an exorcism. He didn't seem to mind. His deep baritone all but disappeared as I stared at my wife. Soon to be wife. Again.

She smiled up at me with those eyes that matched the water beside us. Somehow, she was mine. Our start might have been rocky, but we were solid now. She'd been coming out of her shell more and more as the weeks went on and I was as much in love with the woman she was becoming as the one she'd been.

We recited our vows, ignoring the sniffling coming from the women in the crowd. Her eyes were dry and perfect as I professed my love to her. Her voice was clear and strong as she promised to be my wife until death do us part. Death would have to go through me to ever get near her. Nothing would touch my family while I was alive to protect them.

Our family cheered when I dipped Sloane then kissed her until she was breathless. We stayed down on the beach, wrapped up in each other as everyone headed up the cliff to the celebration waiting for us at the top.

Pulling her close, I breathed her in. It was hard for me to imagine that only a few months ago, I'd been single and thought I'd been happy. Now I knew I'd just been waiting. Stuck in a perpetual pause until I found my angel. Now was when life began and I couldn't fucking wait to go through it all with her.

CHAPTER 35

Sloane

If you had told me a few short months ago that I'd be on the beach, dancing with my husband while the waves lapped against the sand, I'd have told you that you were lying. Yet, here I was. Riptide had me in his arms, his phone was playing soft slow music through the speakers, and I'd just promised to be his and meant it with every fiber of my being.

The first time we'd gotten married I'd been forced by Ethan. My people had watched as I'd taken my vows and while I'd honored them, I hadn't willingly said them in the first place. What kind of games had fate been playing in order to deliver me the perfect man? The kind I'd dreamed of in my youth, but given up on ever finding as an adult?

Rip fit my childhood requirements to a 'T'. Handsome, brave, kind —at least to his family—and dangerous to those who threatened his loved ones. Adult me had been thrilled to find out that he also came with the ability to give me multiple orgasms, and a set of six pack abs.

I ran my hand under his shirt and over the ridges of muscles. We'd both put on jackets after the ceremony, but I didn't let that deter me. Casting him a flirty look, I asked, "How are we going to consummate this marriage with so many people staying in our house?"

"Looks like we'll have to sneak down here," he told me with a wicked grin. "That rock over there looks like a good spot."

Frowning at the rock he was pointing to, I imagined it digging into my back. "Maybe not there," I suggested.

He leaned forward and purred into my ear. "Then I guess I'll just have to bend you over that log there and fuck you from behind."

My cheeks heated, but the vivid image he created had my heart pumping wildly in my chest. "That sounds better."

He chuckled, then took my hand, leading me along the water's edge. "I want to give you a wedding gift."

"Oh?"

"Anything you want."

I paused, tugging him to a stop beside me. "Really? Anything?"

"Anything," he told me, eyes searching mine.

"I can't believe how giving you are," I replied with a smile. "I've never known a man like you, Rip. I hope you know that I consider myself incredibly lucky that you came into my life."

His hand brushed over my hair. I loved his habit of always touching me. It was like it was a need he wasn't aware of. It made me feel special and loved each time he did it.

He linked our hands again and started walking. "So what would you like?"

"It's a lot to ask," I started, hesitating. He waited patiently until I was ready to tell him. "I want to build a school."

"A…school?"

"One where we can hire teachers for the kids who came from the village and others for the mothers. That way they can all get a good education. Tilly came home in tears the other day because she, Janice, and Audrey had started their first day at a local high school and they were so far behind they said they'd never catch up. The principal ended up putting them in a lower grade, but the kids were jerks to them because of it."

Riptide sighed. "I worried that might happen. You did the best you could, teaching them, but the schools out here are pretty rigorous and you weren't given much to work with inside The Order."

"I want them all to go to school with each other and learn together. They need not just an education, but to learn how to integrate into a new culture."

"We can make that happen," he said thoughtfully. "I think you should set up to be the counselor."

I frowned over at him. "What do you mean?"

"Schools out here often have a counselor. You help kids decide what they want to do after high school. Help them choose a path, a career. You talk to them about their emotional and mental health, pretty much anything they need."

"I like the sound of that," I responded, "but I'm not certified."

"So? It's our school. We can hire whoever we want." He shrugged his massive shoulders. "You can still go to college to get your degree and by the time all the kids are ready to go to school in the city, if they choose, then you'll likely be done with your degree and ready to move on and help other people."

Biting my lip, I gave him an imploring look. "I think I'd really like that. And to be able to help others. I hate to think it, but we can't be the only ones to escape a cult. Or other horrible conditions. I want to help anyone, everyone transitioning back to the real world."

"Then it's done, Angel. I'll get Static to help me figure out the logistics. He's a fucking miracle worker when it comes to that kind of shit."

"I thought he was a lawyer?"

"He is," Rip said with a laugh, "but he knows people. He'll have someone who can help with this project. I'm sure of it."

"Okay," I told him, happy that this was a possibility. "Thank you so much. I'd like to give you something, too."

He turned to me and placed his big palm on my belly over my

dress. "You've given me everything, Angel. I don't need anything but you and our child."

Tears filled my eyes at his words. He showed me every day how much he loved me and I vowed to myself that I would do the same for him. There wouldn't be a time where he'd feel lonely. I'd fill his life with so much love he wouldn't know what to do with it all.

We walked along for a few more minutes, each lost in our own thoughts.

"Oh!"

The worried expression on his face had me finishing the thought that had materialized in my mind.

"Do you think you and Lockout could do me another favor?"

"Possibly," he said. "I need to know what it is and will have to talk to Lockout before agreeing..."

"I wanted to see if we could have a barbeque with the MC and my people every couple months. Some of the kids are really missing their dads. The men of The Order were assholes for the most part, but these kids have been stripped away from everything they knew. They're not old enough to realize how cruel their fathers were, they just know that there are no men around. It's strange to them. I think it would do them some good to be in your guys' presence and just... hang out."

Riptide grinned and nodded his head. "Yeah, I'm sure Lock wouldn't have any trouble agreeing to that. We were sort of thinking the same, but didn't want to force ourselves on them in case some of them blamed us for their fathers' deaths."

I sat down on a log that had washed onto shore and stared out at the water. "It's sort of a weird situation. I think most of them are just pretending that their dads are still living out at the compound. They haven't come to grips with their fathers' deaths yet. The older ones will understand. The younger ones will have a harder time adjusting. You saved our lives," I told him, squeezing his hand.

"We'd do it all over again," he replied. Something was weighing on him.

I could see it in the depths of his eyes. "What's wrong?"

His jaw tightened, but then he sighed. "I'm worried about Ricochet. I didn't want to tell you, because you knew everyone we fought, but he ended up killing Jarrett, John, and Gary that night."

"Oh no," I whispered. My eyes closed and I brought forth their faces in my mind. The kids were already brainwashed and indoctrinated, not to mention mean. There hadn't been anything we could do to save them. That didn't mean that I wasn't upset about their deaths.

"He didn't realize they were kids. It's hitting him really hard."

"I can only imagine. But…if he hadn't killed them, what would've happened?"

"They'd already shot Hellfire. They wouldn't have hesitated to kill both him and Ricochet."

"I agree. Ricochet did the only thing he could do in that moment. He must know that."

"He knows that, deep down, but it's not the first time this has happened to him. He's got some shit he has to work through and this didn't help matters."

"You and your brothers will help him through it," I replied. "And if I can help in any way, I'd be glad to."

"Thanks, Angel."

"If you don't get up here and cut this cake, I'm eating it whole!"

We glanced over our shoulders and up to where Seek was standing at the top of the bluff. Her hands were on her hips as the wind carried her words down to us. We started laughing at the indignant look on her face. Only a pregnant woman could look that offended about uneaten cake.

"We'd better go. She didn't get breakfast because of the morning sickness."

"How have you been feeling?" he asked as he pulled me to my feet.

"Fine, so far, but we'll see how it goes as I get further along." I placed a hand over my belly.

"I can't wait to see you all swollen with my kid," he said with a grin.

"Let's see if you still feel that way once you have to help me up from the couch," I replied with a grim look.

"I'm signing up now to help you up from any surface when you need it."

We headed up toward the party and the family that was waiting to celebrate with us. I couldn't wait to learn more about these people who were already becoming irreplaceable in my life.

CHAPTER 36

Riptide

"Open your eyes," I told Sloane with a grin.

Her eyes snapped open and the smile dropped off her face. We'd spent the first two days of our honeymoon in bed and I didn't regret a single moment of that, but I'd woken her early this morning, telling her I had a surprise for her.

"This is my surprise?" she asked, trying not to make a face at the wetsuit I held out for her.

"Part of it," I confirmed. Grabbing her, I grabbed her clothes and started stripping her down to the bikini she had on underneath.

"Rip! It's freezing out here. And there are people," she said, casting a quick glance at a pair of guys walking from the parking lot down to the beach.

I'd brought her to Long Beach. It was the perfect place for what I had in mind. The waves were small and easy to navigate, and you couldn't come to the Long Beach Peninsula without seeing the longest beach in the world. Or so the arch over Bolstad Street proclaimed. It wasn't actually the longest beach in the world, but it was the longest on a peninsula. Either way, it was worth visiting.

I didn't bother to answer her, just started helping her into the wetsuit.

"What is this for?"

"I'm going to teach you to surf."

The way she froze had me looking up at her, a foot in my hand as I tugged the wetsuit up over her sexy thighs. "What's wrong?"

"I-I don't know how to swim," she whispered, shame covering her face.

"That's okay, Angel. I'll teach you, we'll start there."

"How can I go into the ocean when I don't know how to swim, Rip?" She put her hands on her hips. It was such a cute, aggravated stance, I straightened up and kissed her nose.

"Because I'll be there with you," I told her.

"What about the baby?" she asked, new worry masking her face.

"We have a friend over in Austin who's a doctor. I asked her if this was dangerous. Ming said as long as you don't hit a rock or drown, there's no problem. Long Beach doesn't have any rocks in this area," I pointed in that direction, "and I'm not going to let you drown."

She seemed nervous and hesitant but put her hand in mine and walked down to the water with me. I brought her out until the water was hitting our hips. She shivered as the cold water filled her suit, but she never complained. She was a real champ.

"Flip onto your back like this, take a deep breath, and just float," I instructed, showing her how to do it.

She watched me as though she were studying every detail. I loved the way her mind worked. She soaked in everything around her so that she'd perform any task perfectly on the first try.

Sloane let her legs come out in front of her and floated on her back. Her bright blue eyes met mine and excitement shone there. "This is easy."

"The wetsuit helps your buoyancy, and if you feel like you're sinking you can take a deep breath. Your lungs can act like flotation devices. Another thing is, if you're on your back, raise your stomach like there is a string on your belly button and you'll float easier as well.

We spent some time floating around so she could get more comfortable with the water.

"You started without us?" a deep voice called from the shore.

I grinned and helped Sloane get her feet under her before I charged toward the sand and the man standing there. He met me halfway, water spraying everywhere as he moved toward me. We slapped each other's backs hard in a bro hug.

Sloane came up behind me, keeping my body between her and the newcomer.

"Sloane, this is Trip. Trip, this is my wife, Sloane."

"It's nice to meet you," Trip said, his voice softening instinctually. Sloane seemed to bring this softness out of people without even trying. She wasn't a wounded bird or anything, but they just knew they could let their guard down around her. "Sorry we couldn't make the wedding."

Sloane reached out and shook his hand. "That's okay. It's nice to meet you, Trip." Her eyes darted to mine. "Is he a part of the MC?"

"He's a part of our Austin Chapter," I told her.

"Actually, Drew and I went Nomad," Trip corrected me.

"No shit?"

"Yeah. We offered to go after Eric."

My chapter had gone over to Austin to help their group with some trouble that had popped up and we'd taken the majority of the trash out. Eric had been part of that trash, and had gotten away. Before I could ask how that was going, Trip turned and motioned to a beautiful woman standing on the sand, waiting for us.

She came forward and gave us a soft smile. "Hi, I'm Marina."

"Marina's my old lady," Trip said, a hint of pride in his voice.

"A lot has changed," I replied, shaking Marina's hand. "You look way too good for this dirtbag."

She laughed and shook her head. "I'll never get used to the way you guys insult each other."

"It's their way of bonding, I've come to learn," Sloane said, introducing herself to Marina.

"Trip is here to surf with us," I said, ignoring the women's comments. There wasn't anything weird about me and my brothers casting digs at each other. At least not from my point of view, but then again I'd grown up around an MC.

"I'm not sure I'm ready for that," Sloane said with a shy smile. "I still don't even know how to swim."

"I can help you, if you'd like," Marina offered. "I'm a dive instructor."

"A...what?" Sloane asked.

"Scuba diving," Marina clarified.

"She's like a fish in the water," Trip said in agreement.

"I'll take any help I can get," Sloane agreed.

We spent the next few hours horse playing and swimming around. As long as we were moving, it wasn't too cold. I started off with my arms around Sloane, letting her doggy paddle around while I held her afloat. It didn't take her too long to start getting the hang of it. I was reluctant to let her go. Having my arms around her felt too good. But she'd insisted so she could start learning more swimming techniques.

Trip and I went back up to the parking lot to haul down the chairs and coolers and set up in front of the women as they kept practicing. I'd packed sandwiches and drinks in preparation for the day.

"I like your girl," I told Trip, taking a huge bite from a sandwich and opening my beer.

"I like yours, too. She's sweet." He caught the beer I tossed him. "Lockout mentioned something about you going undercover?"

I quickly relayed the story while the girls emerged from the ocean and stripped out of their wetsuits as they walked toward us. Sloane nearly had me choking on my ham on rye in her bright red bikini. I'd taken her shopping in town for swimwear and had insisted she buy this one. It covered more than most people at the beach wore, but it accented her gorgeous body. She was becoming much less self-conscious about her scars, though she was seriously considering getting some tattoos to cover them. She said she wanted to cover some of the bad with something pretty and new.

Her hair streamed down her back, sleek and wet. I had to shift in my camp chair or anyone passing by was going to see my hard-on under my swim shorts. My woman was a menace, in all the best ways.

Her eyes met mine, then dipped down to my lap. She gave me a sultry look and I considered ditching our friends early, carrying her all the way home, and cashing in on the promise in those blue eyes. I watched in disappointment as she dried off as much as she could with her towel, then tugged on one of my sweatshirts. It covered her all the way down to her thighs.

"You ready for some lunch?" I asked, trying to curb my wayward thoughts. If we got too cold, we'd head up to the vehicles and eat there. Living in Tucson for so long, I wasn't used to the cold anymore, and neither were the others, but for now it was a gorgeous, but cold, day.

"I'm starving," both women said at the same time.

"The water and fresh air will do that to you," Trip said with a nod.

"After lunch, we're going to try some surfing," I told Sloane, judging her reaction. There were still some nerves, but now they were mixed with excitement.

"I can't wait."

We sat and chatted while we ate and let the food digest. Once enough time had passed, I stood and held my hand out. Hauling Sloane to her feet, I pulled her against my body. "You ready?" I asked quietly, so the others wouldn't overhear. "If you're not we can always do this a different day."

"No. I think I'm ready."

"There's the brave woman I love so much," I told her, kissing her nose.

"Aw, aren't you sweet," Trip said, dramatically batting his lashes.

"Fuck off, asshat," I told him flipping him off. Then I dipped Sloane back and kissed her.

A heavy sigh had us looking over and Marina was watching us with hearts practically floating over her head.

"Uh oh," I said with a laugh. "Looks like you better step your game up."

Trip gave an uncomfortable laugh, then sighed. "You're going to end up forcing me to propose early," he muttered at me. "Knock it the fuck off. I have a whole thing planned for when we get home."

I laughed and elbowed him in the side before we all stripped off our extra layers and managed to wrestle our wetsuits back on. Taking Sloane's hand, I dragged her off toward our boards. Picking one up, I brought it to the water's edge and ran her through how to lay on it and paddle. It was a good thing it was still early stages of her pregnancy and she wasn't showing yet, or she wouldn't be able to do this. Poor Seek would probably roll right off the board at this point and she was only a few months ahead of Sloane.

"You ready?" I asked twenty minutes later.

"It's now or never!" she said and ran into the water.

"You forgot the board," I yelled at her. Shaking my head, I grabbed it and hauled it into the water.

"I'm going to go with you the first time, okay?"

She nodded and laid on the board. I hopped on behind her, my chin right above her ass. "Maybe I need to do this more than the first time."

She gave me an unamused look over her shoulder. "I'm ready. Let's go!"

I couldn't help but laugh at her impatience. We paddled a little ways out and turned around. "Okay, here comes a small wave. Stay laying down and I'll steer us in. Give you a chance to feel what it's like on top of the wave, alright?"

"Okay!"

Her laughter filled the air as I caught the wave and we sped toward the shore. "This is so fun," she shouted to me, a smile splitting her face.

I was glad she was enjoying herself. There were a lot of people who would have been complaining about the cold the whole time. She never uttered a single complaint, just went with the flow. Her beautiful smile was worth every minute.

Once we slowed down, I hopped off and steadied the board. "You ready to try alone?"

"Yes." She gave me a determined look.

"Okay. Remember to snap upright and lean forward on the board."

She nodded, then turned the board and headed out. Trip and Marina came over; we were all standing in waist deep water watching as Sloane made her way out. Marina didn't seem to be worried about the cold water, but Trip was shifting back and forth to keep himself warm. We watched as Sloane picked her spot and sat, waiting, on her board.

"Here comes a good one," Trip said.

I nodded, leaning forward a little as I watched her lay back down. "Paddle, paddle, paddle," I muttered. My breath caught in my lungs as she hit just the right spot and popped up on the board. "Fuck yeah!" I yelled as she dropped in on the wave. "That's my girl!"

"Yes!" Both Marina and Trip were cheering for her as Sloane steered the board toward the shore.

The waves weren't massive and the one she caught was the perfect beginner wave, but to come from a place where she hadn't been allowed to do shit, to conquering fears and dreams, it was huge for her. I was so fucking proud of everything she'd accomplished so far and would continue to do.

She cared so much for people and I knew she was going to make the perfect confidant for those who were struggling. She'd start with her own people, but I knew she'd branch out from there. The world was hers for the taking and I'd make damn sure I was there to back her up every step of the way.

I stormed forward as she dropped down on the board in front of us and grabbed her up in a hug. Spinning her around, I crowed with pride and laughter. "Great job, Angel!"

"Thank you," she gasped out, holding onto me for dear life until I stopped spinning. Then her arms tightened around me. "I want to do this forever, with you."

"Surf?" I asked, a brow arching.

"Try new things," she corrected. "Have fun. Live life to the fullest. I want it all. At the same time, I just want you."

"I know exactly what you mean, Angel. I'm going to give you everything, and you'll always have me."

We headed back out, just the two of us, with Trip and Marina watching, to catch the next wave. Our lives were going to be full of waves and we'd tackle the highs and lows together.

* * *

Thanks for reading!

Sign up for my newsletter to receive an updates on new releases and much more! https://www.cathleencolenovels.com/bonuses.

Join The Book Bunker-A Cathleen Cole Reader Group https://www.facebook.com/groups/thebookbunkercathleencole

Keep flipping to find a sneak peek for book four of The Vikings MC: Tucson Chapter, Ricochet. It's available for pre-order now!

SNEAK PEEK

RICOCHET

My breath hissed out as the cold water sent shivers down my back. It created a sharp chill that cascaded throughout my whole body. I reached for the shower knob and rolled it back. The water got even colder.

I wasn't one of those masochist types or health nuts that took cold showers for the fun of it. I could tell you I did it to cool the rage inside me, to ice down the monster within. That would be bullshit, too. At least it would be *good* bullshit. Almost believable. It made me sound like I was doing humanity a kindness. I wasn't sure I was capable of being gentle or caring any longer.

No, I did it because it was something I could *feel*. Really feel. I didn't enjoy being cold, but I enjoyed numbness even less. And I'd been living without feeling and emotion—besides anger—for too long now.

Letting my skin take the punishment of the cold water and taking on that pins and needles feeling as the spray hit my body was far better than the emptiness in my soul. Before all this I wouldn't have subscribed to the theory of souls and shit, but once you fuck up the way I had? You started to believe. The absence of it was driving me insane. I spent my days unable to connect with anything or anyone around me. Not even my MC brothers, and they were some of the most important people in my life. That numb aching feeling was getting worse. I wasn't sure how much more I could take before I did something drastic and stupid.

Standing in the shower, now that I was accustomed to the temperature, I went about the business of scrubbing my ass. Getting worse was an understatement. A black inky weight was slithering over that part of me I once thought was mythical. All I wanted to do was find my enemies and torture them until they writhed in pain. Finish them once they couldn't absorb another moment of torment. Let them bleed out and die. That wasn't normal, right?

My head dropped, heavy with the weight of my urges, and the water pelted the back of my neck. Icy cold fingers spread over my skin, creeping down my body until they disappeared through the drain and it started all over again. I didn't have any enemies at the moment, they were all dead, but the urge was still there. I needed to find new enemies. Someone to expel my rage onto. Needing that couldn't be good either.

Last night we raided the cult. Executed the extremists and freed the women and children. I thought I was ready to get back into the fight. Hell, it sounded easy enough. Crazy cult leader, fanatical men who rape and abuse women. I had no issue with killing those types. That wasn't the problem.

I hadn't been ready for what was actually going to happen. Butcher tried to warn us, warn me, that with these cults it's never that easy. I thought we'd be fighting crazy men. *Adult* men.

I wasn't ready for the kid. Ten, maybe eleven years old. I had a nephew that age. Still playing with Legos but not yet looking at girls. In a different world the kid from last night could have been going to school with my nephew, they could have been friends. In any sane world he should have been in with the group of women and children we were rescuing. The other two—while still young—had been old enough to make their choices. The kid... The kid, though, shouldn't have been there. Shouldn't have shot at Hellfire.

I reached for the knob and rolled it back slightly. A new round of shivers engulfed my body with the colder water. It was the only thing that was helping to chase away the memories.

No. This was the real world. At least the one that boy had lived in. The one I'd helped take down. And he'd been carrying a rifle. He'd gripped that gun, and he'd been ready to use it. He *had* used it. When I saw him I froze. In my life, in all my service with the Navy Seals, my time on the teams, I only ever froze once. When I had, my best friend had been killed. I was the reason his wife was a widow. His children were growing up without their father. My best friend had died because I'd hesitated.

Swallowing hard, I squeezed my eyes shut, as if that could block out Jack's face from my mind. As if that one movement could somehow erase the fact that he was gone. He was buried in fucking Arlington, and I was still here. The cold and memories bled together, making it hard to breathe.

Last night when I saw that kid, I froze again. Hellfire was nearly killed because of it. My limbs had weighed a ton and it was as though I was anchored to the ground, and because of that the kid shot my brother. I honestly wasn't sure for a minute if I was awake, or if I was stuck in the middle of one of my fucked up dreams. Then I'd heard Riptide. I was able to move again. My training kicked in and I killed a kid. Again.

That was when I lost it. I wasn't sure I was ever going to regain my sanity after this. Killing does something to a man. When you're forced to end the life of someone who was so young and should still be innocent of the evil in this world? It did things to you. Things I never wanted to experience again, but they were my constant companions. Voices inside of me, whispering all the fucking evil things I shouldn't think about.

Behind that kid had been a man giving orders. My brain went from sluggish and unable to process to hyper efficient. I saw the man —Bruce had been his name—and realized he had been the one to arm the kid, to make a child soldier. He had been the one to put me in a position to kill a kid for the second time.

Berserker is what my brothers call it. When I lose my shit the way

I did last night. A blind rage overcame me. Some guys called it seeing red. I didn't see much of anything, other than the target of my rage. I'd beaten Bruce to death. With my bare hands. Broke two of my fingers and dislocated two more. This wasn't the first time I'd gone berserker, but it certainly was the worst. I'd get into bar fights, lose my temper, and take it too far. I'd just lose sight of when to stop. This rage, this fear always took hold, telling me that if I stop, the person I'm fighting will hurt someone else that I care about. So I didn't stop.

Looking down at my hand, I flexed it. Crash—a special forces medic we'd known from back in the day—had reset the two dislocated fingers and splinted the other two. The pain hadn't registered. Crash was a bit of an oddball. Even Butcher gave him a wide berth, when possible, but the look he'd given me when I'd refused any pain relievers told me he thought *I* was the crazy one. He wasn't wrong.

My knuckles were scabbing over, but a few hours ago you could almost see bone. That was a new one for me. I'd never hurt anyone that badly when I'd gone Berserker in the past. It was building, growing…getting worse. I wasn't sure how deep this rage and numbness could go. Or what would happen when I lost it.

Usually I just beat someone's ass, wounding them, maybe breaking the occasional rib. I'd never beaten someone to death with my fists before. Killed plenty of men, and I wouldn't feel bad for that. Not for killing for my country, or for my club, but men were entirely different than what was haunting me. Or should I say who?

According to Riptide, if anyone deserved what happened to him, it was this Bruce fellow. His death didn't bother me. The blind rage and lack of control was worrying. It was a problem, both for me and for the motorcycle club.

I knew my brothers wouldn't just throw me out. But they couldn't rely on me. Pain stabbed through my heart, making me gasp out loud. It'd been so long since I'd felt a fucking thing besides that rage, the zip of emotion physically hurt me. My brothers couldn't trust me. Why should they? I couldn't even trust myself. Soon we would have to deal with this. And I had no clue how to begin.

Leaning my arm against the wall, I rested my head on it, closing my eyes and trying to block out the images from last night. My ears were filled with the sound of water and static. Nothing penetrated my bubble so long as I was in here. But I couldn't live my life in the fucking shower. At least I wasn't using up all the hot water.

I shut the shower off and stepped out to begin drying myself. Walking past the mirror, I refused to glance over. I was in no condition to look at that guy right now. Instead, I went to my phone. I had a text from my sister. Despite living in the city, I hadn't seen her in some time. She wanted to know if I was free to come visit.

Somehow she always knew when I needed her. I used to be able to tell the same for her, but that instinct had been silent for a few years now. Ever since I'd gotten home from my last deployment. Since Jack's death. Since the last time a death from my hand had haunted me.

If there was anyone who could calm the raging beast inside, it was my twin sister Gwen. Staying with her and my nephews might help me keep myself under control. Fuck knew I couldn't be here right now. All it would take would be one pitying look and I'd lose the tumultuous hold I had on my control.

My MC brothers were my world, that didn't mean I didn't need room to clear my head. I always needed space, more and more so over the years as this disease grew inside me. How could I join my brothers and enjoy life when I never knew when the rage would break free?

One thing I knew for sure, I'd kill myself before ever laying a hand on my twin or her boys. They were safe from me. I couldn't say the same for my brothers at this point. It didn't matter how much I loved them, something was broken inside of me. I was afraid more than ever that in my spiral I'd take them down with me. They wouldn't abandon me, they would allow themselves to fall before leaving me. I couldn't allow that either. They deserved better.

Decision made, I dressed and packed a duffel bag. I'd stop and talk to Lockout on my way out. He'd understand. He wouldn't stop me from leaving. I knew it would be a short reprieve—because Lockout wasn't going to let me slink off like a dog with its tail between its legs—but I needed it. He'd understand that. My president was far too fucking perceptive for his own damn good. And mine.

* * *

I made my way downstairs, moving slowly. Glaring at the lightbulb as it happily shone overhead, I tried to figure out why the room looked draped in shadows. It was noon and I could see the ambient light bleeding through the windows. That one light fixture that needed the bulb replaced was flickering like it always did. So why was it so fucking dark? I rubbed at my eyes, wondering what the hell was wrong.

Lock had forced me to go see Crash last night to get patched up. There was no way I was heading back on my own just to get my damn eyesight checked. I avoided doctors at all costs. Continuing on, I glanced around, careful not to lock eyes with anyone. It would have been too easy to say I was creeping around. I just couldn't stand the thought of running into anyone.

As soon as I made it down the stairs, I realized there were already people in the main area. It was the middle of the day, so it wasn't all that surprising. I'd just been hoping to get the hell out of here without seeing anyone. I knew Riptide and Hush were worried about me. Smokehouse and Kit were still with Hellfire at Crash's as far as I knew, but if they were here my closest friends would be dragging me back up to my room to talk sense into me. That was the last fucking thing I wanted right now.

I moved past the bar, scanning faces as I went, taking stock of who was around today. I didn't see either of my friends. Guilt pinched as the thoughts invaded my mind. I couldn't face them right now. Smoke and Hell knew me better than anyone. When I'd tried to avoid making close friendships, they'd bulldozed right past my defenses. It'd been too fucking hard losing Jack, but those assholes didn't give a shit. They'd forced me to care. As much as I could right now anyway. It wasn't the same way I'd loved Jack. Nothing was the same since I'd lost him.

SNEAK PEEK

Still, those two and I had just clicked. All of the MC members were my brothers. I'd give my life for any of them, but the relationship wasn't the same between every man. I saw Lock and Hush as mentors. Men I could go to when I needed something. People I respected more than anyone else. Rip, Priest, Butcher, and Toxic. They were great. I knew they'd go to bat for me. Every member would, but I always held myself back from the rest.

Hell had been the one to approach me on that first day when I'd started prospecting. He'd watched me as I'd completed my first task set by Lockout, guard the gate. No time limit had been given, so I'd sat there for just under twenty-four hours. Hell had come out with a beer. Smoke had later joined us with some sandwiches. Eventually, Riptide had come out, realizing I'd been forgotten out there and released me. Ever since that day, Hell, Smoke, and I had been each other's shadows.

I can't handle seeing him.

Bile rose in my throat as the image of him wavered inside my mind. It kept intermingling with the memory of Jack—lying still, eyes open, but empty, staring at nothing—and the idea of losing Hellfire made my stomach roil. The shame was too much. The fear, overwhelming. I'd failed him. Eventually I'd have to face him, just...not right now.

I grunted a hello at the others, but kept my eyes averted and moved forward. My limbs were shaky and wooden, making my gait stiff. I knew any one of my brothers would talk if I asked them to. I could feel Priest's eyes on me, burning into my back as I turned and made my way down the hallway. Some would talk to me even if I *didn't* want to. Which was why I was avoiding eye contact.

In a way, I was fortunate and I knew it. Too many guys in my position had no one. They faced this alone. I had brothers who would support me. Who would talk—or beat—sense into me, depending on what I needed.

Even in Afghanistan, when Jack was killed, there were people there. People from my Seal team, hell, even some Army pilots became unexpected friends. I'd been surrounded by people who just wanted to help. It'd been a shock, but welcomed.

SNEAK PEEK

It wasn't a lack of support. That wasn't my problem. I just couldn't see burdening them. I was a child killer. A lowly piece of shit who didn't deserve help. Damaged goods. These men, they were heroes. Legit pulled a baby and her puppy from a burning building type of heroes. They were the best men I knew. The last thing they needed was to be babysitting me. I definitely didn't want their pity. Deep down, if I allowed myself the slightest bit of hope, what I really wanted was an end to the numbness. That would only happen through redemption.

Last night was supposed to be that redemption. Instead it was Afghanistan two point zero. I was fairly sure it'd done more harm than good. I didn't know anymore how to fix myself. What could I do? For now, hiding out was my only option. Gwen offered the only safe place for me to go. I could always stay here, but then I'd feel like a burden. It was better that I left.

I got to Lockout's office and knocked on the door. It was open already so I leaned my head in.

"What's up Ricochet?" Lockout asked, motioning for me to come inside.

"I- uh- I just got off the phone with my sister. I haven't seen her or her kids in some time.

"Far too long," Lockout agreed, his sharp eyes watching every move I made.

I swore the asshole could read minds. It made me fucking nervous. I loved the man with every fiber of my being. He'd taken me in, treated me better than I could have ever hoped. He was like an older brother to me, but he still made me nervous. Everyone did. When you had so many secrets you weren't sure you could name them all, you tended not to trust anyone fully. Not with that dark part of you that could snap at any time. No. That got tucked away, pretending like it didn't exist, until it forced its way forward from time to time.

"She wants me to come by, maybe stay with them for a little while. I thought that maybe it would be ok, what with us not being as busy right now."

"I think some time with your sister and family would be good." He gave me an understanding smile, but there was a lot left unspoken. I could see it in his eyes. He didn't need to say more, and I didn't need to ask. We were both hoping that maybe she could help me in ways the club couldn't. If not, we both knew Lockout was going to step in and take over.

I wasn't sure what that meant for me, and I *was* sure I didn't want to find out. Somehow, I needed to figure out how to unfuck myself. That was easier said than done. It was also a problem for another day. I had enough weighing me down right now that I didn't need to contemplate that.

With the small talk over with, I made my way out to my bike. I didn't stop to talk to anyone, I just nodded and grunted as I passed. Stepping outside, I realized it was gloomy outside. It was unusual to have cloud coverage this time of year, but today it was thick enough to block out the sun. Fitting. It matched my mood. If those clouds got any darker, they'd match my soul. At least it made me forget about the darkness inside the clubhouse. In a place that should be bright and make me happy, all I knew were shadows and pain. I had to get out of here.

Hopping onto my bike, I made my way across town. The city was quiet, barely anyone was on the road, just the way I liked it. I skipped my way through some red lights. There was no point in stopping. If someone came along and slammed into the side of me, I'd come back long enough to thank them for ending it.

Gwen lived on the west side, near Picture Rocks. It was a beautiful area, and still pretty vacant. Not too many people lived this far outside the city limits, but Gwen preferred to be out here. I'd bought this house for her years ago, when I'd still been in service, and continued to make the payments. She and my nephews deserved the very best. She'd had a rough go of it so far, and I hadn't been about to let my only family struggle. Not when there was something I could do about it. The house was in her name. I didn't need any kind of credit or acknowledgement. It was enough to know they were in a safe neighborhood and happy. I rolled up to her house and shut my bike off.

The thing about a Harley is that you can't make a quiet entrance. I wasn't even off the bike yet before the door burst open and the kids were on their way out.

"Uncle Gage!"

I put on my biggest grin, hoping they wouldn't see through it to the dead man underneath. Despite my mood I had no desire to ruin their happiness. Maybe some of their innocence would rub off on me.

Fake it 'til you make it right?

I grabbed Sean and swung him up into the air, bringing him full arc and onto my shoulders. The screeching and giggling was a nice change to the silence I normally had.

"Me next, do me!" Grace was screaming from the ground. I picked her up and swung her in the same manner, then held her upside down by her ankles in front of my face. I studied her as she giggled and swatted at me. I tickled her exposed belly. More screeching and laughter filled the air.

"Ricochet, it's so good to see you! We've missed you." My sister said, walking up with a big smile on her face. Even though she'd known me as Gage her entire life, she'd switched over to my road name as seamlessly as if I'd been born with it. She'd always understood me more than anyone. More than our parents, though they'd done their best while we'd had them.

Her arms wrapped around me, somehow avoiding the kids and managed to give me a hug. We were a mess of tangled limbs. I gave myself a moment to relax into her embrace. To soak in the love and contentment, so I could almost feel it for myself.

"You look good, Gwenny."

She made a face at my childhood nickname for her. "Thanks." She made no move to release me. It was almost as if she realized I needed this comfort. We'd always had that twin bond. Some didn't think it existed. We knew for a fact it did.

The night Jack had been killed and I'd been back in my barracks, staring down the barrel of a pistol, she'd called. From halfway around the world, she'd known something was wrong. She was the reason I was still here. She'd saved me that night, and every other. We'd lost our parents when we were younger and I wasn't going to be the reason she lost the rest of her family. I made a choice, every-damn-day, to fight and to stay, for her. For my nephew and niece. For my brothers. Maybe one day, I'd want to stay for myself. That was the hope anyway.

Over my sister's shoulder I spotted a woman walking out the front door of the house next door. Long raven hair and forest green eyes met mine. They reminded me of the trees from back home. The home we'd ended up leaving to come live with our aunt in Tucson. I'd had a treehouse built in my favorite tree on our property. It had been my escape. Her eyes brought me right back to that little wooden shack stuck up in a massive tree.

My heart nearly stopped. The sun had chosen that moment to emerge from the clouds and shine on her hair. It was so dark the highlights almost looked blue. More importantly the brightness of it made me squint. Whatever was going on with my eyes seemed to have resolved itself. She sauntered down the walkway, smiling at our reunion.

I almost dropped the kids. Grace let out a squawk of indignation, so I set her down, followed by Sean. I nearly walked through Gwen as I moved toward the beautiful woman.

She made her way over to us, ignoring the way I was staring, and waited patiently.

Gwen let go of me and laughed. "Sorry, manners, Ricochet, this is Jordan, my neighbor. Sweetie, this is my brother."

"Hi." It was all I could manage to mutter. I reached out and took her offered hand. It was soft and warm. A warmth that spread through my own, up my arm, where it unfurled inside my body. Her cheeks pinkened and she glanced away. It made me wonder if she'd sensed something sparking between us like I had.

I wasn't sure what was happening, but for the first time since Afghanistan it wasn't only numbness, pain, and rage inside of me. Somehow she'd managed to bring out more. Staring into her eyes, holding her hand, I knew this was something I didn't want to let go.

ACKNOWLEDGMENTS

A huge thank you to my partner in crime and Co-Author, Frank Jensen. I couldn't do this without you.

To my amazing beta reader Heather Ashley, thank you so much for all of your time and effort you spent helping me make these books the best they can be!

Also a heartfelt thank you to my editor, Ce-Ce Cox of Outside-Eyes Editing and Proofreading! Thank you for catching everything I always seem to miss, especially those pesky commas.

Thank you to the awesome Kari March of Kari March Designs for giving me gorgeous covers each and every time.

To my wonderful and perfect fans! Thank you all for giving an unknown author a shot and for reading my books! I hope you love them and I can't show my gratitude for you enough.

Lastly, to my family, you're the best. Thank you for the love and support.

ABOUT THE AUTHOR

Cathleen and Frank live in SE Oregon where they have a family farm. They split their days between working with their animals and writing. Both left a law enforcement background to pursue their passions and for Cathleen that meant picking back up a long-forgotten hobby with writing. They strive to bring readers steamy, action-packed stories that provide hours of entertainment.

ALSO BY CATHLEEN COLE

The Vikings MC Series

Heart of Steel

The Viking's Princess

All's Fair In Love & Juárez

'Til Encryption Do Us Part

Bass & Trouble

War & Pieces

Heavy Is The Crowne

The Vikings MC-Tucson Chapter

Hush

Priest

Riptide

Ricochet

The Discord Series

Havoc

Inferno

Deviant

Malice

Soldiers of Misfortune

Captured By The Mercenaries

Protected By The Green Berets

Saved By The Marines

Kept By The Agents

Printed in Great Britain
by Amazon